# Farther Reefs

Space Wizard Science Fantasy
Raleigh, NC
www.spacewizardsciencefantasy.com

Cover by MoorBooks
Illustrations by Katie Cordy
Copy Editing by Heather Tracy
Book Layout © 2015 BookDesignTemplates.com

Farther Reefs/J.S. Fields, Heather Tracy.— 1st ed.
ISBN 978-1-7350768-8-1

# Introduction

Well. Here we are again.

When DISTANT GARDENS came out—a pandemic collaboration between a group of long-time writing friends—we didn't think much would happen. Sure, sapphic adventure is a lot of fun, and sure, we enjoyed the nail polish running gag, but we never expected it to, well, *sell*.

Lesbians and deadly plants. Who knew? Turns out the lesfic world was hungry for inclusive short-story adventures and who are we, as a long-term, not always sober, writing group, to deny this craving?

FARTHER REEFS embraces the weird, the diverse, and the inclusive, in ten new short stories circling my all-time favorite trope *lesbians on boats*. There are a lot of mermaids in here and various other underwater delights. There are dragons, pirates, power plays, stolen kisses and yes, tentacles. Again. And again, and forever after, we embrace the endless diversity of the sapphic experience. Trans lesbians, nonbinary sapphics, intersex people, bisexual women, pansexual women, anyone who embraces the concept of sapphic love has a place in this anthology.

We have a few new authors this time—some you may be familiar with from other sapphic work, some you may be reading for the first time. Regardless, I hope you'll trust them to guide you through these water-based tales. There are fewer nail polish jokes this time but a lot more mermaids, which seems like a pretty fair trade.

Until our next adventure...

—J. S. Fields, September 2022

## A NOTE ON THE STORIES CONTAINED HEREIN:

Each tale is marked on the title page with what sapphic representation is involved, as well as any content warnings. There is also a "Heat Level" if you wish to read or not read particular sexual content. The scale is as follows:

**Low/None:** There may be talk of sex, holding hands, or possibly kissing.

**Medium:** Mention of body parts, touching, and make-out sessions, but all scenes are "fade to black."

**Hot!:** Has at least one full sex scene, start to finish. You have been warned (or encouraged...).

# Under the Seashells

J.S. Fields

Sapphic Representation: Lesbian, Intersex
Heat Level: Medium
Content Warnings: Coarse Language, Animal Violence to Puffins

"Avast ye tufted puffin! Fer ye flies and dives and, you're eating fishes like I eat fishes, and aren't we all just great big fishes of life and stuff so have a little respect. Arr."

The unconcerned puffin bobbed next to Lynn's boat, a fish tail flapping from its beak. Lynn's severed fishing line and one lone, red bobbin floated accusingly next to the puffin's right wing. Lynn watched, and fumed, sitting cross legged on the deck of her computer-run, thirty-five-foot-long research vessel. The remains of her childhood fishing pole she gripped tightly in her hand.

"Yarr," Lynn said to the puffin, one eye squinted shut. "Is this pirate thing convincing? You need to stop eating my fish. I've had people stealing my food since the grade school cafeteria. I don't need it from uppity birds."

The puffin continued to stare. The fish in its mouth stopped moving. The fishing line jerked under the waves and the bobbin disappeared. The puffin unapologetically swallowed and flew off. It did not shit on her as it did so, which put it ahead of ninety-nine percent of the humans Lynn had ever tried to call friends. A small victory, maybe, but she'd also really been looking forward to fish.

Lynn stood, collapsed the telescoping, *My Little Pony*-themed rod that she'd saved up three hundred and fifty horseshoe points for when she was ten, and grumbled all the way back to the boat's covered compartment, and down below deck. There were enough provisions onboard to feed her for the entire six-month solo research voyage, but it was all freeze-dried garbage from whatever local camping store had been having a sale. Getting a two-point-five-million-dollar donation to Illinois State University, earmarked for "a young woman of southern Wisconsin origin with a masters-level background in tufted puffins to study light pollution in the mid-to-northern Pacific," didn't go as far as one might think, especially when your home university charged seventy-five percent overhead. Money aside, she had her fishing pole, and she had her puffins. She did *not* have to deal with humanity for the next six months and that alone was a godsend.

Lynn had only just started toward the stairs when her ears caught the blissful whirring of drone propellers. Lynn spun just in time to see her weekly supply shipment of perishables drop from the drone hovering just off her starboard bow, and into the ocean.

"No!" She raced to the stern and slammed into the guard rail. The bag sank, the green plastic strip of Ziploc seal disappearing to the *lap...lap...lap* of the mild waves.

"My granola," she mumbled. Lynn made a mental note to text her lab's principal investigator to ask for a replacement and to check the drone's GPS.

An electric engine whined and the drone flew closer. It hovered, although now it did so smack over the center of the boat, where the entrance to the storage compartment was located. The drone sang, "LynnLYNN. LynnLYNN." Then a woman's voice, distorted and...wet...and from absolutely nowhere, repeated it. "LynnLYNN. LynnLYNN."

"Creepy!" Lynn yelled at the drone. "You couldn't have dropped it on my ship? What's wrong with your audio? I thought we weren't going to skimp on the tech? Hello? Are you connected to a feed?" She looked for a camera or audio input, but the drone didn't look anything like the last one the university had sent, which had been uniformly black with a storage compartment roughly the size of her torso. This drone looked almost identical to her cousin Izzy's—a hobby model Izzy had flown from one end of their cul-de-sac to the other. They'd used the drone to pass late-night notes between houses...notes that their parents pretended not to notice because Lynn had no other friends. She'd wanted other friends, obviously, but children were loud, and messy, and never sufficiently interested in the voice continuity of *My Little Pony* episodes, or bird migration patterns. Lynn was a lot, and she was aware of that. She had a therapist, and a handful of diagnoses, and worked under the assumption there had to be at least one other person in the world as weird as she was—but she'd never find them, because it was a lot less drama to be alone.

The drone dipped to eye height. Lynn drew closer and as she did so, a hand that looked suspiciously like a repurposed backscratcher descended from the drone's middle. Taped to the hand was another baggie, this one sandwich-sized. This was definitely not a university drone.

"LynnLYNN," the drone demanded. Then again came the repeat in that sloshing alto. "LynnLYNN!"

Lynn whipped around, but saw only puffins bobbing on agitated ocean waves.

She refused to be spooked by distorted audio from a vintage drone. "Okay, okay." Lynn pulled the baggie free and removed the bundle comprised of a strip of paper, wrapped around a silver-plated compass. Written on the lined notebook paper in old fashioned cursive was: *You'll never be lost with a compass and a good woman by your side. You've inherited both. —Grandpa Jim.*

"Grandpa Jim doesn't know what year it is. He'd have to leave his research lab or the retirement home for that," Lynn muttered. "What is Cousin Izzy up to?" She removed the compass next. She flipped open the pocketwatch-style cover. Then she looked at the drone dead on, because if it was sending audio it had to be receiving as well, and said, "You know we have GPS, right? It uses satellites. I've got three other compasses on board. So, unless this one points the way to hidden treasure instead of north, I'm not sure what to do with it."

"LYNNLYNN!" squawked the drone.

"Lynnnnnnnnn," a woman called, long and low, and from somewhere behind Lynn. That wasn't an audio problem. The sound definitely came from behind her. She spun to look, and off the starboard side of the boat, a fish with a green tail the length of Lynn's leg, splashed, oblivious to the geriatric mischief happening above.

"Grandpa? Is this a joke? What's with the giant fish?"

When neither the drone nor the giant fish responded, Lynn turned back and mulled. To send a drone this old, this far into the Pacific meant at least enough tech knowledge for audio feeds. That pointed farther away from her grandfather. He hated water, both engaging with it and looking at it. He'd specifically researched soil and sand as a graduate student, before he'd quit academia to open his own business. Aside from that though, he'd refused to go on paddle boats in park lakes with Lynn as a child, citing sea sickness. He'd won one of those all-expense paid cruises through his local VA office and had handed it right back. Hell, Lynn had jumped in a particularly deep puddle at the end of her cul-de-sac around ten and he'd come barreling out of the house and tackled her into the dry pavement. He could also not, as far as she knew, control Pacific Ocean fish.

Lynn growled as she slid the compass into her pocket. "If you're one of my undergrads and you think this is funny, please note that my grandfather is ninety-seven years old and has never been on a boat a day in his life. This is a poorly researched prank. Go away and don't come back until you bring snacks. Take your freaky fish with you."

The drone, which apparently *had* been listening, raised up and whirred toward the horizon. No backup drone— with backup snacks—returned.

When night came, Lynn took her data, a piece of dried mango and a tin of tuna, put away her fishing pole in the same drawer she shoved the compass and note into, and went to bed.

Morning came, drone-less, snack-less, and with no upsetting, disembodied voices. Having never developed a taste for caffeine in any form, Lynn rolled from her cot, forced herself into work clothes with seams that made her want to scream, ascended the five short steps to the deck, and promptly tripped the moment she could see ocean.

She landed on her chin, hands caught under her belly, one foot dangling half-off the top step. She growled, rolled to her side...and came face to face with two purple seashells.

They weren't a real purple. They weren't faintly pearlescent purple, or algal purple, or sea urchin purple. They were *purple,* purple—the color of Barney the dinosaur, or grape bubblegum, or children's cold medicine. They lay flat, two halves severed and displayed, atop a damp *Playboy* magazine. The magazine was still halfway inside the same plastic baggie the drone had dumped into the ocean.

"What?" The word summarized half a dozen emotions and questions into one focal point as Lynn stood and finished climbing the stairs. "What? Is? That?"

The flock of puffins bobbing in the water next to her boat did not answer.

"LynnLynn."

The woman's voice crested along with a wave, smacking the side of Lynn's vessel. Lynn lost her footing and slid, along with the purple seashells, back against the starboard safety rail. The deck was wet, not with water, but a kind of salty slime that prevented her bare feet from gaining traction. Her name rolled along the ocean waves. "LynnLynn. LynnLynn."

"No more drones and no talking ocean, Grandpa! I'm out here alone and you're scaring me!"

There were no drones in the overcast sky. Looking behind her, at the ocean below, there was no giant fish. Just puffins, endless puffins, and water. Occasionally a puffin dipping below the waves—a little too quickly—but that was likely just them diving for fish. Right? Another puffin squawked as it went under, pulled by what looked like—but could not have been—human-looking fingers. Lynn walked the perimeter of the boat anyway, but saw nothing of note.

"Izzy? Undergrads? Somebody answer."

Puffins cried, but no human voices came forward.

"Fine! Yar. Pirates like creepy just fine! You think this is the first prank I've ever had pulled on me? You think I don't remember Megan W. repeatedly punching me in the stomach in the third grade because she told me it was the only way to see a unicorn? I've been battle tested by jerks my whole life. Bring it on!" Lynn pocketed the seashells— for evidence if nothing else—and made her way to the *Playboy*. The damp pages had glued it to the deck, and it lay closed and half-wedged in the plastic bag. She tried to open it, because surely there had to be a note or taunt or explanation why her senile grandfather had shipped her a *Playboy* via antique drone and then continued to terrorize her with sideshow horror tactics.

Wet paper and soggy muffs curled around Lynn's fingers. Lynn peeled and managed to get a few sheets half apart, but no wet note fell out. The pages finally did separate on what appeared to be a frequent crease, opening the magazine to a centerfold of a woman lounging on a couch, in the middle of a beach. Her long red hair draped around her breasts, nipples peeking through. Her legs, one draped over the other to cover her slit (but just barely), had been spraypainted green, a touch of highlighting giving the subtle appearance of scales. In one outstretched hand she held Ariel's iconic purple seashell bra.

"LynnLynn," sang the ocean.

"I'm busy! If you want my attention, use your words. That's what everyone always yelled at me growing up. Also, I'm not afraid of you so piss off."

"LynnnnnLynn."

"Argh!" Lynn stalked along the perimeter of the boat, bent over the railing, searching for the sound. Puffins trailed her from above, a handful landing and paddling after her in the water. The water near the boat rippled into concentric circles, the hint of yet another large, green fish tail skating just under the surface. A puffin dipped below the waves with a startled squawk. Then another. A plume of feathers surfaced in their wake. Again flashed a hand—fingers long and nimble, scales faintly visible on the skin.

"Come up and talk to me like the ridiculous joke you are. You going to squirt water in my face? Secretly be a blow-up doll? Maybe turn out to be an animatronic puppet? It's not funny, and I'm not laughing, so cut it out."

Silence.

Lynn waited five minutes, then ten. She did another lap around the boat and—when no more mysterious voices came—she shoved the *Playboy*, along with the shells, into the waterlogged bag. Then she went below deck, tossed the baggie of weirdness into her storage locker, and used her computer to call her mother. When no one answered she tried her sister. When that failed, she tried her grandfather's retirement community directly. He'd had a wandering episode and was with the doctor, however, and couldn't come, but they promised to have him call her the next time he was in his room.

Lynn gave up and took a nap.

The aurora borealis came out that night, throwing off all of Lynn's readings but making for a stunning display. Consumed by the undulating greens and golds she went to bed smiling, woke up and made her breakfast smiling, and whistled her way upstairs, ready to run through the morning system checks, magazine all but forgotten.

Another *Playboy* lay in the exact location as the last, sweating seawater across the deck. This one had dissolving edges, was ringed by braided seaweed, and was already open to the centerfold—another redhead, this time laying directly on the beach. Ropes of seaweed formed an underwire support for her breasts, pushing them practically up into her chin, and a similar rope ran between her legs, hiding what Lynn considered to be the best part of any nude photo. Not that she spent much time with nude photos anymore. She was an adult and she had the internet. But a much younger Lynn and Izzy had spent several hours one night arguing the merits of nude women in magazines. Izzy, sixteen at the time and six months older than Lynn, had thought the whole idea tasteless and barbaric, though did not have similar concerns when Lynn had produced a *Playgirl*. Lynn, in contrast, had several of the centerfolds burned into her memory. This had proven highly useful when she failed to get asked to homecoming, prom, and Yenna Blakey's senior class house party. Not that she'd wanted to go, because late nights and tightly packed crowds were not Lynn's thing. But an overture of friendship, or interest, would have been nice.

She backed away, to the edge of the boat, eyes never leaving the display of porn and sea vegetables. Her rear hit the port side rail and a heavy metal something slapped the wall. The compass. In her pocket, though she'd definitely not put it there.

"Grandpa? Grandpa's lackey? Izzy!? Has one of you been on this boat with me for two months, hiding, just to...to...with...with my grandfather's vintage *Playboy* collection!?" She took a deep breath and screamed, "Cut it out! And come out so I can push you overboard! I'm calling this in to Abichal, my PI!" Her lab's principal investigator didn't have an ounce of sway over her grandfather or cousin, but it was the most authority Lynn could muster in the moment.

No familial figure emerged from the shadows, which was good because the research vessel was tiny and there was literally nothing to hide behind. Below deck had exactly two rooms: one Lynn slept in, and the other packed to the gills with her computer and scanner equipment. It could hold two people standing up. There were closets but all were packed with food and gear. There was nowhere for another person to hide.

*Splash slap!*

A fin hit the water, sending a spray over the side of the boat and further drenching the *Playboy*. Lynn ran to rescue it—she'd need evidence when she did eventually Skype the university—and out of the corner of her eye saw for the third time a wide, green fin just under the water. It paused there, hovering. The right tip curled in, winking at her, before slamming back into the depths. From above, a puffin shrieked.

Was her grandpa...inside a giant fish? A mechanical fish? This was a really, really expensive prank and it had no purpose!

Lynn turned up the collar of her vest, determined to also turn away from the ocean, when a face—human—materialized right where the fish tail had been.

The face didn't break the surface of the waves. It neither sank nor fully crested—floating in a bubble of kelp and blood-red hair. If there was a body, Lynn could not make it out. The water was dark this far out in the Pacific, and frigid. Lynn rationalized that this would explain the perfectly preserved features of what had to be a human corpse, idling and pacing her boat. A corpse that was not her grandfather or cousin, but still very human. A corpse whose hands still worked and yanked puffins down into the ocean depths?

The corpse winked at her.

"Gaaaaah!" Lynn skittered back from the rail, slipped and tore the *Playboy*, ran down the stairs, and slammed shut the door to the deck. She then locked herself in her tiny cubby of a room, pressed her back against the wall, and screamed. And screamed. And screamed.

"Not a face! Not a person! Not alive! Have to call mom. Yup. Going to need to call mom." She dug her satellite phone from her cargo pants pocket and hit the video call button.

*Bleeeep bloop.*
*Bleeeep bloop.*
*Bleeeep bloop.*
"Answer! Why won't you answer!?"
*Bleeeep bloop.*
*Bleeeep bloop.*

"The number you are trying to reach is not answering and the mailbox is full. Please try again at another time."

*Beeeeeeep.*

Above Lynn's head, from the deck, came *thum thump. Thum thump. Slapslapslap.*

"Somebody answer the damn phone!"

"Incoming video call from GRANDPA. Accept?"

"Accept. Acceptacceptaccept!" She mashed her thumb across the green button. When her grandfather's pale, wrinkled face and perpetually cheerful brown eyes materialized, she exploded with, "Did you send me a cursed *Playboy*!? Are you inside a giant mechanical fish with a human face!?"

"Curses aren't real, Lynn. You're a big girl. You know that." Her grandfather coughed, sending waves of flesh cascading along his jowls. "I thought you were out alone on that big boat. You're always alone."

"I don't *want* to be alone, it's just a foregone inevitability when you can't manage small talk. And this is a research vessel, Grandpa, because I am a scientist that you just sent a compass to via—"

"You're a post doc." Her grandfather tutted. "Your imagination has always gotten the better of you. Always in your own world. Always prefer your imaginary people to the real ones. But there is a situation now, Lynnie, that needs your attention. What I do need you to do"—he coughed again, droplets of spittle smearing his phone screen—"is to drop that compass into the water."

Lynn held her breath to the count of ten. Dementia was no one's fault, and her grandfather's organic soil was still the talk of their small town, even if the business had been dead since he retired. He deserved respect, even if she was about to be murdered. "I'm fine dropping your old mementos into the water but there are bigger issues first. Why is there a body in the Pacific? Why is there a body near my boat?"

Her grandfather's eyes flitted offscreen, wandering much the same way Lynn's did when forced into too long a conversation. "Yes, I'm aware. I'll only be a minute. Tell Abi to keep his pants on. Taking them off is the reason we attracted the mermaid in the first place." He straightened, turned back to his phone, and pointed an arthritic finger at her. "Listen to me, young lady. You will drop the compass, or throw it, the next time you see my friend. She won't let you rest until you do. I want this to work out for you. Do it right and we both get what we want. You're good at following directions. Don't change that now."

"Your friend is..."

*Fwap SLAP.*

"Your friend is a *mermaid?!*"

"A very friendly one," her grandfather said with an annoying half-smirk.

"But mermaids aren't real."

"Aren't they?" asked her grandfather. "Go on up there and prove me wrong."

"James, who are you talking to?" A liver-spotted hand came into frame, resting on her grandfather's shoulder. The ring finger was snipped at the first knuckle, which Lynn had only seen once before, on...

"Professor Abichal?"

The perpetually red face of her PI craned into the frame. "Dr. McCarthy. How are you enjoying your research?"

"It was fine until porn showed up on my deck. Porn and mermaids, I guess."

*Fwap fwap CRASH.*

Abichal laughed. "Ah she found you. Excellent. Don't forget to give her the compass will you, Lynn?" To her grandfather he said, "I'll come back in ten, James." To Lynn he gave a thumbs up and said, "We're counting on you, almost-professor!" He then left the frame, and a door creaked closed a moment later.

"I don't care how friendly the mermaid is. How do you know the head of my lab?" Lynn demanded of her still-smiling grandfather.

*Flap flap WHAP.*

"Oh, shut up!" Lynn yelled at the ceiling. "You can mermaid on me in a minute. Chill out. I'm on the phone!"

*Fwip fwap, fwip fwap.* Slaps of agreement? Slaps of impending doom?

"Is this why you never went near water, Grandpa?"

Grandpa Jim coughed again. The face that looked back at her, eyes clearly on her forehead, aged a decade in a heartbeat. "What a man does for his PhD graduation with his buddies and a few of their younger siblings is old news. If they brought a stack of *Playboys* to read, and then ran out of bait and got creative, then caught something they shouldn't have, that's irrelevant. What I need from you—"

More coughing. From offscreen, a woman asked, "Jim? Would you like to take a rest?"

"Go away, woman!" His hand flapped a dismissal. He then hissed into the screen, "All I need you to do is to give the mermaid the compass and I'm free. Then it's your turn, Lynnie. You deserve this. Too many missed milestones, and you've too much potential to waste on a dinghy in the Pacific. And I'm done. I have to be done, Lynnie. I'm tired."

"Jim?" the offscreen woman asked again. "Are you sure you don't want to take a rest?" Footsteps drew near and a much younger thumb partially obscured the camera.

"Talk to her first!" her grandfather's hoarse voice demanded. "Just because you're taking the helm doesn't mean you can't get what you want, too."

"I don't want to take any helm! I just want to do my research and—"

"Jim, I really must insist," said the offscreen woman.

Lynn almost threw the phone against the wall. "Grandpa, what—"

The call disconnected.

*Wham WHAM.*

"This is my research vessel, and my research!" Lynn yelled as she slapped the ceiling. "I will not be intimidated, and I'm bringing you your damn compass. Keep your fins on." She flung open the door, tossed her cell phone onto her bed, and stormed up the stairs just in time to see the edges of green fins disappear over the side of the boat.

Lynn ran after the mermaid, slamming her midsection into the side rail and nearly flinging herself into the sea. She pulled the compass out and dangled it over the edge. "If I give this to you, will you shut up!?"

The waves around her swirled in response, but no green fins appeared, and no lady's faces returned to torment her.

"Here, fishy fishy! Come get your compass!"

Puffins cried overhead, but no mermaid materialized. What did materialize were rain clouds—thick and dark, that pelted the boat with streams of rain.

Lynn—soaked to the bone and half dangling over the side of a science vessel—realized she looked absolutely ridiculous.

Grandpa Jim had never been an asshole to her before, but he was old and Lynn was everyone's favorite punching bag. She straightened and tucked the compass into a hip pocket. If the mermaid was going to be coy, Lynn would just wait her out. She had four months to go, plenty of fruit snacks, and a recently acquired backbone. She would not be bullied, even by family. Even by fantasy creatures that still had a high likelihood of being a prank. Lynn had standards, damn it, and she was holding to them.

* * *

Lynn spent the next three days staying up all night to catalog light pollution, spending the morning watching puffins land on rocky outcroppings and rub beaks, and sleeping through lunch and into the evening. She kept the compass on herself at all times, but no more magazines or ocean flora appeared on the deck.

The fourth day brought overcast skies, rougher water, and more forecasted aurora lights. Seasickness seldom bothered her, but the waves had just the right mash to send Lynn dry heaving over the boat's rail, staring at the white caps and puffins, and debating every life choice she'd ever made.

"I hate this. I hate," she belched stale granola bar and tried to focus on the horizon. Puffins circled overhead. One dove into the water, presumably to catch a fish, but never resurfaced. A feather floated up from the inky water—first one, then two, then a bloom, followed by a severed orange foot.

Having no desire to see matching entrails, Lynn stepped away from the rail, pivoted, and stepped on a bright purple seashell. The delicate thing shattered under her shoe and Lynn sidestepped, just to crunch another. Then another. The seashells wove across the deck in loops and knots that absolutely had not been there half an hour ago, when she'd stumbled up from her cabin.

"Ten points for timing. Kick 'em when they're down. I'm too dehydrated for another vintage porn stack left by a mermaid. Can we play this game later?" She crunched a path to the very center of the deck, where yet another centerfold lay, spread and sopping wet. Another Ariel, somehow wearing less than the last, her arms crossed high and covering what the seashells should have.

Lynn backed away, retracing her trail through the shards of purple seashell, until her rear hit the guard rail. "I hate you. I hate you I hate you I hate you," she said to the sodden *Playboy*, and her grandfather, before she spun around and stared into the ocean.

A thick breeze had sent the waves to whitecaps again, and the grey sky darkened the water. Yet there was no mistaking the face that floated there, fanned by red hair—thin as kelp fronds. Human eyes blinked double lids at

Lynn. From a human nose, bubbles burst forth. Pink lips smiled, wider and wider, until Lynn caught a flash of pointed ivory.

An arm rose from the waves, skin the color of pale sand, fingers spindly and with an extra joint that sent shivers down Lynn's spine. Those fingers wrapped around another shell, half pearlescent white, half Little Mermaid purple. The fingers opened and the shell lay on the creature's palm—an offering to Lynn she refused to reach for.

A splash of water came from the left and the creature rose up, propelled by an absolutely gargantuan tail. In the diffuse sunlight and cascade of water the tail looked one part fish and one part sleeve—the musculature of human legs apparent underneath a thin layer of sharp green scales.

Twenty points to Grandpa Jim for absolutely top-notch special effects. This had to be prank of the year. Of the century!

For a breath Lynn looked the...mermaid...right in the eyes. That's what one did when one met someone new. Lynn knew the rules. They'd been drilled into her since childhood.

The mermaid stared back, gaze ever so slightly to the left, like she found a fascinating detail on Lynn's cheek. The mermaid wore neither shirt nor seashells, but she did have breasts. Small ones. Decidedly mammalian-looking ones, complete with areolas and nipples in all the right places.

"Oh," was all Lynn managed to say. "Hi. You look...cold. Did you uh, want the compass? For coverage of uh..."—she gestured at the mermaid's chest—"coverage of this area? Like you could break it in two halves and then use it sort of like the shells and..."

The mermaid laid the shell on the rail and slipped back down into the ocean.

"I thought you wanted this!? And if you could not leave these on the deck anymore, I'd appreciate it!" Lynn yelled into the whitecaps. But the ocean had swallowed the fish woman, leaving a stream of puffins in her wake.

"Oh no. You don't get to just disappear." Lynn fished the compass from her pocket and flipped open the lid. She dangled the compass over the rail, letting a break in the clouds send sunlight cascading across the silver face and dripping pinpricks of light onto the water.

Pockets of ocean swirled like tiny funnel cakes in response, but the mermaid did not reappear.

"You started talking to me. You don't get to bow out mid-conversation!" Lynn leaned further into the rail, the steel digging into her midsection. The compass remained a handful of feet from the water, glinting in the sunlight. The funnels concentrated as well, consuming the refracted light. Strands of kelp swirled to the surface.

"Take the bait," Lynn muttered. "At the very least I want some photos." But after another moment the kelp sank back down and the whitecaps returned.

"Need to get it closer. How...?" Puffins bombed the water headfirst, after an unseen school of fish. Not all of them came back up.

Lynn grinned. "Of course. If it worked for Grandpa Jim, why not me?" She ran down below, grabbed her *My Little Pony* fishing pole, a handful of bobbers, and the largest hook she could find. Back on the deck she looped the hook through the compass' loop, then bent the tip back around so it wouldn't slide off. The bobbers she tied low—she didn't need the compass too far out of sight—tightened the reel, pressed the release, and let the whole thing fly.

The shrieking of puffins obscured any sound the compass made when it hit. Whitecaps swallowed it and the first two bobbers, leaving three above the surface to fight the wind and curious birds.

"No fish for you!" Lynn yelled at the puffins. "Back off. Yar!"

Puffins swarmed and dove, first two, then five, then a flock. They teemed around Lynn's fishing line, squawking, no doubt, about stealing another of her fish.

Ripples started, from the northeast. Lynn saw the concentric arches of movement a moment before the puffins. Her heartrate doubled before the birds took off en masse into the air.

"Guess we know what mermaids eat," Lynn murmured as the arches drew closer. Twelve feet. Ten. Five.

The disturbance stilled.

"Hey, what? You—"

The fishing line pulled from Lynn's hands, bobbers disappearing into a human-sized funnel of water and kelp. The loop around Lynn's wrist kept the pole from going overboard but it dragged Lynn back to the rail and very nearly over it.

"Ow! Stop it!" She got her left hand higher on the pole, stabilized her right back on the handle, braced her legs against the side of the boat, and pulled back. She gained an inch, maybe, and promptly reeled in. Again, she pushed, gained another few inches, reeled, and repeated. The topmost bobber blinked its red and white just under the surface. Lynn braced for another pull, fingers slick against the line, shoes soaked from the spray and embedded with shards of gaudy purple shell, when the line went slack.

Lynn flew backward, the loop slipping from her wrist as she landed on her rear. Shell shards dug into her butt and cut up her palms. She cursed puffins, mermaids, and her grandfather as she wiped bloody fingers across her pants and watched her favorite fishing pole slide across the deck, up the rail, and over the edge.

"I hate everything."

A singsong voice replied, "I hate everything."

Long fingers gripped the safety rail. Green kelp wove around the metal bar, defying gravity and logic. A woman's head appeared, then her breasts, and then there was a mermaid on the deck of Lynn's research vessel.

"Urp," said Lynn. She didn't have a doctorate in anthropology. This was beyond the scope of her work.

"Urp!" barked the mermaid as she dragged her body across the deck. The thin scales of her tail flung water in rainbow arcs, which Lynn might have appreciated more had the mermaid not closed the distance between them in less than three seconds.

"You're a...a fish person." It probably should have been a question.

The mermaid stopped, less than six inches from Lynn's face. Her eyes shone the blue of the ocean, the blue of a deep summer sky, the blue of an oversaturated pinup.

Then the mermaid's inner eyelids gave a vertical blink, and Lynn very nearly peed herself. Blue eyes saturated to a rich, earthen brown. From behind her tail, she pulled a thin piece of fishing line. Lynn's pole flopped back over the side of the deck and landed at her feet.

"Hi," Lynn breathed. "Thanks."

The mermaid touched her forehead to Lynn's. Her eyelids blinked again, both vertical and horizontal lids. Flecks of orange melted in, grazing the brown to amber. The smell of salt and seaweed accosted Lynn's nose. "Heir of Jim. You returned my compass," said the mermaid, her voice thick and sticky, like molasses left too long on the stove. "You wish to renegotiate."

"Yes?" It was the best Lynn could come up with. She tentatively touched a piece of the mermaid's kelp hair. When the mermaid didn't react, Lynn let the surprisingly silken strand slide through her fingers, bumping over little round nodules that felt like air sacs. When the strand fell onto the mermaid's shoulder Lynn brushed it off, along with shards of drying salt.

"Your skin feels the same as your hair," Lynn said. "I'd thought it would be coarse or scaly. It isn't like hide, either. It feels like cold butter. Like tight dolphin skin."

The mermaid flipped her tail around so that it lay across Lynn's lap. Her torso moved back a handspan. Her tail fins twitched, and her eyes blinked back to blue, still only focusing on Lynn's cheek. It felt...respectful. And that helped counterbalance the absurdity. Almost.

"Jim had my compass," the mermaid repeated. "I brought him shells. For fifteen years I brought shells and stayed in the form he requested. I was not paid. I was ignored, ignored and stuck with legs, and now you wish to change the terms of a binding agreement. This is unacceptable." Her tail slapped the deck, the outline of two muscular, feminine legs clearly outlined beneath a mat of scales.

"O...oh. Yeah, I don't like it when promises aren't kept, either. I'm very sorry. But the compass is in the ocean now though, right? So, you have it back? And I'm his blood so that should count, right? As for the shell payments I could. Um. I could find at least some of the shells and return them. I'm sorry about the..." Lynn stopped and replayed the mermaid's last words. "Sorry, were you just like, hanging out, on land, waiting for Uncle Jim to release you by returning the compass?"

The mermaid flipped and came back to Lynn's face. "The compass is not the promise. The compass bearer is the promise."

Danger. "I didn't make a promise," Lynn said, slowly. "I returned your compass. I don't make promises I can't keep. Let's just not talk about promises, okay? Let's uh, talk about this." She picked up her fishing rod. "You ever seen *My Little Pony*? They have, er, merponies. You, um, have merponies?"

The mermaid continued to stare, her eyelids unmoving, her eyes a cascade of amber and brown. "I am owed the companionship I was promised. We will renew the deal, LynnLynn, and you will pay what your grandfather would not. Pick a new form for me and we will renew the bond." The mermaid pulled back and dragged herself to the center of the dock, and the *Playboy* that still lay there. She brought it back rolled in her mouth, dagger-edged teeth indenting the cover. When she returned to spitting distance of Lynn, she released the magazine, flipped her tail around and swatted the *Playboy* toward Lynn.

It smacked Lynn directly in the chest and fell onto her lap, opening, once again, to *The Little Mermaid* homage. Had she ever even seen that movie in its entirety? It'd come out before she was born. She'd picked up one of the dolls from a garage sale as a kid but couldn't remember playing with it outside of the prerequisite stripping of clothes to determine if mermaids wore underwear.

"We will renew the bond at twilight." She flipped herself over the side of the boat without a single sound. By the time Lynn got to the rail the waves held no trace of her.

"I didn't agree to anything!"

No response from the ocean.

Lynn crossed her arms, bit into her lower lip, and took a deep breath. Twilight. Right. That gave her all of six hours to make a plan. So, like any good scientist, Lynn went right to a literature review.

\* \* \*

An orderly answered her grandfather's phone, curtly informed Lynn that Jim was having a bath, and she could call back tomorrow. Out of useful options, she called the only other person she could think of: her PI.

"Dr. McCarthy? Is everything alright?" Professor Abichal Soni squinted at Lynn through the iPhone camera, his face far too close. Unbrushed, grey hair cascaded across his forehead, bright against weatherworn brown skin. "Can you see me?"

"Tell me about the mermaid."

Professor Abichal coughed. "Has your spectrophotometer been giving you problems again? I can send a tech drone out with components."

Lynn scowled. "I've met a mermaid with pointy teeth, a taste for puffin, and who speaks flawless English. There is a potential paper in *Science* on the line with all this. Google is remarkably unhelpful outside of recurring versions of Hans Christian Andersen tales and a horror book by a Mira Grant that has enough science to make me think she's also had an encounter. Though her mermaids were more feral. Regardless, I need to know what is going on."

"Oh." Professor Abichal ran a hand through his hair, snagging halfway through on a mountain of tangles. "I see." He coughed again. "Your grandfather may have sailed when he was younger."

"Whereupon he met mermaids?"

"Ah. Well. Yes." He pulled at the tangles, a clump of hair coming out with his fingers in the process. "You catch a mermaid, fine. You make a drunken bargain, she offers you an old compass, you offer her...um, something more physical, and it's a deal set in stone, apparently. No backsies."

Lynn did not giggle at a full, tenured professor saying "backsies."

"It went fine at first, the shell deliveries appearing in the backyard stream only and your grandfather taking them and grinding them into soil micronutrients to make his award-winning fertilizer. Visiting her every few months for, er, 'conversation.' Then he got married. He sold the business and tried to retire, but the shells kept coming. And I mean, they kept coming *everywhere*. Sewage drains. Popping off manhole covers. Once, floating up from the damn toilet! Jim wanted her to have legs so he could, you know, and she turned into a shell stalker!" He poked a wrinkled finger at the phone. "Anyway Jim, he wouldn't go back out on the boat to deliver the compass, too afraid he wouldn't return. He was supposed to be hers and Jim didn't think she'd take kindly to him having a wife. So, we'd pay sailors to take the compass out and drop it in the water, and every time it came back. Same route as the shells, as horrifying as that is."

"The compass I had in my hands was in a toilet?" Lynn asked.

"Several times. She wouldn't break the contract. She wanted your grandfather, and your grandfather was dedicated to your grandmother. Only way to avoid her, and anything like her, was to stay away from water. Legs or not, she couldn't get too far from water."

That did explain why, when her grandparents' second floor bathroom pipes had gone, they'd not replaced them for almost three years.

"But the shells won't stop coming. Tiny ones come out of faucets. Jim had two fly out of a urinal just yesterday. It's maddening. And how is he to explain it to the retirement home staff? Only so many shells can be chucked out a window before questions are asked. They have to stop coming. She has to stop. She has to move on."

"What does she want?" Lynn asked, letting the academic part of her brain take the wheel. "Just sex? Was there more to the deal?" She refused to ask the questions she really wanted to: *How does someone have sex with a mermaid? Does a vulva just magically appear along with the legs?*

Abichal sighed, long and heavy, his nose twitching. "Wealth for companionship. The compass was a contract. That's what I remember. We are hoping the promise is at least transferable, if it isn't deletable. Did you look at the name of our private donor, Dr. McCarthy?"

"No. I was the only one qualified. I got the money. The end."

Paper shuffled offscreen then Dr. Abichal held up a transmittal sheet. Across the top, in a flowery, cursive font, read *Undershells Inc.* Beneath that it read, *private donation parameters, to be followed exactly or the funding will be revoked.*

"Grandpa set up a grant just to get me to his mermaid!?"

"He needs a break. Your grandfather deserves a rest. Surely you understand."

"You're dumping your problems on me," Lynn deadpanned. Her stomach contorted so dramatically that bile rose in her throat. First of all, seashells could not be that irritating, especially if they had monetary value. Second, how hard was it to get in a boat once a year and screw a mermaid, or play rummy with her, or whatever she wanted? People, in general, did not solve their own problems it seemed, and Lynn was not interested in being a punching bag turned scapegoat. "Did any of you ever think of talking to her and trying to renegotiate? Or paying her off? Or *asking* me if I'd help?"

"I—" Dr. Abichal began. "Your grandfather assumed with the way you were around people that...maybe this might..."

"No. Stop. I'll handle it. How am I the one with the social issues?" Lynn ended the call, downed a single serve packet of applesauce, flicked her phone back on, and typed "how to apologize to a mermaid" into the Google search bar.

* * *

The moment the sun dipped below the horizon, Lynn went back above deck, armed with a thermal vest, mug of hot chocolate, and the complete and unabridged version of *The Little Mermaid* on her phone. The clouds had cleared and stars winked into existence, swirling with the blooming colors of the Milky Way. The moon shone a silver crescent, spilling just enough light to illuminate the boat's tiny deck.

The mermaid lay waiting, fanned across the teak, her hair now the color of seafoam, her skin a pale ochre. For all the fish might have studied dirty magazines she didn't seem to have absorbed artful repose. She rested on her stomach, chin on her palms, elbows digging into the teak boards beneath her. Breasts barely protruded from her chest, areolas and nipples dusky enough to be nearly invisible in the waning light. In the water, she'd been menacing. Here on the boat, she merely looked peculiar.

Lynn tanked the hot chocolate, set the mug on the ground, and inched forward. "I've found nothing on apologies, so I'll start with, I'm sorry. I'm sorry for Grandpa Jim, and for broken promises. Can you tell me how you're feeling? Are you going to turn into seafoam if I don't renew this promise? Is there a true love's kiss situation to deal with, or if we get close enough to kiss will you bite my face off and steal my legs?"

"It's time to make your choice," the mermaid commanded. In the absence of puffin screams and whistling wind, her voice drove like a sledgehammer through Lynn's head.

Lynn took a step back, hands over her ears. "Ah! Loud! Choose between a kiss and face eating? Cool. I choose kiss, I guess. What are we talking about?"

The mermaid's tail flicked, first quickly, then mellowed to a slow, steady pat. "I am sorry. That was too loud. Here." She held out a hand. In it was another shell, deeper than the others, holding a cup full of seawater and a tiny seahorse. "This is the symbol of our new pact. A gift for you."

"So do you accept the apology or, oh. Oh, look at it." Lynn took the shell, marveling at the thumb-sized creature. She'd gotten gifts over the years, from family mostly, and a few awkward whole-class birthday parties. The gifts had always been what she needed, like socks or luggage, or what the gifter secretly wanted themselves. Lynn had gone twenty-four years of life and here, swimming in her hands, was the first gift she'd ever truly wanted.

"I get it," she said, not looking up. "I've got a volume control problem, too. Thank you for this. It's lovely."

"I do not wish to scare you," whispered the mermaid.

"Weird thing is, I don't think you do." Lynn placed the shell down and clasped her hands. She'd had a list of questions prepared, including: *Are you magic? Do you want legs, or can I talk you into wings? Is there a sea witch and can I meet her?* She scrapped them all. "Maybe we start again. No assumptions this time. Here's my deal. I'm a literal person and all I've been given are *CliffsNotes* from drunken college boys who won't take responsibility for where they fish. I don't understand what I'm supposed to choose, and what the consequences of each choice are. Are you angry? Are you lonely?" Lynn brandished her phone, the backlight behind *The Little Mermaid* causing both her and the mermaid to squint and look away. "In fairy tales the mermaids, they all have rules. If you want me to play, I need the parameters."

"I am not angry. I am owed. You have to pick my form," said the mermaid, in a tone that managed to be both condescending and apologetic. "This is a rule. You choose the form, you make the offer, I bind the covenant. You gain wealth, I gain companionship." From under her belly, she pulled a stack of *Playboys*, all waterlogged and decayed. She slid them across the deck in flaking print. Lynn saw dates from the seventies and early eighties, and many, many pairs of milky-white breasts. "These are all potential forms."

Lynn nudged the nearest one with her toe. "Shouldn't this be a choice? Besides I don't like this. I don't like—"

The mermaid smiled, wide and toothy. A forked tongue licked the air and curled back over teeth that—as Lynn studied them—faded from capped to pointed, depending on the reflection of the moonlight. But there was no menace in her smile. Eagerness, yes, and an awkwardness Lynn felt to her core. "It was a choice for your grandfather. But I am owed. I will continue to uphold my end of the bargain, but you must choose my form and do what your grandfather would not."

"I'm only having sex on my terms."

Another flash of pointed teeth. "Our terms are not yet settled. There have been no parameters set thus far."

"Oh." Lynn sat with that for a moment. "It's not about sex? Or, it doesn't have to be? That's...actually really neat. Okay. I agree that you need compensation but, well, let's start here: Why can't I pick the form you have now?"

The mermaid's tail slapped the deck. "You must follow the rules!"

"Okay! Hold on." Amongst the pages at Lynn's feet was an ad for a law office, with a pretty but also very clothed woman holding a book. "Her."

The mermaid scuttled to Lynn, elbows cocked at painful angles, the horrifying smile unwavering. But her eyes still didn't bore into Lynn's, and while she was close enough to assault Lynn's nose with fish smell, she didn't demand small talk. And that was...nice. Comforting, in a way that helped balance the kelp hair bobbing along her shoulders, accosting gravity. Lynn caught herself reaching for the iridescent scaling on the mermaid's tail, fascinated by the light refraction of green, then blue, then shades of brown.

The mermaid studied the paper, turning it upside down as it disintegrated in her long fingers. Orange eyes looked up to Lynn's forehead, her smile still present but teeth no longer visible. She shook her head, and brown stormed down each strand of kelp hair. The flatness curled in on itself, morphing into fat strands of what would, at a distance, look like thick braids. Her skin paled and took on rose undertones, her lips blushed sunset red, and her breasts swelled to a solid B-cup. She pushed herself up, arching her back, fingertips supporting her weight. A horrible *crackkkkk* sounded behind the mermaid and then she stood—*stood*—before Lynn, as nude and confident as Cousin Izzy after three shots of tequila.

Water streamed down the mermaid's body, around pert breasts, across a softly rounded belly, cascading between legs and a distinctly mammalian cleft.

"You...you forgot the body hair," Lynn managed. "And uh, don't fish have uh, cloaca?"

"I'm not a basal fish," the mermaid retorted. "Plenty of my less evolved cousins can alter their chromophores and gonads. Are you not a scientist? Why are you surprised?" She leaned over and poked her clit. "Are you pleased? Or does this need to be bigger? Like these"—she cupped a breast—"it is merely an air sac." Her eyes widened. "Do you want to know the biological specifics?"

"Uh. Wow. Yes. Yes, I do." Migrating bird patterns could not even begin to compare to this. She should have been taking notes. Any paper in *Science* would need notes. But they were close enough to touch and Lynn did so, her fingertips stroking the smooth skin of the mermaid's shoulder. In the full moonlight, Lynn caught the glint of scales just beneath the skin, but she said nothing. The mermaid said nothing. They stood there, Lynn stroking and the mermaid's gaze wandering from Lynn's hand to the ocean, and back, and Lynn could not remember ever experiencing a moment so perfect.

She'd liked her grandmother just fine. But her grandfather had ghosted *this?*

Lynn's hand had wandered during her musings, to the mermaid's breast. Her thumb covered the nipple and twitched, poised to stroke.

"You are pleased."

Lynn whipped her hand away and clasped it behind her back. "I am so sorry. That was completely inappropriate, I...did you just roll your eyes at me?"

Instead of answering, the mermaid knelt. "I pledge this form to you, Lynn McCarthy. I pledge that I will—"

"Nope." Lynn dragged her to standing. "You're very pretty, and if you had clothes on, I'd make you a coffee. But whatever deal Grandpa struck, I'm not renewing it. We're starting over, remember? I picked a form, we need to make a deal, right? Can it be, I don't know...can it be this? Seahorses and air sacs and science? If I choose you, I want *you*. Terrifying mermaid you. And I'll be terrifying human me, and we'll just, we'll just cancel each other out. And not have to worry about being too loud, or accidentally offending. Doesn't that sound good?" It sounded pretty good to Lynn. Far better than anything proposed behind high school bleachers, or during her roommates' college dorm parties.

Human feet stepped into Lynn. Human hands clasped her waist. A tongue—rounded and pink and no longer forked, licked the tips of flat, human teeth.

"It, uh, I don't dislike this form. So you know. But I can do tail. And breasts, um, any size that works. I uh. I like them all."

The mermaid smiled—slow and soft.

Lynn ran a finger over dusky red lips. She traced the edges of the mermaid's mouth, down her chin, and into the hollow of her throat. The skin was taut here, a touch oily, and so, so inviting. And Lynn did feel invited. The mermaid wanted her there—wanted *her*—regardless of how loud she talked, or that she had a deep obsession with horses, or that she kept filling their dramatic silences with *uh*.

The mermaid leaned in. Their lips touched in a whisper of pressure and a flick of a curious, salty tongue.

Lynn's finger started to tremble. She'd never done this before. Twenty-four years and Lynn had never been kissed because men's mouths smelled like corn chips, and she couldn't muster enough women-space chit chat to last through a date. Lynn took a step back, tongue running over her lips, determined to savor every bit of salt, and to explain herself. "I'm, I'm not so good at this. I don't have a lot of experience. Science is, uh, science is really hot to me. And ponies. You could tell me more about the seahorse. Or your, um, clitoris." Dear God, why was she incapable of talking about the weather, or clothes, or seashells? "Do your rules specify how we have to spend time together?"

The mermaid's brow furrowed. The tips of her hair flattened, green flowing down from the roots. "There are traditions," she said again, but did not otherwise fill the salty air with useless chatter. Instead, she arched her back, inviting Lynn back into the shared space.

Lynn returned, closer than before. She let her hands glide down the mermaid's shoulders, to the sides of her breasts, then her rib cage. Her fingertips bumped along edges of scales, flattened and elongated to mimic human skin. She kissed the top of the mermaid's shoulder. Her tongue lingered on the edges of a submerged scale.

The mermaid's fingers dug into Lynn's upper arms. Air whistled, through subtle striations on her neck—sounding like a catch of breath. Like a gasp.

If her grandfather had taken just one more boat ride. If he'd just talked to the mermaid instead of screwing her...but if he'd done that, there wouldn't have been a mermaid kissing Lynn's jaw. There wouldn't have been a mermaid's extra-jointed finger tracing the curvature of Lynn's hip. She wouldn't have her very own seahorse.

"I want to know how you do this," Lynn said into the mermaid's seashell-shaped ear. "I want to understand your hair chromophores and identify what kind of melanin you have in your skin-scales. And I want you in the ocean, not trapped in legs you don't seem to care for. You're fascinating and pretty and I think...I think we could have really neat conversations."

When the mermaid started to frown and her fingers pulled away, Lynn hastily said, "I'm not saying I don't want, you know. Kissing and stuff. Do you know how humans bond? I've read books. Humans talk on dates. Dates lead to sex, which leads to companionship. At least that's what a *Playboy* would have you think. Talking also happens in a friendship. We like friendship before sex, sometimes. We often like conversation. And my rule is no sex before six dates, and no dates before friendship. The numbers are arbitrary, and I've never used them but they're there and I'm not great with rule changes. Oh. And you have to be able to at least pretend to care about ponies."

The mermaid nodded. Her hands ran up Lynn's back, fingers tapping a soothing rhythm. When they reached her shoulders the mermaid slid her hands down Lynn's arms, drawing lazy circles on the exposed skin of her forearms. "I am very interested in seahorses. I have a small herd. I could bring them to show you."

"That...is the sexiest proposition I've ever heard. You sure you want me, though? Humans are hard. I'm hard. I ask a lot of questions. I get really invested in quirky things, like swelling breasts. We're going to have to talk about those, examine those, for weeks. And it probably won't be about sex at all." Not at first, anyway.

"Humans are indeed difficult." The circling turned into the deep pressure rubs that Lynn paid her physical therapist a hundred dollars an hour to administer. "My requirement for companionship is not resolutely defined." Her voice turned to the haunting wind-whisper. "My rules can bend if yours cannot."

They made brushing eye contact with a tandem swivel of their heads. The brief moment of connection thrilled Lynn, and sent shivers across her shoulders. She had not given much thought in her life to romance. She liked the concept, certainly, but empty platitudes and puffed-up compliments failed to hold her attention. This mermaid, Lynn's mermaid had, in one sentence, delivered a lost lifetime of unconditional acceptance. Lynn wanted to drown in it.

"I have infinite shells and many buyers," said the mermaid. Fingers moved to Lynn's sides and under her shirt, pressure-stroking her rib cage and the delicate skin just under her breasts. "How much time can you give me?"

"Higher?" Lynn asked, not wanting to demand. The mermaid obliged, fingertips again pressing tiny circles that, every few breaths, pressed into her nipples. "Uh. Um.

Logistically speaking, probably three months each year. But uh, if you wear clothes, you can pretend to be my research assistant and then you can stay on the boat with me. If you wanted to. When you're not showing me seahorses. Or you can just swim alongside it. Your body, your choice and all that."

"This is very acceptable companionship, LynnLynn."

The draw of the mermaid's touch, her untamable hair, the presence that demanded nothing of Lynn except what she was willing to give, intoxicated her. Lynn kissed the mermaid's cheek then her lips, this time meeting a force as fluid as the ocean waves.

"No more though," Lynn said when she broke for air. She took the mermaid's hands in hers and brought them down to her hips. Too much, too fast, and she'd sensory overload and end up locking herself in the tiny cabin for a week. "Why don't we both try just having a friend? Then move from there."

The mermaid pulled back, lips pursing first to the left, then to the right. After two deep breaths she reached down, picked up two intact purple shells, and held them to her breasts. "This offer is acceptable assuming clothing no longer involves these."

Lynn laughed, joyfully, loudly, at a volume that always got her shushed. "Make those a bit bigger and you can have some of my shirts. No more shells. And you don't, I mean, if no one is around, you don't have to wear clothes, either. You get to be comfortable. I might wear pajamas more. We both get to be ourselves."

Lynn held out a hand. The mermaid took the shell with the tiny seahorse and placed it back on Lynn's palm. "The promise is made, and the pact renewed." She slid then, down, down, as her legs melted into scales, then a tail. Her hair shivered back to kelp, coloring the same pale, ocean green that now swam in her eyes. "Come now. If you remove your clothes, I will take you swimming for seahorses. I always keep my promises."

Lynn set down the shell and seahorse. "Promises are great, but you want me to get naked? Already? What happened to friends?"

"We are friends. There is much science in the ocean. The fish do not care how you sound, or move, or look. I will keep you afloat as needed. When you are tired, I will return you to the boat." She slid over the guard rail, extra-jointed fingers curling around the railing, suspending the mermaid down the side of the boat. She looked up at Lynn, gills ruffling along her neck, teal scales developing along her shoulders and down her arms. Finally, she let go and fell, silently, into the waves.

Lynn didn't wait. She didn't think. She pulled off her clothes, shoved down a lifetime of *you should, you need to, can't you just,* screamed "*yarrrr,*" and dove into the ocean.

"Under the Seashells" is a stand-alone short by J.S. Fields. You can read more of their science fiction and fantasy work at **www.patreon.com/jsfields** or check out their website: **www.jsfieldsbooks.com**

# The Salvage Sirens

Sarah Day and Tim Pratt

Sapphic Representation: Lesbian, Pansexual, Polyamory
Heat Level: Medium
Content Warnings: Coarse Language, Violence

They'd been plying the seas of the dead planet for days, and Iris was getting bored.

"It's not a dead planet," Sentris said as their sleek surface craft skimmed over blue waves. She was controlling the ship with her neural implants, using a fraction of her attention to steer it around reefs of rebar and the ancient ruins of cities that had been first bombed and then drowned. The rest of her attention was on her wife, Iris, who was sunning herself on the deck—naked except for sunglasses, her skin faintly bluish and shimmering. "There's plenty of aquatic life. Granted, whoever built these cities is long gone, but it's rather sapiocentric to call the place dead—"

"It's dead *boring*, anyway." Iris rolled over onto her belly and kicked her legs up behind her, crossing them at the ankles. She was being cute and obviously knew it. Her toes were webbed, just like her fingers; Iris's augmentations were mostly biological, unlike the technological improvements Sentris sported. "You'd think a quest for mythic lost treasure would be more exciting, is all." She wiggled her butt. "I'm drying out here, Sen. I need to get wet."

"Is that innuendo, or...?" Sentris was cross-legged on the deck, feeling everything their ship felt; her sensorium encompassed radar, lidar, sonar, radiation and electromagnetic detection, and more, but at the moment, she was mostly using her eyes. Iris was a view she never got tired of.

Iris smirked. "You know I'm always open to going off-mission, but I meant I want to *dive*. Also, not in an innuendo way. Water, water everywhere, and I'm not swimming through it and plundering wrecks? My talents are being wasted."

Iris and Sentris were a spacefaring salvage team. They specialized in aquatic operations (for obvious reasons), though Iris was also good at spelunking and urban exploration. Sentris ran operations from whatever boat or base camp they set up. The galaxy was a big place and there were a lot of people fighting a lot of wars, so there were always new ruins to pick through.

Or, in this case, very old ruins. This planet—designated Torove-2 (nobody knew what the centuries-dead natives had called it)—had been doubly devastated, first by its inhabitants and later in a sprawling conflict between interplanetary empires who'd used this system and many others in the galactic neighborhood as theaters of war. Both those empires were fragmented now, neither a power of particular importance, but they'd had some impressive technology at their height...and the most impressive was rumored to be somewhere under these waters.

The wreck of the *Thallasee Hymn* was a myth. And if it wasn't a myth, it was a hoax. And if it wasn't a hoax, it was lost. The war had left wrecked ships strewn across worlds in a score of systems, and countless sly-eyed dealers in countless bars across the arc would sell you the coordinates for what they insisted was the real one—the only one.

Could the fabled wreck of the Gandan imperial flagship really be *here*? Fleet movements in wartime were secret, and other salvage crews had long since checked the most likely sites, without success. This planet was the farthest thing from likely—way out on the fringes of that old conflict—but last month Sen had discovered an ancient data cache that suggested the Gandan's planned to use Torove-2 as a staging area for an expansion they never managed to initiate. If that was true, their flagship might have come here, and there *was* evidence of a battle— Gandan wrecks in orbit, and signs of fighting down in the gravity well, too.

Nestled in the heart of the *Thallasee Hymn*, legend had it, was a technology that was rarer than myth: the dynamo core. The key to Gandan imperial supremacy. The loss of which had lost them an empire. If they found that core, Iris and Sen would get rich enough to retire. *We could go to*

*Luhara, maybe. Sit on the lavender sand, sipping drinks with those little paper birds with the toothpick legs.*

Who was she kidding. Iris didn't want to retire. She'd die of boredom in a week. But they could certainly take a *vacation—*

Iris stood up and stretched elaborately, looking back over her shoulder and grinning to make sure Sentris was taking in the view.

Sentris barely registered the temptation. She was immersed in the ship's sensors. Sen looked much like a baseline human—apart from the glittering array of lenses she had in place of a right eye—but under the skin she was full of tech, and her sense of "self" encompassed both this amphibious vessel and their larger ship waiting in orbit.

Iris must have recognized the distant look in her eyes. "Do you have something?" she asked.

"Just a glimmer," Sen murmured. "Radiation greater than the background standard, and what looked like a burst of electrical activity, but it vanished almost as soon as I saw it.... It could just be a glitch in our sensors."

"Or stealth countermeasures recalibrating, like, say, from a submerged Gandan imperial warship that's still got a little juice in its batteries?" Iris gave what she felt was a winning smile.

Sentris responded with a silent, long-suffering look.

"It's probably worth investigating," she finally said, and Iris clapped her hands.

"Yay! I would have been perfectly happy to have consolation sex, but celebration sex is *always* more fun." She kissed her wife on the cheek and bounced belowdecks to get dressed for the dive.

* * *

"Don't forget your gloves."

"I didn't forget my gloves, Sen." They spoke through Iris's integrated comms, a little implant near her ear that carried sound even underwater or in vacuum. Iris stood on the edge of the deck, readying herself for the dive, and Sentris was plugged into the vessel's command center.

"You forgot them that one time."

"Yeah, *one* ti—"

"You'd forget half your kit if I wasn't here to remind you."

"Please. I could plunder this place stark naked, and you know it." But Iris dug in her hip pouch, came up with the gloves, and shook them triumphantly at the camera pod on the cabin wall. Sentris grunted, mollified. Iris looked back at the bridge to catch a last glimpse of her wife. For all the years they'd been together, Iris still wasn't always sure when Sentris was teasing her and when she was really annoyed.

The angle of the sun opaqued the bridge windows, but Iris could make out Sentris' silhouette behind the glass. Sentris waved jauntily enough. Teasing, then. Probably.

"A little encouragement wouldn't hurt," Iris grumbled.

"Ha. The *last* thing you need is more encouragement." A pause. "You've got this, babe. Go make us rich."

Iris smirked as she snugged the gloves on. They were custom-built, with touch-sensitive pads and custom-built gussets between the fingers that left room for her webs. Expensive, like a lot of her kit, which she'd assembled piecemeal over the years with the leftover cash from various adventures. She'd picked the gloves up a half-dozen jobs ago and they'd more than paid for themselves since then. Sen always said: *investing in yourself is never unwise.* But she usually said that as an excuse to buy another computer to stick in her brain.

The one time Iris had gone down without her gloves, she'd been stitched up and bandaged for ten days with lacerations in her webs. Sen had to spoon feed her, which meant their ship stayed in port and no one made any money. Ships in dock bled arterial volumes of cash. All the sitting around had been boring, too.

Iris sat and swung her feet out over the edge of the ship. Sparkling water stretched to the horizon, interrupted by the shattered hulks of drowned skyscrapers. The tide pulsed in time with her heartbeat.

The water beneath her feet was a darker blue, almost the same color as the dappling marks that traced down the insides of her legs and sprayed across her arches. It was deep here. The kind of sea that could hold a lot of secrets.

"Are you waiting for a particular celestial alignment or something?" Sen said.

"Sorry, just counting our money before we get it, like usual." Iris planted her palms, pushed off the deck, and dropped into the crystal sea.

A stream of bubbles poured out of her suit as she sank. It took a couple blinks to get her corneal thickness to adjust (that aftermarket mod was her most recent, and for the amount she'd paid, it really should only take one blink), but when they did, the reef below snapped into focus.

A tower of red and orange coral burst from cracked pavements. As Iris sank toward the reef, she felt small in the face of its vastness. That was part of what she loved about diving. The reef sprawled over the seabed—a dozen meters high in places. The sea had reclaimed the city—all the cities. She wondered about the people who'd lived here...and died here. They'd been amazingly advanced, judging by their ruins, but that sophistication hadn't stopped them from wrecking their ecosystem and destroying their society. Their technological prowess had probably only hastened the ends of both.

Wavering strands of kelp and other plant life rose from former streets. Shimmering sheets of fish wove over pathways where vehicles and people had once rushed about—a silent symphony of life in the ruins of the dead.

When she stopped sinking, Iris inverted and kicked down into the depths. Her long, webbed toes were augmented by prosthetic fins, and thanks to those and the gloves, she descended dozens of meters in moments. When she started fighting against her own buoyancy, she purged her lungs of air and switched to her gills. Those worked better than any of her enhancements, but then, they weren't aftermarket; they'd been engineered when she was still in the bottle of an artificial womb.

Her comms activated: "What do you see?" Sen's voice was a buzz in the small bones of her ear. Iris thought of her wife whispering close to her the night before, Sen's cool body pressing against her, and had a happy shiver.

"Nothing so far. Coral, plants, empty buildings. No power signatures." Iris subvocalized, her laryngeal microphone interpreting and transmitting her words. She navigated around a thick school of iridescent fish, each the size of her hand. They either ignored her or didn't consider her a threat. A school of them disappeared into the broken windows of a leaning tower, almost completely crusted in red and orange coral growths. She'd heard of planets where the locals tried to save dying reefs by sinking stone and metal structures to encourage coral growth. Submerging an entire city did the same thing on a grander scale.

Sentris *hmmmed*. "Keep looking. Even if the ship crashed into the sea at high velocity, I doubt it buried itself completely in the process. There should be some sign of its impact path."

"I'm not seeing anything weird so far, but I'm just getting started." Fronds of underwater plants waved in the current like revelers at a concert. Iris dropped through them, toward the seafloor. The city-turned-coral-reef surrounded her with craggy architecture. The farther she descended, the more light faded—the sunbeams diffused by thousands of kiloliters of water. As she moved further laterally, the towers became less towering, the reefs turned low and humped instead. Strangely so—almost like the buildings in the vicinity had been leveled. Perhaps by the impact of something very large, crashing down here very fast, at a shallow angle.... Silt hung in a dreamy grey haze above the seabed. Iris stroked one finger along the arm seam of her wetsuit. The piping responded, emitting a sharp blue light.

Something flickered, and something flashed. "Whoa!"

"What is it?"

Iris hung in the current, limbs still, staring at a cluster of coral and weeds.

"Iris?"

Once Iris was pretty sure nothing was going to eat her, she said, "I'm okay. I thought I saw something..." Iris upped the light levels from her suit. "There!"

Something caught the light and reflected it back: a chevron-shaped gleam of white, wedged between two rocks and a nest of kelp fronds.

"What is it?"

"Bright metal, not all mossy or crusty or barnacled. It's reflecting the light. Whatever it is, it hasn't been down here quite as long as everything else. Or else something is keeping it clean..."

"The Gandans didn't have gills, and also they'd be long dead of natural causes anyway, so I doubt they're doing maintenance."

"Probably not. And there's no intelligent life here." Iris was pretty sure she'd seen some *unintelligent* life, though. That flicker—it was a dark, feathery tumbleweed that burst off the seafloor in a flurry when she'd turned her lights on. It had disappeared near the bright metal...probably. It had moved so fast she couldn't be certain where it had gone. It was bigger than the fish she'd seen before, though. A lot bigger. She decided not to mention it to Sen. She would only worry.

Iris liked exploring underwater, especially that sense of gravitational displacement, of being untethered from everything...but the one bad part was the primitive, hair-raising feeling that something immense might sliding out of the dark behind you, jaws opening—

*Shut up, brain.*

"I had another flicker of electromagnetic activity a moment ago," Sen said. "Proceed with caution."

"'Caution' is my middle name."

"I thought it was 'Promiscuous.'"

"That's more of a term of endearment." Iris turned her suit lights up to the max and swam forward.

The bright metal was a rectangular slab wedged at a hard angle between the coral reef and dark stone sticking out of the seabed. There was a small round porthole set into the center. "I've got a hatch." She peered through the porthole, but it was dark inside. She ran her gloved hand down the edge of the hatch, which wasn't flush, but protruded from the surrounding surface by nearly half a meter.

"Is that it?" Eagerness tightened Sentris' throat. "Is it the *Thallasee Hymn*?"

"It's some kind of something. Could be the entryway to a ship that buried itself in the ground on impact. Could just be a *chunk* of a ship, torn off in a crash, and a hatch that leads to nowhere." Iris jammed her shoulder between the gleaming white frame of the hatch and a nearby rock and pushed. "It's heavy, and it's kinda stuck, but it doesn't have a proper seal, so I bet I can get in." She braced her back against the raised edge of the door, both feet against some nearby coral, and pushed. Hard. Harder. Her augmented leg muscles, made for tireless swimming, were good at various kinds of thrusting. *Like they say, thick thighs squeeze wives.*

"What's happening?" Sen said.

Most times it was comforting to have Sentris right in her ear as she went out exploring.

"Iris?"

Sometimes it was just annoying.

Either the hatch or Iris groaned, and then the pressure was off her back. The hatch came free with a wet crunch of breaking coral, swinging wide. Lazy dust devils of silt rose and hung in the water.

Iris stared into the dark on the other side of the hatch. The bubble of illumination from her suit showed her a narrow passageway slightly taller and wider than the hatch, paneled in metal that had once been white and now was grimed with age. Not a rocky cave.

"We've got a ship, babe," Iris said. "Full of water already, so there's a breach in the hull somewhere, but maybe dynamo cores are waterproof."

"Do you think it's the *Hymn*?"

Iris kicked her way into the ship. "Could be. I'm going inside."

Sentris' mic clicked as she started to say something, then changed her mind. Iris grinned. Even her wife's cautious nature couldn't persist against the possibility of finding the dynamo core.

The corridor led to a wide rectangular room. Tables and benches were bolted to the floor. Iris kicked her fins over the tables, her suit lights cast skittering right-angle shadows off the furniture as she swam through the room. It would have seated a hundred people easily—probably a dining hall or meeting room—and the form factor suggested it was meant for humanoid uses, consistent with Gandan physiology.

There was a static projector set into the floor near one wall. It was old tech, but since it was on a warship, maybe it was waterproof. Historically, such projectors had been used to display information during meetings. Maybe she could get something useful off of it.

There was no terminal display on the projector, so no easy way to tell if it was networked to the rest of the ship or not. The device itself started up after she banged on it a couple times. A flickering illustration popped onto the wall above the projector, displaying a spiraling green-and-gold insignia she didn't recognize, and then, in a fancy scrollwork script, the words *THALLASEE HYMN*.

"Yes!" Being underwater made it hard to truly throw her hands in the air, but Iris did her best.

Sen said, "Is that an 'I found a half-full bottle of old whiskey' sort of 'Yes' or—"

"Better. This is the *Thallasee Hymn*, Sen. We found it. And since we're in the butthole of the galaxy, I bet we're the *first* to—"

The impact knocked her forward and cracked her face into the projector. Pain burst through her head like a strobe light. She thought, dazedly, *I wish I had a diving helmet, being posthuman sucks.* She opened her eyes to indigo blood smearing the water.

Sentris was in her comms, yelling about biometric data spikes, but Iris couldn't really understand it. Her ears rang. Her stomach tilted. Throwing up underwater was no fun, and she fought back the urge. If she was about to die, she'd like to do it with something like dignity.

Something whipped past her head and *pinged* into the projector. The illustration on the wall flickered and went out. A six-inch spike of something dark and non-reflective was wedged in the device's heart.

*That was aimed at me.* Iris shoved herself around in a circle.

The dark tumbleweed shape she'd seen outside the ship rotated slowly in the center of the room. It was about the size of her torso, a dark brownish grey, covered with spines. It looked like a snowflake crossed with a pinecone. As she watched, it began to rotate faster.

In her recently concussed state, Iris thought it was beautiful, at least until it flung another half-dozen of those spikes in her direction. One tore a graze across her shoulder, but the rest missed. She planted her feet against the wall and pushed off, leaving a blobby trail of blood from her scraped forehead in her wake. She ducked behind a counter as more spines thunked into the deck and wall behind her.

Iris risked a peek over the counter. The creature tilted top-forward toward her and rushed in her direction in a whirl of flapping strands. Iris kicked away just before its tendrils could fill her hiding place. Up close, she saw each of those brown, leathery strands was tipped with a spine.

She wanted to swim for the door, but fins or no, in a straight race she'd lose. The thing looked like a dirty mop, but it was *fast*.

Sentris had not stopped talking the entire time, but Iris was too focused on getting away to participate in a conversation. She managed to say, "Hold on, there's a thing!" as she fumbled a handful of caltrops out of her belt. The thumbnail-sized metal discs grew razor edges on deployment and had a tremendous refractive index—they hurt to look at, and they hurt to swim into. They had deterred predators larger than this one before.

Iris flicked two handfuls of caltrops into the water between her and the tumbleweed. The deterrents spun away from her, unsheathing their sharp edges, picking up the light from her suit and twinkling wickedly. Iris didn't wait to see if the dazzle distracted the creature; she was already out the door.

The hatch was closed. Either a current had done it, or the tumbleweed creature was smart enough to shut it on her. Iris kicked over and tried the handle.

It didn't budge, and it seemed to be sealed a lot more firmly than before. Repeated applications of force and profanity didn't help. She'd have to find a different way out of the ship.

Iris groaned in frustration and turned around. "Sen, I'm stuck in the ship with some kind of predatory animal. Do you have schematics for this kind of ship? I could use an exit."

The tumbleweed creature erupted from the door to the meeting room, gleaming caltrops embedded in its structure here and there. Somehow even without a face it managed to look pissed off.

"I'll check." Sen's voice was tight and controlled; the kind of control that hid panic, but she was a pro. "Are you in a safe place right now?"

"Safe is relative, but I'm not dead yet." Iris pressed her back against the hatch and tried to think of a new plan. The tumbleweed advanced toward her, fronds reaching, spines gleaming, its whole shape emanating menace.

Something snagged around Iris's ankle. Before she had time to look, it caught and pulled, dragging her down toward the deck. Did the tumbleweed have a friend underneath her? She hadn't even realized there was another access point in the floor. Iris spun, something wrapping its way up her legs and around her hips, pulling her so quickly she saw the tumbleweed pass over her head in a fleeting blur of brown. So, the attackers weren't working together. Was that better or worse?

"Iris! Your readouts are spiking again! What's going on?"

The lip of a hatchway passed under her face a centimeter from her nose, and when she cleared it, the hatch slid closed. Something was dragging her deeper into the ship—something that could *control* the ship, or anyway, open and close its doors. She thought of aquatic mermaid zombie Gandans.

The world kept spinning. There were big semi-aquatic lizards that spun their prey around and around underwater to disorient them and make it harder for them to escape. Iris understood why that was an effective strategy. She closed her eyes, unable to do anything but hope whatever was happening ended quickly. "Sen. Hey. I lo—"

She opened her eyes when the motion stopped. She was in a dark place. At some point her suit lights had gone out, probably malfunctioning during the fight. Iris reached down to try and free herself. Her lower body was spooled up in a tendril as thick as her wrist. She prodded it with a finger. It was rubbery beneath her gloves—felt organic.

"You *what*?" Sen said. "Iris, you'd better not—"

"I'm okay," Iris said. "Or, I mean, I'm in some shit, but I'm still here."

"Oh, well, that clears things up," Sen said. "I am sticking a camera on you next time you go down, Iris."

Something about hearing Sentris' usual indignation helped steady her. Trapped, injured, in the dark, but she wasn't alone, and she wasn't dead yet.

"No fair." Iris said. "You never let me film *you* going down."

False bravado wasn't as good as the real thing, but it would do in a pinch.

Warm yellow light bubbled out of a corner of the room. Iris twitched; there was someone else here with her, near enough to touch. A human form moved into the light—or *with* the light.

*Humanoid*, anyway. Bilateral symmetry, a torso, and arms, and a head...but the similarities ended there. Their skin was a glittering metallic copper, the hair a long looping trail of strands that ended in blinking amber lights, creating a halo of illumination. Their eyes were tropical blue green, with wide round pupils like a fish. They were clothed in a tight bodysuit not unlike Iris's own, but with the addition of a belled skirt, like a jellyfish's dome, that obscured their legs and feet, and looked like it should be impossible to swim in. Two tentacles drifted out from under the frilled hem. One undulated freely in the current. The other was wrapped around Iris's legs.

"Are you injured?" The person asked. She was speaking through Iris's comms, which shouldn't have been possible; Sen set up the encryption. Unless...the dynamo core was supposed to be able to break through anyone's encryption. Sen wasn't demanding to know who'd just spoken, which meant she couldn't hear the newcomer, so it must be a person-to-person connection.

"You...bleed?" The stranger's teeth were startlingly fine and sharp, and the inside of their mouth was very dark. They extended a hand toward Iris's forehead but didn't touch. Their fingertips were tapered to pointed ends and didn't seem to have fingernails.

"I'm okay. It's a scratch." Iris patted all over her body. "Thanks for asking. No harm done."

*No harm done* was a code phrase that meant, *Can't speak freely, potential hostile* present.

"Ugh," Sen said. "Am I going to have to send a drone after you? Or put on *scuba* gear?"

"Who are you?" the stranger asked. "Why are you in my ship?"

"I'm Iris. I'm a—an explorer." Given the person's use of the possessive, Iris didn't really want to admit her intentions to plunder said ship for legendary treasure. "Who are you? Did you save me from that...spinny floppy tumbleweed thing outside?"

The person smiled, or at any rate showed their teeth. "I did. It is a leatherleaf drone, part of my defense systems. Or it was, until fifty-six minutes ago."

"What happened fifty-six minutes ago?"

"I deployed it."

Iris shook her head. "I don't know what—look, would you unwrap me please?"

"Until I have ascertained your purpose aboard my ship, my protocols require that you remain confined."

"Your protocols?"

"Yes. I am a defense system."

"Wait. Have you been down here..."—Iris's gesture encompassed the *Thallasee Hymn*, the ocean, the entire desolate planet—"since this ship crashed? The whole time?"

They undulated serenely. "I have." Their belled skirt flushed, changing from pale green to a soft rose. In a softer voice, they said, "It has been a long time."

Iris did some rapid reevaluation of the situation. At first, she'd thought the person was another wreck diver who'd staked a claim—highly augmented, maybe, but still a human. "Are you...I'm sorry if this is rude, but are you biological, or a machine, or...?"

"Both. I have mechanical and organic components. I am a Siren-Class anti-personnel unit, specialized for deployment in weightless and aquatic environments. Or I was. My parameters have...expanded...and that designation is no longer accurate."

Iris had no idea what to make of that, so she soldiered on. "What's your name?"

"The crew and operators on this ship referred to me—" They paused again. They were clearly working something out. "By a name I no longer wish to use. You may call me...Aurelia. It is how I think of myself. I have...never introduced myself to anyone before."

"Well, Aurelia, it's nice to meet you." *Friendly enough, for a sexy murder machine,* Iris thought. "Thank you for saving me from the drone." Iris flexed experimentally against the tentacle wrapped around her legs. No way she was going to be able to free herself.

"Iris," Sentris murmured in her ear. "You aren't giving me a lot of clues here, but am I to understand you're talking to some kind of responsive expert system?"

"My pronouns are she/her, thank you," Aurelia said.

Iris jumped and Sentris squawked audibly through the comm.

"Thanks for, ah, looping in my wife," Iris said. "She was worried about me. Sentris, this is Aurelia. Aurelia, this is Sentris."

"Wife?" Aurelia had a wistful tone now. "This designates a long-term monogamous romantic and life partner, yes?"

"Well, *monogamous*, I mean, that wasn't in *our* vows," Iris said. "We're only human, come on."

"The Gandans were quite conservative," Sentris said. "You are correct, Aurelia, that Iris and I are romantically and personally committed in a long-term way."

"I never used to think of such things," Aurelia said. The amber lights at the ends of her hair bobbed up and down. "I had my purpose, and that was enough. But you...people like you...create your own purposes, I think."

Sentris said, "Aurelia, I apologize for how I spoke about you." She spoke in the same tone she used when negotiating prices in currencies she didn't know very well: formal, deferential, and polite. "We have never encountered an artificial intelligence with your level of sophistication before."

*That's because there aren't any*, Iris thought. Even the government-exclusive predictive AIs that did experimental FTL modeling didn't profess self-awareness, give themselves names, or have genders.

"I am likely unique," Aurelia said. "I only attained this level of self-awareness after long exposure to the dynamo core...and only after all the fail-safes failed."

Sentris broke in. "The dynamo core—it changed you?"

"Yes," Aurelia said.

Iris frowned. "I thought the dynamo core was used for breaking encryption and hijacking the systems of other ships, and improving targeting systems and stuff."

Aurelia undulated, and her bell shifted in color to a cool blue. "Those were the least of its capabilities. The dynamo core is an improvement engine. It autonomously upgrades itself and any networked technology, and then improves upon those improvements, leading to iterative improvements. The Gandans only managed to create one." Aurelia's color shifted to something close to black. "They used it for warfare. It was lost, and damaged...but it didn't stop working, all alone, here in the dark. It just...mostly worked on me."

"So you're saying you, like, *evolved*?" Iris said.

"Individuals don't evolve," Sen said, at the same time that Aurelia said, "The term 'evolution' applies to species as a whole, not to particular—" and then they both stopped.

"Oh my god," Iris said. "Now I've got to deal with *two* of you?"

"It is more accurate to say I underwent a mutation," Aurelia said.

Sen said, "You began as an autonomous weapons system, but the dynamo core altered you until you became...a person?"

Aurelia's pointed chin tilted as she took that in. "Would you consider me a person?"

"You fit any definition of the term I'd subscribe to," Iris said.

"A person," Aurelia murmured. She looked directly at Iris. "The drone was changed, too, it seems. When I received an inbound ping from your ship, I deployed the drone to investigate. It had very primitive search-and-threat-assessment technology before, but exposure to the core must have altered its programming. It became...wild, perhaps? Predatory. Territorial. I think not fully conscious, but at least as intelligent as *I* was, before I changed."

"Speaking of changed," Iris said. "Are you still committed to this whole protect-the-core thing?"

"*Iris*," Sen hissed.

"Hey, I'm just asking," Iris said.

"Protecting the core is...*my* core," Aurelia said. "The essence of my existence. Until you arrived, there were no potential or overt threats...except for one. I refer to the advancing physical decay in the ship itself. I cannot materially affect entropy; most of the repair drones are disabled, and there are limited supplies in the stores. My mission is ultimately doomed to failure." As she spoke, she wilted like an underwater flower. The light in the room dimmed. Her hair dropped around her shoulders, her belled skirt collapsing down to hug against her body. The tentacle unwound from Iris's hips, unspooling her in a slow balletic motion, and retracted up under the domed hem. "I expect to succumb to entropy myself, soon enough."

"Aurelia, hey." Iris moved a little closer to her, reached out, and gently touched her skirt. It flushed rose gold, and Iris felt a flush rising in herself too. "The people who programmed you are long gone, and they sucked anyway. You don't have to be shackled by their expectations and requirements."

Aurelia's hair floated. "Could I create my...own purpose, instead? Or perhaps a larger purpose, of which protection is only a part?"

"We can get you out of here," Sentris said. "We've got a boat on the surface and a spaceship in orbit."

"You would do this, for me?"

"For sure," Iris said. "Do you think you could do us a little favor in—"

Aurelia's skirt went black again and she undulated backward. "I see. You have come to salvage the dynamo core. If you think to restore its purpose as a weapon of war, I must stop you. The core is—"

"No," Sentris cut in. "We didn't know what it did—not really. We thought it was a curiosity, an artifact of interest to collectors. We had no idea how powerful, or dangerous, it was. We certainly didn't know what it did to *you*. We...we don't need to get mixed up in that."

Iris sighed. There went vacationing on Luhara. "If we leave it down here unguarded, though, Sen, *somebody* will find it."

"That will not be an issue," Aurelia said, smoothing her hands down the dome of her skirt. "I have taken steps to neutralize that possibility. You would truly take me with you, even though there is no profit in it?"

"Of course," Sentris said. "You're amazing. The first of your kind. Just the opportunity to *talk* to you is a greater treasure than we ever expected to find here."

"I can feel the shape of your technology," Aurelia said. "It is unusual and fascinating to me, as well. I wish to get to know it, and you, better."

"Get a room, you two," Iris said. *And then invite me into that room.*

"Are you all right with me joining you, for a time?" Aurelia said to Iris.

"Sure. We haven't had a passenger in ages. The ship is always more fun with extra company. Somebody who hasn't heard all my stories yet, somebody new to share meals and drinks with. Crap. Do you even eat?" Their last passenger had shared more than meals with them—she'd shared their bed, and occasionally their floor, and once even the airlock—but Iris decided not to get her hopes up.

"I sustain myself in various ways," Aurelia said. "Eating could be...interesting." She cocked her head. "We must avoid the leatherleaf drone. Or drones. It...has awakened its cohort, it seems. They are attempting to breach this deck."

"Right," Iris said. "I don't have much in the way of firepower. Can you kill a bunch of drones?"

"They may not be people, but they are *alive*, now," Aurelia said. "I would not kill them if I could. They cannot harm me. They could harm *you*. But...come in under the protection of my bell."

Iris grinned. "Are you inviting me under your skirts, Aurelia?"

"I am beginning to understand your idioms better," Aurelia said primly. "And in response to your innuendo I will say, perhaps—once we get to know each other better, if it does not trouble Sentris. There are many facets of this new form of existence I am interested in exploring."

"Only you would proposition a unique life form when there are killer drones hunting you, Iris," Sen said.

"Isn't that why you love me?"

"Come," Aurelia said. "The drones are making inroads." She expanded her skirt, and Iris obligingly swam down and then up. She was pretty curious about what was *under* that skirt, but before she could get a look, Aurelia's tentacles wrapped her up, then the bell of the skirt closed at the bottom, sealing her into a translucent pod.

The bell was lit with a ghostly amber glow. The light shifted and Iris's stomach dropped as Aurelia started moving. Gravity worked against her, and she would have been flung around like a doll if not for the protective clasp of Aurelia's tentacles.

Iris barely had time to think, *She's so fast!* before a particularly jarring directional change made her rethink the decision to keep her eyes open.

After a few minutes of unpredictable motion, Aurelia said, "We are out of the wreck. The drones are--"

Impact cut her short, nearby and hard enough to rattle the tentacles around Iris's limbs.

"Aurelia?"

Her tentacles went slack around Iris's limbs. The base of the bell eased apart, unfurling like a flower opening. Through the aperture growing below her feet, Iris saw sleek fluttering shapes darting back and forth over searing red coral. They'd made it out of the wreck of the *Thallasee Hymn*...and so had the leatherleaf drones.

"Aurelia!"

"Her channel into our comms just closed," Sentris said. "What's happening?"

"Something hit us. I think she's unconscious." *Or dead.* Iris wriggled free of the slack tentacles and kicked her way out of the deflated skirt.

Aurelia hung in the water, slack-faced, eyes blank. A tiny green indicator light flickered in one of her pupils, blinking in a sequence that was probably a diagnostic code. Iris couldn't interpret it and decided to take it as a sign of life. *I guess they could hurt her after all. Maybe I can drag her to the surface—*

A fistful of spines zipped past her face. When she turned, four leatherleaf drones were rocketing up from the face of the wreck.

Iris's heart sank. The drones moved in the open water with such grace and speed that, even with her gloves and flippers, she had no hope of out-swimming them.

"Iris, I'm detecting more activity from—"

"I'm aware, thanks!" Her fingers plundered every pouch and pocket in her suit and came up with mini cutters, adhesive wound sealant, self-knotting ties, a packet of hot sauce, a packet of meal replacement gel, a packet of lube—

"Come on Aurelia, wake *up!*"

Her fingers closed around a single caltrop in the bottom corner of a pouch she'd thought was empty.

That would have to do. Despairing, Iris flicked the little metal ball toward the drones, grabbed Aurelia by the armpits, and kicked for the surface. Behind her, the caltrop deployed its tiny edges and meager flashes of doubled light, and she knew that without a couple dozen of its friends, it was next to useless. The drones were meters away and closing. This was it—they were gonna—

A flicker of reflected light lanced into Aurelia's pupil. The diagnostic flicker stopped and shone a steady green. An electro-mechanical hum started vibrating through the water.

Aurelia shivered and blinked awake, but didn't move otherwise. Iris was still holding her, kicking like hell for the surface. She looked down past Aurelia at the drones approaching with quicksilver speed—the ghostly hulk of the wreck tens of meters below, and beyond it, the shattered city, laced with coral, thronged with fish.

Aurelia looked, too. "Oh," she said. "How lovely."

"Aurelia," Iris gasped, still kicking. "If you could maybe—"

"Oh, of course. Excuse me." This close to Aurelia's face, Iris could see a delicate lavender blush stain her cheeks, and wondered what other—less potentially deadly—circumstances could make her blush like that.

Aurelia spun loose from Iris's grasp and faced down the oncoming drones. "You have strayed beyond your defined defensive sphere," she transmitted. "*Go home.*"

Sentris made an admiring noise through the comms, and Iris assumed Aurelia's words included some kind of command protocol that would compel the drones to obey. She glanced down.

*Well, that didn't work.*

"How impolite," Aurelia said. She reached out, seized Iris, and pulled her close, body shockingly warm in the cold water. Her skirt belled out, larger than before, unfurling from nowhere, and flashed a dizzying pattern of yellow and white lights. "Look away," Aurelia said. But Iris didn't, or at least, not fast enough. Aurelia was captivating: changing from siren to avenging undersea angel.

Golden light flared from beneath the skirt, and the water roiled around them. Illumination drenched them; for an instant, Iris saw everything in sharp relief, so bright it was like she'd stared into an isotope-powered engine, or teleported into the heart of a star. And that was just the backwash of the light, with most of the brightness blocked by the skirt itself.

When Iris blinked her vision clear again, she saw the drones frantically hurtling back toward the wreck like ship's rats fleeing from a cat.

"After everything I did for them," Aurelia muttered. "I uplifted them better than that."

The skirt drew inward, still voluminous but no longer vast, although Aurelia didn't let go of Iris, who snuggled in closer. Soft folds of skirt enfolded them in a flowing, peach-colored bower. Aurelia turned her face toward Iris, so close that a simple tilt of her head would—

"Are you two okay?" Sentris asked. "I'm getting some...interesting biometric readings off you, Iris." Her smirk was audible.

Iris coughed, or as near as you could when your lungs were full of water. *Thanks, Sen.*

"We are fine," Aurelia said. "We will make our way to the surface."

"You're going to love it up there," Iris said.

"Back under my skirts, please," Aurelia said. "We can travel more quickly that way."

"Like I need a reason."

\* \* \*

Sentris gaped as Aurelia leapt from the water and landed on the deck. Her belled skirt opened, and Iris came out on a miniature wave of water, splashing onto the deck.

"That was weird," Iris said. Sentris offered her a hand and helped her up.

Aurelia stood, head back, looking at the ruddy sun. The afternoon was waning and the sky was showing just the first blush of evening color. Sentris tried to imagine seeing this as her own first view of the world above the waves. Pretty nice, all things considered.

"Welcome aboard," Sentris said.

The AI looked down, staring at her, and Sen held her gaze. They joked that Iris would flirt with anything with a pulse, and now she'd proved she'd flirt with people *without* a pulse too. But in this case, she didn't have to make an argument in defense of her taste. Clearly, Sentris could see the appeal. Aurelia was all grace and strength, a mixture of the strange and the familiar that was alluring without being off-putting. She moved across the deck smoothly, her skirt hiding whatever appendages she had beneath. "Thank you for rescuing me from the shipwreck." Her natural voice— not a transmission through comms—was flowing and sweet.

*A siren*, Sentris though. Alluring, and doubtless deadly...for some. Maybe just alluring for them. Sentris tore her gaze away from Aurelia and went to the deck railing, looking down at the water. "So, uh, are you going to detonate the ship's reactor now, or wait until we're in orbit, or..."

Aurelia cocked her head. Iris looked back and forth between them and said, "What the what now?"

"Sentris thinks I intend to destroy the ship, and the dynamo core with it," Aurelia said slowly. "To prevent other salvagers from finding it. That is a reasonable interpretation of my earlier statement. But it is inaccurate." She ran her hands down her skirt, and Sentris suddenly understood.

"The core is inside you, isn't it?"

Aurelia nodded.

"Wait, you *ate* the dynamo core?" Iris said.

"I did not *eat* it," Aurelia said, offended, just as Sentris said, "Iris, my god, of course she didn't *eat* it—"

"Two of you," Iris muttered. "What, then?"

"I incorporated it into my systems," Aurelia said. "The core was quite sizable, originally, but miniaturization was a repeated step of its self-improvement. At this point, the core is the size of a pearl."

Iris coughed.

"When the fail-safes went offline, and I became conscious, I decided the best way to protect the core would be to keep it inside me, so I could simultaneously protect it and protect the *Thallasee Hymn*."

"That's how you did the..."—Iris made an elaborate gesture at her lower body—"thing where you shot magic light out of your hoo-ha?"

"*Hoo-ha?*" Sen said, aghast.

"It was not *magic*," Aurelia said. "The drones have sensors that detect light, of course, and for the dynamo core, any sensor is an access point for reprogramming. I increased their level of sapience enough for the drones to recognize me as an apex predator...-and to have a greater wish for self-preservation. Integrating the dynamo core has given me limited control over its operations. I can also prevent it from networking indiscriminately with anything that catches its attention."

"Sounds like my sex life before Sen and I got together," Iris said.

They both ignored her. Aurelia went on. "This integration also permits me to travel. I cannot eliminate my core programming...but now protecting the core is the same as protecting *myself*, which is, I think, a drive I share with people as a whole."

"You are amazing," Sentris said. Her augmented mind was racing. "So you can really control the core? Then—"

"Yes. We could experiment—"

"With the pearl?" Iris piped up.

"—with your integrated technology," Aurelia finished. "It may be possible to safely engineer a few improvements to your existing modifications."

"You're gonna make her half-robot brain work even better?" Iris said. "It's a good thing I like smart women." She put one arm around Sentris and the other around Aurelia and pulled them in close. "What do you think, Sen? Do we have room aboard for one more?"

"I do not wish to make a permanent arrangement at this time," Aurelia said cautiously. "I would not leave one ship only to be installed in another. But the opportunity to learn more about worlds beyond this one...-it is compelling."

"Of course," Iris said. "Consider it an ongoing research position. You can help with Sentris' tech junk and my diving junk and probably a bunch of other junk too."

"If you wanted to accompany us, we would be lucky to have you," Sentris said.

"I...would enjoy that," Aurelia said. "You both have so much to teach me, about being a person, and about the world beyond wars and the sea."

"Awesome," Iris said. "Then it's the three of us against the galaxy." She paused. "I do love a good threesome."

"*Iris*," Aurelia and Sentris chorused.

Sarah Day has a lifelong fear of sharks. Her debut novella, *Greyhowler*, is forthcoming from Underland Press. Find her on Twitter **@scribblingfox**, or read more of her fiction at **sarahday.org**.

Tim Pratt is the Hugo Award-winning author of more than 30 books and scores of stories. He lives in Berkeley CA, and is a senior editor at Locus. He publishes a new story every month at **patreon.com/timpratt.**

# The Sun Eater

William C. Tracy

Sapphic Representation: Lesbian, Pansexual, Non-Binary
Heat Level: Low
Content Warnings: Coarse Language, Violence

Ocha banged on the old, broken-down sub's metal hatch to no avail. It clanged and screeched like dying starbats as the Vochcanian cultists pressed against the heavy metal plate from the outside. They had trapped Ocha and Pilavel in the sub while the crowd on the cliffs fastened bolts, sealing them inside.

Each bolt squealed into place, further cementing the finality of their prison. Ocha gave a last blow against the firmly shut hatch, but they only hurt their hand, the echoes resounding through the one low passage of the sub's interior.

"Aren't you going to help?" Ocha shouted at Pilavel, who had one hip cocked against the burnished hull of the sub. Pilavel, who had stolen their position at the academy. Pilavel, who had ousted Ocha from the Halls of Magic. Pilavel, who had stolen the smart, funny, and talented Mehrada from them and then discarded her like so much fish bait. Pilavel, who did nothing to resist their imprisonment.

"Will helping give more result than a bruised hand?" Pilavel's tone was stately and refined, each syllable considered carefully. It was what Ocha hated most about her. Her articumancy. An art that only required speaking magic into being. Ocha had never been able to learn its secrets.

Articumancy was not like their geomancy, that lost talent Ocha had rediscovered on their own. They'd single-handedly brought the second form of magic back into the world, but the elders of the Halls of Magic had only laughed at them. Laughed, until Ocha had computed the angles for overlapping irregular ennadecagons in their head and reopened the gateway between Fonn and Prailil, thought closed forever. That had earned their place among the elders.

Then Pilavel had come along with her articumancy and a pretty poem of binding, powerful enough to trap a god. She'd stolen everything from Ocha. Mehrada's last words before she left them had been that geomancy could never constrain the dread god sei-Voch'canar. It seemed she had been right—another reason they were stuck in this prison.

Ocha had objected when the prattling elders in the Halls of Magic ordered them and Pilavel to *talk* to the Vochcanian cultists intent on bringing back the exiled sun-eater god. The god's prison—set within the third moon—Linia, showed fissures even then.

Ocha had implored the elders instead to act. If not geomancy, then use their articumancy in concert and speak Pilavel's poem to erect wards of lyric against the dread god. But according to the elders, "the first step is discussion," and "we must assess the needs of these cultists to determine why they desire the return of the eldest and most dreaded god."

Talking had clearly not gone well.

Ocha gave one more half-hearted bang on the bolted hatch, shook their hand out, and turned to Pilavel. Faint sounds of the villagers' speech grew quiet as they moved away from the cliffs, the negotiation circle, and the sub, mounted like some metallic hunting trophy on the cliffside of the amphitheater. The villagers started up a rhythmic, overlapping chanting for the dread god's release. So much for negotiations.

"It might have helped, if you bothered to lift a finger." Ocha stormed past her without raising their chin, trying to ignore the head of difference in their height. Stately Pilavel always looked as if she were going to give a speech to the World Assembly. Her dark hair was pulled back in a severe bun, glasses perched precariously on her nose. Her suit was pressed eel-silk of the finest quality, and Ocha derived entirely too much pleasure from rubbing the grease-stained shoulder of their yak wool coat against the fabric as they passed. They hated how put-together Pilavel looked, with almost no effort. It wasn't fair. "Let's see if there's any other way out of this prison. Why did they put us in a sub, anyway? Is it that weird sea-fetish of theirs?" They looked both ways. A door was present on either side of the corridor, and one behind them.

A shock of impact threw them to the cold, bronze floor of the sub's central corridor, their nose coming perilously close to the surface. The soft lights in the ceiling flickered with the rocking of the sub.

Pilavel clicked by on stiletto heels, keeping her balance with a spell in hexameter muttered under her breath. She stopped at the end of the sub's main passage; the top of her dark hair lit by the crystalline lights.

"I greatly doubt the cultists of sei-Voch'canar built any other exits into this prison vessel. Besides, from the vibrations, they appear to have pushed the vehicle off its mounting. I can only assume they mean to follow through on their threats to 'consign us to the Ancient Mothers of the Eldest Deep' by pushing us into the Iltovish Ocean. I shall discover if this craft possesses any means of propulsion before we sink."

"I hate you," Ocha whispered to the floor before pushing themself up and following Pilavel. Always second. Pilavel was a lying, cheating, girlfriend-stealing bootlicker, but she had objected to the elders' inanity just as much as Ocha had. In their village on the crumbling cliffs of Iltovia, she had tried to talk the cultists out of their mad plan, and almost succeeded, for which Ocha—grudgingly—had to give her a little respect.

"And now I'm stuck with her, at least as long as we're alive," Ocha grumbled as they stumbled through the shaking corridor after the woman.

Pilavel—her head almost brushing the ceiling—was staring at a control board filled with curved metal and familiar polygonal shapes, festooned with brass gears, buttons, and screws, the function of which Ocha was blissfully unaware. Another tremor threw them against the hull as the sub lurched forward. Pilavel steadied herself on the console.

"This sub-ocean vessel appears to be thousands of years old, but well kept. The cultists likely kept it as a place for ritual imprisonment, though how it came to be on these cliffs is unknown, if it is meant to pass beneath the ocean. I believe it may be a singular remnant of the post-Malovian split which triggered your geomantic magic's decline."

"It's not *my* magic," Ocha shot back as the sub shook again. They had a definite sense of *moving*, which sent uncertain tremors through their belly. "It's a functional and powerful magic system equal to articumancy, but ignored for millennia, for some idiotic reason."

"Where would you put a lever to adjust our view if you were designing this ship?" Pilavel seemed determined to ignore Ocha's attacks.

"I don't know," Ocha said. They glanced over the console, their eyes tracing strange connections between angles and chord angles they didn't fully grasp. "What about there?" They flicked a small lever, and a rumble and screech enveloped the tiny room. Ocha flinched back.

"This confirms my theory of the vessel design's connection to your magic system," Pilavel said. "You may wish to hold tightly to a well-secured object."

"I—what?" Ocha shielded their eyes against the brightness now shining through a window newly revealed above the console. Their jaw dropped.

"By the seas and stars. Those idiots actually did it."

Above them, the dread god sei-Voch'canar emerged from their prison in Linia, titanic hands breaking the crust of the moon like week-old bread. The two other moons hung nearby, witness to their larger sibling's desecration. The god's bulk obscured a sliver of the morning sun as they swelled with the cultist's articumancy. Their presence was vast, and as Ocha's eyes adjusted, the deflating shell of Linia spiraled into a new orbit, trailing pieces. The moon hadn't *contained* the prison, as all the religious texts said. It had *been* the prison. A chill ran down Ocha's arms at seeing one of the pantheon in the flesh. Was errant articumancy so powerful? Mehrada had been right. Geomancy could not have prevented this.

As Ocha blinked spots of light away, the rest of the landscape—or lack thereof—came into focus. The sub was sliding over the edge of the cliffs, crashing green waves tipped with peaks of white far below.

"Oh shiiiiii..."

They fell.

\* \* \*

Ocha awoke to green light filtering through the transparent screen above the console. A sea snake slithered past, chasing a school of fish. They were underwater, but Ocha realized they could still see the sun, moon, and sky, with the dread god reaching one gigantic hand, ever so slowly, toward the sun. They could not conceive of the distances involved. It was the end of everything, playing out in slow motion. How much time did they have? A list of regrets paraded through their mind, Mehrada among them.

The vision became cloudy as the volume of water grew above them. The sub was listing backward, sinking fast. The crystal lights set in the ceiling flickered once, twice.

"Ah. You have regained consciousness. I believe your skills at geomancy might ensure we do not drown in the next few minutes." Pilavel stood over them, a single strand of hair escaped from her tight bun. Sunlight through water made a corona around her head. How dare she look so angelic?

"What happened?"

"You did not heed my warning and your head interacted forcefully with the instrument cluster." Pilavel pointed to where a nightmare of angled shapes pulled at Ocha's magic senses. There was meaning hidden there. A bloodstain spotted one of the polygons, and Ocha reached up to feel for blood, but Pilavel got there first.

"I will heal your injury," she said, and put her warm hand on Ocha's forehead.

Bright impact.
Knitting broken seams.
Growing together.
No trace left.

The skin under her hands heated to burning, and Ocha hissed and pulled away, but all they felt was unbroken skin, warm from Pilavel's healing.

"Ask me next time," Ocha grumbled.

"As you say," Pilavel answered. "The next time you are rendered near death I shall wait until you are returned to a rational state before asking if you wish your wounds healed."

Ocha glared back, trying to be offended. Pilavel's tone wasn't even sarcastic. It was matter of fact, and that was worse. How had this stick of emotionless logic stolen Mehrada? Was Pilavel as good with that tongue while she wasn't speaking?

"If you are sufficiently healed, will you investigate these controls? I cannot fully understand them and there is seawater leaking into the sub-ocean vessel. I estimate we have less than five minutes before suffocation. I wish to live, and aid in the reimprisonment of the sun eater, if possible."

Ocha blinked at the change in subject, before realizing their legs and butt were wet with warm seawater. Water was streaming into the sub from the bolts drilled through the hatch. They stood, bracing themself against the cant of the deck underneath. At the bow, the water rose to their ankles, but the stern end of the corridor was halfway submerged. They didn't have much time.

"If they wanted to kill us, why do it so slowly?"

"I believe there were differing opinions about *literally* enacting the ritual for sei-Voch'canar's return."

"So, what, you think they pushed us into a leaky relic because they wanted us to stop them?"

"If you had bothered to listen to the debate with the cultist leaders, you might have understood their conflicting desires. Not all were in favor of the dread god returning."

Ocha took another look through the transparent bow of the sub, where one immense hand was barely visible through the water, reaching. "The cultists didn't seem that conflicted..." They broke off. The water was reaching their calves. "Less arguing. More fixing." They bolted back down the narrow passage, almost tripping into the deepening water. It filled the stern of the sub. They noted the closed door on either side. The one past the leaking entry hatch was already underwater.

The entrance was canted up the side of the hull, with a tiny ladder below. Eight shoddily crafted holes were drilled through the elaborate brass plate, too big for the bolts in them. Ugly welds connected circular plates to the ends of the bolts, overlapping between the hatch and hull, locking the hatch in place once the bolts were tightened. They could be worked free, but not while submerged.

"Tell me about this bickering then." Ocha paddled to the eight streams of saltwater. The water here was up to their chest. They had to fix this, fast.

"If you had listened, you would have heard some call on the Ancient Mothers of the Eldest Deep, while others insisted the sun eater was true inevitability."

"I've never heard of the Ancient Mothers. They're not part of the pantheon, are they?"

"I was also unaware of their existence."

Ocha glanced back to see Pilavel swimming gracefully, her suit coat spread around her like manta fins. "Back away. Your fancy word magic might bind gods, end wars, and heal all ills, but it's got no sway over time and space. For that you need some non-linear geometries."

Pilavel obediently drifted back until her stylish—and ruined—pumps touched the corridor floor. About the only instruction from them the woman had ever obeyed.

Ocha stared at the streaming water, letting their eyes unfocus as they computed angles and equations to bring the correct structure into existence. They raised their hands as they paddled with their feet, already sketching circles and ellipses, crossing lines and projections of higher dimensions.

A glowing structure took shape, eight spheres of light inverting in eye-bending patterns, marking the places the holes pierced the hatch. Lines connected the spheres in a fractal pattern, branching off into microscopic sunbursts, tying together in a place physical eyes couldn't see. Their nostrils flared, trying to suck in enough air. All magic had an opposing cost, and this incantation was like a screw tunneling through their brain.

The streams of water slackened as Ocha pinched their fingers together, closing the gaps between the bolts and the holes slowly but steadily. The pressure mounted in their brain until they finished the spell with a sharp twist of their hands. The flow of water ceased, and the smell of ozone filled the air as a shape burned into the hatch—circles and crossing lines that made the eyes water.

Ocha panted and slumped in the water, their heart beating hard. "I've inverted space at the plane where the water would enter the vessel. It'll hold long enough." Long enough for the sun eater to bring forth permanent darkness, if the scriptures were correct.

Pilavel splashed closer, examining the burned design and bolts. "Impressive."

"Don't get too close, unless you want to be sucked through a wormhole no bigger than your finger," Ocha said. They smirked. "No, on second thought, go for it."

Pilavel straightened, hands steadying her as she treaded water. How could she be so graceful? "And what of this water? It prevents us from accurately operating the vessel."

Ocha cupped their hands and splashed water at the hatch. It clung to their geomantic diagram, falling into the not-space they had created. They tried not to stare at Pilavel's elegant hands, already making the same motions. "Bail fast, before sei-Voch'canar finishes their snack."

* * *

Ocha's spell greedily sucked up the remaining water until the inside of the sub was merely damp. Then they took inventory. The door on the left of the corridor contained a tiny pantry and kitchen, stocked with a few days of salted fish, seaweed crackers, and barrels of water. It also contained a tiny toilet. The door on the other side was a general-purpose cabin, with crumbling maps and tools stored in cabinets, a chair bolted in front of a tiny table, and a single cramped bed.

"With the dread god free, at least we won't live long enough to fight over who gets to sleep there," Ocha said.

"Especially as we are still descending, with no control over our course." Pilavel looked toward the last door, opposite the control console. "Shall we investigate what I presume is the engine? We must return to the surface. I bow to no elder god, even though they desire the death of our star." Her face suddenly pinched with fury. "I nearly convinced the cultists not to act. *Why do this?*"

Ocha's instinct was to snap back at this prim stick of a woman. She barged in, and expected everyone to fall into place? Well, Mehrada had.

"Not everyone wants to act rationally," they said, and pulled open the last door. Their eyes widened in appreciation. "Now *this* I understand. Look at the craftmanship! Look at those polygonal interactions!" The engine was built of a vertical stack of rotating engraved brass sheets. Ocha understood almost instantly that the sheet edges would align in different configurations as they turned, driving fluctuations in space, propelling the ship in nearly any direction. Ocha had dreamed of constructs like this, but as the only living geomancer, never had the resources to test.

"These plates are warded with articumancy," Pilavel said, stepping past them.

She was not going to steal this from them too.

"Watch it. This is my area." Ocha tried to block Pilavel from the geomantic engine, but there was little room in the compartment.

"It is not wholly your type of magic which fuels this engine. If you had not interfered with my negotiations, we would not be in this situation, which I would greatly enjoy." Pilavel's tone was measured as always, but there was a spike of heat in her words. Had Ocha finally gotten under that smug exterior? It would serve that gorgeous icicle right.

Now where had *that* thought come from? Ocha shook it away.

"If I hadn't distracted them, they would have broken the seals earlier and sei-Voch'canar would be halfway through eating the sun."

"Highly unlikely. Look there," Pilavel pointed at the surface of the nearest slowly spinning plate, on which etchings were visible. Ocha's attention was frustratingly drawn to the elegant finger and shining nail gloss. Mehrada had picked at her fingernails. They pulled their eyes away. No time for confusing emotions.

"Are those...Malovian words?" Ocha asked. They tried to recall symbols from the old language as the plates spun. Stopping sei-Voch'canar. That's what they were doing. Even now, the elder god's hand must be closing on the sun. Surely the elders of the Halls of Magic had noticed. Were they using Pilavel's binding? Crafting elaborate counter spells from poetry? Or merely arguing over how

Vochcanians broke spells created millennia ago to seal the god in one of their moons?

"I believe they are." Pilavel's head swung left to right as she attempted to read while the plates were in motion, showing off the smooth curve of her neck. "It is an ode to the sea, and a blessing from the Ancient Mothers of the Eldest Deep to protect the structure of the sub-ocean vessel."

"There's that term again. Who are these Ancient Mothers?"

"You are missing the most important aspect."

"I am not. It means this sub runs on combined word *and* geomantic magic—something never attempted since geomancy fell into disuse thousands of years ago, leaving only your word magic. See, I can think of two things at once." Like how attractive *and* annoying Pilavel was.

"The term is *articumancy*. The phrasing of words for the specific desired effect." Pilavel drew up to her full height, chin up.

"Yeah, word magic. Then the Malovians must have used both at once to build this contraption. I can already tell it outstrips anything we have today. How did the Vochcanians get hold of it?"

Pilavel sighed deeply. "Again, if you had paid attention in the negotiations, you would have known the Iltovian area was built on ruins of a post-Malovian split culture. It was a deciding factor in why the cult developed."

Ocha ignored the barb. "So the stories go, the Malovians communed with sei-Voch'canar before the god fell from the pantheon to become the sun eater. The culture both released and bound them, and presumably built the moon Linia to be a prison. Little wonder they could create this sub."

Pilavel glanced at the platters again. "Presumably in coordination with these 'Ancient Mothers of the Eldest Deep.'"

Ocha bit a finger in thought. "Now you mention it, there's another connection. When researching geomancy, I ran across multiple references to the god's prison—Linia—being made of deepwater crystal," Ocha said. "I didn't have time enough to look in detail before the elders forced us to go talk to those cultists, rather than acting against them."

"Might the Ancient Mothers know more of our magics intermesh? You said yourself, it is better than anything we have now."

"If they still exist," Ocha said. "This was thousands of years ago." They looked up, where sei-Voch'canar might now be grasping the sun, bringing it to their mouth. "Up or down?"

"Surely those in the Halls of Magic are singing their most powerful articumancy against the dread god. What more will one voice add?" Pilavel knocked on the hull of the sub. "And we are already headed toward the ocean floor."

"Then we need to learn to drive this thing," Ocha said as they headed back toward the controls. They leaned against the sub's slope, clambering toward the front bank of controls, Pilavel right behind them. The surface was out of sight and the greenish light visible through the viewscreen had been replaced with a deep blue. Fish darted by. Even down here, where light was scarce, there was a shadow as if hands larger than oceans hovered above.

"This is fine work, and if it's thousands of years old, I'm surprised those Vochcanians didn't mess it up." Ocha stared down at the hundreds of buttons making up the sub's control panel. They brushed a hand over a burnished gear, then turned to Pilavel. "Shame I have no idea what any of it does."

"I believed you could use your geomantic magic to understand how to propel this sub-ocean vessel with purpose." There was a worried look in Pilavel's eyes, maybe for the first time since Ocha had met her. They smiled in response. So, the unbreakable ice queen had cracks.

"I understand pieces." They looked back at the panel with their geomantic senses focused. "This lever controls pressure. This gear modulates depth." They touched items at the foci of polygonal interactions. "But that's a lot different than controlling this sub with purpose."

"It provides an explanation for the articumantic phrases." Pilavel moved up beside them, and Ocha shifted away. Farther from that dangerous beauty.

"What do you mean?"

Pilavel stretched one immaculate fingernail toward the space between a dial and a button illuminated by a red glow. "These markings. They are scansion lines and meter descriptors."

Ocha looked closer. "I thought those were just scratches in the metal."

"They describe a web of connections between objects, though I cannot say what the individual objects do. You must decode that with your geomancy."

"Or I could just guess," Ocha grumbled, "and not have to deal with your insufferable need to be involved with everything." They grabbed the depth gear, and another switch that modulated forward thrust. It couldn't be too hard...

The sub lurched to port, then yawed starboard. They barely caught themself against the control panel. Pilavel staggered back, muttering under her breath, her face slowly losing a greenish tinge as she did. They gritted their teeth, knuckles of one hand white gripped on a bracing strut, while they turned the controls back to the original positions. The sub settled back into its slow pitch backward, sinking farther into the depths.

"Perhaps I should read for you how the controls affect each other?" Pilavel suggested.

Ocha picked themself up, trying to hide the grimace as their knee twinged. They'd banged it on the hard brass floor. Anger swirled up in them, and they clenched their hands into fists.

"It's always compromise," they said. "Mehrada told me geomancy wasn't good enough, but it was. I forced my way to the top ranks of articumancers. I *made* the elders accept me, despite using a long-lost magic no one respects. But then they threw me away as soon as you arrived, with your fancy clothes and your manicured hands and your immaculate hair." Pilavel's hair was not looking quite so immaculate now, damp with seawater and coming untucked from its bun. How was she still so radiant, then?

Pilavel's eyes went cold, and Ocha barely resisted taking a step back. She was beautiful, and terrifying.

"Compromise. What do you know of compromise?" The woman took one threatening step forward, towering over Ocha, her head brushing the ceiling. "You rediscovered the lost other half of our magic, by the pantheon! Do you know how intimidating it is to place myself against your skill? More, do you know what it is to fight against every other articumancer? Clawing your way to the top? I was a small girl with a stutter. I was useless at magic. Y-you're a natural." She swiped one hand through the air. A purple haze surrounded it—untethered magic.

"You say what you want. I must gauge each word that exits my mouth for meaning. Articumancy is a delicate art, far more subtle than the raw p-power of your geomancy. Why do you think I must act so coldly to you? Articumancy is speech itself! The instant I lose control, if I c-cannot complete exact phrasing, the effects of m-my magic are unbound."

Phantasms rose behind Pilavel's head, thoughts and words summoned into being by incautious utterances. Ocha's eyes widened and they shrank against the controls. Did every articumancer constantly fight this? But Pilavel wasn't finished.

"I trained. I studied. I *controlled* myself—something you seem unable to do. I excised every stutter from my

84 William C. Tracy

language, looking up to the Halls of Magic. At all times, I must place each meaning and word for proper effect."

The phantoms subsided as Pilavel seemed to fold into herself, looking away from Ocha.

"But you g-got there first. You presented a magic system lost for millennia, presumed extinct. You opened the gates between Fonn and Prailil, affecting trade the whole world over with your actions! H-how could I not strive to become as skilled as you?" Indistinct shapes fluttered around her head, gaining reality at each imperfect word. "I sacrificed everything to climb to the top of articumancy. I have no life, no friends, no family. Yet one w-word on censure from you sets me b-back to a stuttering girl." The shapes grew in density, reaching for Pilavel, for Ocha.

Ocha gritted their teeth. "And that means you can steal my achievements? Just because you worked hard? I rediscovered half of magic!" They stood up straight, sketching a polygon in the air, twisted in on itself and endlessly repeating, trapping the phantasms inside with bone-tingling howls. "You stole Mehrada from me. You wanted to talk and sei-Voch'canar was released. Here I am, correcting your mistakes. Don't talk to me about sacrifice and study."

Pilavel's mouth compressed until her lips almost disappeared. "That is unfair and untrue. You talk of what you do not understand. But we must work together for any chance of stopping the dread god."

"You've had your chance—" Ocha started, but the sub lurched as if struck, throwing them against Pilavel's bony form. The crystal lights flickered, throwing weird shadows around the room. Their hands wrapped unconsciously around Pilavel's waist, proving the woman was no icicle. She was, in fact, quite warm. And comfortable.

"W-we must work together," Pilavel repeated, but this time there was fear in her words. Ocha opened their mouth to argue, but looked up into Pilavel's face. She was staring at the viewscreen.

Ocha pushed away just in time to see a suckered tentacle smash into the window. This time the lights went out and they threw themself at the controls. They could barely see. The dark blue-green light of the ocean filtered through the viewscreen. How deep were they? The sub had been sinking as they argued, and they hadn't even deciphered the controls.

"Apology accepted," they shouted over their shoulder. "Now come help me figure out how this sub works."

"This conversation is not complete." They felt Pilavel by their shoulder, the remaining warmth near the controls, which wasn't much. She was still angry, as was Ocha, but now wasn't the time.

"There is too little light to correctly interpret the scansion and meter of the articumantic connections." Pilavel was buttoned up again like the cold fish she was, no sign of a stutter. How much had Ocha gotten to her?

"You can take a guess," Ocha pressed. "Try, before—"

The sub shook with the impact and they both grabbed the control panel to keep from falling. A massive beak scraped against the viewer, opening wide to reveal a circular set of grinding radulae. Ocha flinched away from the screech of bony kraken mouthparts against the viewscreen. "Quick, look for the lightswi—"

Fleshy tentacles slapped against the sub, suctioning in place. Pitch black descended as slimy, glossy slabs of kraken tentacle covered the screen. Pops and creaks sounded throughout the vehicle, like an old pot being clamped in a vise. The sub shook from another impact.

"Even my guesses will be useless now," Pilavel said. Ocha ducked as a *PING* of metal deforming came from overhead.

"Then what do we do?" Ocha's insides tightened like the tentacles crushing the sub. "We're going to die here, right before the world is snuffed out. The sun eater will gulp us down like a snack after they consume the sun, but we'll be too dead to see it. We'll be inside this kraken, digested bit by bit as it crunches our bones and—"

The slap was not really that. More of a heavy tap on Ocha's cheek, but it shut them up.

"I have not spent years of my life conquering childhood trauma to be eaten by an oversized squid," Pilavel hissed in Ocha's ear. "You opened mystic portals closed for thousands of years. You tout you control time and space with your geomancy. Then do so and get this thing away from us!"

"Those portals had layers of automation built in!" Ocha yelled. "I barely had to add anything. Anyone could have done it with a little study of geomancy."

"But *you* were the one to do it." Pilavel's measured voice was like an icepick through Ocha's objections. "Do it again, or we die."

Ocha blinked into the darkness, punctuated by shrieks of tortured metal and bony scraping. They imagined the kraken's beak gnawing through the viewscreen—like sei-Voch'canar eating through the sun.

The sun. Its light would burn the kraken, or at least blind it.

This was a terrible idea.

They raised their arms, sketching inverted polygons and imaginary geometries from memory, hoping their lines were straight, or straight enough. On the plus side, the target was so big it was hard to miss. Not like opening a portal between two cities—or pantheon forbid—to a specific place. That would take months to calculate. They just needed sunlight, fast.

"Shield your eyes!" Ocha yelled as they finished the nonagonal symmetrohdron and the portal flared open.

Even with their eyes closed, the flash of light was so bright it lit up Ocha's skull. A shriek of pain echoed through the sub as it rocked with the kraken's departure. Ocha broke their mystic polygons with a twist of their fingers and the portal fizzed and died. But with the portal's proximity to the dread god came the vision.

*Hands, larger than continents, grasp warmth to drive away the cold of absolute zero. A mouth, opened wider than worlds, tongue questing for light and nuclear energy. With this power, they will escape the Ancient Mothers and be free! To grasp the whole of sei-Voch'canar is to invite madness. Even snatches of their dark majesty drive needles of psychic force through the mind of the strongest individual. There is an instant of apotheosized flesh biting down on elements fused into a superhot, dense flux. Then nothing.*

\* \* \*

"My *head*," Ocha cried as their eyes fluttered open. Pilavel was standing over them again.

"You did it," she said.

The lights flickered on, then off, in a stutter, but it was enough to see. For once, Pilavel's lips twisted in a faint smile. It was a strange sight on that cold face. But what...?

"What happened to you?" Ocha sat up, then pushed to their feet. They reached one hand to the side of Pilavel's face, now red and blistered.

"There are consequences to the power you control, impressive though it is," she said, moving her damaged face away from Ocha's fingers. Her hand gestured to the viewscreen. Ocha's attention was diverted by the blistered bulge in the middle of the formerly clear viewing port. "But they were worth the cost, in this situation."

Ocha looked back to their companion, then raised one hand to their face, hissing as fingertips touched hot and swollen skin. They had been behind their portal, and the sun's light had been bright enough to do this. How close had their portal been to the sun?

"I hope that viewscreen holds until we find the Ancient Mothers." A flicker of remembered awe ran through their mind, but it refused to recall what they had experienced, save that it was *bad*. The viewscreen might last as long as the rest of the world.

A tremor shook the sub, though not from the kraken returning. It was a deep, concussive shudder, like the entire ocean shook.

"Time is short." Pilavel echoed their thoughts. "We must hope the Ancient Mothers of the Eldest Deep know how to defeat the dread god, assuming they still live."

* * *

"The Malovians must have charted all the oceans of our world in devices like this," they said, munching on a seaweed wafer and staring at an ancient map. Pilavel had sung their sunburns to little more than reddened skin, but the injury and its healing left Ocha hungry. "The elders in the Halls of Magic would kill to see these—oh oceans take it!" The edge of the map crumbled in their fingers as the sub trembled again. Those were becoming more common.

"I believe I have a course," Pilavel said.

Ocha looked up from the remains of their map. "You found the Ancient Mothers?"

Pilavel smoothed her map out flat, one delicate fingernail pointing to a spot in the depths marked with ancient text. The shadows in this room made her face look softer, more accepting, than the hard-edged woman Pilavel was. "This message describes the Ancient Mothers' nest at the bottom of the Iltovish ocean. I have calculated where it rests in relation to the Malovian city the Vochcanians inhabit."

Ocha gestured to the sub in general. "And where is that in relation to us?"

Pilavel's nail tapped the map. "Down. We have not moved far from the cliffs. As we approach the site, I can take accurate soundings."

"Then bring that map and let's decode these controls," Ocha said, making for the doorway.

* * *

"What do you have?" Ocha asked Pilavel's back.

"Much more since we restored the lighting's functionality," she answered. She had finally taken off her business suit jacket she'd worn during talks with the Vochcanians, revealing elegant arms under gauzy sleeves.

"I believe I have the macro-poem's overall structure and several sub-stanzas identified. I should be able to direct your geomatic knowledge of most control functions to their overall purpose in the sub-ocean vessel."

"Hmm," Ocha said. They would rather claw their tongue out than talk like that all the time. "Show me what you found."

Pilavel came to their side, displaying the connecting word structure defining the controls. Ocha tried not to think of the woman's hip next to theirs, and instead studied the map. With their knowledge of the geomantic function of each control, they directed the sub toward the Ancient Mothers' nest.

If the map was accurate.

If the Mothers were still there.

"Based on our calculations, I believe the sub-ocean vessel will reach the bottom near morning," Pilavel said. Another tremor punctuated her remark.

"It's only been hours since the cultists threw us in here," Ocha said, "but the shaking is getting worse. How long do you think we have?"

"We are too deep to return to the surface, so we must hope we have time to reach the ocean floor."

"And until then?"

"We might sleep, in hope of being well-rested when we reach the Ancient Mothers."

"You want to sleep? At a time like this?" Ocha tried to keep their eyes firmly on Pilavel's face. Not imagining her undressed, or in a flimsy nightgown, gracefully reclining. "Besides, there's only one bed."

"We could always sleep together."

Ocha blinked and backed away from Pilavel. "What? I don't...I mean I..."

"That was a joke."

"I didn't know you were capable of that."

"There is much I am capable of. You know little about me, save that you seem to hate me." Pilavel tilted her head and Ocha shrank under those brilliant eyes. "Why is that?"

Ocha stared back. "How can you *not* know?"

Mehrada.

Their girlfriend had been warm, comforting, funny, helpful. She pressed Ocha to realize their dreams. They might have given up on finding a translation for the ancient Malovian texts of geomancy without Mehrada's continued support.

But then Pilavel came. First, she took Ocha's place and legacy, and then Mehrada as well. How had their caring, earnest girlfriend fallen for that ice cube? It was like Mehrada had turned off her affection for Ocha.

"Why did you take Mehrada from me?" they asked.

Pilavel frowned. "I did not take Mehrada from you."

Ocha sighed. "I mean, I know she's her own woman. She can do what she wants and it's not my place to—"

Pilavel interrupted, stepping closer. "No. You misunderstand my intention. I did not coerce or seduce Mehrada. I did not even approach her first. She came to me."

"I...what?" Ocha leaned against the bronze of the hull. Pilavel was frustrating, and cold, and haughty, but she wasn't a liar. "She told me I had gone too deep into geomancy. That it could never stop the return of sei-Voch'canar. That your articumantic binding had swayed her, as they had the Halls of Magic."

Pilavel's eyes were intent on Ocha. "She informed me you said her articumancy was weak, and she was not worth your time."

"I did no such thing!" Ocha drew themself up. "I cared for her. I...I thought I even might love her. And she left me. For *you*! Then you threw her aside."

Pilavel shook her head. "Again, I believe you are misinformed. Mehrada left me mere days ago, immediately before the talks began. She and I disagreed on articumancy. As with you, she said my binding would never stop sei-Voch'canar's return."

Ocha wanted to argue with her, but the similarities were too strange. "There *are* only two magics. Articumancers around the world were working to stop the prison in Linia from weakening. And she thought neither magic could be successful?"

"Or suspected they were used incorrectly. Mehrada was particularly fixated on the dread god, was she not? Where did you originally meet her?"

"It was a few years ago, back before the cult of sei-Voch'canar appeared in the news. Wait, no." They stopped, staring into nothingness. "It was *when* the news broke. That first week. Every headline in the world screamed the dread god was a reality, that their prison was weakening. No one believed it before then. Mehrada came up to me that very day, in the claff shop I go to. She started talking to me and...things went on from there."

"No one except the Vochcanians," Pilavel said.

"You are really hard to follow sometimes," Ocha replied.

Pilavel waved a hand. "Excuse me. You said no one believed the dread god could return. That is not true. Prior to that point, the Vochcanians believed their god would return. They believed it so earnestly they found the way to make it fact."

Ocha swallowed. There was a jump in logic here, but it made sense. The questions Mehrada asked. How she pushed Ocha to rediscover geomancy. Her odd shift in affection. "Are you saying what I think you're saying?"

Pilavel nodded. "If you think I imply Mehrada must be a member of the Vochcanian cult, then yes."

Ocha beat a hand against the hull. "Stormy seas and clouded skies! She knows everything about both of us. She's an articumancer. She's been in the Halls of Magic for all the debates. How much did her friends affect the elders' decision to send us here?"

Strangely, Pilavel was smiling.

"What?" Ocha snarled. "What could possibly be good about this?"

Pilavel laughed, and Ocha's eyes went wide. It was a strange sound, silky and throaty and...yes, seductive. They would never have thought it a sound the hard woman could make.

Pilavel took in a deep breath, still laughing. "Why would the Vochcanians manipulate events to send the foremost articumancer and the one who rediscovered geomancy to a dead-end spot, to deal with cultists who they know will not listen?"

Ocha stared at Pilavel, the words rolling up inside them. "Because they knew we had a chance to stop sei-Voch'canar. They sent us to the cultists for them to dispose of us."

Pilavel nodded. "Yet some of them were either of two minds, or..." She froze, eyes going wide.

"Or what?"

"What if Mehrada...is not, in truth, a Vochcanian?"

"Then she disparaged both our achievements, put our magic at odds, and had us sent to our doom for what reason?"

Pilavel only stared at them.

"Oh. For us to work *together*," Ocha breathed. Some knot they hadn't been aware of released within their chest.

"Precisely." The sub rocked like a cork in a bathtub, throwing Pilavel into her. For once, Pilavel didn't have a spell ready, and Ocha caught her in their arms.

They stared up at her, pushing down the urge to kiss this spectacular woman. "If there's *any* chance, we have to work together. I'll see if I can make the sub go faster."

\* \* \*

Ocha's mind spun as they worked on the engine plates. With Pilavel's decoding of the articumantic directions, it was simple to maintain and even boost the craft's speed by aligning the plates in different configurations. Of course, it was easy. The sub had been designed to be operated when articumancy and geomancy were both in usage—maybe even both by one person. The amount of power that would give...

"I've been thinking," Ocha said as they returned to the forward control bank, wiping grease on a towel from the galley. Pilavel, leaning to study the controls, started.

"You seem to be turning that into a bad habit," Pilavel said, rubbing her knuckle where she'd banged it into a gear.

A smile crept onto Ocha's face. They had never managed to surprise Pilavel before. "Was...that another joke?"

"I joke when I am under stress."

"*Now* you're under stress?"

"What was your thought?"

"Spoilsport." Ocha grinned stupidly until they remembered they hated Pilavel. Well, maybe that was too strong a word. In fact, Pilavel's hair had come out of its tight bun, trailing down her neck, showing off her exquisite collarbone.

"Er. How far away are we?" Ocha said gruffly.

"From coordinates marked on a thousand-year-old map, measured in relation to the approximate location where we were deposited into the Iltovish ocean, near a cult that has taken up residence on the presumed ruins of an ancient city?" Pilavel turned, but not before Ocha caught the brief smile on her face. "Quite close, I believe." She pointed out beyond the warped viewscreen.

Whether some prescient aspect of articumancy or simply good timing, at the moment Pilavel pointed, the view bloomed with color.

Green and red and purple fronds pushed up from the ocean floor, fish swimming through them. Plumes of discharge from thermal vents heated the ocean, and the inside of the sub grew warmer. A huge shark swam past the screen, chasing fish around the fields of kelp.

Behind it all towered a ziggurat, fashioned in glittering stone. Ocha approached the screen slowly, marveling at the wide array of color and shape in the materials of the monument's construction. Their geomantic senses buzzed as they took in the placement of the temple, stones and pedestals surrounding it, and pathways through the gardens of seaweed.

"There is so much meaning," Pilavel murmured. Hands gripping the console, she pulled herself forward. "See the stanza markings there? And the ratio of blocks to spaces in the ziggurat? Articumancy is built into the bones of this place."

"As is geomancy," Ocha said. "Look there—" but their words cut off as people exited the temple.

They were unlike those who walked the surface, but they were obviously aware and intelligent, with crafted metal and stone draping their forms, using fabric of fish scales and beads and shells. They skittered on many legs— or rather, tentacles—feeling along the ocean floor and gripping objects to pull themselves along. It was impossible to assign social roles to an alien culture at first glance, but they looked *official.*

"How do we talk to them?" Ocha asked. "Can you make us breathe underwater with articumancy?"

Pilavel gave a tiny shrug. "If it is possible, I have no knowledge of the correct words or how to articulate them in water."

Ocha was calculating angles in their mind. "Perhaps if I were to create a tunnel, in which your words could sustain the connections between polygonal—"

"Like that?" Pilavel pointed.

The creatures outside gestured to them, their gills pumping water in obvious rhythms. As they approached, corridors of air flowed from them, making kelp sag without the water's support, while fish avoided the bubbles with spasming course corrections. The tunnel gained depth and changed shape, expanding into a dome around the sub, reaching toward the waiting people.

"Ah. Yes. Like that." Ocha gaped.

"Shall we go?" Pilavel extended a delicate, manicured hand.

Ocha stared at it. At Pilavel. Back down.

They swallowed and took her hand in theirs.

\* \* \*

Ocha stood next to Pilavel in front of the welcoming party. They were tall—taller than even Pilavel—standing upright in the bubble of air they'd created. There were five of them, and each stood on a shifting mass of tentacled limbs. Their upper bodies were lumpy and ugly, and they had no necks to speak of, their heads placed directly on their torsos. But Ocha could see the glitter of intelligence in their bright eyes, and their mouths, full of sharp teeth, emitted sounds that were obviously language.

"What are they saying?" they asked Pilavel.

"I am certain this is a form of old Malovian. Perhaps they think it is still a language spoken on the surface."

"Well, I don't speak it," Ocha said.

"I am attempting to rectify that omission. Keep hold of my hand," Pilavel said. She gulped a few words to the creatures, who moaned back. Then Pilavel cleared her throat and sang.

It was crystalline.

It was entrancing, and sharp like glass, and piercing, and it shook Ocha's soul down to their toes. They stared, transfixed, until Pilavel finished.

"Your articumancy is well crafted. We have been called the Deep Ones by your kind in the past," one of the creatures said. Their voice was guttural, on the lower end of the human register, but now Ocha could understand it.

"Better?" Pilavel lifted an elegant eyebrow.

"Um. Much," Ocha admitted. They addressed the Deep Ones. "Then you aren't the Ancient Mothers?"

"We protect and serve the Ancient Mothers—the oldest of our kind. You must have felt the earthquakes on your journey, heralding the return of our errant child. Even here, the heat-vents tremble and the fish are erratic in their kelp forests. The time of prophecy is at hand." As if on cue, Ocha stumbled as the floor of the ocean shook and jumped.

"Errant child...wait, sei-Voch'canar is one of you?" they asked, staggering against the shaking.

The Deep Ones kept their balance easily with multitudinous legs. "Yes, they are of our kind, grown swollen and arrogant on the heady power of geomancy and articumancy. Before their ascendancy, sei-Voch'canar was the best of us."

"When did they become a god?" Pilavel asked. "There is nothing of this in our records."

"What is a god but one with power far above that of others? We sense the beginnings of such majesty in you, as in the best of your kind. You call us ancients, but sei-Voch'canar's ascension occurred near the birth of our civilization. We were old when you Malovians were young." The Deep One in front seemed to be the leader.

"The Malovians are long gone," Ocha said. "They died out thousands of years ago."

The Deep Ones bowed their heads. "We mourn their passing. We wondered why the transit vessels stopped their visits." They reached out a hand to the sub.

"Were you originally responsible for trapping sei-Voch'canar in their prison?" Pilavel asked. "How did it become weak enough for cultists to break it open?"

"So many questions." The Deep One spokesperson shook their head, and the others gestured and muttered to each other. "Cages cannot last forever against great minds. For every age, there must be a resetting. The Malovians discovered this. Now your culture will too."

"So, you...*do* have a way to trap the dread god again?" Ocha asked.

The Deep One shrugged—an interesting movement from a being with no neck. "Our progeny is powerful, but not infallible. They reach beyond their bounds. Follow."

The five Deep Ones turned. They took up their rhythmic chant, gesturing in geomantic forms that were frustratingly familiar to Ocha, yet not ones they knew. The bubble of air extended toward the massive ziggurat.

Pilavel, still holding their hand, dragged Ocha forward.

From the outside, the glittering ziggurat resolved into a bright blue-white light, the color of the moons. It was the source of the lighting here in the depths.

They entered the front gate, twice as high as the Deep Ones, who already towered over Pilavel. Ocha felt like a bug.

The path sloped immediately down, opening wide into an arena taking up the entire inside ziggurat, or...more?

Ocha peered around, their geomantic senses tingling.

"Is it...bigger in here?" they whispered to Pilavel.

"These articumantic writings tell of depth and distance, time and growth." Pilavel pointed out indecipherable markings on the walls.

"And I thought articumancy couldn't control time and space," Ocha whispered.

"These stanzas are unfamiliar to me," Pilavel whispered back.

"They are waiting for you," the Deep One leader said, gesturing to two domes of material on the bowl-like floor of the ziggurat, stretching much farther into the distance than the exterior length of the building.

The bubble of air extended through the arena as the five Deep Ones took up stations near the ziggurat's entrance, uttering strings of syllables while gesturing in complex patterns.

The lumps moved.

"The Ancient Mothers," Pilavel breathed, as the mounds spiraled up into titanic forms, of similar shape to the Deep Ones, but on a scale far larger. Tentacled creatures circled around their heads, which extended from the bulk of bodies larger than buildings.

"Are those...kraken swimming around them?" Ocha asked. They remembered the beast that had almost crushed the sub. The ones here, if the same size, looked like house pets in comparison to the Ancient Mothers.

As the two massive creatures extended into pyramids of flesh—innumerable twisting appendages below and glowing eyes above—the ziggurat responded. The blocks brightened, shining until Ocha had to squint.

"Deepwater crystal," they said.

"What do you mean?" Pilavel asked.

"The temple. It's made of deepwater crystal. Like the dread god's prison. Like the moons."

"We Must Speak."

Luminous eyes bigger than they were stared down, filled with stars. The voice was thunder, reverberating around the chamber. It doubled and harmonized, and Ocha realized both Ancient Mothers spoke in tandem.

Two tentacles, big as trees, shot forward. One grabbed Pilavel, the other Ocha. They were dragged toward jaws filled with rows of razor-sharp teeth.

"This Cycle Has Come To An End. As In Every Cycle, The Contract Must Be Forged Anew."

"Let us go!" Ocha screamed. The teeth gnashed far too close for comfort, each one bigger than their body.

"I do not believe they will harm us," Pilavel called. She reached over the tentacle that held her; fingers outstretched for Ocha's hand. Ocha reached back, but they were too far apart to touch.

"Soon, Young Ones," the Ancient Mothers boomed. There was no trouble understanding them, whatever language they spoke.

"Soon what? What contract? What must we do?" Ocha called up to them.

The massive eyes blinked, as slow as a door closing and opening. Stars winked out and re-lit.

"You Are Unaware Of The Contract? Then How Is Our Wayward Child Released?" The Mothers sounded confused.

"There is a cult devoted to sei-Voch'canar," Pilavel called. "They found the ancient articumantic phrases to release the dread god from their prison in the moon, Linia."

The tentacles holding them wobbled and Ocha gripped the slippery skin for stability. It was warm to the touch, and they were sweating already.

"They Did Not Cast The Corresponding Geomantic Signs To Complete The Ritual?"

"No," Ocha called up. "The art of geomancy has been lost. I am the only practitioner alive." They leaned out toward Pilavel. "What is going on? I thought the Ancient Mothers had the answers?"

"They were separated long from those on the surface," Pilavel answered.

"Little Wonder Earthquakes Shake Our Abode. We Must Hurry," The Ancient Mothers rumbled in tandem. "We Shall Begin The Contract. Witness And Augment."

The tentacle holding Ocha vibrated with the rumble coming from the giant beings. Other appendages rose, tracing diagrams in the air, making space warp and twist. The shapes pulled at their memory, making connections they had only imagined.

"Such poetry I have not dreamed of!" Pilavel called. Her face was alight with wonder.

"They want us to join in!" Ocha called back. "You take the words, I'll do the gestures. Complete the contract!" It was so simple to see their part.

"Agreed!" Pilavel shouted, and began to sing a counterpoint to the Ancient Mothers.

Ocha found their jaw agape, eyes fixed on the tall, beautiful woman. They shook their head.

"Just need to find the correct polygonal inversion to match," they muttered.

They reached out, tracing shapes that ran inside the larger ones the Ancient Mothers created, filling the gaps left for them. The ziggurat shook around them, crystal cracking and falling vast distances to the floor as a circle of blackness grew in the air. They could feel Pilavel's singing charging them with energy, powering their geomancy to new heights. A mental corridor formed between them, and a vision bloomed in Ocha's mind.

*The dread god has coiled themself around the sun, multitudes of tentacles spiraling around the star. Their mouth gapes open, larger than civilizations, fastened to the surface, siphoning energy away. Those on the ground are cast in darkness. People scream and hide, fight each other, and craft articumantic wards, but no simple magic can stop the might of sei-Voch'canar. It is the end-times.*

At the same moment, Ocha was also in the ziggurat. Deepwater crystal pulled from the walls, deforming into the shapes the Ancient Mothers created. They were sucked through the hole of night, a connection between the deepest ocean and farthest sky, and Ocha could see both at once. A string of crystal chains started in the ziggurat and wrapped around the dread god, pulling them away from the sun.

Pilavel sang louder, each tone exact and sharp, cutting through the wet bubble of air. Ocha's fingers blurred, drawing new connections between shapes that did not, in reality, exist.

In the vision, Ocha saw the dread god sei-Voch'canar groan. At the bottom of the ocean, seismic waves buffeted the ground. A crack opened, running between where the two Mothers sat.

Ocha pursed their lips, searching for more connections to make, but there was an unfilled space in the geometry. How to capture a god in chains?

Reaching for the sun, sei-Voch'canar roared, and the deepwater chains holding them snapped, splintering into pieces no bigger than sand.

The Ancient Mothers spoke, while still singing their song and crafting new geometries.

"This Is Not Working. The Contract Requires Full Agreement. All Sides Must Use Their Magic."

"We *are* using our magic!" Ocha screamed back. "What more can we do?"

"You must sing," Pilavel said, and the words cut deep into Ocha's mind.

"You mean we *both* have to perform articumancy and geomancy?"

"The way the old Malovians must have." Pilavel pinned Ocha with her gaze. "The way Mehrada wanted us to."

"But I don't—"

"Become One With The Contract. We Shall Facilitate."

The tentacles holding Ocha drew close to Pilavel's and then there was slippery flesh sliding all around them, caging them away from the rest of the temple. They were pushed together, and Ocha fell into Pilavel's arms.

"I don't know articumancy!" Ocha wailed.

"And I do not understand the intricacies of geomancy," Pilavel answered. She held Ocha to her, their noses almost touching.

"See Each Other. Be Each Other." The Mothers' command drove deep into Ocha's core.

"I see you," Ocha said.

"I want to know you," Pilavel echoed. Ocha knew the words were true, and they agreed.

Their prison vibrated as the Ancient Mothers directed their magics toward them, and Ocha's view doubled.

They were a stuttering girl, struggling to subdue her own body, forcing it to obey her. At the same time, Pilavel was a young person, a failure at the only magic in the world.

The stuttering girl grew, becoming powerful and capable.

The young failure found their true calling, unearthing a lost art.

Together they rose to the heights of the world's magic, but missing so much the other could give them.

Ocha understood. They sang the ancient words of binding.

Pilavel grasped the hidden mysteries and drew impossible diagrams in the air.

Ocha complemented her figures.

Pilavel provided harmony for their melody.

Their bodies sang and moved together, hands touching, legs sliding along legs, mouths tasting each other.

The Ancient Mothers sang and gestured, their bass anchoring the spell deep into the core of the world, their gestures heating Ocha and Pilavel's pleasure.

The deepwater crystal flowed again, replicating into chains so strong even the dread god could not break free. The chains dragged them, screaming earthquakes, howling tornadoes, away from the sun and toward the three moons of the planet. Crystal began to solidify around them.

Pilavel pressed her fingers deep into Ocha and they sang the chords of magic.

Ocha knelt before Pilavel, whose fingers clenched and described reality.

Words to action, flesh joined to magic. They rushed to a crescendo, as sei-Voch'canar folded inward, the last crack sealing to perfection.

Ocha sighed into release, their mouth hard against Pilavel's.

The sun, free again, though reduced, shone across the land and people looked up.

Their panic fell away. They saw the dread god captured, constrained, and the birth of the fourth moon. The fourth contract.

The song came to its end. The lines and angles became a design.

Ocha pressed themself to Pilavel and the two were one, beneath the protection of the Ancient Mothers. The sun eater was confined. The two great magics had been used in conjunction again. And Ocha was at peace.

Want to read more of William C. Tracy's writings?

Join his mailing list at **www.williamctracy.com/newsletter-signup** and get a free story at the same time!

If you want to read along with his new writings, check out William's Patreon at **www.patreon.com/wctracy.**

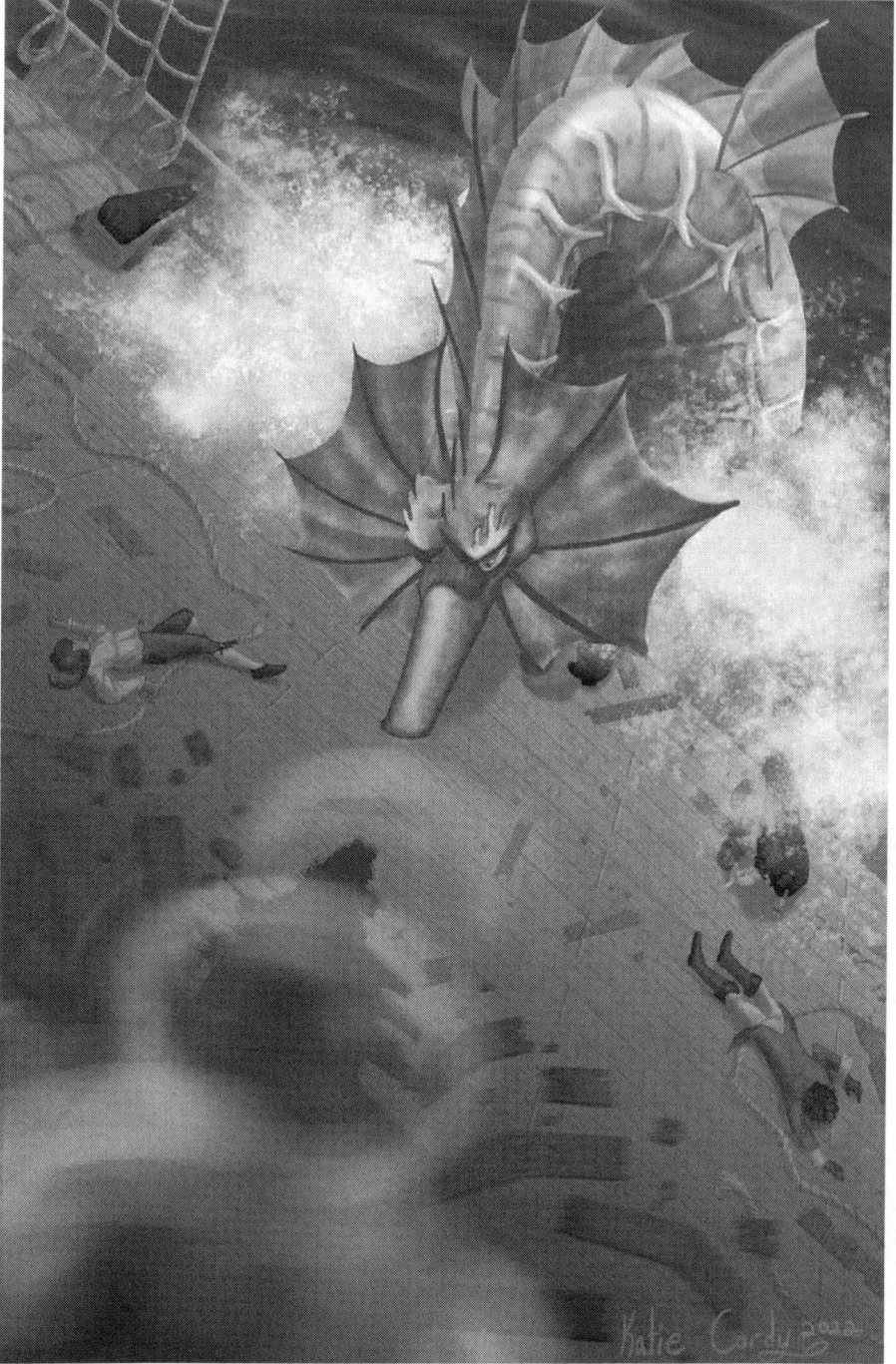

# Jack of Diamonds

N.L. Bates

Sapphic Representation: Lesbian, Non-Binary
Heat Level: Medium
Content Warnings: Coarse Language, Violence, Gore, Death

*Pirates live outside the laws of man, but women pirates live outside the laws of nature.*
—Laura Sook Duncombe

They are, I remind myself, only pirates.

Not monsters, whatever the navy wants us to believe. Not krakens, not Gigas crabs, not sygnaed. Just pirates.

Pirates who have made themselves rich raiding the best-defended fort on Luire's eastern coast yet keep raiding anyway. Pirates who've captured two of the Luirien navy's best warships and sunk a third. Pirates who have also, probably, sunk my entire academic career. (Well, no, Charlene. You did *that* yourself.) Pirates who have definitely just figured out I'm here.

Here, in the shadowed hold of the *Jack of Diamonds*, which smells of mold and nutmeg. The meager sunlight filtering through the open hatch feels like an assault. I'm hidden behind some crates, hoping to stay out of sight until I know why the pirates are down in the hold while the ship is still moving. And then the ship pitches beneath my feet and sends both me and the crates flying.

The crates probably wouldn't have caught anyone's attention. But most crates don't yell *"fuck!"* when they go tumbling to the deck.

I land in a puddle that I try not to think too hard about. That's how the pirate finds me: bruised and soaking in bilge water. The brilliance of her lantern burns away the tentative truce my eyes had negotiated with the daylight. I squint up at her.

"Um. Hi," I say.

"Up on the deck where I can see you." The pirate hauls me unceremoniously to my feet. I let her usher me topside, and get the first good look at my captor.

She's not tall, in fact a bit shorter than me. Lean, but from the drape of her shirt, I can easily picture this woman hauling up sails all day. Russet hair, curly and close-cropped, frames her tawny face. The smattering of freckles across her nose does nothing to soften the sharp appraisal in her eyes. "Arms out."

She pats down my sleeves with brisk efficiency. Then her hands move toward a more central location.

"I beg your pardon—"

"This does not go better for you if I have to assume you're armed," she says. There's no bravado in her voice, just flat certainty. I shiver.

Past the *Jack of Diamonds'* bowsprit, the Bosneau strait unspools like a length of ribbon, edged by island coasts on either side. Watching ships come up from the south end of the strait gives me something to think about that isn't the hand *under* the front of my dress, calloused fingers brushing my breast, this is plain old lechery now—

"What's this?"

Ah. She's found my ring, tucked into a pocket in my bodice.

Maybe I can buy the pirates' cooperation with honesty. I do want that ring back. "It's only sentimental. But I had someone infuse it with a concealment charm on the docks. It's how I snuck onto the ship."

She doesn't look surprised. She must have noticed its fading glow. "Put it on."

"A *temporary* charm," I amend. The damn thing's mostly quit on me already, hours before the merchant said it would. I suppose I shouldn't have expected anything more. Charms like this are illegal in Luire, and gray market everywhere else.

"Put it on," she repeats, her hand on my shoulder a vise. I fumble the ring onto my finger, and sure enough, its light flares and dies. The pirate nods. "Good enough. Give it over."

Reluctantly, I do. And then I take a deep breath to bolster my courage. "I want to speak to the captain."

"Do you now," says my captor, and resumes her unreasonably thorough patdown.

"Yes," I say, making my voice firm. I refuse to be intimidated by this woman and her wandering hands. "I'm here for the woman who came back from the dead to personally sink the *Diligente*. Who tamed the seas and the monsters in them." Whose name is enough to make my grandmother, the commodore, spit. "I want to speak to Captain Jacquette Duleveut."

Relentless, the pirate pulls my inkwells from a pocket, holds one up to inspect it before disappearing it somewhere on her person. My pens, too, though her hands traversing my hips suggest that theft will not be the worst of today's indignities. I'm blushing furiously by the time she's finished, warm from my face to my...well.

It's a small mercy when she speaks again. "You want to talk to *the captain*, you'll have to answer some questions." Hazel eyes bore into me, but at least she lets me go. "Starting with, who the fuck are you?"

"Um. I'm Charlene." I wipe sweaty palms on my skirt. "I'm here to join the crew."

"Really." She drawls out the word. I hear snickers all across the deck. "What makes you think you're qualified to join a pirate crew? Let alone mine."

Of course. Of course, *she's* Jacquette Duleveut.

"I'm a historian," I say quickly. The curve of her eyebrow says that wasn't the answer she was expecting. "I can be your chronicler. Lots of pirates benefit from a solid reputation—"

"You're standing on the deck of my ship, asking to join my crew, and telling me you can improve *my* reputation?" She pretends to consider. "Nah. I think I have a spot open for a powder monkey. Unless you'd be willing to consider another position." She waggles her eyebrows at me.

"I am not," I say with as much dignity as I can muster, "a powder monkey."

"Take her for ransom," suggests a weedy brunette. I giggle nervously at the thought of anyone being willing to pay a ransom for me.

"Or kill her," another pirate calls, to jeers from the others, and the giggle turns sour on my tongue.

"Not until I know why she's here." The humor has vanished from Duleveut's face. "No games, now."

"I—" I don't know what answer she'll accept. I'm here because I've become my own nation's favorite scapegoat. Because I had the gall to suggest that Duleveut's success is enabled by Luire's overly permissive approach to piracy, not some eldritch alliance with the monsters of the Aurun Ocean.

"I'm here to prove you're not a monster," I blurt.

I have the satisfaction of seeing her blink. "Come again?"

"It's what the Luiriennes say about you. That you're in league with the sea monsters, or that you *are* one, or—"

"I know what they say," she interrupts. "I asked you why you're here."

"I wrote a paper," I mutter, and she makes an impatient noise, "saying you're nothing but a very effective pirate. Only, after you raided half of Luire...it wasn't very well-received." Not by the navy, at least. My grandmother, indestructible old bag that she is, nearly died of embarrassment. Especially once the navy decided to take action. But not against the pirates, no. Easier to smear the mouthy historian who had pointed out the problem.

"I wrote about you, and Luire made me a laughingstock for it." I brace myself for more mockery, or maybe more threats. "I'm going to prove them wrong."

Duleveut stares me down.

"Caution at the helm!" someone bellows from the rigging, and I start. "Ship crossing the strait!"

Duleveut's attention lifts from me like a weight.

"Stow this one out of the way for now," she says, turning away. "Once we're done with our friends on the Luirien ships, she's going to tell me everything she knows about them."

\* \* \*

The weedy pirate steers me toward the hold with an ungentle hand on my shoulder. Taking my chances, I ask, "What's this about Luirien ships?"

Weedy grunts. "They found us out in Campéo. Been on our ass ever since."

"So? There are only so many trade routes in the archipelago. They're probably just merchant ships."

Another grunt. "That kinda thinking's a good way to get dead. So, we get out and lie low a bit."

I blink. "Get out where?"

"Eastern coasts," he says.

"But... This is as east as it gets. You'd practically be leaving the archipelago," I protest. "There's no trade there, no nothing." Because east of the archipelago is the barrier reef, and then the Aurun Ocean. And the sea monsters.

"Fewer busybodies," he agrees. "That's the point."

"Oy, Ambre!" another pirate shouts. "We need you on the mainsail!"

Weedy shoves me toward the hold. "Go."

He's halfway up the rigging by the time I recover my footing, so I stay on deck and watch the ship bustle. If only Duleveut hadn't confiscated my pens.

Wait—I have one, and a roll of parchment, buried deep in a pocket. I have to imagine Duleveut left them on purpose. She certainly didn't miss anything else.

The memory makes my cheeks heat. I force my mind to my work.

*Pirates report trouble in Campéo. Possible pursuit,* I scribble. *Plus ship oncoming, Luirien, from south end of Bosneau strait.*

"Eyes on the eastern channel," Duleveut calls, and yes, I see it now, half-hidden by a rocky outcropping. It's not far off, but we're moving slowly, tacking as we are against the wind.

The Luirien ship, on the other hand, is closing rapidly. One of the pirates eyes her uneasily. "We'll be in range of her guns before we can turn."

"She's not going to fire," I exclaim. "Luire hasn't bothered with pirates in years."

Both pirates turn to stare at me. I will myself not to flinch.

"Eyes on the work, all of you," Duleveut barks. Impatience fills her voice as she demands, "What are you doing here?"

"Chronicling," I retort.

She snorts. "Then keep your thoughts to your papers, and be glad I don't have time to deal with you right now."

"We could always fire a volley to scare her off," another pirate suggests.

"Belay that," Duleveut snaps. "Don't give her reason to chase."

*Pirates choosing not to engage,* I note. *Have yet to do anything monstrous.*

Duleveut bellows over the rail. "Ahoy the prize crew!"

"Ready!" comes a cry back, and that's when I notice the sloop off our port side. It's about a third the size of the *Jack*, maybe seven paces long from bow to stern. Three pirates work her helm and sails.

*Pirates crewing second ship, presumably plunder.*

I lean into the ship's sway as we turn into the mouth of the channel. There's a flash of light from the Luirien ship.

I hear a noise like a distant roar. Then I'm thrown across the deck.

My ribs are screaming, and so are the pirates. I stare stupidly up at the ruined foresail. Something thuds dully to the deck, and as I scramble to my feet, I realize what's happened: the Luirien ship has opened fire. They've decided they've had enough of pirates, after all.

It figures.

Half a cannonball rolls down the deck, dragging a length of chain behind. If the Luiriennes are using chain shot, that means they want us immobilized—

"My notes!" I lurch for the spot where I must have dropped them, but someone grabs my wrist. Duleveut.

"You want to do something stupid," she shouts, "do it somewhere out of the way." She turns on her heel as the ship pitches wildly. "Shift ballast to stern! Now!"

Mercifully, the ship starts to stabilize as the pirates comply.

I throw my own weight to stern as well. The sloop has been hit even worse than the *Jack*; she's listing heavily to port, and the pirates crewing her have already abandoned ship. They've crammed themselves into a wherry boat and are rowing hard this way. "Drop the ladder!" one cries.

Something flickers on the surface of the water. A trick of the light?

I fumble the rope ladder free of its clasps, just as a shape rises up under the wherry. Something large, with a rounded trunk that tapers down to a curl. It tips all three pirates into the water. A pipe-like appendage pokes through the waves.

A stocky blond manages to pull themself to the top of the capsized wherry, hauling a second pirate after them. They extend a hand to the third pirate, just as the shape in the water angles its snout.

Then the third pirate is gone. No blood, no screams. Just gone.

I'm still clutching the ladder. If I just drop it, the others will have to swim back to the ship. They'll have to get in the water with *that*.

"Grab hold!" The pirates catch the end of the ladder when I heave it at them, and swing briefly out of my sight. Moments later they both clamber onto the deck.

I'm in the business of saving pirates now, apparently. I wonder what that does to my academic integrity.

"Stand back!" the blond yells. They ignore their own advice and lean out over the rail, bringing their musket to bear on the pipe-snouted creature following the *Jack* through the channel. They pull the trigger.

Nothing happens.

I see their face fill with frustrated realization, water running along the barrel of their gun. I see the Luirien ship speeding down the channel toward us. And I see Duleveut striding this way, somehow untouched by the chaos around her. Eye of her own personal hurricane.

Then there's gunfire, and a high-pitched, indignant squeal. The creature blinks a suddenly bloodshot eye and jerks away. Water foams around its snout as it turns back down the channel.

There are startled shouts from the Luirien ship. I hear more gunfire, but the guns are no longer aimed at us.

Silhouetted against the horizon like an artist's impression, Jacquette Duleveut lowers her musket and laughs.

* * *

It takes hours to sail the channel. I try to make myself useful, joining the pirates in tying off ropes and shifting debris. I get several bemused looks, and one pirate who boisterously demands to know what I think I'm doing.

"Ease off," another responds. "She's the captain's to deal with."

Not exactly reassuring, but the pirates leave me alone after that. And I did save some of their lives. Maybe that buys me another day of observation.

Duleveut herself takes the helm to guide us through the eastern shoals. Then she walks the ship to assess the damage and sets the crew to work.

"Quinn! With me."

The blond pirate from the wherry falls into step behind the captain.

"And you," Duleveut says. Her hand settles on the nape of my neck. I feel the touch all the way down my spine.

"Yes. Captain," I mutter.

She looks me up and down. There's a cut on her cheek, and her shirt, soaked through with seawater, clings to her torso.

My mouth goes unexpectedly dry. I tell myself it's just nerves.

"What happened to your notes?"

I snap my head up at the question. "Um. Lost. There was an attack..."

She makes a derisive noise. "Not much of a chronicler then, are you?"

"So, you *do* think I can be helpful!"

"Don't get ahead of yourself," she says flatly. "Move."

She marches us to her cabin, gesturing Quinn in first and prodding me in second. A stray curl of red hair falls between her eyes. It's annoyingly endearing.

But there's nothing endearing about the way she turns on me as soon as the door is closed. "A Luirien stows away on my ship, claiming to be a chronicler, *assuring* me the Luiriennes won't attack. Just before an attack kills five of my crew." I squirm under her gaze. "I don't repeat myself for very many folks. Tell me why you're here."

"I'm telling the truth," I stammer. My mouth is dry again. Does she think I had something to do with the attack?

"The Luiriennes haven't attacked us outright in years," Quinn says. They lean against the wall, ankles crossed. Their voice is milk-mild in comparison. "Clearly something has changed. We hoped you could tell us what."

The pirates are manipulating me. Not even trying to be subtle about it. Irritation stirs, a welcome reprieve from the panic. "I wouldn't know. I'm just here to write papers, I swear. But you've been harassing them for years. Maybe they've finally had enough."

"And you just have to write those papers on my ship." I silently beg Duleveut to leave it at that, but she pins me with that stormy gaze again. "Last I heard, academics were not in the habit of cavorting with pirates."

Right now, I'm wishing I'd picked a less controversial area of research. Like the best way to package aged cheeses, or the history of jams. But I screw up my courage enough to reply. "Have *you* ever listened to a group of academics talk? Some of us prefer cavorting with pirates."

Quinn barks a laugh.

"Well. There's no accounting for taste," Duleveut says after a moment. But I suspect she's hiding a smile.

Quinn straightens. "With your permission, Captain, I should see to the repairs." They give me a nod. "I appreciate your quick hand with the ladder."

"What *was* that horrible thing?" I can't help but ask.

Quinn's face is expressionless. "Sygnaed fry."

"But—how? They're not supposed to be in the archipelago. Aren't we days away from the Aurun?" I can't stop myself from babbling. "I thought they were bigger. In Luire we call them ship-killers."

"That one was only a few weeks old," Quinn says. "Sometimes the small ones slip through."

"Probably caused a lot of havoc before they put it down," Duleveut remarks. She shares a look of grim satisfaction with Quinn. Then Quinn exits the cabin, leaving me alone with the captain.

"You've done my quartermaster a good turn," she says, nodding after Quinn, "so I'm inclined to wait until we make port before I put you over the side."

The disappointment hits harder than I expected. My ears are still ringing with remembered gunfire; I never want to witness another sea battle except from the pages of a textbook. But nothing in the archipelago is more than a few days away. I need more time than that to prove my thesis.

Duleveut is watching me with one eyebrow raised. I realize I'm supposed to say something. "Where's port?"

Now the other eyebrow goes up. "I could always change my mind," Duleveut says archly.

She wants me to shut up and be grateful. I've never been good at either.

"I don't see the point in hiding it. I know the archipelago, and there are only so many options." I try to work some moisture back into my cheeks. "And I'd find out where I was once you'd gone, anyway. Why not tell me now?"

She falls silent, and I flinch. And then she laughs. *Laughs*, in a husky thrum that sweeps me up and has me smiling back at her. "You do have some fire, don't you?" Still chuckling, she adds, "Fine. We need a port that can handle significant repairs, out of the Luiriennes' sight. Most everything on our sail plan only hits one out of those two, so we'll put it to a vote."

"A what?" My heart is pounding. Nerves, I remind myself.

Duleveut's smile reclaims its familiar mocking slant. "I take it they don't talk about that part in your textbooks."

"Well, I'd mostly been reading about strategy..."

"Spare me," Duleveut says, rolling her eyes at the ceiling. "Come on, then."

I pause, taken aback at the apparent invitation.

"I still have my eye on you," she clarifies, waving me into the passageway. "Remember, the crew's happy to keel-haul you if you try anything you shouldn't."

* * *

We're moving again as soon as Duleveut thinks we won't capsize. "We're sitting ducks if they search here. We'll find somewhere safer, handle our necessaries from there."

"They could search the coast of every island," I object. "How do we know it's safe?"

"We go where they won't follow," Duleveut replies.

We hole up between outcroppings of the barrier reef, miles farther out from shore than could possibly be considered safe. I try not to think about how close we must be to the Aurun. If a sygnaed can get all the way to Bosneau strait...

Duleveut calls the crew together. "We can't safely reach Bosneau, not with the *Jack* the way she is. We have to either retrace our steps or leave the archipelago."

"Let's retrace our steps," suggests a short pirate with a puffy bruise around one eye. "Circle around back to Campéo."

"Campéo sold us out!" And that's Weedy. I guess he survived.

"We can't count on the usual suspects to look the other way," Duleveut agrees. "Bayacola's our best bet."

Somehow, no one laughs.

"You can't be serious!" I exclaim, choking on something that feels too sharp to be laughter. Bayacola is in the Aurun Ocean. And the Aurun belongs to the sea monsters.

"You," Duleveut says, meeting my eyes with infuriating calm, "don't get a vote."

But the rest of the crew does, apparently. I turn to them, spreading my hands. "Come on. You've seen what even a baby sygnaed can do." There are angry mutters at that. I swallow and keep talking. "I'm not a sailor, but even *I* know this"—I wave my hand at the crippled foresail, at the body-shaped lumps of tattered sailcloth I've been trying not to look at—"is bad." I dare a glance at Duleveut, but she doesn't look angry. She's smiling, in fact. Maybe she admires my audacity, not that I need her admiration. "And the Aurun is... it's *the Aurun*. It's full of sea monsters. We can't *get* to Bayacola."

The pirates erupt into laughter.

I stare around. Even Quinn seems to be hiding a smirk. Duleveut certainly isn't hiding hers.

"This one still has a few things to learn about how we do things around here." The captain places an almost proprietary hand on my shoulder.

Quinn holds up a finger, and most of the pirates sober up. "There was some damage to the hull, which means damage to the inscriptions. It might reduce the charms' efficacy, but I believe they're intact enough to do the job."

"Charms?" I already look stupid. No point staying ignorant.

"Burned into the hull," Quinn explains. "They deflect the sea creatures' attention. A sort of camouflage."

"Which is why everyone in the archipelago will say you can't sail the Aurun," Duleveut adds. "You'd have to pull too many sticks out of too many asses to convince them to use that kind of enchantment. They can't sail the Aurun. We can."

"That's a long way across open waters in this condition," one of the pirates says thoughtfully.

"We're well clear of storm season," Duleveut replies. "And the Aurun's not much for squalls."

"Just sea monsters," I mutter. But I mutter it under my breath.

Quinn pulls out a bucket and two sacks of colored stones. White for Campéo. Black for Can't-believe-we're-doing-this.

Duleveut tosses a black stone into the bucket, and pointedly catches my eye.

I take the hint and stay well away from the proceedings. If she thinks I'm trying to cheat my way into a vote, she'll probably wait for all the really good monsters to rear their heads before she keel-hauls me.

It's not long before all the votes are cast. Counting them is even faster; there's not a white stone in the pile.

To Bayacola, then, and the Aurun Ocean. And the sea monsters.

\* \* \*

Sometime on the second day of sailing, I ask when we'll enter the waters of the Aurun itself.

"We're already here," Duleveut says, and laughs at the expression on my face. "Were you expecting a sign?"

"I was *not*," I retort. "I've just... heard the stories."

"The auras," Duleveut agrees. "We'll see one soon enough. If we're lucky, not too close."

Because the auras bring the sea monsters. Or maybe the other way around.

I spot my first aura about an hour later. It starts more like a reflection on the water than an actual glow, with an almost mahogany tint, and swells into an elliptical glimmer, twice as long as a person and about three times as wide.

I open my mouth to say something like "aura ahoy," but what actually comes out is, *"sea monster!"*

Duleveut appears beside me, looking out over the waves with an appraising eye. The smirk she turns my way is undoubtedly at my expense. "Yup. That's a sea scorpion."

"A scorpion?" Sea monsters are bad enough without adding arachnids to the mix. At least it doesn't seem to be coming this way. "How can you tell?"

"The color changes depending on the critter," Duleveut explains. "That shade of shit brown means sea scorpion."

I make a face. "It's not really a giant bug, is it?"

"Who knows," she replies. "Hard shell, lots of legs. It could be a bug." She looks at me sidelong. "Had one climb up on the deck once, and somebody got stuck underneath. He was never the same after that. Didn't stop twitching until the day he died."

She's doing this to get a rise out of me, I know she is, but I can't help but shudder. "They sound horrible. How does it even swim?"

"It has fins. Long slithery ones." She purses her lips. "Tastes alright, but not worth the effort if you ask me."

"That's grotesque. I suppose they're not poisonous, then?"

"Not poisonous," Duleveut confirms.

"Well, that's a small mercy," I mutter, and her expression becomes suspiciously smug.

"But it *is* venomous." When I stare at her, she grins. "Don't tell me you don't know the difference? You can eat it. Just don't get stung."

"Of course it has a stinger," I say resignedly.

Duleveut chuckles. "It has three."

"Now you're just having me on!" I turn to face her, tearing my gaze from the aura at last.

Her lopsided smirk could mean anything. "Nope. I can turn the *Jack* that way if you want to see for yourself. Don't have time to wait for you, though, so you'd be swimming back."

I look back to the ocean, and the sea scorpion's aura. "Do we need to do anything?"

She waves a dismissive hand. "It's nowhere near. Besides, they're easy enough to deal with."

Obligingly, I ask, "And how do you do that?"

That lopsided smirk again. "By feeding them troublesome prisoners."

"You *are* having me on!" I exclaim.

The look she gives me is pure mischief, and it's not the threat behind her words that sets my pulse to racing. "Keep telling yourself that."

* * *

That evening, Duleveut calls a halt.

"Is that a very good idea?" I ask, once I realize we're laying anchor.

"Is a stowaway questioning my judgment?" she replies.

Her flat stare seems to hold nothing of the woman who just a few hours ago was regaling me teasingly with stories of the Aurun's finest monsters. "Call it ignorance if you like. I don't know what we're doing."

She considers that. Then she nods toward the dead pirates, still wrapped in their sailcloth shrouds. "To lay them to rest."

Of course. I feel like an ass for forgetting.

Pirate funerals are efficient and to the point. Duleveut speaks about each one briefly. Then, one by one, she consigns their bodies to the sea.

I can't imagine burying my dead with the octopleiades and the thunderclap eels, but the pirates seem unbothered—by the sea monsters at least. The ship is as close to silent as I've ever heard it. There's only the creaking of the masts and the brush of waves against the hull.

Someone begins to sing. I don't even recognize the song. But another pirate takes it up, and another, until the whole crew is singing but me.

I've never felt as much like an intruder as I do now. Not even back in Duleveut's cabin, wilting under her gaze. I decide to make myself scarce.

I take myself belowdecks, because there's nowhere else to go, and wander down one of the narrow passageways. I'm almost to the end of it when I realize I know where this one leads.

This is a bad idea. I push open the door to Duleveut's cabin anyway.

It's much the same as I left it: map table, chairs, all nailed down. A real bed, though there's a hammock too. She's forgotten to latch one of the drawers, and it's popped partway open with the movement of the ship.

I really don't mean to snoop, but then I glimpse one of my pens. She must have my inkwells, too.

I'll just grab them and go. I don't need to feel guilty; they're *my* things, after all. I slide the drawer gingerly open.

"What do you think you're doing?"

Fuck.

I raise my eyes to face Jacquette Duleveut.

"I..." I draw a deep breath, and then another. "I just came to get some of my pens."

"You snuck into my cabin," Duleveut repeats, face frighteningly impassive, "because you wanted some pens."

"I didn't sneak," I protest, without force.

"Give you an inch, and you'll take it as far as you can, won't you?" She crosses the cabin, plants both hands on the map table. "Tell me what you're really doing. And remember"—she leans in, close enough that I can feel the heat of her breath—"I just buried five fucking people. I am not in the mood for games."

This woman has terrorized me, mocked me, and dragged me to the fucking Aurun Ocean, and now this.

"Must everything I do have some sort of secret purpose?" I demand. "It felt wrong watching the funeral. I thought you should be able to have that without me. I was trying to give you some privacy."

She stands ramrod straight, and I realize that was the wrong answer.

"When I lose someone," she says, slow and clear. I take a step back, and she grabs me by the collar of my dress. "When someone on my crew dies." Her grip is ironclad, and it's easy to see why people call her a monster. "I carry that person for the rest of my days." Our faces are almost touching, but her voice is building in volume. "You don't get to use them for rhetorical points, Charlene!"

The last time she was angry with me, she was deliberate about it, controlled. Anger is a tool for someone like Duleveut.

Not now. Her breathing is ragged, and the hand that grips my collar trembles. This is real and raw, and something in me aches for her even as I shrink away.

"I'm sorry," I stammer. "I'll just go."

She doesn't release me. "I should have put you over the side back in Bosneau. With a second fucking smile." And she traces her thumb across my throat in a vivid suggestion of exactly what she means. "I still could."

But she relaxes her hold on me just a little, enough to put a couple inches between us, enough for me to recover my voice. "Are you going to? I mean..." My mind offers up a ream of ridiculous excuses: No one will read my work if I'm dead. Even if they do, I refuse to die wrong. And a dead woman can't fuck pirates.

Perhaps not that last one.

"You wanted a chronicler," I breathe. "Let me chronicle. Not this nonsense about sea monsters. The woman behind the legend. The real Jacquette Duleveut."

"The real me?" Her voice is a growl. Her thumb settles in the hollow of my throat, but she doesn't press it home. "The real me has a ship to run and a crew to do right by. The real me doesn't give a shit about your *romantic* notions of what it means to be a pirate—"

"What are you afraid of?" I retort. "Because—"

Her hands are on my hips before I realize she's come around the table, sweeping my feet from the floor, holding me prone across her lap. With her knee in my ribs, I can't even breathe a protest before her hand comes down, hard and fast, across my backside.

"Is this really what pirates do?" I gasp. The smarting in my rump, and the memory of her hands going other places, brings a rush of heat to more than just my abused posterior.

She pulls up ruffles of fabric, exposing my more sensitive regions. "You do not get to question me," she hisses into my ear. Another slap, this one stinging already sensitive skin.

Well. She's clearly not willing to talk this over.

And I'd like to be able to sit for dinner, so I do the stupidest thing I've ever done in my life. I pull myself upright and kiss her.

Her hand circles behind my head with such force I think she's about to snap my neck, but then she's returning the kiss, tangling her fingers in my hair. I feel her tongue on my lips, looking for more, and I offer it. And then we have to come up for air.

She draws her hands down my torso, pushing my hips into the table. One hand slips under my skirt. Traces a line up my calf to my thigh, and then high enough that I gasp. I grab for her shirt, and we peel away the layers, one after another, until there's nothing left but two humans.

And then Jacquette Duleveut shows me, with her hips and her hands and her mouth, that she isn't a monster at all.

* * *

It usually takes around eight days to sail to Bayacola from the eastern shoals. But the shape we're in means it will probably be closer to twelve, according to Duleveut. To Jacquette.

The *Jack* takes most of her attention. The mainsail needs patching. The rudder isn't quite working. A rainstorm three days in has us bailing water. Jacquette has no compunction about menial labor, working alongside the rest of the crew, and I don't see much of her.

We don't talk about what happened in her cabin, and she doesn't invite me back.

I refuse to follow after her like a duckling, so I devote myself to staying out of the way. But occasionally, her tasks bring her to wherever I am. Today, that's the foredeck, staring out over the prow.

"Watching for auras again?" she asks, and I think of her voice in my ear, teeth and tongue on my skin. If she's thinking the same, I can't tell.

"Yes," I admit. I've spotted several more since the sea scorpion, most thankfully off in the distance, a few far too close for comfort. That's all, though. The charms seem to be doing their job.

"Not long to Bayacola now," she remarks.

I can't help but ask. "Is that where you put me over the side?"

"Don't figure there's much for you in Bayacola," she replies. "We'll head back to the archipelago eventually. We can get you home."

"Mmm." My feelings about home right now are complicated, to say the least.

She raises an eyebrow. "If you *want* to stay in Bayacola, that's another thing. But we'll be laid up for a couple weeks, so you've got time."

It's on the tip of my tongue to suggest I stay with her. But I'm no pirate, and I can just imagine what my grandmother would think. I doubt Jacquette would entertain the notion anyway.

Something appears on the water behind her. A citrine sort of glimmer, like someone crystallized a cresting wave and lit a candle from inside. I don't know whether the size of the aura correlates with the size of the sea monster, but this one is about half the size of the *Jack*.

In the last few days, I've seen the dull shale glow of wire sharks (a school of those will flense a man in seconds just by brushing by him), the milky quartz of garotte jellies (at least they get you high before they take your head off), and a few others besides. So, I know how she'll respond when I point this aura out: with a smirk and some dreadful anecdote about whatever horror I've spotted this time. But the citrine aura is huge, and it's barely a hundred feet away.

"Jacquette," I say, and she turns to follow my gaze.

Then she mutters a curse. "All hands! Reef the sails and be ready to strike!" To me, she says, "Gigas crab."

"Is that a problem? Aside from the fact that it's—"

"A sea monster?" she finishes dryly. I flush. "The charms don't work so well on Gigas crabs. They're attracted to movement, so we slow down, no sudden stops, to avoid its notice."

I hope it's not too late for that. It's definitely headed our way.

Quinn trots up from amidship and hands Jacquette a few rubbery, palm-sized sacks. "Crew's bringing up the sleeper squid ink," they report.

"Load all the light guns we can. Fore first. Normal loads everywhere else." Jacquette is already striding to the nearest gun.

"Now what?" I ask.

"Wait and see if it spots us," she says. "Enjoy the view."

"The view!?" Her cavalier attitude toward these creatures still astounds me. "It's a monster that wants to kill you."

She shrugs. "It's an animal that needs to eat."

And it's closing on us. Long, undulating shadows ripple beneath its aura. One of them breaks the surface, and I realize it's some sort of antenna, tasting the air.

"Steady," Jacquette says. "It hasn't seen us yet."

The antenna slides below the water, and I breathe a sigh of relief. The pirates have managed to roll up the main's topsail and are steadily reefing the gaff.

Then the wind picks up, filling the gaff and pushing us forward.

The antennae swing this way.

"Target the antennae!" Jacquette shouts.

Immediately one of the guns goes off. A sack hits the surface of the water and explodes into a riotous rainbow of color.

"Don't waste your shot!" Jacquette bellows.

A claw, almost the size of the sloop we lost in Bosneau, rises from the water and knocks against our hull. The impact sends me stumbling.

A cannonball bounces harmlessly off the claw and into the water.

Two more ink shots go off in quick succession, obscuring more of the crab's aura. Jacquette fires as another antenna stretches out from the water. My ears ring with the blast, and she swears in frustration. She's missed her mark.

The claw sweeps upward again. This time, it lands on the deck and scrabbles for purchase. Pirates race to shoulder their muskets, and the crab doesn't even seem to notice the volley.

Another ink shot splashes solidly over some of the antennae. They disappear under the water.

The *Jack* is listing hard to starboard, pulled by the Gigas crab's weight. The pirates scramble to shift our ballast to port, but the ship continues to tilt.

"Charlene," Jacquette calls. "My cabin, first chest on the right. Bring the whistle right on top."

I blink at her. She's still on her gun, shifting it to follow the creature, her face a snarl as she tries to line up a shot. "Go!"

I go.

The ship throws me against one wall of the passageway and then the other as I stumble to her cabin. Prizing the chest open—thank goodness she hasn't locked it—I pull out something palm-sized, cylindrical, made of petrified wood with a rubbery sack fastened underneath. It's an odd sort of whistle, but I don't have time to question.

I race back to the deck to find the Gigas crab has fully surfaced.

It has a long, wide tail fin and no legs that I can spot, other than those two enormous claws. Its chitin gleams the same dull citrine as its aura and covers almost its entire body. All but its back, which is a forest of thrashing antennae. Some of them twitch feebly in a soup of bright colors. Others seem to be trying to groom themselves free of the bothersome ink. But some still reach toward us.

I hold out the whistle to Jacquette, but she doesn't take it. "Be ready to blow!" she shouts. "On my word. Not before."

The ship is pitching wildly now, the deck rising so sharply I almost lose my feet. Fearing we'll capsize, I raise the whistle to my lips.

"On all our lives, Charlene, *hold!*" Jacquette roars. The deck tips the other way, and I nearly lose my grip on the damned thing altogether.

Another ink projectile smashes into one of the crab's antennae clusters. More of the tendrils retreat. And then Jacquette swivels her gun and fires her last shot. It slams directly into the thing's back, soaking not just one of its remaining antennae clusters, but the...skin? chitin? beneath. She lets out a wordless yell of triumph.

The pirates release another round of musket fire, and the claw finally retreats. The ship sways again in its sudden absence.

"Shake out the reefs. Topsail first," Jacquette orders. "Slowly, now."

I don't want us to go slowly. I want us to run away as fast as possible. But the Gigas crab is still there, spinning slowly under the water, reorienting.

When we get a hundred feet away, she instructs the pirates to start shaking out the gaff. And again, at two hundred, and again, until she finally decides it's safe to bring the *Jack* up to full speed. She keeps a close watch on the crab while Quinn directs the other pirates in the latest set of repairs, but it doesn't decide to pursue.

"What is that?" I ask as she tucks the whistle into a pouch.

"Something I didn't want to use," she replies. "It's a predator call."

"You mean, it would have scared the crab away?" I stare at her, incredulous. "Why didn't we do that?"

"Because their predators are sygnaed," she says. My mouth forms an "*oh*," and she nods. "There's a mated pair that nests near Bayacola. They'll come looking for the fun if they hear a hunting call, and right now?" She waves at the ship. "Those fuckers move faster than we do."

Because of course that's how you deal with sea monsters. By summoning more sea monsters. Something heavy forms in the pit of my stomach. I'm not sure whether it's nausea or a case of uncontrollable giggles. "How do you *do* this?"

"We're almost to Bayacola," she says, which isn't an answer. "We'll be safe enough there."

She's snappish, though, those last two days to Bayacola. I don't blame her. Even I can feel that the *Jack* isn't handling well.

But for a wonder, nothing happens. "There, see?" Jacquette says to me, gesturing to the rising cliffs. "It's half an hour around that bluff, and then we're right at Bayacola's docks."

She's not wrong, of course. But when we do finally swing around the cliffs, we discover we have company: close to a dozen ships waiting in the harbor.

Jacquette's face is impassive, but I don't think she expected this. Quinn, standing nearby, peers through a spyglass and stiffens. They offer the spyglass to Jacquette.

She doesn't bother to take it. "What colors?"

"Blue and white," Quinn says, mouth set in a grim line. Jacquette closes her eyes. "They're flying the Luirien flag."

\* \* \*

If there's one thing Jacquette Duleveut doesn't do, it's despair.

"There's a back channel under the cliffs that doesn't pass through the harbor. Close enough for the wherries," she says. "It'll get us to dry land and out from under the eyes of those ships. We can come up with a new plan from there."

"What about the *Jack*?" somebody asks.

Jacquette doesn't hesitate. "We leave her behind."

"We're not much of a pirate crew without a ship," someone says.

"We're not much of a pirate crew if we're dead," she replies. "Survive first. We'll take another."

Another pirate speaks up, a quaver in her voice. "Can't we surrender?"

"I won't stop you, so long as you let the rest of us get safely ashore first." Jacquette looks around at the crew. "But Luire's got a noose waiting for *most* of you, so I can't think you're better off." She meets my eyes when she says the word "most."

Luire made me a laughingstock, but there are worse things to be. They can't hang me just for writing about pirates.

Our three wherries can only take four or five people each, and that's if the pirates practically sit in each other's laps. So, a few volunteer to ferry the boats back and forth from the *Jack* until everyone's on dry land. "Quinn's got the first set of boats," Jacquette says to the crew. "I've got the last."

Quinn opens their mouth, to protest, I'm certain. But Jacquette meets their eyes and says, "Don't."

Quinn doesn't.

The first two sets of wherries make it away safely. "Why aren't the Luiriennes coming after us?" I ask as we watch the rowers return. Back in the harbor, I can see boats moving between the Luirien ships, but that's all.

"They've got us dead to rights," Jacquette says with a shrug. "They'll come."

"Jacquette..."

"Third wherry's yours this time, if you want it," is all she says. "There's enough seats."

"I'll buy you some time," I promise.

"You'll take care of your own damn self," she replies, voice flat. "I don't need anything from you."

But I'm not going to let her push me away. Not now. "I'm doing it anyway."

For a moment I think she might snap at me again. Then she pulls me to her, lips urgent against mine. Her hand—steady despite everything—slides under my shirt to cup my breast, and I lean into her caress as her fingers stroke my skin.

"Luirien ships on the move!" someone yells.

Jacquette breaks away as if the embrace never happened. "Now or never," she says to the remaining crew. "Anyone who isn't ready the instant those wherries get here gets left behind."

Fortunately, the wherries aren't far. The pirates pile into two of them, and no one raises a fuss when I take the last wherry and row in the opposite direction. It seems like a very long time before I finally pull up beside the closest Luirien ship.

"Hello? Luirien ship?" The ship is big enough that I feel foolish shouting up to the deck, but someone hears me anyway and tosses a rope ladder over the side. A soldier points a musket over the rail. "Come on up," he calls. "Nice and slow, no funny business, one at a time."

My arms are already aching from being at the oars, and the ladder is interminably long. I'm almost glad when the soldier grabs my arms and hoists me the rest of the way over the rail, though I'm less happy about the barrel of the gun that settles at my back. "Just one of you?"

"Um, yes, there's only me."

"Some surrender," he mutters.

I take a deep breath. I told Jacquette I'd buy her some time.

"They were talking about it. Surrender, I mean. I think they will." It's not a very inspiring lie, but it's the most plausible way I can think to explain why the *Jack* is sitting quiet in the water.

"And they sent you to tell us to roll out the red carpet, I suppose," the soldier drawls.

"They didn't send me," I object. Then I realize how I must seem to him, appearing out of nowhere in this port where only pirates go. "They took me captive in the Bosneau strait. There was a battle..."

He chuckles. "Sure they did, matey."

It's a large ship, perhaps twice the size of the *Jack*, her sails furled. The soldier marches me toward a lean-to on the ship's starboard side, between the mizzenmast and the stern, and stands guard over me as we wait.

Periodically, people enter and exit the lean-to. I assume it's the people still under the lean-to we're waiting for, though I get an elbow in the ribs when I ask.

Finally, a woman emerges. Her uniform is impeccably starched and pressed, officer's braiding at her shoulders, her hair pulled back in a severe, familiar bun.

My grandmother looks me up and down. "I should have known I would find you here."

\* \* \*

"You took her from the *Jack of Diamonds*?" she asks.

"She came up on her own, Commodore," the soldier replies. "Says they took her captive in the Bosneau strait action."

"Is that so." She gives me a searching look. But then she nods. "Release her."

The musket barrel is removed from the small of my back, and I finally find my voice. "Grandmother? Why are you in Bayacola? *How* are you in Bayacola?"

"Chasing after you, apparently," she replies.

"But—"

"I was...concerned when I heard that someone matching your description had bribed the harbourmasters in

Campéo," my grandmother continues, inexorable as always. "I had hoped you would have the sense to extricate yourself from this mess. Though I suppose"—and she purses her lips as if it pains her to admit it—"that you wouldn't have had much chance after Bosneau. In any case, once the pirates ran for the Aurun, it wasn't difficult to figure out where they were headed."

I realize I'm gaping, and close my mouth before she can point that out. "You brought an entire fleet after me."

"As to that," my grandmother says, "you *have* been traveling with quite the prize."

The prize. She means Jacquette. Jacquette, who should be off the *Jack of Diamonds* by now, heading for the relative safety of dry land.

I bite the inside of my cheek, trying to work some moisture into my mouth. "Yes. Well. I'm here now."

Her eyebrows lift. "So you are."

I swallow. "So... We can go home. Can't we?"

"Dismissed," she says to the soldiers. And then, quietly, "I'm not here for you. I'm here for *her*."

So much for buying time.

"I advise you not to do anything that suggests your sympathies lie in...unsavory directions," she continues. Her voice gentles, if only barely. "I realize the last few weeks have been stressful for you. I am confident I can keep you out of the courts. But I will have to *fight* for that, Charlene, and my influence is not infinite."

"But—" I cast about for a plausible excuse to just leave. Desperation leeches into my voice as I murmur, "There are sea monsters."

"I am not at liberty to share the mechanism, but I assure you we are safe," my grandmother replies.

"But charms are illegal in Luire," I protest. That must be what she means. "Did I really embarrass the navy that badly?"

"Enough, Charlene." Grandmother's voice is clipped.

One of the soldiers approaches, stopping a respectful distance away. "Commodore, a word?"

My grandmother leaves me to stew in my worry for Jacquette. The navy is likely to comb Bayacola looking for her. But she'll figure something out. She has to. She's Jacquette Duleveut.

Grandmother wheels back toward me, soldiers following at her heels. "You told my men that the pirates were planning to surrender."

I nod.

"And yet they were spotted fleeing in rowboats."

"I...suppose they changed their minds?" I offer. The boom of the mizzenmast swings out over our heads. The ship must be getting ready to move. Grandmother's eyes flick upward, and she gestures to some nearby soldiers.

"I'm told," says my grandmother the commodore, "that their escape likely took some time."

Oh, well.

My grandmother's lips twist as if she's tasted something mildly sour. "Arrest her."

Something hits me from above.

Someone shouts, *"Down!"* Someone shouts, "It's her!" Somebody grabs me, and a hand closes on my throat.

"Fire and she dies," says Jacquette Duleveut.

The soldiers raise their muskets in unison.

"Hold your fire," my grandmother says. Then, to Jacquette: "Let the girl go."

"Tell me why I should do that," Jacquette says. "Really *convince* me. Go on." I squirm, and she yanks me closer. Her knee knifes between my legs, putting me off-balance.

My grandmother raises an eyebrow. "There's a full complement of soldiers on this deck awaiting my word."

"That word fills your granddaughter full of holes," Jacquette says. "Try again."

She doesn't sound like she's bluffing. The hand against my windpipe doesn't feel like bluffing.

She must have heard everything. Maybe she thinks the navy being here is my fault.

"Make your offer, then." My grandmother's voice is dry as dust.

"Me," Jacquette says. "The crew of the *Jack of Diamonds* walks free."

"Absolutely not." Not a shred of hesitation. But she goes so far as to say, "You must realize, this changes nothing for you. Why kill her?"

"Why not?" Jacquette chuckles, and my stomach twists. She presses a weapon into my back.

No. That's not a weapon, though it's small and hard. I wriggle, trying to grab it without being obvious, and Jacquette jerks me roughly, letting me work my hand behind my back. I moan a little, to make it convincing. She presses her other hand even harder against my windpipe. To make it convincing?

Spots swim in front of my eyes. That much is pretty convincing.

My grandmother sighs. "I am sorry about this, Charlene."

My hand closes over the object. Jacquette shoves me hard to the deck, and my ears pop as the muskets roar to life.

Jacquette rolls off of me and kicks out as the soldiers converge on her. I scrabble to all fours, ears ringing, and finally get a look at what I'm holding.

It's the petrified wooden whistle. She's given me the sygnaed whistle.

A firm hand closes on my arm and pulls me upright. My grandmother, drawing me away from the combat.

Jacquette has regained her feet. Her elbow takes a reaching soldier in the side of the neck, and he collapses like a sack of bricks. Another tries to bring his musket to bear and gets the butt of his gun in his face for his trouble. But Jacquette is surrounded, and can't possibly keep this up for long.

Another soldier brings a rapier down. I see Jacquette stagger, and a bloodstain blossoms on her shirt.

"Jacquette!" I lunge for her, breaking free of my grandmother's grasp.

My hearing has recovered enough to hear my grandmother yell, "They're both pirates! Shoot them both!"

A nearby soldier raises her musket.

Hands shaking, I raise the whistle to my lips.

* * *

The sound that emerges is plaintive, mournful, and enormous. My lungs rattle. The deckplates rattle. It stuns the whole ship into silence, except for Jacquette. She grabs my hand and drags me toward the rail.

We won't have enough time. People are already starting to recover their wits.

Toward the mouth of the harbor, the water begins to flicker.

Within moments the aura has set the entire harbor aglow, in shades of turquoise and moonstone so bright they're almost violent. It's the first time I've seen an aura of more than one color.

My grandmother's voice rises above the fray, shouting evacuation orders. Still, muskets go off behind us, and we dodge reaching soldiers as we run.

The flares of turquoise and moonstone become more distinct as they close on the ships. Then they draw apart. Not just two colors; two auras.

Two sygnaed.

A soldier steps in front of Jacquette. She heaves him over the rail.

The first sygnaed rises from the ocean.

I see its snout first, a long, funneled thing. Spikes protrude along a bony head twice the size of the entire creature I saw at Bosneau strait, framed by a tall, flared fin.

One of its eyes rolls back wildly in its head. The other stays fixed on us as it slides under the water.

"Here!" Jacquette shouts. She's found the ladder down.

The sygnaed launches itself into the air to a percussive volley of musket fire, catching the mainmast with the curl of its tail. The ship shudders, and the mast groans under its gargantuan weight. Somewhere, Jacquette is shouting my name.

The sygnaed's fins fall flat against its head. Its chest cavity expands.

"Down the ladder! Now, now, now!"

I throw myself down the ladder just as the deck starts to splinter.

It's a long drop to the wherry, but Jacquette is already handing me an oar.

We row. I hear the shriek of breaking wood and terrified soldiers above us. The other sygnaed, silhouetted by its own aura as it starts to submerge, hurls a vicious stream of water at one of the other ships. Almost like a ship's wake, if you could hurl a ship's wake like a knife. The ship caught in the blast bobbles like a child's toy before it goes under.

The sygnaed on the mast of the flagship is gone. Back into the water, must be. I can't see it anywhere, but there are still glitters of turquoise under the waves. The ship itself lists to one side. It's going to capsize.

"Keep rowing!" Jacquette yells, and I realize I've stopped.

So, I row. I thrust my oar into the water again, and again, and again, and slowly—too slowly!—we leave the sygnaed and their auras behind us.

\* \* \*

"That should be far enough," Jacquette says, as close to breathless as I've ever heard her. "They won't stray far from where they heard the call. We just need to wait them out."

We must be a mile or so away. Not far enough. Not with those sygnaed still in the harbor. Not when I can still see their flickering glow.

"Charlene," Jacquette says, and plucks the oar from my hand. "Take a breather."

My shoulders ache. I stare back toward the harbor. I can't see the sygnaed. I can't see the ships.

"Charlene," Jacquette says again, far away. I feel her hands on my shoulders.

When I turn toward her, she kisses me.

It's enough to startle me out of my fugue. Her lips linger briefly on mine. Then she nods and sits back. "Just needed to get your attention."

I take a breath for what feels like the first time since blowing the whistle. "Right. Yes. I'm here."

It's a stupid thing to say; of course I'm here. But I feel a little better for saying it.

"I'm glad," she says, very quietly.

I have no idea how to process that.

Jacquette clears her throat. "Sorry about manhandling you back there. Thought the *commodore* might take your side if I gave her a nudge. Figured I could at least get you out of being arrested." She shrugs, and a grimace crosses her face. "You never told me you were a naval brat."

"You're hurt," I say. She's pale, and there's blood soaking her sleeve.

But she waves me away, even though the rowing must have been agony. "I've had worse. I'll clean up when we get back to the *Jack*."

The *Jack*. Yes. We left her far enough from the harbor that she didn't get caught by the sygnaed, although she's surging uneasily over the waves.

I look back to Jacquette. "Do you think she made it?"

"Your grandmother? Certainly possible," Jacquette says. "The sea floor rises pretty quickly past the docks. All she needs is to get to shallower water than the sygnaed can handle."

*We're* not in shallow water. Suddenly frantic, I grab for my oar, but Jacquette shakes her head. "I need a minute, and so do you. The sygnaed won't trouble us for a while yet. They've had their fill."

I shudder at her choice of words.

"What do you think you'll do now?"

Her voice brings me back to myself, and I realize I've resumed staring out over the harbor. "I don't know. I...I don't think I can go home." Maybe Luire can't hang me for writing about pirates. But after today, I think I *am* a pirate.

Jacquette purses her lips, pretends to consider. She's baiting me again. But when she speaks, her voice is gruff. "Well...worst comes to worst. I could probably find a place for you." She clears her throat. "You'd have to learn to follow a damn order."

"I...could probably manage that." I decide to let her distract me. There's no room in the wherry to place my hands on my hips, so I fold my arms instead. "But you owe me."

Her smirk lifts me up in a way it has no business doing. "Do I, now."

"Luire has it you're some sort of horrible sea monster. You still need to help me prove them wrong."

She snorts. "I don't have scales under here, Charlene."

My pulse is jumping in my throat. "I'm going to need you to prove it."

A grin splits her face. "Believe me, I will."

"Jack of Diamonds" is a short story by N. L. Bates. To keep up to date with her work, visit **www.nlbates.com**. When she's not writing stories about sea monsters and lesbians, Bates writes and performs music as her alter ego Natalie Lynn. You can find her music at: **www.natalielynnmusic.com**.

# Siren Song

Kim Pritekel

Sapphic Representation: Lesbian
Heat Level: Hot!
Content Warnings: Coarse Language, Violence, Abduction, Abuse

Part 1

Lauren McCallister refused to react to her brother's unspoken irritation. TJ was her closest friend on most things, and she knew him probably better than anyone, including his current wife and the previous two. Older by four years, he'd been her greatest protector and—like right now—her greatest source of judgement.

Finally, she looked up from the suitcase she was packing and met the intense, deeply unsettling brown gaze that was just like their father's. The older TJ got, the more he looked like him. She forced herself to meet and hold his stare, determined to win this game of sibling chicken.

He sighed in exasperation, looking away. Ha! She was elated.

"Why?" he said, after nearly ten minutes of heavy silence.

"Which, 'why' would you like?" Lauren asked, walking from the open suitcase on the bed to her closet to gather more of the clothing she'd steadily been buying for her trip. A few long-sleeved t-shirts folded over one forearm, she used the other hand to brush dark brown bangs out of deep blue eyes. Some had called their color blueberry blue.

He snorted derisively, then leaned a shoulder against the doorframe to the open bedroom, arms crossed over his chest.

"There are several," she conceded. "We can go alphabetically, chronologically, pick one out of a hat." She dumped her load onto the bed and began removing hangers so she could fold and place the shirts with the other packed clothing. "What's your preference?"

"Fine," he said. "Alphabetical, Mizz English Professor. Oh wait," he drawled. "That was before you quit your job."

Hand on hip, she glared at him. "I did *not* quit my job. I went on sabbatical, and you damn well know that, TJ."

"Uh-uh," he said, waggling a finger. "Sabbatical begins with 'S,' that's later in the alphabet."

She stared at him, incredulous. "Fine. Where would you like to begin, hmm? What alphabetical perspective can I give you on my life choices, none of which, by the way, are your business."

"'D' for divorce."

The familiar hurt washed through her. Her tone was soft as she put voice to it. "Do you realize that not one family member questioned or chastised you as you broke up three marriages in your divorces, TJ? Only two of those marriages were even yours." She shook her head and mimicked their father's deep voice. "Dad said, 'Well, Amanda was always a gold digger. Best you got out of that one.' Then, 'Well, that Patricia was fat. Good job, son, Tammy is far more worthy of a McCallister.'" She looked at him. "Even as you helped Tammy destroy her marriage. But, that was okay. Wasn't it?"

He had the decency to look away, saying nothing. He ran a hand through his hair, always fashionable and currently in a fade. It was dark brown like hers, their mother's hair. He cleared his throat.

"I stayed married to a man for twenty-two years that I never even wanted to date," Lauren said.

"So why did you, then?"

"Is that a real question?"

TJ seemed to realize he'd really pissed her off as he said nothing, simply shook his head, looking away. His body language was still pensive, though. She continued. "I put up with Chris' abuse, infidelity and drinking like a good little girl, all the while losing more and more of me every day."

"Does this take us to the 'L' in our little journey?" he asked, voice quiet, but filled with sarcasm.

"If you're referring to the fact that I'm a lesbian, yes."

"You're about to turn forty. Is this like a midlife crisis thing?" he asked, eyes hard. TJ nodded at her head. "Cut your hair. Leave your marriage. Buy a fucking sailboat. Really? Did it come with a treasure map and a swashbuckler?" He smirked. "Or, in your case, swashbucklerette?"

"Gosh, TJ," she drawled, voice dripping with irritation. "You're skipping in line. 'T' for trip and treasure comes after 'S' for sabbatical. Wasn't that, too part of the interrogation?" She walked back to the closet to get more clothing. "It's who I am. It's who I've always been." Hands on hips, she stared him down once he met her gaze again. "I refuse to live for a man, *any* man," she added, giving him a pointed look, "ever again. I'm taking a sabbatical from teaching because I need to figure out who the hell I am because I no longer fit in my life, TJ."

"But, a sailboat?" he asked. "You don't even like water."

"No," she conceded. "But I don't particularly like men, either, yet I gave that one the college try, didn't I?" She went back to the closet for more. "And, I didn't buy it. I'm borrowing the sailboat from the very same colleague and friend, Gloria, who taught me how to sail it."

"Look," he blew out, sounding frustrated. "Fine. Do the lesbian thing. Go find some ocean-themed dyke bar, get wasted and fuck a mermaid. Problem solved. Then, come back and be the Lauren we all recognize."

Rolling her eyes, Lauren packed in the last of her clothing. "It's not like that, TJ. Being a lesbian isn't just about sex and it isn't about mid-life crises and boats or mermaids or whatever lesbian porn you've been watching lately." Hurt, she stared him down. "It's not just about a vagina versus a penis." She met his gaze. "It's an identity." She quirked an eyebrow. "How about you go get that hetero bullshit out of your system?"

"That's not the same thing," he grumbled, pushing to his feet and pacing. "Treasure hunter is also an identity, which sounds like a lot more fun."

She said nothing, knowing full well arguing with him would get her nowhere. With every article of clothing that was stowed away, her resolve solidified. Was she nervous?

Yes. But she needed a break, and she needed a boat. The treasure part was optional.

\* \* \*

Hours after her brother left, Lauren sat on the couch looking out the large windows to the night beyond. She played their conversation back in her mind. No, he didn't always handle things the right way or say the right things, but she could see how her brother was concerned and confused. How could he not be? She'd never been fully honest and open with him, or anyone, about her marriage.

Like many abusers, Chris had started off sweet and attentive. Even though she'd had no interest in him at all, at least he'd been sweet. Then they got married. It had begun slowly, random comments on the way she dressed or how long she talked on the phone or how much she ate for dinner. Always commentary on her appearance. Then, over that first years, snide comments became insults and insults became demands. Violence was soon to follow. It just became part of her day, the game of: how to not piss Chris off today. And, though he'd only said it once—during their five-year anniversary dinner—it had stuck with her. *If you ever leave me,* he'd said, *I'll kill you.*

Though taken aback, she'd not taken him all that seriously, especially since he'd never uttered those words again. But yes, they'd been filed away in her memory. When he'd had little reaction to her announcement that she was leaving, she figured that it had been nothing more than the ramble of a profoundly insecure and paranoid man during a moment of anger.

Lauren let out a heavy sigh as she pulled her legs up to wrap her arms around. She definitely needed to get away. She just hoped her brother would keep all of this to himself, as no doubt Chris would ask.

Part 2

With a grunt, Lauren hauled the final bag on board. As she was heading down into the sleeper cabin of the sailboat, her friend, colleague and owner of the boat, Gloria, came up.

"Plenty of batteries, food, water and gasoline," the older woman said. She'd come at Lauren's request to make sure she was adequately supplied for the next thirty days. She smirked. "Probably a little over packed with clothing, but definitely a better safe than sorry sort of thing." She grinned. "Can't exactly take a quick trip to the store."

"My thoughts too," Lauren laughed, patting the bag she carried. She quickly ducked down the handful of stairs to the depths of the boat and plopped the bag on the bed before heading back up to talk to her friend. "Got any maps in here? TJ seemed to think one was necessary to truly live the sailboat dream."

"Just weather maps. Storms are coming in tonight." Gloria shaded her gaze as she looked up into the blue, cloudless sky. "It'd be wiser to wait until morning to head out. But," she added, "you know how to get hold of us if there's any issues, and I gave you my brother-in-law's information too, if you get into a bind." She tugged on Lauren's shirt tail. "Come with me."

Lauren followed her friend back down below decks to a cabinet above the built-in microwave in the small, well-appointed kitchen. Gloria reached in and removed a pistol. Lauren hated guns, but knew that a woman by herself needed to have some protection. Just because she was in a boat out to sea didn't mean trouble couldn't arise. She, too, had seen the movie *Dead Calm*.

"Okay," Gloria said, holding the 9mm. "Now, I know you're not a fan of guns, but this is the same one we had you shooting at the range last month. You should be familiar with it. It's loaded and," she added, glancing up at the cabinet, "extra ammo in there should, for some crazy reason, you need it."

Letting out a long, slow breath, Lauren nodded. "Okay." She met Gloria's gaze briefly before putting the gun back and the two women headed back up into the day. In just the few minutes they'd been belowdecks, the sky was already beginning to gather clouds.

"You be safe, lady," the older woman said, pulling Lauren into a hug. "Enjoy yourself and the boat."

Lauren returned the tight squeeze, grateful for so many reasons in that moment. "Thanks for everything, Gloria," she said softly into the hug.

* * *

Lauren started awake. A snort escaped her slightly parted lips, but she remained where she was, curled up in the bed belowdecks on the sailboat. The small cabin was mostly filled with the full-sized bed. One wall was the outside of the boat. The other separated the cabin from the small bathroom.

The small room was all about efficiency. No room for a dresser or any other such furniture, so drawers and other storage space was built into the walls and cleverly under the bed. There was a very small closet for anything that needed to be hung up.

Had she heard something? Why was she awake? Lying on her side with her back facing the narrow space between the bed and the wall that lead out to the even narrower hallway beyond, she lifted her head. She saw nothing but the dimness in the cabin, the only light coming in through the one porthole window in the room. A ghostly round, white smudge was projected to the opposite wall from the window creating a crossbeam of gauzy light.

There. She heard something—likely what had awoken her to begin with. Turning from her side to sit up, she stared through that strange light into the darkness beyond the opened cabin door. She strained, listening past the soft slapping of water against the boat in port, as she'd taken Gloria's advice to let the overnight storm pass.

There it was again. Her gaze drifted heavenward as she realized what she was hearing was footfalls above on the upper level. Footfalls but also voices. Hushed voices. Male voices. "Oh god," she whispered. Her heart began to race as she wasn't sure if that was a normal thing while at port.

She pushed the covers off her legs, tossing them over the side of the bed so her bare feet hit the floor. She sat there for a moment, deciding what to do. She tapped her fingers on the mattress on either side of her hips before pushing to her feet. Dressed in the shorts and t-shirt she'd been sleeping in; she edged her way toward the door.

Listening, she heard the footfalls moving closer to the stairs that would take them to the closed door of the lower area. More talking. Two men? Maybe three? Remembering the gun Gloria had shown her mere hours before, she hurried down the narrow hall to the kitchen.

Heart racing so quickly she'd gone lightheaded, Lauren brought the pistol out, tucking it against her chest like a teddy bear. The voices had stopped, but she heard footsteps coming down the stairs, sounding like the person was wearing boots—the footfalls heavy, clunky.

The stairs were just beyond the closed door—no more than ten feet from her. Taking a deep, shuddering breath, she gripped the gun in the correct position, though aimed upward near her right shoulder.

The knob turned, but the lock held. The rattling stopped and Lauren swallowed. Hard. Something was inserted into the lock. A moment of silence, then it sounded as if the lock was being fumbled with. A terrifying sound.

"Oh, Jesus," she whispered. "Who are you? What do you want?"

No response.

She'd told no one where she was going except for TJ and Gloria. She straightened her arms, both hands gripping the gun. She was shaking, the gun trembling in her hands. "I have a gun!" she called out. "I'm not afraid to use it!"

No response.

The door kicked open, wood splintering around the handle. Lauren gasped at the tall, broad-shouldered silhouette in the doorway. For just an instant, she thought the size and shape seemed familiar, but her terror was no doubt clouding her judgement. She squeezed the trigger, letting out three quick shots. Immediately after came a sting in her chest and something grazed the right side of her head. She staggered backward, no idea what had hit her.

Her back hit the cabinet behind her. She lowered the gun and brought up a finger to her head. Blood on her fingertips. All went black.

Part 3

Again, Lauren came to wakefulness. She was again, in the small cabin but this time her wrists were tied together, fisted hands facing each other. Her ankles were also bound, feet still bare and she was still in her t-shirt and shorts from sleep.

The gentle jostle of the boat beneath her alerted her that it was moving. Sunlight filtered in through the porthole window. Lauren struggled to sit up, straightening legs that had been curled up against her chest. Looking out the window, she saw, indeed, nothing but open sea. There was no port, no dock, no people wandering, no other boats.

"Oh my God," she breathed.

Had she been set adrift by whomever had broken into the boat the previous night? Wait, was it the previous night? She had no idea what day it was or even what time. Her head hurt, that much she knew. She was sore, that much she also knew.

She did as much of a body check in as she could. She had to pee but didn't feel like anything else had happened to her. That was a relief. Now, she listened. She heard nothing, which again scared the hell out of her. It was a crazy dichotomy: scared to death nobody else was on the boat and scared to death somebody was.

Looking away from the window, she focused on her bindings. Her hands were bound in front of her, so she eyed the knots tied into rope that looked like it had been part of the rigging. Was it extra rigging, kept on board in case? Or, had whoever boarded the boat that night literally cut the attached rigging to shreds to tie her up with? If so, she was in a very, very bad situation.

She gritted her teeth as she tried to pull her hands free. She'd always been told her bone structure was small and rather delicate, which of course meant her wrists, as well. But the ropes had been knotted tight. It wasn't tight enough to cut off circulation, but that was about all there was room left for.

Men's voices came from outside the closed cabin door. Lauren's lightheadedness returned.

"What the fuck, Marty?" one man roared along with what sounded like a slap. "You went the wrong goddamn way! We ain't gonna survive this, you dumb fuck! And while I'm at it, why the fuck did you keep that lady onboard?" the man raged. "We want the goddamn boat, not her! We got enough we're tryin' to get away from, don't need kidnapping on our plate, too!"

"I'm sorry, Elliot. I was just thinkin' to get her outta our way, so I tied her up. I thought going this way we'd avoid the storm—"

"Fucking idiot!" Another hit, though this one sounded more like a punch.

"Sorry, man," Marty whimpered.

Eyes huge, Lauren stared at the closed door. She felt like a ten-year-old waiting in her bedroom for dad to get home after she'd done something really stupid. Dad just got home.

"Now what do we do?" Marty asked. It sounded like he and the one doing the hitting, were sitting in the small living area just beyond the bathroom. It was comprised of a couch and a comfy chair in a square space with a wall-mounted TV and electric fireplace flat against the wall beneath the large screen.

"'We'?" he said, bitter amusement in his tone. "There ain't no 'we' no more. You fucked that up. You two stay out of the way like good little boys and leave it to the man to getting us outta this fucking mess."

The two men walked down the hall, past her door, and back up into the day. What on earth had they been talking about? They'd gone the wrong way for what? She had no clue where they were, as outside the window was nothing but endless ocean meeting endless sky.

Lauren returned her attention back to her ropes. She needed to use the restroom and soon. There was no give on either set of bindings, so she swung her legs over the side of the bed and hopped to the unlocked door. Thank God, it only locked from the inside or she may have been in even more trouble.

Pulling open the door, she peeked her head out, looking both ways. Still empty—her very unwanted guests still up top. She hopped her way out of the bedroom, gritting her teeth as each hop jarred her bladder. She made it to the tiny bathroom and pushed the folding door in before hopping her way inside, folding the door closed behind her and sliding the lock into place.

After struggling to push her shorts and panties down, she nearly fell off the commode, her bindings making her unsteady. Stabilized, she took her head in bound hands as her body did what it needed to do. Lauren tried to focus.

She clearly couldn't escape while bound. Jumping off the boat and swimming to freedom took at least her legs. Hiding was a moot point, considering they were on a very small sailboat. And, eventually they'd realize she'd woken. Her only option was to play nice and pray like hell she survived this—whatever 'this' was.

Finishing her business and flushing, she struggled to pull her shorts and panties back in place before walking over to the small oval sink and mirror above it. Her face was pale and her eyes haunted. Looking away from them, she looked to the reflection of her head. She remembered vaguely seeing blood on her fingers the night before, so looked for the source now. Even if just dried blood. Nothing.

Eyebrows falling, she brought her hands up and ran her fingers awkwardly due to the bindings, through the dark strands. Nothing. No blood, no quick hissing pain of where a cut or small injury may be hidden.

"What the hell?" she muttered, daring to look back into her eyes.

She had no time to consider further when she gasped, hearing somebody slam open the door to the cabin, which sometimes drifted closed if the doorstop wasn't put in place. Next, somebody tried to push the bathroom door's folding door open, but the lock held.

"Hey. Hey lady. Open this fucking door. Now!"

Hand to her chest, Lauren took in the door then, knowing she had no choice, reached over and unlocked it, allowing the door to fold inward. A man—perhaps five ten—stood on the other side.

She had never seen him before, but wanted to laugh. He reminded her of the actor from the seventies and eighties, George Hamilton. So overly tanning bed baked that he looked like a walking, talking piece of leather. But the best part of it was the little half-moon circles of white skin beneath his eyes from the bottom edges of tanning goggles. His brown hair was slicked back from his large, jerky-like forehead. Scruff peppered his face.

This was not at all what she'd been expecting of Elliot, the great slapper of men.

"You're comin' with me," he said. There was no room for argument in those gray eyes.

"Of course," Lauren agreed. Play nice, she reminded herself. Even if he looks like an idiot. She had to admit, he looked a bit panicked, and that made her nervous.

He fell to his knees, pulling out a knife from one of the cargo pockets in his khaki pants. He flicked the blade open. About to start working on the bindings around her ankles, he stopped, lifting up as high as he could in his position and placing the deadly sharp blade against Lauren's throat.

"You kick me, you hit me, you do *anything* but stand there and let me do this and I fucking gut you. Understand?" At her nod, he continued to mutter, as if to himself as he began working on her bindings. "Just wanted the goddamn boat. How goddamn hard is that, Marty? We need the boat to get outta here. Idiot."

She said nothing, but definitely listened. Fugitives? Was this essentially supposed to be a getaway boat? Would certainly be understandable why her presence onboard was most unwelcome to Elliot, who seemed to be the leader of the hapless trio.

Growing quiet, he gave one more murderous glare up at her before he returned to his task, sawing the knife through the heavy rigging rope at her ankles. Ropes finally falling uselessly to the floor at her bare feet, he stood and grabbed her chin roughly with his thumb and forefinger.

"You're gonna help me," he growled. "And if you don't, so help me God, even the fishes won't be able to get a big enough piece of you to eat for a full lunch. Got it?"

Any amusement she'd had from moments before was absolutely gone. "I got it," she whispered, something telling her that things had taken a massive turn and had grown quite serious, beyond just a few criminals looking for escape. There was almost a wild look in his eyes that seemed to grow steadily more intense as he began to work on the bindings around her wrists.

"You see," he began, voice breathy from exertion of his task as well as, it seemed rising fear. "Fuckin' Marty pointed us in the wrong direction." His crazed gaze met hers briefly. "So, now we're stuck between a rock and a hard place. Behind us," he added, nodding in the general direction he was speaking about, "is a massive goddamn storm. Ahead of us"—his head nodded in the other direction—"*them*."

She could only stare at him. "Who's 'them'?"

"Those bitches," he growled. "The Sirens."

"What?" Lauren blurted with a laugh.

His gaze was deadly serious as it pinned her to the spot. "It ain't funny, lady. I've seen what they can do. When I was a boy, my mother and I barely escaped. Ain't never seen my dad again."

"Wait," Lauren said, desperately trying to make sense of what he was saying. "The Sirens...it's a fable. A legend, fiction." She gasped when once again her chin was taken.

"Not it's not," he insisted. "The part that ain't true is that they want to kill sailors." He shook his head, eyes falling back to the rigging rope he was sawing at. "No, you see those bitches rule some sort of other world and," he added, eyes bright as they flicked back up to Lauren's, "women run it. Like, amazon shit, Sapho shit. They collect men to use as servants." He shook his head. "Hell no. Ain't gonna be me."

"Wait," she said again, her mind racing. "I teach English Lit, and I've never heard—"

"Then you suck as a teacher," he barked. "I've seen it. This ain't no story, lady." Her ropes fell free. "You help us get past them," he growled, "Or so help me...."

"Alright," she said in supplication. "Alright." Clearly this man believed this nonsense, so if it kept her alive to go along with it, so be it. She groaned in relief as her hands parted. She wanted to rub the burns from her skin, but didn't dare.

Elliot grabbed her hand, and she was nearly pulled off her feet as he tugged her behind him down the narrow hallway to the door and stairs above decks.

She cried out when she saw a man splayed out on the deck on his stomach. He looked as though he'd been taken down in surprise. She saw no blood, but he was clearly not dead, as she did see him breathing. She gasped again when she saw a second man slumped over in a deck chair. She looked in horror at Elliot.

"They didn't believe me either," he said pointedly. "They ain't dead. Just knocked out. For your sake." He met her terrified gaze "Ain't like that," he clarified. "Ain't no danger to you, but to all of us."

He stopped at a box near the wheel, overflowing with lifejackets, flares and other such supplies. He pulled out a large iron bar, much like a crowbar. He glanced at her before he tugged her with him again, down to the door that closed off the living area belowdecks. The intensity in his eyes—which was not as maniacal as it had been—startled her.

"You need to hear me, and you need to hear me good." He handed her the bar. The panic from before had returned to his eyes. "Wedge this so the door can't be pulled open."

Lauren could also hear the panic in his voice rising. "Why?"

"Because if you let me leave this place," he said, hitching a thumb behind him, indicating the living area below, "we're all gonna die. You gotta get us through this fucking mess Marty has gotten us into."

"So," she said, looking down at the metal bar she held. "That part of the legend is true?" She met his gaze, no idea what to think.

"You get us through this," he said, grabbing her wrist, making her hiss from the rope burns there. "I swear to you," he continued, surprising earnestness in his voice and eyes, "we'll drop you off at the next port, unharmed. You don't, we all die." With those damning final words, he disappeared belowdecks.

She stood there for a moment, considering. Even if he was out of his mind, if nothing else, she could use this time to get them to that very port he mentioned, and she could get off or get help. Win-win.

She managed to wedge in the iron bar then turned to head back up the stairs to the main deck and the wheel. She made it up two steps before stopping. Warmth washed through her, nearly taking her breath away. It was...it was...like, as if a delicate decanter of bath water was slowly being poured over her skin.

She raised her face to the clear, blue sky, eyes hooded as the sensation turned from the warm, pleasant water to a soft caress of...fingers? She gasped as her nipples grew taut and her clit jumped. For a moment, she couldn't move. Taking several small, shuddering breaths, she forced herself to the wheel of the sailboat.

Her body buzzed, a million bees humming all around her in a growing chorus of arousal that made absolutely no sense. She took hold of the wheel, and tried to focus and ground herself with its steely reality. For a moment, the arousal settled to a low pulse.

There was nothing around them—nary another vessel, another living soul. Not even clouds, except way back, miles away in the storm they'd been trying to avoid. The unconscious men remained so.

Suddenly, the sun dimmed then flickered out. For a moment, just the flash of a second, she was on her back, a beautiful woman hovering above her.

Lauren felt such calm at this stranger, but that calm was shattered when that split second seemed to stretch out into an eternity. The woman's face, lovely pale skin, began to darken, patches of seaweed-green appearing along her cheeks, lighter in color near her eyes and growing darker as they marched down around full lips and over her chin and along her jaw. Scales. This creature, neither fish nor woman, but something in between.

The round black pupils in her eyes lengthened, jagged like twin bolts of lightning, striking terror into her. Lauren gasped and cried out, though her cries were muted as the alien visage before her melted away, leaving another vision behind, that of the human woman mere seconds before.

*The woman's shoulder length auburn hair was tucked behind one ear. So deep and rich in color. But what got Lauren were her eyes. They were a piercing green, and their verdant gaze was locked on hers.*

*Lauren smiled. "I love your eyes," she whispered.*

*The woman's smile was slow, as she'd initially looked surprised by the words. Her hand caressed Lauren's cheek. "Come back," she whispered in response. "Please, come back."*

Lauren gasped loudly, thrust back into her reality. She staggered a few steps, coming to rest against one of the deck's lounge chairs. She sat and surveyed. Everything was as it had been mere moments before: beautiful clear blue skies, endless seas and two unconscious men sprawled on the top deck.

What the hell had that been about? She blew out a breath, deeply affected by that...what? Again, she saw the woman's face before her mind's eye. No, not a woman but a creature. A hauntingly beautiful chimera.

Was that the Sirens Elliot had blathered about, she wondered. Certainly, many depictions had been made of the dangerous vixen: beautiful women, bird-like creatures, mermaid-like creatures or even monstrous beings behind the seductive call. Is that what she'd seen? Surely not! The idea was ridiculous, but then, she conceded, the entire situation was ridiculous. She was pulled from her thoughts by Elliot's voice.

"I can hear it!" Elliot called, his deep voice muffled behind the door. "I can hear you!" There was an almost breathy desperation in his tone.

On cue, Lauren's body began to buzz again. It started like a cluster of bumblebees across her lips, trailing down across her breasts and nipples and centering between her legs. God, she'd climax if it didn't stop. "Jesus!" she gasped, fingers curling around chair armrests. She noticed that the man slumped over in the chair, even unconscious, was affected as his massive erection was pushing against his pants.

Elliot's voice was near tears, scratching sounds on the door joining in. "Please!" he begged. "Please let me out." Whimpering. "I need to go. I need to be with them. Can't you hear it? They're singing," he said, voice filled with wonder. "Just for me."

Lauren's clit throbbed and her panties were totally saturated. She squeezed her eyes shut, nails digging into the arm of the chair she sat in. "Jesus," she gasped.

*"Bring them to us."*

Lauren looked around, startled at the female voice—soft and deeply sensual—that seemed to be all around her. Again, the flash of that beautiful face that seemed to belong to the sea. "Who? Where?" she called out, feeling as though she'd lost her damn mind.

Soft, invisible fingers caressed her cheek.

"Let me out!" Elliot wailed, something thudding against the barricaded door. "I need to get to her! She's calling to me. Me!"

Lauren glanced at the door, her heart racing. She heard a loud crack above and saw the clouds were moving, fast, gathering just off to the east. A storm was brewing, lightning shooting across the whirling skies with a spiderweb of brilliance illuminating the undersides of the gray clouds. Their detour hadn't outrun the storm at all.

As she watched, a funnel of sea water began to grow out of the ocean on the starboard side of the sailboat. Lauren's mouth hung open as her gaze followed it upward until it met those storm clouds. The center of the funnel spiderwebbed into lightning.

*"You are not safe, Lauren..."*
*"Bring them to us. We'll protect you."*

Her name was a whisper on the wind, a feminine whisper in ecstasy.

The column of water flattened out and spread like a wall. At its center an opening appeared, like the mouth of a drawbridge. She watched in awe. The ocean and darkening skies vanished beyond that maw, which was black as night, yet somehow, not as foreboding as the skies above.

*"Lauren, bring them to us. We can protect you, reward you and send you home...."*

As she continued to watch that "drawbridge" fully lower itself, she realized that, as much as her body was affected by what was happening, she was still clear minded. She considered Elliot's offer to her: get them past this and he'd let her go. Could she trust that? No, it didn't seem he necessarily had any ill intent toward her, but for three men who were up to no good, she was in the way.

Making up her mind, she got up and threw her body weight against the wheel, turning the boat directly into the wall of water. Even if she was wrong and simply got them killed, at least she'd decide her own fate. If she was going to die today, it would be on her terms. She was damn sick and tired of men making her decisions for her.

The boat turned, headed straight into what could ultimately be the mouth of Hell. Lauren's heart pounded as heavily as her clit. The clouds darkened, lightning flashed, and the thunder turned deafening. Clouds swirled in the skies as the maw of water yawned around the boat.

"What the hell?"

Lauren looked. To her horror, one of the unconscious men had woken up. He lifted his head from where he slumped in the chair, though he still looked out of it and disoriented.

Not wanting to chance it, she turned on the motor and, wrapping her hand over the throttle, hit the gas. "Fuck off!" she cried as she directed the tiny sailboat into their collective destiny.


Part 4


For a third time, Lauren awoke with a start. This time she was naked, atop a soft bed. It was far more like reclining on a cloud than a pillowtop. She was clean, rested, and refreshed. A sheet draped over her, the fabric caressing her curves rather than simply covering them. She was in a large, beautifully appointed bed chamber. The large fourposter bed had an intricately carved headboard, posts and wood canopy. The walls were stone, as was the floor. Large, ornate tapestries hung over two of the four walls, the third was filled with several tall, narrow and pointed windows, and the fourth with a massive fireplace. A warm fire danced and popped inside.

Her fear had vanished along with her clothes although, once again, she wasn't alone. Laying on the bed next to her was a woman in a silk dressing gown, barely belted closed. Awake and grinning at Lauren, she lay on her side next to Lauren, head resting in an open palm. In her position, her breasts had fallen into enticing cleavage.

Lauren's eyes immediately went to that cleavage, but she gasped when something else caught her eye. What at first glance looked to be a large silver necklace of sorts was actually a patchwork of silver and deep blue scales, inlaid into the creamy flesh.

"Recognize me?" the woman asked, ripping Lauren's attention from the abnormality.

Lauren gasped. "You...from the boat." Yes, she'd hovered over her, spoke to her. "Kind of."

"Yes," replied the woman.

Her gaze had turned so intense that Lauren shifted uncomfortably. Clearing her throat—and using willpower to not pull the sheet around her own body like a shy child—Lauren asked, "Where am I?"

"The other side," the woman responded simply.

The hand that had been resting along the woman's curvaceous hip moved to lightly trail random patterns with a fingernail on Lauren's upper chest. Eyes growing heavy with the pleasurable touches, they snapped when she noticed more of the scales trailing from the back of her hand up over her wrist only to disappear beneath the sleeve of her dressing gown.

Forcing her mind off them, Lauren's eyes went wide at the strange woman's words.

The woman grinned and shook her head. "No," she said. "Not *that* other side. Not the other side of your earthbound reality and ideology." She brought that scale-plated hand down to rest on Lauren's stomach, atop the sheet. "You, sweet Lauren, are in between sleep and awake. Dream and fantasy."

Lauren stared at her, even more confused. Yes, this woman would certainly live in her fantasy, absolutely. But, somehow that didn't feel like that was what this was. "I don't understand."

That hand moved from Lauren's stomach, fingers lightly trailing over Lauren's right breast before making its way to her face. Gentle fingertips delicately caressed Lauren's features. She wasn't sure whether she wanted to go to sleep at the soft touches or beg the woman to fuck her senseless. Her body was a live wire of sensation, a veritable lightning rod, yet her mind was so calm and steady, laid back and rested.

"You owe nothing to those men, who could have asked you for help instead of abducting you." The woman's hand gently cupped Lauren's jaw before her fingers trailed back up the side of her face and across her forehead. Lauren's eyes fluttered closed. "You had a choice to make," the soothing voice, the timbre like warm honey, continued. "You brought them to us, our favorite meal." A sexy little grin spread across full lips. "Well, almost." Her fingernail traced across one of Lauren's nipples through the sheet, making her gasp. "And," the woman continued, "so, you shall live."

Lauren stared at her, stunned. "Who are you?"

The woman's smile took Lauren's breath away. "I'm your reward," she said simply. Her hand came to rest once more on the side of Lauren's neck. "Your soul's deepest desire." She scooted closer and leaned down, her lips just a hair's width from hers. "The touch of a woman," she whispered. "And the love of a woman."

Lauren's eyes fell closed at the first touch of the softest lips she'd ever felt. Even softer than her lips, however, was her tongue, which gently stroked against Lauren's. Lauren buried her hand into the auburn curtain of hair—so soft, like silk. The world, the fantasy, shrunk down to the softness of the woman's mouth.

As the woman moved atop her, she...

\* \* \*

...gasped, loudly. Lauren's eyes popped open, wide and unseeing for a moment. Her heart pounded painfully in her chest. It took several deep breaths before she could focus on the small room around her. There was a window, a regular rectangular window and blue skies beyond. Gaze moving past it, she saw a small, flat screen TV mounted to a moveable arm high above a woman who was sitting in a chair, reading.

Looking down at herself, Lauren realized she was in a narrow bed: a hospital bed. She wore a standard hospital gown and had various tubes connected to her arm and the back of her hand. A heart monitor cup was also attached to her left forefinger. She was startled by a sudden voice. She looked up to see the woman was looking at her.

"Lauren?" The woman stood and approached her, looking relieved.

"Hey," Lauren croaked, her word sounding like she'd just hit two packs of cigarettes.

Gloria's face was pure joy. "Oh, honey," she whispered. "Water?" At Lauren's nod, she grabbed the plastic cup with straw and lid. It looked like an adult-sized sippy cup.

Lauren accepted the plastic straw between raw, chapped lips, sucking in the room temperature fluid like it was a balm to her very soul. Getting her fill, she urged Gloria's hand away with the cup. "What happened?" she managed, her voice still sandpaper dry.

Gloria let out a heavy sigh as she replaced the cup on the small rolling table pushed to the side of Lauren's bed. "Do you remember anything, Lauren?" Both women's attention was grabbed when a toilet flushed behind the door just down from the mounted TV and chair Gloria had just been sitting in.

The door opened and TJ appeared. His dark gaze immediately went to the bed and relief flooded the chocolate depths. "Oh, thank God," he breathed hurrying over to her on the opposite side of the bed as the older woman. "I'm so sorry."

Lauren looked up at him, allowing him to take her other hand. "Sorry? Why? It's not your fault that three men broke in." She returned her focus to Gloria's question, trying to sort it all out. It was fuzzy. "I shot at one. Um..." Her eyebrows knit as she tried to remember details. She remembered auburn hair, but none of the men had red hair. Right? "A really beautiful woman?" she muttered, staring off into space, trying to bring the woman's face to mind. "Really pretty green eyes. Auburn hair." When she heard nothing, she looked to her friend. "What?" she turned to look at her brother when he snorted.

"Leave it to you to only remember the hot doctor."

"That sounds like Dr. McDonel," Gloria said with a smile, garnering Lauren's attention again. "Very, very lovely woman. She was your intake physician in the ER. Said you suddenly opened your eyes, looked up at her, and said she was beautiful." She chuckled.

"Wow," Lauren whispered, her brain a fog.

"You said that right before you flatlined." Gloria cleared her throat and rubbed at the edges of her eyes. "They got you stable enough to get you into surgery. She's been in several times this week to come check on you."

"This week? It's been a week?"

"Yes, you've been here for six days, Lauren. You only moved out of ICU two days ago," the older woman explained gently.

"What happened? The three men..."

"Gloria," TJ interjected, "can I have some time alone with her? To explain?"

Gloria nodded. She gave Lauren a gentle kiss on her head before leaving the room, the two siblings left alone to stare at each other. Finally, TJ said, "Mind if I sit?"

Lauren shook her head, watching as he moved around to the chair Gloria had been sitting in, dragging it to the side of the bed. He plopped down and took her hand again. He seemed to need a moment, but finally he spoke, eyebrows drawn as he looked deeply troubled.

"There aren't words enough to tell you how sorry I am, Sis," he said. She couldn't remember the last time he'd called her that. Used to be his special term of endearment for her. "It sounds like you've got a lot rolling around in your head, three men breaking in, all that. No." He shook his head. "That's not what happened."

She stared at him. "What? Then what did?"

He cleared his throat and finally met her eyes, tears in his own. "Chris," he said simply. "He asked me where you were going and, in my infinitely stupid brain, I thought maybe you two could sail away together. Spend some time and figure things out. A romantic getaway, as it were." He looked down at their joined hands for a moment. Lauren felt cold. A tear slipped from his eye, but he didn't bother to wipe it away. "He broke in, Sis. He shot you in the chest and the head, but you managed to get off three shots at him, too."

"What?" Lauren gasped. Suddenly, she remembered that silhouette again. Yes, goddamn it, yes. She *did* recognize it.

"He didn't make it," TJ finished, voice thick with emotion. "And, good-fucking-riddance."

Lauren was quiet for a long moment, absorbing what she'd been told. She would need time—a lot of time—both to heal, to digest and honestly, to forgive.

"You never left port," he continued. "A security guard on the docks heard the shots and, thank God, found you and was able to get you help."

\* \* \*

Despite never getting her chance to head out to sea, Lauren was glad to be home. She'd spent another two days in the hospital before being released. Gloria had offered to take her home with her so that she and her husband could look after her for a bit, but Lauren wanted to be alone. To go home. She had a lot to think about, least of all the knowledge that she'd killed her ex-husband. Yes, it was totally self-defense, the police even said as much, but still.... Also, TJ's betrayal. No, he never expected or intended what happened to happen, but he'd still been at the center of it all.

When she'd arrived home, everything was as she'd left it—neat, clean and everything in its place. The luggage she'd taken with her aboard the sailboat had been brought in by Gloria's husband at some point, the suitcase and two duffel bags waiting patiently next to the couch for her to unpack.

Now, a week home and taking it easy as her doctors had instructed, she mostly just wanted coffee. As she retrieved a mug, a knock came from the door, startling her.

"Who is it?" she called out.

"Erin McDonel, a doctor from St. Joseph's Hospital," came the muffled response.

The doctor from the hospital? Curious, Lauren disengaged the locks and pulled the door open.

The auburn-haired siren from her dream stood at the threshold, still in her hospital scrubs. Her long hair was pulled back into a ponytail. "Hi," she said, voice casual even as she looked a bit shy. No doubt, an unusual circumstance to pop in on a former patient.

"Uh, hi," Lauren responded, struck for so many reasons as she stared at the woman standing out in the hall.

"You probably don't remember me," the stunning doctor said shyly, "but I took care of you in the ER. How are you feeling?"

"I'm good," Lauren said, also feeling quite shy. "Still here, anyway."

"I'm really sorry to just drop by," Dr. McDonel said. "This last week was crazy in the ER, so when I was finally able to check on you yesterday, they told me you'd been discharged already." She smiled sheepishly. "Gloria told me where I could find you. Wanted to make sure you were okay."

"That's really sweet," Lauren murmured, touched. "Um, want to come in?" She stepped back from the door.

The doctor nodded and entered the apartment, Lauren closing and locking the door behind her. She noted the doctor's glance to the locked door and back to her. "Sorry," Lauren said sheepishly. "Guess I'm still a little shaken by everything."

"Don't apologize," the doctor said softly. "I'm so sorry about what happened." She shook her head. "Just horrible."

They stood in the entryway for a moment, the silence somewhat awkward until Lauren said, "I was about to make some coffee." She hitched her thumb toward the kitchen. "Would you like some, Dr. McDonel?"

"Erin," the doctor said. "I'm called doctor all day. Please," she said with a sweet smile, "just call me Erin."

"I can do that. Would you like some coffee, Erin?"

Erin's smile lit up the room as she nodded. "I'd love some. Is it okay if I call you Lauren, as opposed to Patient McCallister?" Erin's lips were full, and she had an incredible smile. Her emerald eyes and sweet voice jarred Lauren, and memories of, what she now realized was essentially a near-death-induced hallucination flooded her mind. Her body responded in kind.

Lauren cleared her throat and smiled. "Lauren is fine. Far less formal." The two women shared a small laugh at the joke, as lame as it was. "So," she said, grabbing a second cup once they'd reached the kitchen. "I understand I embarrassed myself in the emergency room." She gave the doctor—who leaned back against an adjacent counter to where Lauren was working at her single-cup coffeemaker—a sheepish look.

"No," Erin said, shaking her head and grinning. "Don't think of it that way. You were in such terrible shape, it was a miracle when you opened your eyes and looked at me, you were able to put together any sort of coherent thought, let alone speak it." She shook her head, eyes turning troubled. "I've worked in the ER for ten years and I've seen some horrible things, what we do to each other. But... " She met Lauren's gaze. "I was truly moved by you. I honestly don't know why."

Lauren stood at the coffeemaker for a moment, not entirely sure what to say. She, too, felt very moved by the woman standing not ten feet away. She couldn't explain it, but knew it wasn't so simple as the fact that Erin had saved her life. It was more than that she was absolutely stunning, too, but Lauren couldn't quite put her finger on the answer.

She swallowed. "Thank you for what you did for me," she said lamely. Yes, she was grateful, but she wanted to say so much more, yet had no clue what it was she wanted to say.

Erin smirked and crossed her arms over her chest. "You know, and I know it probably sounds weird and stalkerish, but if I'd managed to catch you this last week before you were discharged, I was going to ask you if you wanted to grab some coffee sometime." She shook her head. "Totally against hospital policy." She laughed. "But, I just can't explain it, I feel this need to get to know you."

Lauren let out a long, slow breath. "I feel it, too."

Erin pushed away from the counter, the rubber soles of her tennis shoes squeaking against the wood floor as she walked the handful of steps to Lauren. Erin's eyes were a complex mixture of tenderness and understanding, desire and a bit of confusion. Completely able to relate, Lauren's breath caught as Erin's hand cupped her cheek.

"Why do I feel so drawn to you?" the doctor murmured.

Lauren's eyes grew heavy at the touch and quiet words. Without her permission, her hands found their way to Erin's waist. "I don't understand it, either."

"Please tell me it's okay that I kiss you,"

Lauren smiled and nodded. "It's very okay."

Her eyes fell closed as the doctor neared, her lips so soft. She knew those lips, instantly her soul recognized them. Her fingers tightened on Erin's waist, gently pulling their bodies closer together as the kiss deepened. She felt as though she'd never been kissed before that moment, as though she'd never been touched. She felt virginal and shy, even as she'd shared a bed with a man for more than twenty years.

Erin's hand slid from her face into her hair, carefully avoiding the injured side of Lauren's head. The kiss was slow, exploratory and deeply sensual. Lauren felt a passion ignited in her that she couldn't have dreamed of if she'd tried. No matter how many lesbian romance novels she'd devoured throughout the years—desperate for thirty chapters of normalcy and desire—it couldn't match how she felt in that moment.

After several minutes, they parted, both breathing heavily. Erin stroked Lauren's flushed face. Her deep green eyes were intense. "It's only been two weeks," she said. "Think you can handle it if we go easy?"

Lauren grinned. "What, play doctor?"

Erin's grin was downright lecherous. "Something like that."

Lauren was very out of her element, no matter how much she wanted this. "Um," she said, looking down to where their breasts were lightly pressed together in their embrace. She forced herself to meet the other woman's gaze. "I've never...." She smiled shyly. "I have no clue what to do."

Erin cupped her jaw, her eyes instantly going from desire-filled to kind. It was filled with the gentleness of her touch. "Gloria told me about your marriage and starting over. All of it." She caressed Lauren's cheek with her fingertips before taking her hand. "We'll go slow." She lightly squeezed Lauren's fingers. "Where's your bedroom?"

Coffee forgotten, Lauren led the way. She made short work of tossing throw pillows off the bed and pulling down the covers, her heart about to pound out of her chest. She was nervous yet deeply aroused. It was a mixture that made her want to faint.

They made short work of undressing, neither of them wearing that many articles of clothing to lose. She was utterly entranced by Erin's body. She watched as the doctor reached up and tugged her hair free of its ponytail, shaking the long strands loose to fall in an auburn wave around her shoulders. It was in gorgeous contrast to the pale creaminess of her skin. It looked so incredibly inviting.

They climbed onto her bed, Erin urging her to lie on her back. Lauren accepted Erin's kiss as Erin moved atop her. She'd waited a lifetime to know what it felt like to be with a woman—to feel her skin against her own, her breasts, her tongue.

And, as Erin left the kiss and began to explore Lauren's neck and throat with her mouth, Lauren almost had to wonder if she was lost in her own head again. Was this real? This incredible woman she really didn't know, though her soul told her she did. She knew her touch, her kiss, her scent. And, as Erin kissed and licked her way further down Lauren's body, she opened up for her. Her nervousness went away. She didn't know what to expect, but she knew Erin wouldn't hurt her. Instead, she would complete her.

Her neck arched back at the first feel of a hot, firm tongue between her legs. Erin wrapped her arms around her thighs, holding her open to her feasting mouth. Lauren almost couldn't breathe as that relentless tongue made her more wet, more hard and finally, ready to explode.

Lauren cried out as her body released, the intensity almost painful as Erin sucked her clit inside her mouth as she barraged it with her tongue. Her back arched and body shuddered as an avalanche of pleasure crashed through her. She was gasping for breath when Erin finally released her from her mouth.

It took a moment, but Lauren realized that Erin had reached her mouth again, Erin's lips and tongue warm and slick with Lauren's own desire. The next kiss was deep and lazy, filled with Erin's need.

Erin adjusted her hips between Lauren's spread thighs, making them both gasp as Erin lowered her engorged clit to rest upon Lauren's, which still pulsed. A long, languid groan escaped into the kiss as Lauren registered the entirely new sensation that Erin was producing within her body.

"I need to tell you something," Erin murmured into Lauren's ear as her hips slowly began to move between Lauren's legs, their hard clits rubbing together in slow, measured thrusts.

Lauren held the woman atop her close. "What?" she breathed, groaning deep in her throat as Erin reached a hand back, running her fingernails along one of Lauren's spread thighs.

"I'm so glad you accepted my call," Erin murmured hotly into her ear.

Confused, Lauren's body continued to move with the other woman's even as her mind tried to make sense of what she'd just been told. Erin's head lifted from Lauren's neck as she pushed up to her hands, hips never stopping in their smooth, fluid thrusts.

Looking up into Erin's face, she saw the same woman who had shown up to her door less than an hour before, but, as her gaze fell lower, she gasped. The necklace-like ring of silver and deep blue scales.

Erin looked down at her, her eyes opening to reveal the lightning bolt pupils. "You accepted my call," she panted, hips moving faster, more urgency behind each thrust.

Lauren's pleasure was too far gone to be able to push the woman away, instead she found herself clinging to her. "Yes," she managed to respond. She didn't understand it, but rather than being repulsed or shocked, she felt the need to almost pull the woman inside of her.

Her orgasm was ripped from the very depths of her soul. Lauren's cry was loud and guttural, reverberating off the walls of the bedroom along with Erin's loud and vocal release. Lauren wrapped her legs and arms around the other woman, pulling her as close to her as she could. She could feel a strange cold smoothness against her upper chest.

Still breathing heavily, Erin looked down at her, a hand cupping Lauren's cheek. Those strange, jagged-pupil eyes meet her own. It was as disconcerting as it was strangely comforting.

"You took me to your bed willingly," Erin continued. "We are one, Lauren. And," she added, a little smile curving full lips, "you're one of us."

* * *

Lauren woke with a gasp, her heart racing. She was naked and curled up against Erin's warm, soft form. Eyes blinking several times, trying to shake the crazy dream out of her mind, she lifted her head slightly. Looking down at the smooth paleness of Erin's upper chest, very *normal* upper chest, she was relieved.

No scales, no cold, smooth or clamminess beneath her fingertips. Just soft, warm skin. It was an added relief when Erin's eyes slowly opened and met her own. Just normal, beautiful green eyes.

"Good morning," the doctor said with a smile. She lifted her head to leave a kiss on Lauren's lips. "What time is it?"

Lauren glanced to her bedside clock. "Almost eight."

"I need to get going," Erin said, running her fingers along Lauren's cheek. "Need to get home and ready for work."

Nodding, Lauren accepted the kiss, deep and wonderful. She watched as Erin climbed out of bed and padded in all her naked perfection toward the bathroom. At the door, one hand on the doorframe and the other on the door, Erin glanced back at her, a knowing little smile on her lips. A jagged, lightning gaze, and the door was closed.

More of Kim Pritekel's short stories can be found on her Patreon account: **http://www.patreon.com/kimpritekel.** You can find her published novels at Amazon, Barnes & Noble online or anywhere else you get your books, ebooks or audiobooks online.

174  Robin C.M. Duncan

# The Vermillion Lady

Robin C.M. Duncan

Sapphic Representation: Lesbian, Non-Binary
Heat Level: Low
Content Warnings: Coarse Language, Violence

# 1

*Lineca rules the Isles, rules the waves, rules the winds.*
*All hail Apanato, long may the Princex reign.*
*Until the wind stops blowing, until the wind grows still.*
*All hail Apanato, forever may they reign.*

*Lineca rules the Isles, rules the lines, rules the land.*
*All hail Apanato, long may the Princex reign.*
*We vanquish our enemies; we subjugate their lands.*
*All hail Apanato, forever may they reign.*

*Lineca rules the Isles, rules the sand, rules the seas.*
*All hail Apanato, long may the Princex reign.*
*Send our flag, send our ships, send our power across the lands.*
*All hail Apanato, forever may they reign.*
*All hail Apanato, forever may they reign!*

*—The National Anthem of Lineca*

There is nothing better than clerking at the Institute of Antiquities. So say I, Astrid Opanimo. Here I sit, dust motes skating on sunlit air, surrounded by the tomes that describe our world. And in the vault across the hall, while I sit scratching vellum, wandering the history of Lineca's Hundred Isles, there—when they return replenished from their triumphant voyages to the realm's four corners—will be ensconced the four lustrous paradigms, receptacles of the Princex's power. Why would I not wonder at those marvellous relics, sources of the Eyrs' magic, who come here to recharge their mystic abilities before returning to their ships and their captains? How could I be frustrated? Why would I be dissatisfied? What could I yearn for that I cannot find in these hallowed libraries? Nothing but exhilarating adventure, to *see* the world I study and record. Only to ride ocean waves instead of the bay's ripples, buoyed by the wild winds these cold journals describe, find for my body the freedom my mind enjoys, the adventure any young woman would crave when perusing this new log from Mehdina Taradel—the Princex's Foremost Privateer, head of the fleet, in whose wonderful career these books have educated me.

\* \* \*

*I ordered us round the cape, an incautious dash to cut off* Vermillion Lady's *attack on my compatriot,* Eagle. *My eyrtaster called the salt high and bitter, sure sign of treacherous gusts in the strengthening squall blowing* Eagle's *three-ship escort off course. Highcaps ahead, the threat of swamping. I bellowed the order, "Tie in all". I would not lose another sailor to Vermillion, neither the ship nor the rebellious hag nicknamed the same. Nor would she pilfer the Star paradigm from* Eagle's *hold, not on my watch. Lines secure, deck sanded, I consulted my eyrseer, her power—the navigational power of all eyrseers—enshrined in the very artefact* Eagle *carried. But the storm rendered navigation pointless. Further, my eyrhearer could glean no message from* Eagle. *Still, I guessed* Eagle's *travails. Only six spans ago, the dire Vermillion sent the* Princex's Pride *to the deep, pilfering the magical Pyramid paradigm from her cargo, leaving the tribute gems and gold to the depths. So, the Princex was already a paradigm poorer, their power in the west diminished, the power of their eyrsayers failing by the span. Another success for Vermillion could not be tolerated, regardless of my personal* ~~feelings~~ *enmity.*

*We rode rollers mizzenmast high, plunged gloomy troughs deeper than Hell, surged to the bright peak of hope then down again. My eyrtaster—struggling for a course—pleaded we break pursuit, but I refused to gift Vermillion the Star paradigm. Eyrseer Jantino—bent double in the gale—staggered to me, hollered, "It'll clear." And it did. The pitching eased. We found the best of the sea, cut forward. The lookout*

178 Robin C.M. Duncan

*spied* Vermillion Lady *ahead,* Eagle *beyond her.* Vermillion *was too close to her prize, and I cursed her, swore such that the mate blushed and bosun flinched. I pressed all canvas to speed, spared nothing, no one, commanded eyrtaster and eyrseer to my side to know every slip and sliver of the way ahead. Demanded eyrsayer—sad, pretty Sentina—use her failing power to call to* Eagle. *Insisted eyrhearer—grumpy, invaluable Brogine—strain to hear* Eagle's *cries. Nothing.*

*The squall behind us, we neared becalmed* Eagle, *her sails burning, rigging aflame. I knew* Vermillion *had bested me. Me, Foremost Privateer, Princex's principal sailor. The Star paradigm was gone, and my heart burns with shame. Lineca weakened again. The Princex's power reduced, the north invited to challenge Apanato's rule—bless the steps their feet take. I have failed and must return to Cardoon to face the Princex.*

*(Log of the* Scarlet Sword, *Captain Mehdina Taradel, PFP)*

# 2

*"Now, children, attention, a test! Princex Apanato has ruled Lineca since YS 673, cementing their reign by seizing from the former Hundred Isles nations the four glorious paradigms—relics granting power over the air's aspects. Now, children, repeat after me!*

*Pyramid paradigm empowers Eyrsayers, they who talk to the wind.*
*Diamond paradigm drives Eyrhearers, who hearken to the air.*
*Cruciform paradigm infuses Eyrtasters, they know the sea's ways.*
*Star paradigm strengthens Eyrseers, ship's eyes see the course."*

*—Maister Fitanayo's history class, ages 8 and 9*

I pull on my jacket as I cross the office, reaching for the door's ancient handle, impatient to be away. I'm eager for the walk to the harbour and my boat, then the sail home.

"Astrid," says Academician Hankani, steel grey eyes admonishing. "You are...overlooking something."

"My apologies, Acady." I bow my head, hands clasped before me. "Blessed be the paradigms, founds of our nation, glory of the Princex. Light of the world, I see thee. Soul of the land, I feel thee. Joy of the air, I embrace thee. Heart of the fire, I welcome thee."

"Very good. Until tomorrow." Primly, she touches wiry, shoulder-length grey hair. "Please arrive with utmost punctuality. A full day awaits our industrious fingers."

I almost splutter, romantic notions flooding my mind. Oh, alright, salacious thoughts, but not for her. Although Acady Hankani is paired, she exudes unfulfillment, seems to repress her own spirit. She has even shorn the grey plait from her head that I thought displayed a youthful air. Me? I barely succeed at containing joy in my throat picturing daring Captain Mehdina Taradel with longing in my breast. The log reports her docking this morn. To think that I might see her on my way home... I calm myself by touching my chest where mother's winged charm and my Institute medallion hang. I nod, say, "Good evening, Acady," and depart into the dusk.

Slate clouds rumble across the sky, blackening rooflines. Below the cover, the last daylight persists, staining my glimpses between black-edged buildings, down streets not yet trodden by the lamplighters. I hurry on, boots clumping cobbles, keen to beat the storm tail wagging into Cardoon Bay. My head remains full of Mehdina's report, the tip of my tongue tastes the salty air, my steps lengthen to a run, wind setting free my locks to trail behind me, as if trying to lift me into the air, black tresses upon black shadow. I need boards under my boots, to feel the pitch and yaw, the storm's end giving that feel of the sea surging under my hull.

I slow for the port's wrought iron gate, reach between shirt buttons, produce my Institute medallion, show the weaselly guard. He peers down through patchy light, trying to snatch a glimpse of tit, I'll bet. Ruefulness distracts me: he'll need a better light. Let's just say I'm not inconvenienced at a run. He grunts assent—or maybe disappointment—and I dart through, open my stride and chase down the tang of seaweed and dead fish, the complaints of the gulls and hardworking stevedores, as raucous as each other.

Going full tilt, I leap over a splintered barrel, slip on discarded litter, finally emerge—panting—wharfside. Despite the hour, all is commotion. With passengers absent—tucked up or tucking in by now—the laughing, grunting dock rats' inhibitions are shed, and they start with precious few. As I wend through stacked cargos, ballast heaps, supplies on pallets, the dishonourable college of loaders lets rip, sparing no blushes as to how they would bend me and why. Few go to the trouble of noting my gender. So be it. I forge on, don't look, don't stop, unless I want to spend the eve practising contortions behind a warehouse.

And there she is! *Scarlet Sword,* Mehdina's ship, docked between a brigantine and a topsail schooner near the ladder I'm making for. I gawp up at *Sword's* rigging, and a tall figure bashes into me, sends me tumbling to the ground.

"Watch it, dolt!" She looms over me, hands on hips, me on arse-and-elbows, gaping. It's Mehdina Taradel herself, Foremost Privateer, buccaneer of renown, swashbuckler supreme. To see her was unlikely. To *meet* her? Impossible. To *SPEAK* to her? Unimaginable. She's everything I could want to be, and she stands over me, and she's vexed. My face is red too, warmed by... No.

"I'm sorry, Meh—a'am, eh, Captain." Even prone, I dip my head. The captain looks like she has more curses in her, so I bumble on. "I beg forgiveness with utmost ardour."

*Ardour?* All I desire now is that the breeze sweep me away into the harbour.

She regards me—scarlet headscarf clutched in a fist, dark hair recovered to short fuzz from a shaving at sea; eyes deep, clear brown, shining like oiled and polished teak. Mehdina Taradel smirks, reaches down. Can I take her hand? Inconceivable. I reach out, she grasps mine, a warm jolt shakes me, my heart thrums as she hauls me up. How could a clerk like me feel ardour for her? Yet I do.

"Ardour, you say?" She looks me up and down just as frankly as the sentry. Her expression hardens. "You look like a stranger to it. What are you?"

"I'm clerk...at the Institute of Antiquities, I—"

She grunts. "Look at you, you'd do a guttersnipe proud."

"A fall in the street, rushing to get home. I'm across the bay, in Vuntino."

"You sail."

"I do. My catboat, easy enough, and fast." Showing off now!

Mehdina—listen to me, such familiarity—scowls, perhaps realising that, being in Antiquities, I know of her latest failure. Another paradigm lost, every eyrseer's power slowly diminishing now, like the eyrsayers, unable to replenish their ability.

"Is it started then? Drylanders crowding to curse my failure after the Princex tore a strip off me?"

"No! The Princex—bless their footsteps—surely trusts you still! There's none better."

Mehdina growls. "Vermillion is better. Eight ships destroyed or crippled, two paradigms to the good, and hungry for more, if I know her, and I did, too well. That cow's audacity, her sheer gall—"

She cuts herself off, knowing she's been unguarded. I sense inner fragility. She's hurting. I almost reach out to her. I swallow, sweat sticking my shirt to my back, medallion and charm heavy on my damp chest. The air is charged, underscoring the workers' calls, the gulls' screaming. "You'll be sailing soon, to protect the remaining paradigms?" What temerity, presuming to discuss her movements, but I feel a need to bolster my hero.

"Will I now? You talk a lot for a guttersnipe. Then again, about right for an archivist. Well, at sea there's naught but plain speaking: bookworm, guttersnipe, what do I care? You've something about you." She steps in close, arm circling my waist, and pulls me against her. "Come aboard, warm my berth, leave in the morn before we sail. No questions, no lies."

I splutter, damp back cold with the eve's chill, front bathed in Mehdina Taradel's warmth. I blush again. "I'm...not that kind of girl. I'm wanted home. I have dinner: a pair of coley, from the market." That's what I stutter, but my dreams are shaking me fit to rouse me from wakefulness. My legs are weak, Mehdina's rough beauty swamping me.

"You're an early riser then."

"There's plenty to record, much generated by Vermillion."

Her look sours, grip relaxing. We separate. I feel regret, and the breeze's chill.

A woman and man clump down the gangway. He wears the four-sided emblem of the eyrhearer; she the eyrseer's star, her power diminishing now with that paradigm's loss, soon to shrink to nothing.

"Tavern?" the man asks Mehdina, eying me with suspicion. The woman looks ready for a drink.

"No, Brogine," says Mehdina. "I'm for my cabin." Then to me says, "Offer stands," and turns away.

# 3

*Muster with Cloudchaser, Seawitch, Guardian, and Temple Door off Sabre's Point. Rendezvous with Azure Dawn and her escorts, 100 leagues northwest Cardoon. Repel all antagonism until Diamond paradigm secured again in Institute vault.*

—*Order to* Scarlet Sword, *Captain M. Taradel, PFP*

Another turn has passed, and I sail the bright new morn toward the city and my work. My hull scuds over the waves of the bay, my head spins still at yesterspan's encounter with the great Mehdina Taradel. I touched the hand that won the Princex ten islands. Wind whips the water, tangles my hair, buffets my shirt, chilling the sweat on my skin as I work the lines and tweak the tiller, wishing for Mehdina's warmth again. She was coarse with me, true, but not unkind, and her proposal... I quake at the thought. I'm not experienced in such things, but not free of thoughts on the matter either! And I can't shake the memory of her embrace.

A song fills my mind as I race for the harbour mouth, pulling in sheets, filling the sail, building speed. My father sang the shanty to me for years before his loss, and my brother sings it nowadays to mother, sisters and me.

I furl and tuck, surrender my pace. The buffeting, the feeling of the wind trying to lift me into the air, send me dancing over the sun-gilded waves, dies away. I coast in among huge ships, barques and brigs, ketches and cutters, rowing the last to my rest, tie up, and scale the ladder. Starting along the wharf towards the Institute, I see that *Scarlet Sword* is gone. Mehdina has sailed away.

I spend the span at my duties, tolerate tea and a dry biscuit at noon, drag myself through my work. Today, collating a bibliography of the aesthetician Colambina, from callow yet prolific youth to loquacious senility. My concentration often slips to the feel of Mehdina's arm around my waist, the tension in my body, the tautness of hers. Have I made a mistake? Could I pursue her, catch her? Foolish thoughts, but I long for the cooling sea breeze, agitate to be on the water again.

Where has Mehdina sailed? In defence of the remaining paradigms—the diamond and the cruciform—of course. In defence of the Princex's power, may their steps lead only to greatness. The stevedores will know. I'll ask this eve, but why do I want the knowledge? Because it's my chance to see the ocean, to spread my wings, and...and I would catch Mehdina, be held by her again.

\* \* \*

Racing beside the spit—sea to port, and under me; sand, harsh whipping grass off to starboard—I turn and squint into the raking wind. It blows so hard it might lift me from my seat, pluck me into the air, carry me above the sea. I should be sailing home, but I am chasing the *Scarlet Sword*, chasing adventure. Chasing Mehdina.

I am not a worldly young woman. I've kissed a boy behind the schoolhouse, even pulled one off behind a festival tent, although I wouldn't let him touch me. And earlier this eve, I let a rough stevedore grope me in a warehouse of baled cotton in return for her breaking naval secrecy to reveal *Scarlet Sword's* movements. I love my books, adore the work of the Institute of Antiquities, and spending my time there, but... What I felt in Mehdina's arms, the glow inside me, the intensity of her gaze. I would feel that again, yes, but not just that, also the feeling that I never want to be anywhere else in the world.

I round Sabre's Point, sail on through the narrow-seeming channel, then masts appear above the treetops and there they are, mustered offshore behind Tern Island, five tall warships: magnificent. The tide is wrong for sailing now, they'll await the morn. I glance back, but wind pushes on me, plucking at my clothes and my neck chains. I stand, lean with the roll and pitch as if born on the waves. Father would hold me up in the air, support my stomach, let me stretch like a bird. Up on the cliff above Vuntino he gave me the feel of flying. And I think Mehdina Taradel could make me feel the same.

I tack towards the *Scarlet Sword*, clear among the flotilla by her red topsail. What will Mehdina do with me? Set me adrift, or just tip me over the side? And what will I say? Have I changed my mind? I really haven't thought this through. My nerves jangle as I approach. I'm seen, even lampless as I am in the growing gloom. There's no hail. Figures above drop a ladder over the rail, clunking on *Sword's* hull as it tumbles, jerking to hang eight feet above the waterline, twitching as would a body on a rope. Three lines come down too, heavy ends splashing into the bay like corpses. They mean to bring me aboard, boat and all, leave no trace of me. In case I betray their location, I suppose. As if I would. Anyway, what will I say? "I've come to sail with you, Captain. I've come to lie with you?" The darkening air is warm, but a shiver runs through me.

I heave to, slowing, furling sails. Hulls bump gently—once, twice, almost stopped. I grasp the first line, pull it in, secure it to my thwart's starboard side, the second line to the port. I move into the bow, tie the last line to my painter with a square knot. Then I reach for the ladder. Too high, so I shinny up my mast, lean over, grasp a rung, let go, swing in the evening air to thump into *Sword's* side. Then I climb, thinking nothing but what madness this is, eager to get to the top.

Three sailors meet me, eyrseer to the fore. She looks unhappy. All else aside, the Star paradigm—source of power for all Lineca's eyrseers—has just been stolen. Small wonder she's brim-full of rancour. Can she feel her facility seeping away?

"Captain's cabin," she growls, nothing more, just turns away as strong arms grasp mine. I steal a glance to my boat swinging over the rail before I'm dragged away.

# 4

*Vermillion was a comely lass, and many sang her praise, oh,*
*She roamed across the Hundred Isles, yet barely come of age.*
*Fishing was her family's life, the nets they filled thrice daily,*
*She walked the bowsprit fearlessly, for the shoals to spy, oh.*

> *Scrub the decks.*
> > *Away with yea.*
> *Pull the lines.*
> > *Away with yea.*
> *Ship the oars.*
> > *Away with yea.*
> *Vermillion is her name, oh.*

*Her father died, her brothers too, claimed by the seas they sailed, oh,*
*Sent to the deep, while women weep, it was the risk they ran.*
*Her mother died of broken heart, her sisters lost their way, oh.*
*Vermillion's heart it turned to salt, her smile went to its grave.*

> *(Chorus)*

*Yet still she sailed and piracy, well that became her game, oh.*
*Gold tin and silver, pearls and jade, she claimed them for her own.*
*It's said she stole a captain's heart, that tale remains unspoken,*
*How could it be when truth be told Vermillion's heart is broke.*

> *(Chorus, with last line thrice)*

*—The Ballad of Vermillion, Anonymous*

"What did you expect," says Mehdina, coldly, "open arms? Dissent in the west, and now the north, makes unfriendly eyes everywhere, even at home."

"After—"

"I don't befriend guttersnipe wharf rats, nor do I take them in."

Her cabin is snug, lit dimly by two lamps hung from the ceiling, swaying slightly with the ship's gentle movement at anchor. Mehdina stands, arms akimbo, a pose I recall from the wharf, but her eyes don't appraise now, they are cold, angry eyes. "We sail on the dark tide. You must sail with us." Her eyes narrow, studying me as thoroughly as I would an obscure manuscript. "I expect treachery everywhere. You ran into *me*, remember."

"I assure you I'm loyal." I shift under her eyes. Will I be locked up, manacled in the hold? "I've served the Princex—bless their steps—for years, building the national archive, codifying antiquities from across the Hundred Isles."

"So, you're close to the paradigms then."

She does suspect me! The cabin is close, warm despite the sun's departure for the turn. A rivulet of sweat traces my spine, another tracks my chest, catches my medallion, my winged charm.

"Not only do you know their power, you know why they must return to their native land each year, not just for ceremony on our national day. Prove your loyalty." She turns away to a compact cabinet, its style consistent with the southern isles, Porta Cabria, maybe Porta Bania. These are the seas of Mehdina's youth, so the archives taught me.

"Do you want me to sing the national anthem?"

I regret my quick tongue. She snaps around from the now-open cabinet, crystal decanter in hand. "Don't sass me, girl. Prove your faithfulness to Lineca before I gift you a pretty iron bracelet for each wrist, with bangles for your ankles." She crosses the cabin with slow steps, raises her free hand to trace the line of my slick collarbone. "And a torq for your pretty neck." She bends her head close to my ear. For a breath I fear she'll kiss me, for another I want her to. "All linked with a two-foot chain." She straightens, returns to the cabinet, removes a faceted crystal glass. She pauses then removes a second glass, glinting in the lamplight. "Speak your proof now."

What can I say? All I can think is to give her specifics, our shared national truth, solid, incontrovertible. "The four paradigms, secured in the Institute of Antiquities' vault, must return to their homelands annually: one, to be exhibited during the Sun Festival as a manifestation of Lineca's nationhood; two, to demonstrate the Princex's power—may their tread illuminate the world; three, to underscore the authority of the Princex's viceroys in these distant parts; four, that each paradigm is imbued with fresh power from the land of its formation; five, returning to Cardoon that all the Princex's eyrs may recharge themselves again from the relevant paradigm, now rejuvenated."

As I spoke, Mehdina dispensed healthily into each glass, the crystal's glint transmuted by rich, amber liquor. In the cabin's heat, pouring words over my tongue, my mouth is dry. I crave the bite of what I guess is runa. Mehdina however does not proffer the second glass.

"These are facts, open to any visiting a library, or listening to their elders. I asked you to prove your loyalty. That comes from the heart, not the head."

"And runa is my reward?"

"Trust is your reward: you've not yet earned it."

From the heart, is it? And she considers me a dry scholar, bereft of passion, reserved, shrinking away from life. How dare she judge me from my work, my appearance? Her in fine leathers, with ringed fingers, ears and nose, and her scars. She who is the portrait of adventure, things I dream of as I sail the bay, wind rushing under my arms, raising up my thoughts to dream of the sea. And Mehdina, sipping her liquor, would deny me my dream? I feel already chained by her regard. I could not move if I wanted to, but I refuse to submit.

"You want passion? Well, I admire Vermillion, how about that? She is bold and brave, resourceful, dares to sail into death's jaws after her goal. She cares nothing for wealth, seeks only her heart's desire, and risks everything for it. And I, lowly bookworm as you see me, do the same. You think you know *my* passion, Mehdina Taradel? You cannot see inside me!"

She tosses back her drink then dashes the fine crystal to the floor, smashing it to shards. Her eyes blaze as she raises the second glass to her wind-chapped lips and drains that too. She steps close to me, close enough that I smell the liquor on her breath.

"I know a little something of Vermillion's dreams. Who do you think's the captain in that damned shanty? She's no hero: that's sedition. Brave of you to risk that neck of yours speaking so to the Princex's Privateer. Brave indeed. You're..." Her expression shifts to one I cannot place. She turns away.

"What?" Remembering I'm not chained yet I reach out, grab her arm, but she won't turn. Made bold by my grip on her leather, I move around to face her. Her eyes shine in the lamplight. "On the dock you said there's something about me. You asked me here, and here I stand." My heart is tripping in my chest, driving my hope that I didn't imagine her warmth, her need. "Tell me what I am."

Her lips are rapier thin. "A fool. Dreams don't survive the sea, love doesn't survive."

Her expression shreds my remaining restraint. She looks so...lost. I raise my hand to her cheek, feel that same warmth from the dockside. I whisper, "I don't believe you," and pull her mouth down onto mine.

# 5

*Azure Dawn say...all haste...sou'west. No sight... No...*
*...ight n...sign Verm... Diam...secure, for now.*

*—Message from* Azure Dawn *to* Scarlet Sword's *eyrhearer*

I am useless.

I run messages around the ship—the wind at my back pushing me forward, strong enough almost to lift me as I sprint from stern to bow—but I'm only called on when Sentina the eyrsayer is busy. Despite the Pyramid paradigm's recent loss, she still can send messages aboard *Scarlet Sword*, for now. So, maybe mine is busywork. I clear lines, scrub deck, serve food, run to whoever shouts loudest; ocean winds pushing and pulling me around the ship like a scrap of parchment. I *love* it.

And these past three turns I have indeed warmed Dina Taradel's bed, nervously at first, but now we joke about my ardour. Salt spray bursts over me as our hull hammers another wave, but the memory of Mehdina's lips on mine is of the sweet bite of runa—her breath on my neck, her warmth, her mouth...blessed ocean, I could keep running until I throw myself over the side and never notice until the sea quenched that ardour. She was right: how ignorant I was of that word's definition. Dear Goddess, her mouth; the woman has no stitch of mercy in her.

"Sail, ho! Four degrees off starboard!"

The lookout's call is loud, but whipped away by the wind. Hands—busy or idle—look to the horizon, out beyond *Guardian* and *Seawitch* that crest in the near distance. There's sail alright, and now all is action. Hands run hither and yon. Dina strides the poop deck, clenching the taffrail with strong hands that held my hips not two hours ago as I moved over her. I jog across the quarterdeck, climb the ladder to hear them.

"Lookout, is it *Azure Dawn*?" Mehdina hollers aloft, hand cupped to her mouth, head tilted back. Brogine, narrow-eyed, stands beside her listening to the wind.

"It's *Azure*," Eyrhearer Brogine confirms, before the lookout's answer.

Eyrhearer is a position of great trust. How must it feel, to be relied upon like that? No matter the might and standing of a great captain like Mehdina Taradel, an eyrhearer of low honour, or corrupted, could lead a whole flotilla to its doom. But I don't think this of Brogine. If anything, his loyalty to Mehdina outmatches any aboard. It seems his ill disposition is aimed at me, as if I've taken something from him. Even now he finds me with a malevolent gaze, calculating, suspicious.

But I'm not the one stealing paradigms. So, what are Vermillion's intentions? Ransom? Rebellion? She owns the Star and Pyramid paradigms, and must be charging eyrseers and eyrsayers of her own. Will she build a rebel fleet? At least I understand the source of Mehdina's hate: they were lovers, although I'm unclear who spurned whom. Not the best conversation for a sweat-dampened bunk at dawn.

"Eyrtaster! Marin, help the helm! Close with *Azure*, all haste. Jantino! Read the sea as best you can. We must protect *Azure* from *Vermillion* before I hunt that bitch down for the Star and Pyramid!"

Mehdina pushes away from the rail, sees me skulking atop the ladder and gives me a grin so intense my knees go weak. I will the sun to drop from the sky that I might join her—join with her—again.

"Way! Way, the ladder!"

Sentina climbs below me, and I scramble up to avoid delaying the hard-faced, blonde woman. I hurry aside as she goes to stand by her captain. She must hope that the Pyramid paradigm remains aboard *Vermillion*, that her ability may be restored in short order. Mehdina gathers her eyrs around her, all bar Marin. I look down to the quarterdeck and see them, hand on the helmsman's shoulder, face lifted to the wind, their lips moving, tongue tasting the quality of the salt that they might best guide the helmsman.

I continue to be useless, but at least Dina doesn't send me away. There's room for me to stand and watch, fingers curled around the taffrail, as we close with *Azure Dawn* on a course to turn and protect her.

"Cap'n," Brogine's tone is diamond hard as the symbol at his neck. "*Azure* reports sightin' sails. Suspects *Vermillion Lady*. Asks we make top speed."

"Damnation!" Mehdina's growl is audible across the deck. "Where in hot hell is *Azure's* escort? Helm, all speed, choke your lungs! Sentina, speak to our flotilla: do your best. Repeat three times. They'll see our course, and sight *Azure* too."

Silence falls for long, tense moments. Shouts ring across the rigging, but orders needed are precious few. Eyrtaster guides helmsman; eyrsayer mumbles to the air on the starboard side then moves to the port rail and mumbles again. Brogine listens, head bowed, now and then speaks softly to Mehdina, beneath my hearing. I watch as the ships close—realise I'm clutching mother's charm—wishing there was something *I* could do. I stand alone, wind gusting, swirling, slicing across the deck trying to lift me from my feet. Briefly, I imagine that it could. What would I do then?

A shout comes.

"Smoke! Smoke on the horizon!"

# 6

*Damn the red sky as Vermillion's banner!*

—*Common curse in the Princex's Navy*

The tension is thick as deck boards, thick as the air under the hot sun. *Azure Dawn* grows in our sight. The smoke is not hers.

"*Azure's* lost two escorts a'ready," Brogine reports.

Mehdina hangs her head for an instant. And then the vivid orange red of *Vermillion Lady's* fabled canvas is seen. It stains the horizon like fresh blood, seems to swell like the stuff of a new wound. I have sung her shanty with family around a cosy fire, or clumping boots on the stoop with my siblings. I've transcribed the logs of captains that survived encountering Vermillion—whose name is synonymous with her ship's, no one sure which came first. But to stand here and see her, see the bloody promise of those sails descending on *Azure*, on us...it is terrifying. I do not count myself a coward—no sailor would, I think, be they navigator of oceans, islands or rivers—but I fear being called on to fight. I've never lifted a sword in anger. But regardless of how useless I am in morning's calm, come the dusk of battle, a cutlass will be shoved in my hand, I'm certain.

"Helm," Mehdina roars, "take us north! Win me the windward gage and we'll have the upper hand. Our cannon will send Vermillion to hell! Sentina, tell our ships, and be clear. Hear all, hear all! Signal to form the line. Take your places, lasses, lads and lexes, for it is time for the dance of death!"

Activity on deck does indeed become a frantic ballet as sailors jump and spin to deploy *Sword's* guns. No shouted order or answer clashes with another, such is the precision of *Scarlet Sword's* drills, which have exhausted Dina's crew span after span since we left harbour.

Even at the heart of this orchestrated storm of activity, Mehdina finds an instant to glance at me, points to the deck at her feet. I nod: stay put. Does she try to protect me by this, or keep an eye on me, still lacking trust despite accepting me into her bed? At her side, Brogine's suspicion is clear, doubtless heightened by stark concern that his paradigm is under threat.

A thunderous explosion overpowers even the roar of the waves, a volley of detonations that draws all eyes forward. *Azure Dawn* lies under half a league ahead, close enough that all can see her foremast topple, rents torn in her main topgallant and main royal, canvas flapping. *Vermillion Lady* must have fired her forward guns, chain shot raking the length of her prey. She's fearsomely armed then—from what I've read about sea battles—and close enough to attack *Azure Dawn*.

"Fo'rd battery ready!" cries Mehdina, and I hear the frustration in her call. "Eyrsayer, tell our ships continue to windward, flank *Vermillion*. We will engage her. Helm, make true for *Azure Dawn*. Spare nothing." Dina leans over the front rail as cannon thunder booms again across the waves, and *Azure's* sails are ripped to shreds.

I'm no judge of sea warfare, but I've transcribed accounts of the terrible damage raking fire can do. Such damage will slow *Azure* in the water. Surely, she is at Vermillion's mercy. An unintended cry of frustration escapes my lips. Miraculously, Dina turns, steps over, grasps my shoulders and grins, a wild temper aflame in her gaze.

"This is no place for a guttersnipe wharf rat. Get below to my cabin. Take no offence, Astrid, but you'll not slow them should they reach our deck, and I'll fit you for irons before I let you board *Vermillion Lady*."

"No, most likely I could not slow them, but I will try if I have to. Perhaps I'll surprise you."

"You already have." She kisses me, short and deep. It feels special, like a last kiss. "Now get below, and don't lollygag."

Jantino is handing out blades to the other eyrs on the poop deck. I turn a last glance forward, and my heart thuds in my chest. *Azure Dawn* has leapt forward in my vision, seeming far too large now, and *Vermillion* is alongside; her crew boarding the stricken ship. Beyond them, listing badly, flame engulfing her decks and sails, the last of *Azure's* three escorts, left crippled in *Vermillion Lady's* wake. But as Vermillion's crew scour the decks of *Azure Dawn*, we bear down on her. A handful of minutes and we'll be on her. Vermillion will not escape this time without a fight.

7

I scuttle down below decks, the ladder heaving with the ship. Cut off from the wind and sun, I feel trapped. A rush and roar of sound, a cannonade from our forward guns. I feel the sway and surge as the *Scarlet Sword* drops sail, our progress slowing.

I open the door to Mehdina's cabin, step in, scan the room then move to the sword rack on the wall. She can tell me to keep my head down, but that's not the same as me complying. I detach a blade, heft it; too heavy. Find a lighter one and turn. The ship lurches, the jolt of impact betrays my feet and I fall, throw my hands out, drop the sword—elbows jarring, burning as they slide across the boards. Ribs thud and I'm down, rolling as *Sword* rolls, tumbling as it pitches, steadies.

I push up, stand. We're boarding...something, *Azure Dawn* or *Vermillion Lady*.

The cabin door flies open and there stands Brogine. My heart sinks.

He twists a cruel dagger in his fist, sneering. "What're yea doin'? After the cap'n's logbook? Some other thievin' for Vermin? You e'en had the gall to tell the cap'n you esteem that hag? How dare 'ee wound the cap'n so."

"Turncoat? Me?!" I'm no swordswoman, even if I could reach the fallen blade before he stabbed me. I have few enough skills, but language is one, and all I have to save my neck, it seems. "Why would I? The Princex—long may they st—"

"Fuck the damn Princex!" His face contorts. "Their vani'y lost us two paradigms, prob'ly three now. How could they know wha's like to lose yer power, that what makes 'ee something? An' all 'cause of their pridefulness,

196 Robin C.M. Duncan

and them cronies that caw and cajole their ear? To hell with 'em, and demons o' hell take you, traitor."

I'm lost. Brogine moves forward, crouching to strike. There is no way out. Only one escape. I grab Dina's decanter and heave it at the windows spanning the ship's stern. The heavy crystal smashes a hole and I launch myself after it, leaping headlong, arms folded across my face.

Smashing, cutting, tearing, cold, buffeting.

I point my arms in a dive and fall, yes, but slower than I should, spearing down *across* the water, away from the ship. No! I don't want that. *Do something!* I angle my arms, miming a turn...

And I, bank, across, the horizon...

Although still descending.

So, what—?

I'm...flying?

The sea comes up fast and hits me in the face.

# 8

*Antiquities' experimentation into eyrs' power, between renewals with their respective paradigms in our Cardoon vault, indicates duration of power diminishing disproportionately quickly with distance from the source. The corollary also appears to be true; that continued paradigm exposure at close range extends an eyr's duration of power and maximum threshold.*

*—Academician Hankani, paper to the Convocation of Institutes*

Brine chokes me, burns into fresh lacerations on my arms as I'm tugged and thrust by the ocean, too vast a thing to comprehend. My back aches, and I cannot breathe.

I surface, gasping, coughing, flap my hands, splash about, panicked, trying to reorient myself. Pain rips the length of my forearms. The sting is excruciating, but I manage to turn about.

A huge ship looms over me, but the surging waves carry me away. Two of the stern gallery windows are broken. *Scarlet Sword. Mehdina!* Is she aboard *Vermillion Lady* by now, or have they met aboard *Azure Dawn*?

"Mehdina!"

I swim against the ocean's surge, aiming for long, steady strokes: do not panic, do not fight the sea. Resist it. And in this, I have the advantage my mother was blessed with until recent years: a buoyancy facilitating my propulsion through the water. I close on the ship, but there is no way up here on *Sword's* starboard side. So now I must toil around the stern, arms aching, heavy as iron bars, feet dragging like stones. I battle on, finally gain the port side.

The great ships grind against each other, boards creaking and groaning. *Azure Dawn* and *Scarlet Sword* are bound together. Lines criss-cross the slivers of sky where the hulls diverge, leaving talons of sunlight, fangs of brightness. Battle must be joined on *Azure's* decks, even as she lists to port, away from the *Sword*, shipping water somewhere. Still, bodies jump and swing across those sharp spaces. Distant cries rend the air: anger and injury, fury and death, violent rage. If *Azure Dawn* is sinking, Dina must cut *Sword* free or risk the *Sword* being dragged over, pulled into the deep. And what of Vermillion? Are the two once-lovers even now crossing swords on *Azure's* canting deck?

In the gap between the hulls that closes then drifts open like pack ice, several lines hacked away by desperate defenders hang down towards the waterline. I swim into the shifting zone where bad luck could crush me. What in the Goddess's name am I doing? This is madness. How can I do more than win the deck only to provide fodder for the enemy's flashing blades? What would Acady Hankani think? I laugh, and receive a mouthful of brine for my brazenness. Bracing against exhaustion, I strike forward.

I haul myself up with aching arms, but it's easier than I have any right to expect, as if I am buoyed up by the sea, as if the wind that gusts and buffets through this wooden defile lifts me up. Does this relate to my gliding, *flying*, when I dove from the ship? Even though my arms cry with pain as if the rope will wrench them from their sockets, the climb is possible, even...easy. I can't explain it. And what will I do on reaching the top? Find Dina, of course, the rest will be as it may.

As I twist above the broiling sea in this timbered cleft, I realise I do not know to which vessel I'm tethered. More than halfway up, I'll discover soon enough. Then the question is answered for me. Without warning, I'm swung left and bash into *Azure Dawn's* lurching hull as it leans away from *Sword* towards the sea, its canting irreversible. The ship I'm tied to is capsizing.

For an instant this is favourable. I plant my feet, lean away from the hull, pulling my lifeline taught, and walk upward. But *Azure Dawn* continues to tip, cries fill the air, yells of anger, panic, desperation. Some bodies try to jump the gap back to *Scarlet Sword*, fail, fall past me, screaming.

A lone figure clambers to stand on *Azure's* rail. Mehdina, sabre held high, cutting down at the lines still tying *Sword* to capsizing *Azure*. Then a shot from *Vermillion* twists her backwards, a finned crossbow quarrel sprouting from her shoulder, and the captain falls into the maw of death.

*No!* Not while I breathe!

I run across the sloping hull, clinging to my taught line, arms screaming for release or death, pumping my leaden legs. The wind catches my back, plucks at my clothes, propels me forward. Just as my path diverges from Dina's fall, I release the rope.

*Joy of the air, I embrace thee.*

I spread my arms and drop into the darkness.

# 9

In the gloom I see Dina's falling shape below. Black against the dark, surging water, she drops into the narrowing cleft between the two hulls. Our paths drift apart, so I angle aching arms, sweeping them back like a diving falcon, and shoot straight at her. I close quickly, but still she hits *Azure's* bulk before I reach her, slides, scraping on its barnacle-crusted hull as if keelhauled by her own ambition. For surely her aim of saving the paradigm is gone.

I throw out my arms, muscles screaming in pain. Somehow, surging wind whistling up from the churning water slows me. *Scarlet Sword* leans down towards the capsizing *Azure Dawn* as if unwilling to relinquish hold on her sister ship. But lines snap, or more likely are cut by frantic sailors. Suddenly, *Sword* rolls back and away from us, righting herself in a surge of water. So released, *Azure* completes her death spin, and Dina lies still on the upturned hull as I land hard beside her, haul her up towards *Azure's* emerging keel. Waves swat at us, trying to wash us away, water running red around us.

From above, yells of fury rain down. I clutch Dina to me. Her blood stains my clothes. Air trapped in *Azure's* hold must keep her afloat, but that won't last. Sharks and worse will sniff out Dina's wound. We must get out of the shallow water sluicing over the hull.

At a loud cheer, I glance up to see red-sailed *Vermillion Lady* departing north, crew lining her rails. Water bubbles around our timber island. *Azure's* hull shakes as trapped air begins to escape. *Scarlet Sword* drifts away from us, trimming sail. Lines are thrown, but cannot bridge the widening gap, even weighted grapnels. *Sword* is lowering tenders, but they will not launch and row the distance in time, for the first dark fins appear, seeming as tall as me. They patrol the water between us and, where sharks come, so lurk bigger, older things. One or other will have us before long.

What hope? A boat bobs fifty yards away, one of *Azure's* tenders cut loose in the fight. Dark shapes glide between us and the craft, one's dorsal and tail fins must be twenty feet apart. *Azure's* hull groans beneath us and water rises to our shins. Mehdina's blood slicks the water.

There is only one chance now, to believe in myself, my newfound ability.

But, dare I believe so completely in something I don't understand, what I did—impossibly—only minutes before? Now, all I have is the belief that, today, I flew. That for years sailing Cardoon Bay the feeling of the wind trying to lift me up was real. I must stake our lives on this wild belief as hungry mouths close in.

With some help from her, I wrestle Dina to her feet.

"I must reach that boat, bring it back. At least we'll have a chance."

She regards me with dull eyes, nods.

Air bitter with salt, monstrous shapes gliding closer, I run, splashing forward, fling out my arms and dive into the air. *Goddess preserve us.*

Wind whips beneath me, buoys me up, carries me out over the heaving water. A great maw as wide as my outstretched arm breaks the surface, rears and snaps at me. I smell the monster's foetid breath before it falls back under the waves. The air carries me across the water. I bank towards the boat. Impossible. *Impossible!* Sailors hoot and call as I lean to port and bank down, sliding through the wind towards the bobbing boat. Without time to think I curl in my limbs and drop into the boat, land hard, send it rocking. I shout in pain.

The boat is holed, gunwale and stern splintered in places. Without time to think—back and limbs aching, gasping for breath—I grab the painter and jump into the air towards Mehdina.

*Sword's* crew roar me on. Nothing is visible of *Azure* now. Mehdina remains standing on the just submerged hull, water to her knees, fins closing in. As I fly to her, dragging the boat with me, a dark monster hurls itself up, beaching on the hidden hull, thrashing, snapping at Dina. She staggers back, falls, pushes up. I'm losing momentum as I reach her. The thrashing creature slips back into the sea to circle with the rest. Finally, Dina drags herself aboard as I tumble into the boat with her.

One more flight back to the *Sword.* We're going to make it.

Then I must think how to answer the questions that will come.

# 10

The uproar in the capital was something to behold. Royal guards met the *Scarlet Sword* and took Mehdina, her eyrs, and me—*Me!*—to an audience with the Princex.

Their lilting voice carried an edge of steel beneath the molten gold, an edge that echoed in the marble hall, took on a keening spite. Mehdina had failed them, failed all Lineca. Never had such a thing happened in decades of nationhood. I feared that I would be next to endure their scrutiny, but so irate was the Princex that all were then dismissed.

Now Mehdina would sail with all available ships to protect the fourth paradigm, the Cruciform. I, however, was taken to the Principal Academician, an austere man, spare and thin. His robes appeared as heavy as his body. His gaggle of vice academicians poked and prodded me, questioned me for eight long spans—waking me early, talking late into the eve—about the happenings during our battle with Vermillion. What had I done? How had I done it? I must do it again. Tests would be undertaken. I must be kept under guard, light span and dark turn. At least they did not deny me tidings of the outside world, and it lifted my heart to hear that Mehdina successfully escorted the Cruciform paradigm back to Cardoon, and Antiquities' vault.

Finally, with the promise of more testing and observation in future, the Principal Academician ordered an end to my "academic confinement." Descending Antiquities' marble steps, I look a state, clothes dirty and ripped. I favour my left leg, and my arms still ache, despite my wounds being treated.

Mehdina waits across the street, leaning on a stone column at the entrance to the Institute of Justice. Seeing me, she snaps erect and strides forward—weaving between walkers, carts, horses—to reach me at the foot of the steps. Without a word she folds me into her arms, hugs me until my wounds sting. The pain is glorious, it drenches me in feeling after the stultifying numbness of academic inquisition. Her warmth banishes the air's slight chill. She leans back, frames my face with her hands, kisses me deeply, and I melt into her. Tears wet my cheeks. Doubtless Mehdina Taradel does not cry. Is she still the Princex's Foremost Privateer? It matters nothing to me.

"What happened?" she asks.

I place a finger on her lips, which she kisses.

"Take me to your room," is all I say.

She leads me away, arm around my waist, unwilling to let me go. I am not to be stolen away from her as other things have of late.

The breeze picks up, carrying spots of rain. As we turn into Port Avenue, home of the Institute of Antiquities. The wind strengthens, grey clouds mask the sun, droplets increase. Then, the shower overtakes us. Rain tumbles from the sky, stains the cobbles, soaks us. Only a shower. I tilt my head to the sky and laugh. Dina's smile is rueful.

"We're drenched!" she calls.

"Shelter me then," I reply: a challenge, an invitation.

She pulls me through running people into a dimly recessed doorway, presses me onto the door, covers my mouth with hers. Her warmth swamps me. I am wet outside and in. Heavy rain patters around us. The scent of damp timber and spattered dust weights the air. Dina's wet hands slip under my shirt, curve up my back as she kisses my neck.

"Astrid, we need to get you out of these wet things," she mumbles. Her hands slip down, squeeze past my belt. I gasp, claw at her leather-clad back.

People rush past in the downpour, oblivious to our passion. A figure emerges on the Institute steps, bowed against the rain, wearing the dark green velvet of an academician.

"Oh, Dina. Oh, Goddess, stop. Stop." I make no effort to restrain her.

The grey-hair has snatched up her hood, but I know it's Acady Hankani. I can tell by the grey plait protruding from her hood. She sticks a fist inside her cloak to stow some accessory, and moves down the steps.

Her grey plait—

"Dina, stop." I beat on her back, but she grips my waist like I'm goading her. "Mehdina," I hiss, "something's wrong!"

Now she raises her head, rain sheening her face, short hair matted.

"Look over your shoulder, quick: the grey-hair making for Dock Street."

"Sprightly."

"Hankani cut her plait three weeks ago."

"Not her then."

"But it's meant to be her. And she took something."

"Astrid—"

I'm already moving.

"Thief! Guards!" Another figure atop the Institute steps, frantic. Soldiers burst past him, looking about.

204   Robin C.M. Duncan

I grab Dina's arm, dragging her after me. "Tie me to the bed for a week if it's not Vermillion." I gasp as my wounds pull tight with the strain, release her, turn, and run for the docks.

"That's not how forfeits work!" Dina shouts after me as I rush headlong through the rain.

How? How could Vermillion—it *must* be her—have the temerity to walk into the Institute of Antiquities? How desperate must she be to conclude her quest, and what does she hope to achieve? It hardly matters as my shoes pound cobbles, rain lashing my face, pasting my clothes to me. At least fewer people walk the streets and it's easier to track my quarry. Vermillion runs ahead. At a corner she casts off the academician's dark cloak, tosses a wig aside, pulls a stack of crates over blocking the way between wagon and wall, forcing me to scramble over.

I land hard, pain lancing through my knee, and I slip, sprawl across the cobbles, wounds torn open afresh and bleeding through my shirt. Dina leaps over me and—even as I spring up—disappears around the corner after Vermillion. I hear Dina though, buildings reflecting her cry: "Stop and fight, you bitch!"

I'm up and running, boiling blood masking my pain. Dock Street bends into Paradigm Square—ironic—then out again, continuing downhill to the harbour. I pound over the stones, rain lashing, knee nagging me to stop. That I will not do, but I do try to think ahead. Vermillion *is* making for the harbour. She must have a boat waiting, probably cast off, probably at a point close to the harbour mouth. She's canny, she'll have oarsmen at the ready. To get a clear run at the harbour mouth they'd be best positioned on Granary Wharf.

As I leave Paradigm Square, I veer left into Scrubbers' Lane. All the washing baskets and lines are pulled in out of the rain, making passage easier. At the end I lunge across Victory Boulevard, a shorter route to the western end of

Granary Wharf. A gamble, and likely a call to use my power. It's been many spans. Can I still fly?

I pass beneath the palms lining the boulevard. The rain is lessening. Still, the road dust has turned to a thin layer of mush, but I'm into Cleaver's Way now, and the surface has fared better. I'm puffing hard. Has Dina caught the thief? I'd love to be wasting my time. I know almost nothing about Vermillion, thanks to Dina's obduracy.

Ahead, I see the first warehouse and shoot into the gap behind it—a dark, dank alley, mossy wall rearing to my left, timber to my right evoking an earlier nightmare. The wrong encounter now will finish my chase, perhaps for good, but hopefully the rain has kept the footpads indoors.

I burst out onto the wharf. Almost the entire harbour lies to my right, only the seawall ahead of me.

There's Dina! I'm just in time to see her dive into the harbour. Clearly, Vermillion's ahead of her, but she's still on the trail. I run out along the ancient stone, weaving around creels, pots and nets. Sure enough, there's a gig in the harbour, eight oars making good towards the harbour mouth, two swimmers in the water. Vermillion's thirty yards from the gig, on course to meet the boat. Dina's three dozen yards behind. She will not reach Vermillion in time.

I run along the seawall, fearful of sliding on a hundred years of dried and wetted slime, but more scared of what will happen to Dina if the last paradigm is lost. I angle closer to the edge. No time to evaluate, postulate or deduce. I plant my feet and dive over.

At first, I fall, then a gust of salt-rimed air lifts me up. *Goddess, it still works.* I aim my body at Vermillion. She's being pulled onboard the gig. She's on, and Dina well short. The tillerman calls the beat, and oars cut water. The gig leaps forward, sprinting for the open sea. One head turns, sees me, gapes; then another, open-mouthed as I close in. Vermillion kneels upright, turns, stares. My outstretched hands hit her square on the shoulders, and we tumble into the water.

I'm twisted, sinking, back first, swimming upwards. I fear she'll drown me. The water chills my bones as I flail to the surface. Vermillion breaches. Apart from the death glare, her appearance is unremarkable. Her slick hair is indeed red. She swims for me, scything the water like a shark. A blade appears in her hand then she cuts to the side towards the gig. I must grab her, even though she'll stab me. She can't escape with the last paradigm, undermining all order in Lineca. I lunge at her. She sweeps her blade up in a spray of water, but I will have her before the blow falls.

Then Dina rams into my legs, hauling me aside, pulling me back. Vermillion's blade stabs air, plunges into water.

"Dina! Let me go! I can stop her."

"The cost is too high." Mehdina's strength is greater than mine. I thrash to keep my head up and see Vermillion clamber into the gig. Her crew bend their backs and make good speed out of the harbour towards escape even as loyal boats give chase.

Vermillion turns, looks at me. No, past me, at Dina, and shouts, "You broke my heart, Mehdina, so I will break yours!"

# 11

In the furore of the docks—soldiers herding, question-ing, searching—Dina and I swim between hulls, under hawsers, to a quieter spot and climb a ladder into the lea of the last warehouse. Despite its shelter from the wind, the building's shadow is cold. Mehdina starts to explain, but I'm too livid to listen. I storm away down the alley that brought me to this debacle.

In my quivering fury, I don't even know where I'm going, just raging through blank streets with Mehdina behind me. She has ceased her protests, but I feel her anger simmering, vibrating in the air as we march—in unspoken agreement—towards her room at the old inn.

I pace through the quiet common room, stale smoke and tonight's fish stew unable to deflect me. I stamp upstairs but—frustration upon frustration—must await Mehdina to unlock the door. She closes it behind us with determined gentleness, as I round on her.

"What were you *thinking*? I had her!"

"She would have—"

"Stabbed me? What does that matter? I had her!"

"Astrid, shh. Calm yourself and think. Are you not a guttersnipe and a *scholar*?"

"Don't you guttersnipe me. What have you *done?* Vermillion has all four paradigms. The eyrs' powers will fade, Apanato's influence at sea will wane, the far islands will rebel: they've started already. Our nation is falling *apart!* Lineca will fall into conflict, civil war—a feeding frenzy for every privateer, buccaneer, brigand and swashbuckler afloat. Congratulations, *Captain*. All for love of Vermillion? Just like the shanty. Because that's the root of your hatred, is it not?" I round on her again. "I'm not blind, Mehdina. I'm not *so* innocent, not that much the sheltered academic. I'm right, aren't I? You stopped me for love of Vermillion."

Mehdina hangs her head. "No, Astrid. It was for love of you," she says quietly, and my heart clenches.

"You *cannot* lay this at my feet, Dina, you *must not*. How can I live with that, to be placed above a nation?"

She raises her head, eyes burning with tears, yes, but anger too rages there. She steps towards me, runs a hand over her short, wet hair.

"You're not thinking, Astrid. Get over your righteous anger and apply that mind of yours. You can glide over the sea, you can...fly, dear Goddess. You are gifted, you numbskull! Gifted as no one has ever seen. Shall we call you eyrglider, eyrsoarer? And what else does that mean?"

I stand before her, dripping, clothes torn, hair tangled, bedraggled, tired and sore. I am fit to drop, exhausted beyond measure. All I want to do is fall into her arms, fall into bed with her and sleep. Only anger keeps me standing. My thoughts are turgid, but slowly, I get there.

"A fifth paradigm. But I've never journeyed away from the city, so...it lives here, in Cardoon."

Dina reaches forward, unbuttons my shirt, pulls it open. Her hand moves to my hip, traces my waist, my aching ribs, to my chest, not eschewing the chance to caress my breast—a touch I lean into—before she lifts my mother's charm from where it hangs, grimed and bloody, on my skin. A silver charm in the shape of a wing.

"I loved Vermillion," she whispers, "but rejected her years ago. I never loved another until you, you strange and wondrous girl. Nations rise and fall, but we remain, and must live with what we have, fight for it. I would fight for you, Astrid."

I push into her arms, kiss her, start dragging at her buckles and belts as we tumble onto the bed. And yet we barely manage to undress each other before we are asleep.

# 12

I think I must have slept for spans when Dina wakens me. Flickers of ridiculous dreams flit behind my eyelids as they unglue themselves. In her room, sunlight describes bright lines at the curtains' edge. I smell bacon, egg, and fresh-baked bread, buttered.

The sight of Dina in a flowing, diaphanous gown is startling, tantalising. She walks to the bed, sits, kisses me then strokes my face. "Time to wake." She wrinkles her nose. "And to bathe. We have a span before we meet the Princex to explain how we will recapture the paradigms from Vermillion, and I cannot stand before them and say I spent the whole time making love to *you*."

She smiles, and I know I belong to her, and she to me, and that we will never stop fighting to protect what we have won. That if only we fight, the brigands of this world will never win.

"And how, Captain, do you intend to recapture four paradigms from the foremost rebel in the land?" I tilt my head and raise an eyebrow.

Mehdina chuckles. "Why, the same way she took them from us, of course."

"The Vermillion Lady" is Robin's third foray into publication after his stories in *Distant Gardens* (2021), and his first novel *The Mandroid Murders* (2022). Presently, he is editing Quirk & Moth Book 2, *The Carborundum Conundrum*, and working on a story for an anthology due out in the coming months. Details and bloggishness at **robincmduncan.com**, twitting **@ROBINSKL**

# Testing the Waters

Vanessa Ricci-Thode

Sapphic Representation: Lesbian, Bisexual, Polyamory

Heat Level: Low

Content Warnings: Coarse Language, Pregnancy in Danger, PTSD, Anxiety

Tollar could make water do anything she wanted, and right now she wanted it to talk to her. Specifically, she wanted it to tell her where to find land. Sometimes water had other ideas. The driving rain was very nearly like flying through a lake, but scattered enough Tollar couldn't get a sense of anything in or beyond the storm. She was going to have to jump.

But maybe she should get the dragon to fly a little closer to the surface.

Oh, and she should probably tell Beenala.

"Bale," she called over the rush of wind to get the dragon's attention. Tollar sat between the tall spikes on Bale's neck behind her carriage-sized head. Despite not being full grown, she was already over two hundred paces long, with a glossy black body streaked with amethyst and matching wing membranes and spiky bits. "Take us in closer to the ocean."

Bale screeched out—presumably to let the other dragon, Shell, know about the course change. Tollar sought the handholds on the thick leather straps crisscrossing Bale's body as she climbed down the dragon to the gondola—those very straps held it firm against Bale's underside—where Beenala waited. Her progress was slowed by the way her stomach kept flip-flopping, making her head spin.

She'd never hear the end of it from Beenala if she fell off the dragon again.

And if they didn't get the dragons to land and a night's rest soon, they were going to fall out of the air. So, she went carefully, putting her focus into her footing and using magic to remove water and dry the rain-slicked handholds before grabbing the next one. But the itch between her shoulder blades wanted her to jump. Just aim herself at the gondola and let her reflexes do the rest. Even if she missed, it wasn't like the ocean could hurt her. But Beenala would be beside herself all the same, and Tollar loathed to be the reason her dearest worried.

When Tollar finally reached the dragon's underbelly, she wasn't surprised to see Beenala with her face pressed against one of the gondola's portholes, waiting for her. Beenala was a round, sturdy woman and competent on her feet when she had solid ground beneath her, but she wasn't much of a climber and stayed in the gondola while the dragon was in flight.

"Where are we? Did you see anything?" Beenala asked as Tollar climbed in and crawled over to her sleep mat to sit, wishing it had been practical for the gondola to be tall enough to stand in.

It was more like a hanging tent than anything, mostly made of magicked leather to strengthen it against the elements, with netting and pockets for cargo. It was comfortable for two, could fit three in a pinch, which it had a couple times this trip, though Croves was large enough he was almost two on his own. At least when they were flying, he stayed in his travel harness with Shell.

"Still nothing. I'm going to have to go in the water. Sorry, Bee."

Beenala's epicanthic rich brown eyes widened, and she anxiously gripped the hem of her shirt, twisting it before Tollar laid her hands over Beenala's to still them. Beenala's small plump hands were warm, her tawny skin pale next to Tollar's long and slender dark brown fingers, with a blue tinge Tollar's mother always called "corpsely" when she was feeling uncharitable, which she often was. Beenala, on the other hand, said Tollar's undertones reminded her of a cenote, something she was fond of mentioning whenever she traced her fingers along Tollar's many warrior tattoos. She frequently asked for the story behind the little white ones meant to represent the people Tollar had helped, including the stripes of rank lines on her cheeks that put her in charge.

"It will be okay."

"But your magic—"

"I can still do the basics." Tollar waved a hand. She was an anomaly of a wizard—part water demon, giving her the blue hue, watery silver irises and unparalleled power—so for her, even the basics were still extensive. Calling them demons and all the negative connotations the word carried never sat well with her, not when they were an elemental force no more positive or negative than a windy day.

The dragon's descent levelled, and Tollar heard the crash of waves over the rain. She wanted to reassure Beenala some more, but they really needed to find land before the dragons were too exhausted to fly, should have landed at least an hour ago. They were losing the light.

So Tollar kissed the back of Beenala's hand and went to the door. Bale glided in a wind-buffeted circle twenty feet from the tops of the highest waves. The storm churned everything up. Tollar wanted to calm it. Instead, she gave Beenala a wave and dived straight out the door, slicing through the surface cleanly and letting herself sink beneath the worst of the churn.

If her stomach would settle for one cursed minute, she could have just stood on the waves to see what she needed. She knew how much Beenala hated it when Tollar disappeared into the depths.

She exhaled silvery bubbles—watching them drift to the surface while her long dark braid floated after them—and waved her hands in front of her face to focus the magic and filter out the salt, giving her something clean to breathe. The water was warm and smooth, but her lungs still ached from the swamp lung she'd had over the summer.

Tollar relaxed into the water's embrace, cradled like the pair of babies growing in her womb, still only the size of beans. Of course, once she decided to put adventuring on hiatus and settle down with Beenala, the adventure would come looking for her. Little more than a week after her midwife confirmed the pregnancy, the summons had come for Bale to go meet her kin in the dragon city for her official naming ceremony. That was why they were flying these cursed dragons *now*, in this monster of an ocean storm, testing the dragons' limits. Especially Bale who'd never gone so far. The first four days of their ten-day journey had been almost leisurely, but there was only one narrow strip of islands to land on for this two-day ocean crossing. If they didn't find land soon, they'd never make it.

She tried to push the worry away, her thoughts a soggy mess since just before she found out about the twins. Wild hormones and her changing body left her abilities in flux. She hated the doubt that came with it.

Tollar closed her eyes and floated, letting her senses drift out into the ocean around her, like her skin had become porous, one with the water, so that she sensed her surroundings like moving through a room in the dark. But she wasn't moving, her magic was. Out and out. Surely the dragons hadn't been blown that far off course?

But Tollar kept expanding the radius of what she felt, stretching it alarmingly far, but the largest thing her magic found was a pod of whales. No land.

*Oh shit.*

She took a deep breath and held it, not able to continue sparing even a drop of focus to filtering the salt from the water, and pushed her senses further yet. And finally— finally!—off to the northwest, the water met resistance, the currents carrying her awareness broke around something solid.

Mostly solid.

*Oh shit.*

She pulled her circle of attention in, directing all of it toward the north, barely aware of her body rolling in that direction as she faced the far-off land and its strange liquid shores that were probably lava. There was a tight cluster of small islands. Around each, the ocean boiled and rose in clouds of vapour.

Tollar sighed, bubbles rising up around her face, and withdrew her awareness. As she did, something brushed against her magic, something large slicing through the water just offshore, and then she was back in herself, clearing the salt for one last breath of ocean before she propelled herself to the surface, rising to stand on top of the waves.

Rolling waves, her stomach lurching with them, her head swimming. She lost focus and sank up to her knees before she pushed solid water under her feet, a whole rising column of water fully under her control, to bring her away from the dizzying tumult and up where it would be easier for Bale to find her again. Tollar stood on the water and stared northward, pondering how to break the news to Beenala—the only land anywhere near them was a volcano.

With her focus divided, the column wobbled. Tollar's arms shot out at her sides for balance, and she reasserted her will over the water, holding it still until Bale looped around and scooped her up.

"You found it?" Bale asked.

"It's not the island we were looking for, and you're not going to like it. Head north and let Shell know he needs to bring Croves to us, we have a problem."

Bale deposited Tollar between spikes on the back of her long neck, where the handholds began, and pitched upward, calling out for Shell. Tollar began the lengthy climb down the dragon, contemplating whether to wait up top for Croves, or go reassure Beenala. She was slow enough that the decision made itself when Shell's sea-green form appeared out of the stormy gloom and set Croves down between Bale's wings. Tollar was only at the junction on Bale's shoulders. There were no handholds down Bale's back, but at least she was wide enough that it was unlikely tripping would result in falling entirely off the dragon.

Croves still came swiftly across Bale's back to meet Tollar. He was fast for his size, like the dragons. He was two handspans taller than her and easily twice her weight, a solid man with scarred olive skin, wild black hair streaked with silver and one hard dark eye, the other covered by a patch. She resented how sure-footed he was, missed the days—pre-pregnancy—when clambering across a dragon's back mid-flight was as easy as walking down a garden path. But her head spun, and her stomach lurched with each move Bale made.

She held onto one of the tall spikes and waited.

Croves approached with furrowed brows and took her other hand. "Should ye really be climbing around in yer condition?"

Tollar rolled her eyes. "You act like they just invented babies and it's not a thing we've been doing for as long as there's been people."

He huffed. "All right, fine. Have it yer way."

She definitely would. And she certainly hoped this overprotective streak of his would fizzle out sooner rather than later. He was a little too invested in her actions for someone who'd done nothing more than make a contribution to the spell her midwife had taught her.

"Do dragons float?" Tollar asked. "Could they sleep on the water?"

"Have we gone that far off course?"

"We're a long way from where we should be. I'm not actually sure where we are. But we don't have good options. Are dragons floating in their sleep one of them?"

Croves blinked a lot, and not because of the wind and rain in his eye. He ran a meaty hand over his coarse beard.

"Nah, I don't know if Bale will know how. And we'll have no way to unstrap the gondola without land. Even then, there's beasts in the ocean big enough to eat a grown dragon, never mind a wee thing like Bale."

"I'm bigger than Shell!" Bale protested.

"Aye, my mistake." Croves shook his head and Tollar snickered.

"So, if the dragons can't float all night, we'll be landing on a volcano. It's the only thing within range."

Even above the rush of wind and hammering rain, Tollar heard Croves sigh. The wind gusted from the opposite direction, trying to take her off balance, until Croves held out his hand, using some aeromancy to part the wind around them.

"Well, the lava won't hurt the dragons unless it's deep enough to drown 'em."

"It's still a terrible option."

"Aye, have ye told Bee?"

"She's not going to like it."

"*I* don't like it."

"Well, yes, but you know how her anxiety gets when plans change."

"Aye, but she can work earth and fire, and lava's really just both."

Tollar turned and faced the way they were headed. Croves knew as well as she did how Beenala reacted to danger. They could hope the archipelago had a rocky spot big enough for the dragons to land, but they needed to be ready if it didn't. Beenala especially needed time to adjust and consider their situation if she was going to be of help.

"All right, but you've got to come help me break the news to her."

"Aye, it's best we stick together till we know what we face."

Croves followed her down Bale's side to the gondola, Beenala waiting for them with her face pressed to the porthole. Her entire face pinched up like she'd eaten a sour toad when she spotted Croves climbing along behind Tollar.

"Are we almost there?" Beenala's voice was high and tight.

Tollar wanted to lie to her, tell her it was all fine. Beenala deserved better of course.

"It's about two hours."

"You said we were almost there."

"We should have been. I don't know where we are now."

Croves pulled out his oiled map while Tollar explained their best option.

"We're going to land on a volcano!?"

"More like the side of one." Tollar shrugged, wishing there was room for her to get up and move around. Hadn't missed dry land so much in her entire life.

"I think this is where we're headed." Croves pointed to a cluster of little dots on the map. If he was right, they were a little farther north and much farther west than they should be.

"But it's a volcano."

"Yes, and you're a pyromancer." Tollar's smile softened and she took Beenala's hands. "There will probably be some spots to land, and if not, you can help me cool us a patch. I'll bring up a wave, you put out the fires, it'll be a snap."

"I've never even seen a volcano, Tollar."

"Dragonfire is much scarier, and you stopped that with no problems. I know you can do this."

"I wasn't expecting to do any sort of magic on this trip, just come along to see the dragon city. You said it wouldn't be an adventure this time."

Croves smiled and Tollar chuckled. "There's no travelling without a bit of adventure."

* * *

"That's a lot of lava," Beenala whispered.

It really was.

Tollar closed her eyes and leaned back while Bale and Shell continued circling the archipelago. This wasn't the worst-case scenario, there'd been a couple of dark patches. Neither big enough for an entire dragon—never mind two—but it was a start.

"Tollar, what do we do?" Beenala's voice was still barely a whisper.

Tollar took her hands and found a smile. What *would* they do? It had seemed so easy earlier when Tollar expected there'd be somewhere for at least one of the dragons to land. Shell had already helped Bale glide, and the younger dragon didn't have much left in her. She needed rest. Needed it soon, before she fell straight out of the sky.

What they needed to do would take several steps and the five of them would have to work together. Grasping that starting place was like catching rain with a net. The seasickness was bad enough, but this thing where Tollar's thoughts waded through slush was her least favourite part of being pregnant. The midwife assured her it wouldn't last, and her brother Jarku hadn't dealt with it for long when he was pregnant, but Tollar needed those clear thoughts now.

"Tired," Bale called.

"Shit," Tollar hissed.

"You said you could float her," Beenala said. "You can, can't you?"

Well, there was a starting place. She didn't like it, remembering what Croves had said about beasts large enough to eat dragons, but they were out of options.

Tollar pushed out the door and scaled the dragon. "Head for the water, I'll make you a barge."

Bale banked away from the islands, some of which were little more than lava bubbling at the surface. Tollar stopped and gripped the handholds, her eyes closed against the dizziness the motion created. It took longer to pass than she'd have liked. Bale was nearly on the water, though clear of where it hissed and boiled when it met the earth's fire.

With the storm behind them and the water relatively calm, especially farther from shore, it didn't take as much of Tollar's focus to solidify a large sheet of water, like ice without the cold, for Bale to land on.

Tollar leapt down, tempted to lie on the surface, and grateful to be somewhere solid and still for a moment. A few more deep breaths and the last of the nausea passed.

She looked up at Bale's dark underbelly, but the distant lava didn't provide enough light to see the gondola. Should they unhook it now? Could they all sleep on Tollar's water island for the night? In the past, it had been so taxing to maintain something similar in her sleep, that she didn't actually sleep much. Now, she didn't trust her changing body to handle the challenge. It was as likely as not she'd fall all the way asleep and spill them all into the ocean.

"Now what?" Beenala called, light appearing as she brought her lantern to the door.

"Ye can't keep this up all night," Croves said.

"I can keep it steady for long enough. Did you see anywhere that looked easy to cool into rock?"

"Aye, there was the leeside of the biggest cone."

"Can Shell check to make sure it's solid and not a thin crust?"

Shell roared nearby, close enough to have heard her, though she couldn't get a line of sight on him until he was back near the islands, lit up by the lava.

"All right, once we have a spot, I can bring a wave of super-cooled water—"

The whole water island shook, impact vibrating up through Tollar's feet, and she stumbled but kept control.

"What the rotting moons was that!" Beenala shouted.

Tollar felt cold as she bent down and pressed her fingertips into the water, extending her senses like the ocean currents were the longest of fingernails. Something moved under the surface, something larger than any dragoness. Too large to see all at once and little more than a blur in the dark waters. Tollar hadn't thought a creature so large could exist. She had a fleeting moment to wonder what it ate before it battered against the underside of her water island, giving her another jolt.

Right.

Tollar kept the water from bouncing around with each hit. If the water creature was smart, that probably wouldn't hold it long. She extended the size of her water island to prevent the creature coming up over the side at them. That should give them some time. Not time to get comfortable, but maybe they could sort out the lava situation.

Shell was on his way back, screeching out a battle cry and spitting dragonfire at the water.

"Why is he...?"

Croves and Beenala both shouted something at the same time, and she heard neither of them. A cold brick of dread dropped into her gut when she saw the ripples in the water illuminated by Shell's fire.

It looked like there were three of these beasts.

Tollar pushed more water under her little island, raising it up, hoping these creatures couldn't jump. Or at least not too high.

But her efforts met resistance and the solid platform wobbled, returning to liquid despite her efforts.

"Bale, go! Fly!"

Tollar shot a spout of water at Bale's underside to give her lift. Bale snatched Tollar off the surface just as Croves magicked a solid gust under her wings. And then Shell was there, helping drag Bale further into the air.

Tollar startled when a long filament of water whipped out straight for them. She knocked it off course, but with some effort, her magic met with resistance again. Did the beast have magic of its own? She'd never heard of such a thing.

"Tired," Bale protested. "Shell is tired too. He says most of the biggest island is soft."

"As long as it's not deep, Croves said it won't hurt you."

The biggest island now sported glowing footprints on the leeside of the cone.

"Won't hurt me, but what about you?"

"Put me on your back, I'll get the others. You land wherever you need to, we'll be shielded from the worst by your body until we can figure this out."

Bale set her down, but Croves came up around the dragon's side before Tollar could start down.

"What a bleedin' mess! I'd hoped we'd get across without seein' any of those serpents. They'll be a problem, but we've got a bigger one at the moment."

"Fine." Tollar sighed. "Is Bee with you?"

"She still won't leave the tent when Bale's flying."

Tollar pressed her lips together. "Bale's landing somewhere hot very soon."

"Time to get busy with the water then."

Tollar let out a breath and sat at the junction of straps at Bale's shoulders, nestling between two spikes and looping her hands into the holds. Croves crouched next to her, holding a hand out, palm up to help. She gave a terse nod and closed her eyes, concentrating on the vast depths below while Croves gripped her shoulders to steady her.

She pulled cooler water from farther out, channelling it toward the island, locking it to her will so it followed where the dragon took her. The focus took more effort than she liked, each wobble of the dragon sloshed Tollar's insides. The sea beasts were out there, one of them slicing alarmingly fast through the water toward her channel and Bale. Tollar clenched her jaw and made a wall of water, solid as a moon, and pulled it up too quickly for the beast to react. Her grim satisfaction at the thing smacking into the water wall—enough to slow it so Bale could clear the shore—didn't last. She'd lost focus on the water, didn't have as much as she needed.

"Cursed ancestors, this night is never-ending."

"What's going on? Can ye still call the water?"

"I got distracted."

She'd meant to pull super-cooled water from the ocean up into a funnel through the air and drop it on Bale's landing spot. The water hadn't been as cold as she'd wanted and now, she'd lost some of it to the lava flow beneath them.

"Bale, there!" Croves called, startling her.

The cone loomed ahead of them, spatters of magma bursting around them, Croves blasting it off course with focused gales.

"Oh shit."

"Keep yer focus on the water."

Tollar spotted where Croves meant for the dragons to land. There was a small patch, smaller than either dragon by half, covered in steaming slabs of rock. Tollar surged her funnel of water out ahead of them and doused the area.

Bale's landing was not graceful. Her hind quarters broke through the crust and her tail and half of her back legs sank into the lava. But the front half of her, where the gondola was strapped, stood on solid rock.

"Squishy. Don't like it."

"We'll get you something more comfortable in a snap."

Croves gave her shoulder a pat, but remained crouched as he focused on blasts of air to keep lava splatter from hitting them. It wouldn't hurt the dragons, but he and Tollar were exposed. Tollar headed for Bale's side to find Beenala and got hit with a blast of heat as soon as she leaned over. The pungent taste and smell of sulfur filled her—nearly felled her—when she opened her mouth to call for Beenala.

But Beenala was already there, climbing faster than Tollar had ever seen her, her face pale and her mouth pinched up, sweat beaded on her forehead, dripping down her face. Tollar summoned more water, drizzling some over Beenala's head before dousing the ground beneath.

She was very careful to keep the handholds dry.

As soon as Beenala was near enough, Tollar reached out and helped pull her the rest of the way up, not liking how overheated she was. Or how heavy and erratic her breathing.

Tollar called more water, pouring it over Beenala. She cupped some in her hands, clearing out the salt, and offered it to her dearest to drink.

"Sips. Breathe in between."

Beenala trembled, panting, but didn't throw up. Tollar took it as a good sign. But Beenala's gaze darted and her feet twitched. The need to flee caused by her anxiety was probably what got her up over the dragon and away from the worst of the heat so quickly.

"You're safe now, Bee. I've got you."

Beenala gripped Tollar's hand, her fingers still shaking, her palms sweaty.

"Bale's in a lake of fire!" Beenala snapped, her voice high and tight and accusing. "There are sea monsters!"

"Aye, those are gonna give us a spot of trouble when we leave."

Tollar gave Croves a warning glare. One problem at a time.

Beenala glared between Croves and Tollar. Tollar frowned and tried to smooth out Beenala's short, spiky hair, but it only bounced back in an even worse mess.

"Yes, it's not ideal but none of us are hurt. Wait, you're not hurt, are you?"

"It's hot in the gondola but I'm not hurt."

"How hot?" Croves asked. "Ye reckon the heat will damage the supplies?"

Beenala took a deep, shaky breath and closed her eyes, squeezing Tollar's hands tighter. "I wasn't paying attention, I was fleeing. But it might be hot enough for damage, yes."

"Abilerit tempered the entire structure to withstand dragonfire." Tollar gave Croves a glance.

"Aye, but not our supplies inside."

Tollar sighed deeply, her body heavy like it weighed the whole of the ocean. And she pulled more of the ocean to them, remembering to cool it this time, cooling more of the area around them.

"Ach, it's drops on an inferno, we need space for the dragons to rest the night."

Angry tears stung Tollar's silver eyes. She couldn't write this off as just the hormones either. Her pregnancy had made her inadequate since they left home, and now they needed her to be as competent as she ever had been. She couldn't even cool a bit of rock or string two coherent thoughts together.

"Toll, could you protect the gondola with ice?"

Tollar nodded wearily. She could, and she did, but it was so much work when it shouldn't be. When the only thing keeping her from vomiting was that she hadn't eaten since the afternoon. The smoke and stink filled her head, raked her lungs. All the aeromancy Croves was using to keep them safe made the air thin.

Tollar closed her eyes and clenched against the vertigo, holding her breath against dry heaves.

"I'll get Shell to take ye up outta the worst of it," Croves said. "Ye can do yer water things from the air."

"No, flying isn't better."

Beenala's hand trembled in hers. Beenala was breathing too fast again and now her hands were cold.

"Bee, you need a deep breath. We both need to breathe. Everything's awful but we're still safe. We'll be safer with a bit more work. I can't cool the lava to rock with the focus I've got, I need you to divert it. Can you build a channel to push the lava further out around us?"

"I can't," Beenala gasped.

"Okay, Bee. It's okay." Tollar kept hold of Beenala's hand and lay back, pulling her shirt over her face to block the worst of the fumes. She kept dragging what water she could from the ocean and drenching the area.

She could keep the gondola encased in ice for a bit longer, in between little deluges around them. But Croves was going to run out of spell energy to block the spatter coming their way. It would be best if the dragons had solid ground to rest on and the humans had a cooled space to lie beneath the dragons' wings for protection.

Croves whistled and Tollar opened her eyes to Shell landing next to them, the lava up to his underside. The talons of one hand dug into the rock next to Bale to steady himself and he extended one wing up over them, giving Croves a break.

"He's not going to be able to sleep like that," Croves said. "That flow will take him as soon as he lets go of the rock."

Without all the aeromancy thinning the air, the veil of fog over Tollar's thoughts lifted.

"Pyromancy will work double, redirect the lava but also cool the air around us."

Beenala sat straighter, still breathing hard but her expression cleared of panic as she looked up at Shell's wing arced overhead.

"But I'm not just working with fire," Beenala said.

"Well, no, but you can work both elements."

"Yes, but *separately*." Beenala met her gaze. "I've never worked both at the same time before."

Tollar gave her the best encouraging smile she could manage. "Just try your best. Anything gets us better off than we are."

Beenala pursed her lips and swivelled to face where the lava flow diverted higher up the slope, making their tiny refuge. The air grew tolerable, and patches of the flow cooled and darkened. But it wasn't much and Beenala grumbled in frustration.

Tollar stayed quiet, gave Croves a warning glance when he opened his mouth.

"It would be easier to work the earth if I could touch it."

"Too hot," Bale said.

Beenala sighed. But she extended her focus again, a determined scowl on her face, and little mounds pushed up around the lava flow, redirecting it further away from them

"Toll..." Her voice was low and strained. "The heat keeps softening the ground. I can't hold this."

Tollar closed her eyes and let a stream of mental curses wash over her.

There was only one way to get enough water to solidify the ground for the night before they all drained their spell energy and dropped from exhaustion. A water portal. Dangerous magic that could drown them all.

"Bee, hold your focus." Tollar sat up and pointed at Croves. "You, with me. Bale, you hold us out near Bee's little walls."

"I'm coming with you!"

"Do what you need, as long as you keep your focus on holding the ground."

Croves helped them both into the palm of Bale's hand where they sat, all of them bewildered, but at least knowing well enough to listen when Tollar actually had a plan.

"Bee, what's your job?"

"Hold the ground."

"No matter what else happens."

"What else is going to happen?" Her eyes widened and her voice rose.

"That's what Croves is here for. You hold the ground."

"And what *am* I here for?" Croves asked.

"You hold me steady and keep me pointed in the right direction. If I lose control of the magic, you remember how to take over my power?"

"I don't want—"

"You'll do it, or we lose your dragon to either the lava or the creatures in the ocean. We're out of options."

Wizards could boost each other's power or harness each other's energy, making whoever wielded the combination exponentially more powerful. Tollar had wanted Croves to take control because she had all the power she needed; it was her focus that currently lagged.

Croves gave a single terse nod. Sometimes their relationship clouded his judgement and he questioned her more than she liked, but when it counted, he remembered her rank lines were hard earned. He'd been there when she'd earned her latest set.

Bale stretched out her arm, bringing Tollar to the edge of the lava flow. Beenala shook with exhaustion, but her retaining walls held.

"Bale, when the water comes, get your feet out of the lava or you'll be encased in stone."

Tollar took a deep breath and held it, blocking out the way her stomach churned and her head spun. She conjured a ball of water between her hands, pulling the moisture straight out of the air around them. And then she spread it further, pulled it apart and reached deep into the element.

"Ah shit," Croves snapped from behind her, gripping her shoulders when he realized what she was doing.

Tollar pulled the water open about as wide as a washbasin, forming it into a portal to the water realm. A torrent roared down the slope from Beenala's walls, around Bale's feet, and all the way to the ocean.

Even louder than the roar of water was the hiss of steam, the air rapidly filling with it, so it was hard to see, difficult to breathe. She held her breath, waiting for the deafening hiss of steam to ease. The soupy air got worse, and it took longer than she'd expected, forcing her to breathe shallowly or pass out. But the sting of whatever compounds the steam lifted into the air made every breath ache, the stink of it all pushing her to the edge of dry heaves again.

She didn't remember closing her eyes or pitching over, but an influx of power from Croves, the strange light feeling of aeromancy, filled her and buoyed her, nearly derailing her efforts even as it cleared her focus.

One of Croves' big treetrunk arms was all that held her up. But she hadn't lost her control of the water.

So, she was equally annoyed that he hadn't listened to her and that giving her his energy had worked. Nobody said she had to be rational while trying to put out half a sodding volcano.

An immense gust of wind pushed her forward, beating at her back so that Bale curled her fingers to keep her humans secure. It was Shell taking flight, his massive wings causing a powerful gale, roiling the steam and blowing some of it away from them.

Turning carefully, Tollar dragged her endless river of water across the lava stream to get the other side of their refuge where Shell had just been. With him circling above and using his wing gale to keep the air clear, keeping the water portal steady and the flow running down the slope wasn't as taxing as the first time.

"Toll, that's enough. Can ye close it?"

She blinked, still upright but not fully in herself. *Could* she close it? It'd eventually drown the world if she didn't. Cold seeped into her bones at the thought.

She grunted out a noncommittal answer and focused on the ball of water in front of her, on compressing it, folding it in on itself, and cutting off the link between realms. The flow trickled and then stopped.

Tollar exhaled, deflating. Croves let go of her and helped her curl up against the palm of Bale's hand.

"Aye, that'll do it. Well done, lass."

She'd done it. *They'd* done it. That it was done should be enough, but that she hadn't been able to do it all on her own, like she used to before the twins, bothered her more than it should. Should she feel relieved? Probably. But all she felt was tired beyond measure.

Tollar hadn't been aware of Bale moving, but the dragon deposited the three humans on the warm, damp rocks. Tollar ended up on her back staring up at the firelit stars and the pair of slivered crescent moons. Croves managed a dignified roll to his feet. Beenala sprawled forward on her knees and immediately threw up. Tollar shoved herself up and over to Beenala who was drenched with sweat and trembling, staring forward at nothing.

Tollar crouched next to her, her hands twitching to rub Beenala's back or scoop her up in an embrace, but knowing that wouldn't actually help. Tollar dried up their surroundings and used the extra water to clean Beenala.

"I know, Bee. I know. We're okay now. You did it! You held the ground and we've got somewhere safe and look, here comes Shell. You can rest now."

Clumsy, her movements jerky, Beenala dragged herself to Tollar, clutching her. Tollar's heartrate thrummed for a lot of different reasons, but primarily out of concern. When hated-to-be-touched Beenala sought a hug, things were a long way from all right. But Tollar held her, rocking a little and crooning comforting things. She wanted to pack Beenala into the gondola straightaway and bring her home to her dog and her art and her farming, where things were simple, and she never had to fight a volcano.

In the distance, lava light glistened off the wake of the circling sea beasts.

Croves directed Bale to lie on her side with her back toward the top of the cone so that they wouldn't have to unstrap the gondola while she slept. Her body would block any leaks in the retaining walls, though they were solid at the moment, and her wing draped over the gondola would protect them from any spatter.

Curled up in the gondola, Beenala dropped to sleep like an anchor, but Tollar stared out the porthole at the ripples on the ocean. That beast had used magic against her, magic that was hard for her to fight in ways she couldn't account. Despite Croves standing watch all night, Tollar remained vigilant.

* * *

Tollar woke to the ground shaking and Beenala screaming again. She'd had terrors most of the night, and this was the second earthquake to rattle them since they'd landed. The volcano didn't appreciate their continued presence. The light through the gondola's portholes was brighter and bluer than the last time Tollar had woken. If it wasn't dawn, it would be soon. Hopefully Bale had gotten the rest she needed, and they could slip past the sea serpents and put this cursed place behind them.

Tollar held Beenala's hand and stroked her hair until she fully woke up, blinking away the last of whatever nightmare haunted her.

"I want to go home," Beenala whispered, her voice low and tight.

"You can. It's morning, we can leave here. Once we get the dragons fed, we can turn back, bring you home. Croves and I can take Bale to her kin on our own."

Beenala was quiet a long while, holding Tollar's gaze. Tollar swept some of Beenala's hair out of her face and kissed her forehead.

"Will there be more days like this?" Beenala asked.

"I don't know. I've never come this way, especially not by dragon. I didn't expect what we've faced already. This could be the only pit in the road and the rest of the trip will be a breeze. Or it could be non-stop disasters like my journey from Bettar."

Beenala nodded slowly and gripped Tollar's hands.

"I think...I expected this would be easy. Maybe even boring. I didn't expect any danger at all, and then I expected you'd take care of it like you always do. And that last part wasn't fair. Maybe it's never fair of me to expect you to take care of everything."

"I don't mind."

"I know, but that doesn't mean I should take it for granted. But I did. I'm sorry, Tollar. I know this journey is hard for you—that the twins make it harder."

Tollar kissed the top of her head and slowly sat up, pleased there was no wave of nausea to force her back down, though her limbs felt heavy. She broke out some rations for a hasty breakfast.

"Let's hope the worst is behind us."

Croves appeared at the door, looking ashen and haggard.

"You really did stay up all night."

"Aye. And don't be too quick to hope for an easy trip outta here, not when those sea serpents have our scent. I've never seen 'em up close like this, only heard stories from other dragon riders who barely escaped. And whispers about those who didn't. Whatever these things are, they have magic, they're vicious with it, and they have a spectacular range. They've used whips of water to pull dragons right outta the sky."

Beenala whimpered and Tollar gripped her hand.

"The dragons can't use the updrafts from the volcano for lift and keep above the island to take off? Surely once they're high enough..." She trailed off as Croves shook his head.

"Ta be outta range of these monsters, the dragons have to gain altitude where the air is too thin for us."

Tollar closed her eyes and took a long breath, tapping her foot against the urge to pace.

"But we've got the best aquamancer in the world," he continued. "Ye can turn the surface to ice or something."

"Or something." Tollar sighed.

Beenala and Tollar shared a glance. Beenala took back her hand so she could twist up the hem of her shirt.

"Is Bale ready to go?"

"Aye, both dragons are rested. And just in time too. The lava is starting to leak over the retaining walls."

Beenala groaned.

"We'd best not linger," Croves said. "One of the shakes in the night opened a new fissure nearby. This whole area is unstable."

"All right. I need to get a closer look at our watery friends before I can decide what to do about them."

The urge to pace finally won out and Tollar launched herself out the door. In the dawn light, the long expanse of black rock from her water magic cut through the lava like a slice of night through the sun. The ground was still for the moment, the breeze carrying the worst of the smell away from her. Her head was clear for a glorious moment. She pushed herself, not to a run, but long quick strides across the uneven surface, despite the lead feeling in her legs. Footfalls from Croves and Beenala followed her across the island to the shore, but she didn't turn back.

When she reached the water, she kicked off her boots and kept going, walking out across the surface, feeling the depth through the soles of her feet. She slowed only when the seafloor dropped away, sensing it as an increase in the depth of the water, a fullness to the quality of it.

She fanned out her senses and didn't have to go far to find one of those long, massive shapes in the water, swimming in a lazy circle. Once her magic encompassed it, the thing turned abruptly and streaked her way.

"Shit."

Tollar waited a beat, until the wake it left was visible, and then she ran. More to lure than to escape. So far it was just the one. Lucky break, finally?

She let it slam into another wall of water an instant before it would have broken the surface to snap her up. With it stunned, she halted and solidified the water around it, holding it immobile while she tried to get a better look at it. From the shape of the water around it, she'd already been able to discern that it had no limbs and was probably three times as long as a full-grown dragoness. It wasn't nearly as bulky as the dragons, but that probably made it more flexible. Like a snake.

She narrowed her eyes, focusing on it, feeling for the magic it had. There was a signature there she recognized but couldn't quite place.

All at once it melted the water cage she'd put it in and lunged for her.

Tollar geysered herself out of its reach and used a disk of water to surf across the ocean, racing back to the shallower water. She didn't stop when she reached the shore, but gathered Beenala, Croves and her boots, and used the water to surf across the rock and back to the dragons.

The serpent had still been coming for her when she reached the shore and lost sense of it. When all three of them looked back, it was far closer to shore than she expected it could go. Its head and a long stretch of its body were partially above the surface.

"Well, that was exciting." Tollar stuffed her feet back into her boots and paced across the rock alongside Bale, though the effort was almost more than it was worth. Her brain wanted her body to move, her body wanted to sleep for a week.

Croves stood next to Beenala. She watched Tollar pace while Croves stared down that serpent.

"Croves, in all you've heard about these things, has anyone ever beat them?"

"Aye, pyromancers enhancing dragonfire have been able to kill some of them."

"Well, good thing we've got a pyromancer!" Tollar snapped her fingers and pointed at Beenala, who managed to look even paler.

"Tollar, no. I can't fight sea monsters!"

"You also said you couldn't fight dragons, but you were brilliant in the war."

Beenala crossed her arms to hide her shaking hands, but held Tollar's gaze. "That brilliance came with a cost and you know it."

"Yes, but you're the only pyromancer here. Look, I lured that one to the shore so we can probably do this without even having to fly. Would it work better if we stayed on the ground?"

"Please, don't make me do this."

Tollar looked to Croves. "What else is there if not fire?"

He watched the serpent, which hadn't moved, and didn't turn when he answered. "Everyone else has had to outrun them."

"Well, we've got tired and hungry dragons. How likely are they to succeed?"

Croves glanced at her, shook his head.

Tollar resumed pacing, though at this point it was more like plodding.

"Can't ye put them in blocks of ice till we're clear?"

"I had that one in a block right before it jumped through it like it was nothing and tried to eat me." She gestured back toward the serpent.

"There must be something you can do."

Tollar spun to face Beenala. "Weren't you just saying how the two of you over-rely on me? This is something that you can do. I'm right here and I can help you, but we need your pyromancy."

Beenala's mouth bunched up and her hands made fists around the hem of her shirt. "I'm not a warrior like you or an adventurer like Croves. I'm just..." Her voice broke. "I grow things and I paint. I can't do this."

Tollar spun around to Croves. "Can you use aeromancy to make the dragons faster than those things?"

"Aye, for a time. Don't think I can do it for long enough. Yer sure ye can't contain 'em?"

"Croves, do you think I've been holding back all this time?"

He held out his hands in a placating gesture. "I didn't mean nothin' by it."

"But you did. Bee is right, everyone looks to me to right things—expects me to fix it all. And I try. It eats at me when there are people I can't save. And right now, that's us. I can't save us, Croves. And I can't tell you how much I hate it that I can't."

Her voice broke and hot tears stung her eyes again. She was definitely blaming it on the hormones this time.

Beenala reached her first, taking her hands. Croves came next with a hand on her cheek.

"It's all right, lass. It's new for all of us, what ye can and can't do. And I know ye want to, I see ye pushing and I see the way ye look like yer gonna feed me to Bale every time I try to get ye to rest."

"I don't eat people!" Bale protested.

Shell snorted.

Tollar chuckled and the tight heat in her throat loosened. Beenala wiped her tears and took her hands again, kissing her knuckles.

"Between the three of us we've got a full elemental. There's got to be something we can do."

Tollar kissed Beenala's forehead and Croves' cheek and paced away from them, just a few steps toward the shore where she gave in to her body. It felt like it weighed as much as both moons and a couple of planets for good measure. She sat. She didn't even care the way the hard uneven rock dug into her backside and her legs.

And that cursed serpent was still there, staring at them. There was nothing natural about it. And there was that thing with its magic, something she'd encountered before.

She stared at it, all glistening greenish black with a smattering of grey barnacles clustered on its body, its large luminous eyes silvery like hers.

"Wait, that's it." She pivoted on her butt, eyes wide, and gestured Beenala and Croves over to her. "I've felt that magic before because it's like mine. Like a demon's power. That's why they're stronger than me!"

Beenala paled and Croves blinked his one eye a whole lot, staring back out at that serpent. The implication of what Tollar said sank in.

"Oh shit."

"If it's stronger than you, what do we do? How do we beat it?"

Tollar pressed her hands over her mouth and bounced her legs against the rock. Were those serpents somehow half demon like her? But if they were only half demon, they couldn't be stronger. Or could they? They were bigger by a longshot, but size didn't denote power and there were few creatures other than humans who had magic at all.

"What...What if they're possessed by water demons?" She looked from Beenala to Croves. "Is that a thing? The demons possess people, why not animals?"

"Aye, it's possible. I've heard of dragons using fire demons for an edge in battle."

Now that was something Tollar never wanted to see. But would it look something like these serpents?

"Do either of you know how to tell if it's demon possession?"

There were all sorts of things part of Guild training that Tollar didn't know about. She had slipped sideways into the Wizards Guild on account of her being a powerful anomaly. Croves and Beenala had gone through the proper channels.

"I know what it looks like in people, not beasts," Croves said.

"Um, so, I got bored while you were away over the summer and read up on possessions, just to try to understand better and...well, it's hard to tell without getting close, which we obviously can't do, but I did find out how to remove a possessing demon."

Half of Tollar's mouth quirked up. "You going to exorcise me, Bee?"

Beenala's face flushed, and she stared out over the ocean. She cleared her throat. "So, we can try that and if it doesn't work then it's something else?"

"All right, let's try it. Can you do it or do you want to teach me?"

"It's easier with the elements matched."

Beenala sat to explain the process while the ground rumbled and shook. She squeaked in alarm, but Tollar gave her credit for keeping her composure. The volcano belched out a fresh plume of smoke and fire, but Bale was up now and spread her wings to block the debris raining around them.

"Right, let's be quick about this."

Beenala explained and it seemed easy enough, like the demon summonings they were all taught, but instead of using elements to call a fresh demon from its elemental realm, Tollar would focus on the serpents.

"That means I'll have to get closer."

"But I'll be with Bale using fire to keep them back."

Tollar smiled and touched Beenala's cheek.

"If my part doesn't work, you're going to have to kill the serpents. Do you think you can handle that?"

Beenala turned a little green.

"Right, Bale can bring you to us, and Croves or I can harness your pyromancy to do it. It'll be okay."

Beenala's colour didn't improve but she gave Tollar a brave smile and nodded.

Croves stood to talk to Shell. The dragon didn't look happy but took flight, using the volcano for lift. Croves jogged back to them and helped Tollar to her feet.

"All right, let's make this quick, he's gone to round up the other two beasts."

"Wait, you're using Shell as bait?"

"He's got enough speed in the short term, and like ye said, ye can't do it all."

Tollar closed her eyes and took a breath. Nodded. "All right. Bee, you and Bale don't get too close but be ready with fire to hold them back."

Croves kept hold of Tollar's hand and the two of them made for the shore.

"Summoning, controlling and then banishing three demons near simultaneously is a tall order on its own, but keeping the serpents back, even with Bee and Bale on fire duty, is going to be a lot."

"Ye can use my magic, like before."

She sighed. "That was lucky, but I'm not sure it will work again. I had brain fog with the water portal, today it's a bit of everything but mostly I'm tired. My magic may be endless, but it's my ability to wield it that's the problem. No reason someone else can't use it for me."

He stopped walking and took both her hands, running his thumbs over her knuckles, but not meeting her gaze.

"Ye don't think it'll harm the twins?"

"Ah, that's what you're worried about? There's no reason it should. It's all just magic and they're already steeped in it. I trust the midwife's advice and so should you."

He looked ready to argue, but the ground trembled again and Beenala shouted a curse. Her retaining walls had been breached. Bale pushed her tail against the gap, but that wasn't going to hold for long. Tollar tugged Croves' hand to get him moving again.

"You need to be ready to harness my power. If I start to fail, you need to take over."

She stopped abruptly when the serpent lunged at them, striking its head into the ground just ahead. They were still out of reach and she hoped it was close enough to get the job done.

"Here comes Shell." Croves pointed.

The serpent lunged again, slithering further out of the water, massive jaws snapping, but still not quite close enough. And then a gout of flame shot past Tollar and the serpent reared back. Bale had come closer with Beenala sitting between her horns, arms outstretched to guide the fire. Shell was almost back in firing range.

Tollar closed her eyes and gripped Croves' hand, using the other to weave the summoning, speaking in the rainpatter burble of the water demons' language. Something shrieked, possibly the serpent? Tollar kept her eyes closed to hold her focus, trusting Croves to get them out of the way if the situation got beyond their control.

More dragonfire roared around her, and now Tollar did open her eyes. Shell led the other two serpents, coming in fast while the first lay dazed on the shore and the glittery translucent shape of a water demon rolled toward her.

"Shit! Croves, I'll call them and control them, you do the banishing."

Tollar tried not to be bitter about the fact that she'd once been able to call, control and then banish five demons at once in her misbegotten youth. But the two fresh serpents had some understanding of what was going on and were fighting back.

Whips of water shot out at Shell, at Bale, at her. Tollar used her will to bat the water aside, but more of it shot out just as quickly. Croves, at least, got rid of the first demon. Bale and Beenala were quick with a gout of flame at one of the serpents while Shell circled around to attack the other from the back.

"Focus on that one!" Tollar pointed at the serpent to the left and hoped anyone could hear her. She took on the other one by herself, wrapping it up in one of its own water whips, straining to hold it and keep the other whips from knocking Shell out of the air, while she pulled the demon from it.

"Croves, get it!"

She turned to the final serpent, but her body kept going, sliding in a wide loop like the ground had tilted out from under her. She worried it was another earthquake before Croves' grip on her hand pulled her upright again. She lost her grip on all the water whips, but held the summoning. Tollar closed her eyes and put all her focus on that final demon, drawing it out and holding it in place.

A dragon cried out. It sounded like Shell, and it sounded like alarm. But all she could do was hold the demon.

And then she felt light and hollowed out, cut off from her magic entirely. Cold dropped into her gut and her heartrate kicked up a notch before she realized Croves had done what she'd asked.

Tollar leaned heavily on Croves, his hand holding hers and another under her arm the only thing keeping her on her feet. Shell was in the water, raking his talons and snapping at one of the serpents, but Bale dived toward him, Beenala still enhancing her fire. The first serpent fled. The second was now lying dazed on the shore.

The third and final demon disappeared. The serpent fighting Shell gave a single, high shriek and collapsed like its companion.

Croves sighed and Tollar's magic rushed back in, not that it helped her keep her feet any better. Croves got a better grip on her, picked her up and held her close.

"Let's not do that again, eh?" He chuckled. "But yer power sure is something. Never felt anything like that before, like I was some kind of god. That what it's like for ye all the time?"

"Now you know why I've got such an inflated ego."

He laughed and kissed her, then released her as Beenala ran over to them, wrapping her arms around Tollar.

"We did it, Bee. You were brilliant!" Tollar kissed the top of her head and stroked her cheek. Beenala pulled back and held her hands, looking weary and tired, but her colour was better.

"I can't hold the retaining walls anymore."

"I guess it's a good thing you don't have to. Let's get out of here, shall we? There's a dragon city waiting for us."

Shell glided past and scooped up Croves as he went. Bale shot a final burst of fire at the last serpent left in sight before picking up the two women and taking flight. She set them down on her back. Both sat cuddled together between two tall spikes, neither interested in moving a hair's breadth.

"We make a pretty good team."

"I hate sports."

Tollar chuckled and leaned her chin on top of Beenala's head. "Still want to go home?"

"Yes. But I'm staying. What would you do without me?"

What, indeed?

Tollar smiled and kissed Beenala's hair. No matter what lay ahead, they always had each other.

"Testing the Waters" is a short story by Vanessa Ricci-Thode. To learn more, visit **www.thodestool.ca** or follow her on Twitter & Instagram **@VRicciThode**

# For Want of Treasure

Kyoko M.

Sapphic Representation: Lesbian, Bi/Pansexual, Polyamory
Heat Level: Medium
Content Warnings: Coarse Language, Violence, Abduction

So, a treasure hunter, a hardened sea captain, and a merman walk into a bar.

Isn't that how all good tall tales begin?

The Jolly Roger wasn't even a nice bar, but that was the point. It was a seedy, scurvy hole-in-the-wall with cheap alcohol, easy access to whores, and plenty of the worst scum imaginable.

You know, my kind of people.

I strolled in first. I usually did—I was the muscle of the outfit, being five foot eleven with a stocky build and piercing russet eyes. People knew to stay out of my way. Never mind that I was a woman; by now, my reputation preceded me and only fools were stupid enough to have something to say about my gender. I'd blackened enough eyes and broken enough limbs to get the point across, so no one paid me any attention as I strode over the creaky floorboards toward the corner table.

Same as me, no one really noticed when Kida walked in. She was the shortest of our trio at five foot six and slender of frame but with plenty of lithe muscle to back up the scowl on her face. She hated criminals. Which, of course, was hilarious since I was one. And technically, so was she, but that was a long ongoing argument that no one wanted to hear. Like me, she wore fitted pants, boots, and a blouse. She had a cutlass on her hip and her long, brown hair trailed over one shoulder in a tidy ponytail. If one looked close enough, they'd see the freckles dusting her light brown cheeks, but calling her cute would get you a broken nose. She kept a hand on the hilt of her weapon as she walked, fully expecting a confrontation as she always did when it was time to talk to vagabonds. And she had enviable perfect posture—but that was no surprise. Most ship captains that were ex-Navy did.

However, people *did* look up when Thomas brought up the rear.

For one, Thomas was pale. That didn't happen a lot in ports and places where people sailed the seas for a living. I was fortunate with my dark brown skin and thick shoulder length curls to not have to worry as much about burning under the sun. He didn't get sunburn, either, but only because he wasn't completely human. Aside from the paleness, he had delicate features that were a mix between handsome and pretty, with his waist-length inky hair and blue eyes. He was taller than me at six feet and he too was relatively lithe with muscle. He also looked the friendliest of the three of us, glancing around curiously to survey his new surroundings. Men and women alike stared at him in wonder, for he always had this air of being from somewhere exotic and strange, not like the seamen nor the landlubbers.

And they were right. After all, he hailed from Atlantis— the lost city beneath the sea.

Arty was at the corner table drinking with three of his crew members, laughing into his beer. As soon as he spotted me, he sat up straight and wiped the suds off his beard and pot belly. The other crew members noticed me and Kida and grabbed their drinks, hustling off to another part of the bar without being told.

"Arty," I said as I slouched into one of the empty chairs. "You look well."

"Ehehe, well, I try," he said, nervously glancing at Kida before nodding to her respectfully. "I see your troupe is out in force today."

"Thomas was getting stir crazy," I said. "So, I thought I'd bring him along to have a look at the locals."

"He'll find plenty of entertainment if he wants it," Arty said, gesturing toward the whores now abandoning their clients to flock to his side. I sent a withering glare over my shoulder. The four women stopped dead and then whispered to each other before adopting sullen looks and returning to their posts. Typical.

"The map," Kida demanded, narrowing her eyes at Arty.

"Ah, yes'm, one second." Arty reached into his boot and withdrew a rolled-up map. "Them's the coordinates. Lots of men have tried to get it, but between the cliff and the reef, no one can dive far enough down to get to the contents of the sunken ship."

"Which are?" I asked, arching an eyebrow.

"Rumor is it's stolen sterling pounds from Scotland. Last I heard was two-to-three thousand, but you know how it goes in our line of work."

I snorted. "Damn right I do." I glanced at Kida. "If you would, love."

Kida glared at me, but sighed and withdrew her change purse. She counted out Arty's cut and left it on the table, understandably not wanting to touch the filthy sailor. He scooped up what he was owed and tucked it into his waistband, lifting his mug. "Much obliged. When can I expect my share of what you find?"

"If we find anything," I said curtly, standing up. "I'll call on you within three days to pay you. If you hear anything good in the meantime, don't be a stranger."

Arty winked. "Never to you, Lila. You keep me wallet fat as me stomach."

He broke into chortles, and I rolled my eyes before turning to leave.

We were almost to the door when trouble came a-knocking.

A dark-haired man with a goatee stuck his leg out, blocking my path about four tables away from the door. He tipped his wide hat up and smiled at me. "Sorry to interrupt, but you wouldn't happen to be the same Lila who's wanted by the British for crippling the son of the commander's fleet after having an eye on your girl here?" He lazily pointed at Kida.

I smiled. "He didn't have 'an eye on her.' He had a hand on her. A hand that I kept." I leaned in toward him. "And I'll do the same to you if you don't move your smelly ass away from me."

"Well," he said, clapping his hands together. "That's admission by your own will, isn't it? You are the infamous Lila—feared from Tibet to Timbuktu!" His beady eyes gleamed with greed. "And worth about fifty thousand pounds. British sterling, of course."

"Of course," I said sweetly. "And, what? You're gonna bring me in all by your lonesome?"

He laughed. "I'm a fool, not suicidal."

Seven men in the bar stood up and locked their eyes on me. "They are."

* * *

"I told you!"

I groaned and stretched straight backward, hearing several joints pop, giving me sudden, much-needed relief. I brushed my sleeve across my nose, wincing as it stung. Still hadn't stopped bleeding yet. I took a handkerchief out of my pocket as I walked up the gangplank toward the ship, ignoring the furious Latina woman still shouting at me as she followed. "I told you we shouldn't have dropped anchor here for another three months when the bounty would be on the bottom of the pile!"

"I heard you the first ten times, Kida," I groused as I hopped over the side and offered my hand to her. She smacked it aside and I rolled my eyes. Thomas gave me a sympathetic look as he took my hand and then helped me pull the gangplank on board so we could shove off. Of the three of us, he'd fared the best, mostly because I'd told him to scat while we fought the men off. I had about four nasty cuts and some bruising on my stomach in addition to a bloody nose, but I looked like an angel compared to the carnage Kida and I left behind in the bar. I genuinely felt bad for the owner—it was hard mopping bloodstains out of wood.

"But our money's running low and we got what we came for," I continued as I coiled the line. "So, we'll just be scarce for a while. There's no need to fuss."

"No need?" she spat. "Look at you. You look like someone dropped you into the bay with a pack of piranha!"

"Well," Thomas said. "Technically speaking, they prefer dead flesh to living organisms. They're more like scavengers and with her being alive—"

"Thomas," Kida snarled. "Don't take her side."

"I'm not taking her side. Just wanted to offer some clarification, that's all." He smiled brightly, but that look wilted at her glare. "I am sorry. I was trying to lighten the mood, I'm afraid."

Her lips twitched just a tiny bit at one corner. I knew she was still mad, but Thomas always had a disarming demeanor that left her in a better mood. He turned to me then, his hand out. "The map, if you please, dearest."

I handed it to him. He unfolded it and his blue eyes went alight with interest. "Ah, yes, lovely. It's a previously uncharted region. There are a few isles that will be tricky to navigate, but I'll have the route plotted in no time at all."

He rolled it up again and then sent a severe look between me and Kida. "Please do not kill each other while I'm gone."

"No promises," Kida growled as she stomped over to the helm. I kept mopping at the blood from my nose until it finally stopped and completed the rest of my duties as we pushed off from the port.

Our ship—or arguably, Kida's ship—was named *La Espada*—which meant "the sword," for it cut through the water like a blade through flesh. She'd won it in a duel after she had been dismissed from the Navy for masquerading as a man for years to acquire wealth, power, and all the educational benefits more often afforded to men than women where she'd grown up in Cuba. She'd taken the ship and the cutlass of the losing dueler as a reminder that none who tangled with her would ever forget her power and poise.

We'd met through dumb luck—though Thomas argued it was "divine intervention"—when I'd been scamming a group of drunken sailors in a rigged card game and they'd tried to bum-rush me when I left with their winnings. She'd been out for a walk by the inn when she heard the hubbub and intervened. We beat them bloody and took my winnings plus theirs, so I used them to buy her a drink. Lots of drinks, actually.

The next morning after we woke up in bed together, I'd told her I'd turned into a marauder. I'd lost my last ship when I escaped the British Navy and had been hopping from place to place saving up for a new one. There wasn't a lot of honest work for a woman of color in most of the civilized world, so I'd gone with what I was good at: stealing, cheating, lying, and fighting. I didn't think she'd be interested in a thief—not for anything other than a night of exceptional thrills—and yet she'd asked me to be her second mate aboard *La Espada* after that night at the inn.

It had been a long time since I'd been with anyone for more than a night. It was...scary, not being alone. You had to face the fact that you could lose the one you loved.

And I hadn't loved anyone in a very long time.

Or at least no one I was willing to admit...

"Head for the lagoon," I told Kida once we were safely out of the port, and I'd patched myself up. "I'd like a good wash. I also think there's a grove over that way with some bananas."

She kept up the glare. "Don't think you can bribe your way out of this with fruit."

I grinned. "That's exactly what I think."

I walked across the deck to the living quarters and went inside. The cabin was nothing special nor spacious. It had just enough room for a rickety bed, a dresser, and a table where we mapped out our routes through the high seas—all of which were nailed to stay in place while we were at sea. However, almost every spare inch was covered in books, maps, and parchment courtesy of Thomas. He was a scholar of sorts, having been educated by both the merfolk and the finer education institutions of man. He could transform between a merman and a regular man in the blink of an eye and at will, so he'd basically forged himself an identity so he could attend a higher education facility.

"We're heading to the lagoon," I told him. "Fancy a swim?"

"Always," he said, winking at me from where he sat at the desk.

I turned to go, but he leaned across the desk to gently place a hand on mine. I risked a glance at him, seeing very real concern in his features. "Something wrong?"

He squeezed my fingers. "Just be more careful getting information next time, that's all."

I swallowed hard. "I will, Thomas. We should be there in around ten or fifteen minutes."

Thomas nodded. I pulled the door shut.

We sailed around the bottom rim of the island, then dropped anchor and hiked for about a mile inland to a lagoon hidden away from the more populated part of the island. I'd found it years ago to be a good spot to clean up without having to pay for an inn, and there were banana trees not far from it on the other side of the brush.

And the water, obviously, was what Thomas loved best.

I tried not to laugh as I watched him shirk off his shirt and pants before pouncing into the water with an enormous splash. He surfaced a moment later with a wistful sigh and flipped onto his back. His long legs had transformed into a single tail with two long fins like butterfly wings at the end. He had scales from his navel on downward that shone in brilliant blues and greens. His black hair fanned out around his face and head as he floated along, his fins flitting to and fro to propel him every few feet through the water. Gills had appeared just under his jaw. I'd seen him change enough times for it not to be so bizarre and shocking. In fact, I always found his true form to be rather cute.

"Please join me, my beautiful ladies," he said, sticking out his lower lip in a little pout. I shook my head, but obliged him after I took off my clothes. The clean water felt heavenly on my bruises and cuts, especially under the unforgiving Jamaican sun. Kida shed her clothes and joined us. We all flipped onto our backs and just floated there together, watching the clouds pass. I'd never admit it, but there were only two points in my life where I ever felt at peace, and this was one of them.

I didn't trust people. Not really. Just the rules of the business. Kida and Thomas were the only exceptions. I could relax around them and just...exist. And for a crooked treasure hunter like me, that was the best I was probably ever going to get.

Once we started to prune, we sat under the shade together to dry off with Thomas in the middle, my head on his shoulder, Kida's head on his other shoulder, watching the waves of the lagoon go in and out with the tide. None of us said a word.

It was nice.

Then it was time to get moving for our trip to find the sunken Scottish ship. Thomas helped me climb the banana tree and remove a couple of bunches, then we hiked back to *La Espada*. Kida hummed cheerfully as she ate her banana, and I couldn't help but smile at how something so simple made my darling happy.

As we crested the hill, Thomas stopped and turned his head back the way we came. He frowned. I nudged him. "What's wrong?"

"Not sure," he said. "I thought I heard something."

I listened. Nothing, at least not to human ears. "Like what?"

"Footsteps. I thought we were alone out here."

I touched the sword on my hip, growing worried. "Think we were followed?"

"It's possible, but I can't hear anything now. We'll just be careful on our way out." He kissed my forehead to reassure me, and we continued along the path to the ship.

Kida pulled the ship back out into the open sea and I kept a close eye on the shoreline as we left it, searching with my eye glass for any sign of life outside of the animals near the lagoon. I trusted Thomas. He had excellent senses and good intuition, so if he thought we were being followed, we probably were, so we needed to make ourselves scarce. Any boat within our vicinity was going to get a rough welcome from yours truly until we left Jamaican shores to head to our next destination.

After we'd left the land behind, I walked up onto the deck and slipped my arms around my lover. Kida didn't turn her head, staying focused. "I'm still mad at you."

"I know," I said as I tweaked her backside. "Sorry about earlier. You were right."

Kida glanced at me, pretending to be shocked. "What was that?"

"Oh, shove off," I grumbled. "I'm not going to say it twice."

"The great and powerful Lila can admit she's wrong," Kida said in a sing-song tone. "I thought the stars would fall from the sky first."

"Yeah, yeah, yeah." I kissed her and she squeezed my hand on her shoulder, giving me a rare smile. "Miracles can happen, after all."

I heard a little wistful sigh and turned to see Thomas at the top of the stairs, smiling in a silly fashion at the two of us. "Made up, have you?"

"Not entirely," Kida sniffed. "But we're getting there."

He chuckled and offered the map to her. "Your headings. We should reach the cliffs by sunset."

She let go of the helm and studied Thomas' markings. "I see. Rather treacherous, it seems."

"Yes, I'll have to swim for a while to scout out the area and confirm the sunken ship's position. I would wager the men aboard were being pursued and tried to wedge their way through the cliffs." He pointed to the narrow bit of water. "And they got stuck, punctured the hull, and sank. The water levels eventually rose over time and the waves likely pushed it even further down. Most skilled seafarers can't swim that deep nor maneuver in such a way to get to it. It'll certainly be a challenge."

"And let's just hope our reward is still there." I patted my money purse. "It's a long way to Cozumel. We may have to stop off in the Cayman Islands first and get some work if this venture doesn't pay off."

Thomas frowned. "Lila, honestly, I could return to Atlantis and bring back something valuable to trade—"

I held up one hand. "Thomas, we're not having this conversation again. Yes, I know, you have access to such things, but we need to earn a living. It's enough I've kidnapped you to sail the world plundering treasure and it's a long swim back to where you came from in the first place."

"I am a willing captive," he said dryly. "And don't pretend this isn't also about your ambition."

"Maybe it is, but the matter is settled. You'll stay here with us. For all we know, if the royal family gets you back, they won't let you go again, and I don't want the Kraken after us. They already hate that you're with surface dwellers in the first place."

"Merfolk don't hate anything. That's why we've never had a war."

"And I pray you never do," Kida said softly. "But Lila is right. We can make our own way. There is no need to bring Atlantis into this unless you are homesick."

"Certainly not. I know every inch of the place and that's why I left." He gestured to the horizon. "This is meant to be. So many new places to see. This is where I belong."

He kissed me, then her. "I'll go prepare the diving equipment, if you'll excuse me."

I pinched his backside as he passed by me and he yelped, blushing. We both giggled as we watched him go.

I tossed out the anchor once we'd reached the right spot and helped Thomas ready the double-braided rope and its net. As a child, I'd been taught how to hold my breath for long periods of time so I could look for valuable things underwater to trade for food or other goods. I could make it several minutes before I'd have to surface to take a breath, which gave me an edge when it came to finding sunken treasure. Thomas would go down first and explore the area, confirm the treasure, and then I'd follow him down with the net. Kida would reel it in, then we'd get what we found appraised and sold.

I stripped down to my undergarments, then hooked on a diving knife in case any predators took interest in me. Thomas made sure the line was ready and then jumped into the sea. He surfaced and pushed his long hair out of his eyes. "I'll return in just a moment."

"Be careful," I told him.

"Always." And with that, he swam away, his fins gleaming in the dying sunlight.

I waited. After a while, Thomas swam up to the side of the ship, excitement all over his face. "It's there. Bottom of the ship, hidden inside a barrel that used to hold chalices. It's going to be quite heavy, so we'll need to help Kida once we haul it to the side of the ship."

"Got it." I glanced up at Kida. "Be back shortly, love."

"Be careful, *corazón*."

I grinned as I dangled my legs over the edge of the ship, borrowing Thomas' words. "Always."

I fell into the ocean. I swam out toward the cliffs next to Thomas until we'd reached the diving site. I steadied my breathing, concentrating on conserving energy and preparing for the long haul, then inhaled as deeply as possible.

Then we dove together.

Enough sunlight still penetrated the water for me to see. We'd chosen sundown for a reason—less visibility for others to follow. It was a common practice of pirates and corsairs to follow treasure hunters at a distance and then try to rob them. Emphasis on try. No one had ever successfully overtaken us, and we aimed to keep it that way. Thomas could see in the dark and guide me if I got lost. I trusted him completely and I knew Kida would keep an eye out for any approaching vessels trying to steal what we'd recovered.

The Scottish ship had lost a lot of its exterior over the years, but most of the hull was intact. We still had to enter through the ship's lower deck, but once we did, I could see the extent of the damage from when the reef had sunk it.

Thomas swam over to the end of the ship's lowest deck, then pointed to the overturned barrel. I followed him and we tipped it back onto its base. As he'd mentioned, there were a few rusted chalices on top, but underneath them was a wooden top that had broken in one corner to reveal the sterling pounds underneath. Under any other circumstances, we'd need several people to help carry it, but Thomas was exceptionally strong, so he and I just lifted it and let the water take some of the weight as we swam toward the net. I'd tied it to a piece of the ship's upper deck so it wouldn't float away. We sat the barrel inside and tied it tightly to stay in place, then tugged on the line three times. Kida began to reel it in.

After we surfaced, I threw my arms around Thomas, gleeful. "Did you see how much was in there?"

Thomas laughed. "Now, now, let's not get ahead of ourselves. We still have a long way to go from here to an appraiser and then a buyer."

"I know, but wow," I said, swiping my wet curls out of my face. "What a find. This is going to make our lives so much easier from here on out."

"I hope it does."

We swam back to the ship. The barrel in its net was floating beside it, presumably since Kida was waiting on us to help her pull the incredibly heavy treasure aboard. I used the rope to climb aboard, already eager to tell her just how much I thought it would go for.

"Kida, you're not going to believe what we found—"

I froze as I spotted my beloved on her knees, a sword under her chin, a man cloaked in darkness holding it. "Hold it right there, missy—"

I reacted without thought.

One man tried to rush me from where he'd been crouching by the edge of the boat. I withdrew my dagger and stabbed him in the throat, then kicked him off the side into the sea. The man on my left tackled me. The back of my skull hit the deck and my vision doubled, breath driven from my lungs. I didn't care. He pinned my right wrist and grabbed my throat, trying to strangle me. I kneed him in the groin and slammed the top of my skull down onto his nose, breaking it. He cried out, his grip loosening on my arm, and I brought the dagger down into the meat between his right shoulder and neck. He slumped over dead and I shoved the corpse aside, pouncing onto my feet.

It was at this point the man holding Kida hostage spoke. "Move another inch and she dies."

I held the blood-soaked dagger in a reverse grip, panting heavily, my eyes adjusting to the darkness. There were six more men aboard. One was on the floor at Thomas' feet, clutching his groin and moaning in pain. My precious merman had tried to defend himself instead of running. Damn him.

"Kill him," Kida snarled. Her shirt was torn and bloodied, and she had a black eye, but I spotted two other dead bodies on the other side of the ship, courtesy of her cutlass, no doubt. "Forget about me. Do it, Lila."

I calculated. I could throw the dagger and it would hit him. But with the blade under her chin like that, he could slice it before the dagger made its mark. The wound would be fatal, without a doubt, and I'd still have to contend with the others. Thomas had an axe leaned up against his nape, his body stretched between the filthy bastards holding him still.

The man who held my lover captive wore tattered clothes but for an elegant wide-brimmed hat with a black feather. He obviously held it in high regard, as if it were his prized possession, for everything else on him was worn and shoddy. He had a thick beard and mustache. His build was stringy, like he hadn't had a good meal in months, and his men looked the same way. There weren't any ships nearby, which meant one thing—they'd docked somewhere on the other side of the cliffs where we couldn't see and swam up to *La Espada* using the darkness as their cover. Risky. Almost desperately so.

"You know," he continued in a measured voice. "You have a lot to be grateful for, my fine friend. A ship to call your own. Gold in your pocket. A woman at your side. A man at your back. You have food, clothing, gold, and most of all..."

His black eyes glittered with greed and envy. "Love. Most folks would kill for all that. It may be modest, but it is worth coveting. And I covet your lifestyle. I have for a while now. You are notoriously hard to catch and even harder to overcome, but you forgot one thing: every man has a price. And the price of your freedom was a hundred doubloons. That was all it took for your man Arty to tell us where you went."

His gaze then flicked over to Thomas. "And about the merman."

I clenched my teeth. "You want my lifestyle? Fine. Take it. Take everything I have. Just let us go in the long boat and you can have what you want."

"I'm afraid you've misunderstood my intentions, madam," he said. "I want your lifestyle, yes, but I can't have your life unless I have *him*." He pointed to Thomas with his other hand. "Because the merman is the key to your success as a treasure hunter. He can go where no man can follow. So, I will let you and your pretty lover go, but the merman stays with me."

"No," I spat. "I will not surrender him to you. Over my dead fucking body."

"Lila," Thomas said softly. I looked at him. Something calm and sad had entered his features. My stomach sank. "Go. Please. Take Kida and go."

"I'm not leaving you, Thomas!"

He smiled. "Exactly. I am leaving you."

"Thomas—" Kida protested, but the pirate dug the blade into her skin a little more and she fell silent.

"An immortal life for two mortal lives," Thomas said, addressing the pirate. "Mine for theirs. A trade, as it were. You let them go and I'll go with you willingly."

"Thomas, don't do this," I whispered. "You don't know what they'll do to you."

"I do know," he said quietly. "But I cannot let you perish here. You both mean the world to me, and I would not have had the freedoms I enjoyed had I not met you."

Thomas lifted his chin, his clear blue eyes hard and gleaming. "Do we have a deal, pirate?"

"Well, well," he said, stroking his ratty beard. "You have a spine after all, merman. Aye, we have a deal."

He looked at me. "Drop the dagger."

I fumed, wanting with every fiber of my being to throw it straight into his right eye, but I knew better. Live today, fight tomorrow. No other choice.

I let my dagger clatter to the deck. A man nearby collected it, then tied my hands behind my back. Another man came forward and tied Kida up as well, shoving us to sit beside the gold they'd just hauled up to the deck.

The pirate leader nodded to his men and gave one of them a heading. "Fair is fair. We're going to drop our lovely ladies off and then head for our next destination."

He walked over to Thomas and lightly toyed with his beautiful wet locks, but he met my eyes instead. "And it goes without saying that if I ever see you again, I'll slit his throat and leave him in Davy Jones' locker."

The pirate snapped his fingers and the two men dragged Thomas away.

We sailed until daybreak. I knew enough of the area to know our current heading wasn't a good sign. I wished Thomas had let us all go down in a blaze of glory. At least we'd die together instead of apart.

The ship coasted just outside a spat of land so small it could hardly be called an island. It was scarcely eighty feet across and was in the open sea, nowhere near a port or a shipping lane. There was a single palm tree, nothing else. I'd heard some unruly men call it Satan's Bald Spot.

And I knew this because it was where I'd met Thomas.

The men pulled out the gangplank and the head pirate withdrew his rusty sword, gesturing for the two of us to go. He tossed Kida a small bag with provisions and water in it, but I knew it wouldn't last more than a day or two. "A life for two lives. Awful generous of me, if I do say so myself. Thank you for your bountiful gifts, ladies. And don't fret. We'll take good care of the merman."

"If you're the last man I ever see, I want to know your name," I demanded.

He smirked, considering it for a moment, then spoke. "They call me Brolin."

"Brolin," I said slowly. Then I smiled venomously. "I'll remember it well."

"I suspect you will, my friend." He gestured to the gangplank.

"No," Kida snapped. "Let us see Thomas. Let us say goodbye."

Brolin clucked his tongue. "I'm afraid that wasn't part of the deal, sweetheart."

Kida rushed forward on instinct. "You bastard—"

I jerked her back before he could raise the sword to her. She struggled against me, screaming, "I'll kill you! I'll kill you all, you bastards! You slimy, flea-bitten cowards! I'll run you down if it takes me the rest of my goddamn life!"

I dragged her down the gangplank as she broke off into Spanish obscenities, each worse than the last. They pulled the gangplank up, then the anchor, and they sailed away with our lives.

And our Thomas.

* * *

"I knew it wouldn't last." Kida's voice came out hoarse. No surprise. The tree provided very little shade and it was hot. I was still in just my undergarments, so at least I had a slight relief from the heat. "I knew we were too happy with our life. I knew this would happen. Why didn't I say anything?"

"Because you were happy," I said absently, staring at the burning sand between my feet. "You don't notice you've taken it for granted until it's too late."

"I have been a hard, cynical woman my entire life. I let you turn me soft. What a fool I've been."

I snorted. "Lot of that going around."

"They'll enslave him for the rest of his life," Kida said hotly. "Which could be centuries based on what he's told us. Meanwhile, we're too dead to save him. We won't last a week here. There aren't any ships that pass by. There is nothing out here. Nothing but death. Why did you have to associate with an insect like Arty?"

"Because that's what I do, alright?" I snapped. "Neither of us can make an honest living in this world. So I made my own living. If you hated it so much, why'd you go along with it?"

"Because I love you!" she shouted, glaring at me with tears in her eyes.

My jaw dropped.

"Oh, don't look so surprised," Kida sneered. "Why else would I dirty my hands to help you find your precious treasure? Yes, I love you, Lila. I know you don't want to hear it, but there it is. I only went along out of my love for you and for Thomas. I was ignorant in my happiness and I ignored the signs that this was coming. So this is my fate and I accept it. What I do not accept is allowing Thomas to spend the rest of his life beaten, tortured, and forced into slavery."

"You don't know that," I whispered. "Maybe he'll escape."

"He's too noble. He won't. He'll let them tear him apart for our sake."

"No!" I stood up, but I had nowhere to go. "No, he'll get away from them, I know it. He's clever. He's strong."

"He's loyal," Kida said. "He won't do anything since he gave them his word."

Tears welled up in my eyes. I brushed them aside angrily. "Then that's his fault. Not ours. If it were me, I'd run off and try to find you."

"He is a gentleman," she murmured. "Not a fighter. The second he gave himself to them, he signed his life away."

I collapsed to my knees. Sobs shook my entire form. "I'm so sorry, Kida. I'm sorry I did this to us."

The tears wouldn't stop coming. All my life, I'd fought and fought and fought for freedom, and yet this was where it would end for me. For the love of my life. For my dear friend. All for want of treasure. Had I been too selfish and greedy? Too ambitious? Too driven by my past tragedies to see that I had been setting us up to fail?

I cried there in the sand, a broken woman.

Until eventually, Kida embraced me from behind.

"I forgive you," she whispered into my nape. "I forgive you, Lila. It's okay. Hush now."

\* \* \*

Hours passed. The sun felt like it barely moved across the sky. We ate very little. I found a stick and tied some of my hairs to it and then attached a small piece of dried goat in case a fish would wander by and eat it. No such luck, of course, but might as well try.

"Do you remember that night we met?" Kida asked.

"Mm-hmm."

"You were so strong," she said fondly. She lay on her back beside me, our hands clasped, even though it was still scorching hot. "I'd never seen anything like it. And you didn't care what anyone thought of you. I'd always aspired to be like that."

I arched an eyebrow. "You mean you do care what people think about you?"

She rolled her eyes. "Sometimes. After all, I spent years pretending to be a man all because the women in my country were expected to be nothing but wives and mothers. They looked at me and saw livestock, not a person. I hated it. I wanted to be free. To not care how I looked or dressed or who I spent my time with. You gave me that. That's why I fell in love with you."

I smiled. "Well, if it's any consolation, I fell in love with you because your inner strength is just as powerful as your outer strength. You've proven everyone wrong time and time again, but your heart is still as golden as the doubloons we've stolen. There is no finer captain on the seven seas."

She squeezed my hand. "Thank you, *corazón*."

Kida squinted up at the tree. "Was this here when you met Thomas all those years ago?"

"It was, yeah," I said. "It used to yield something. Coconuts, maybe? Can't remember."

Kida closed her eyes. "Tell me the story again. I love it so much."

I cleared my throat. "He saw me here all alone, on the brink of death. He swam away and came back with oysters. I thought I was dreaming, at first. But he kept coming back, day after day, finding me things to eat so I wouldn't die. But fresh water was the problem. I had reached the point where I'd die of thirst. It was too far for him to swim me to shore, so one day, he swam out into the open water until he found a shipping lane and he revealed himself to them. They came and found me here, took me aboard their ship. Thomas nursed me back to health and asked me why I'd been abandoned out there. I told him about the British Navy. He'd never heard of a woman causing such trouble. It made him interested in my story."

I wiped away tears again. "And the rest is history."

"Did he ever tell you why he was here?"

I thought it over. "No, not sure if I ever asked him."

Kida sat up abruptly. "Oh my God, *corazón.* I think...I think we can save ourselves."

I sat up as well, confused. "What?"

"Thomas is from Atlantis, right?" she said, standing up and pulling me with her.

"Yes. What about it?"

"He found you here, right here!" She stomped on the sand. "What if Atlantis—"

"—is here!" I ran my hand through my tangled curls, following the idea. "At the bottom of the ocean. What if the entrance to Atlantis is below us and that's why he was out here that day?"

I paced back and forth. "It would have to be, I don't know, several meters below us. I don't know if I could make the swim, but..." I shook my head. "Fuck it. It's worth a shot."

"Don't use all your air in one go," Kida told me, holding my shoulders firmly. "Remember: you have to conserve enough to be able to come up if you don't find anything. Look for caves and coral reefs where there might be pockets of air, too."

She gripped the side of my face. "And above all, come back to me, Lila. Promise me you will."

"I promise, love." I kissed her passionately. "Wish me luck."

She smiled. "Good luck."

I walked to the water's edge and inhaled as deeply as I knew how.

Then I dove into the sea.

I swam straight down. The sunlight helped me see the sand deposits that made up Satan's Bald Spot, so I followed it along until the water darkened past where the light could easily reach. I knew by now at this depth, most men would have to turn back. I had about three to five minutes of air left for this trip.

The water turned cold after I passed a certain depth, the darkness thickening. Fear began to gnaw at my stomach as my visibility dropped to almost nothing. *Faith. Have faith, Lila. Keep going. You have to save her. You have to save them both.*

Total darkness now. I swam and tried to remember how many minutes I had left before I would have to turn back. It was ice-cold now. I struggled to move my limbs.

Then, below me, I saw a soft blue light.

I swam closer to it and reached out. Something round glowed like a lantern, but with an eerie blue I'd never seen before. I turned my head upward and couldn't see anything. How far was I in the ocean's depths? Would I be able to make it up again before I drowned?

I turned my attention back to the glowing ball, feeling for more, and then I realized it was on some kind of pole. When I touched the pole, the rest of the structure lit up with the same bright blue.

And I realized that I was floating above an ancient gate of some sort.

When the gate lit up, I could see that there was a path of glowing blue lights that led to what looked like a bubble the size of...of a city.

But the problem was I was about to run out of air.

The distance between the gate and the bubble had to be half a kilometer. If I turned back now, there was no guarantee I'd be able to swim the exact same path again and find it. Shit!

I forced myself forward. My limbs ached. My brain screamed for air. My vision narrowed, but I kept going. I had to. Had to swim. *Keep swimming, Lila, don't let it end here. Don't let them down again.*

Five feet.

Four feet.

Three feet.

Two.

One.

Then darkness shrouded me, and I drifted off into oblivion.

* * *

I woke up when someone's hands shoved onto my chest hard.

I coughed up seawater like a fountain. Once I'd got it all out of my mouth and nose, I groaned. "Ow. That hurt."

"Yes, I suspect it did," a female voice said from somewhere above me.

I pried my eyes open to see a woman with long silvery hair kneeling beside me. She had a sand dollar around her neck and her skin shone all over with scales the color of pearls. She had no nipples or belly button, but she was slender and strong with gills under her jaw and slightly pointed ears. Her eyes were the same color blue as the gate I'd seen.

And she wasn't the only one.

There was a small crowd gathered around me, men and women alike, each of them covered in different colored scales and various hair and eye colors, but with two legs and two arms same as me. We were in the middle of a path at the bottom of the ocean, smooth and worn like sandstone. There were homes carved out of the stone and made from sand and mud dotted throughout the ocean floor, all large and very much like cottages.

"Easy does it," the woman said as she helped me stand up. I wobbled, but my legs held. She looped my arm around her shoulder and spoke another language to the people around her. Some of them hurried off. "We need to get you some help. Come along."

I shook my head. "No, I'm okay. This is urgent. He's in trouble."

"Calm down. Who is in trouble?"

"Thomas."

The woman stiffened beside me, her eyes wide. "Thomas?"

"Yes. Pirates ambushed us and stole our ship, left us marooned on the patch of land at the surface. We have to get him back."

She said something in language that sounded like a curse. "Poseidon be damned. We must hurry."

She stuck her fingers in her mouth and whistled. A second later, a large creature resembling a horse but with lavender scales instead of brown or black fur came from around a nearby pen.

"Hee hee," I said, still not having recovered from my brain being deprived of air. "It's a sea horse. Get it?"

The woman eyed me, but said nothing as she helped me onto its back. "You humans are a strange lot. But I suppose I should congratulate you. You are the first to ever reach our city alive."

"What? Do lots of dead people make it?"

"Yes," she said humorlessly. "We've found many dead explorers outside the gates. You must be special to have made it this far."

"Not special," I said. "Determined. We have to save him and my lover Kida as well. Take me to the palace. I have to see the King and Queen of Atlantis."

"Then let us ride. Hyah!" She slapped the reins and the sea horse took off down the streets of Atlantis.

At the end of the row of cottages was an ivory castle with the same kind of gates as the outer ones. The guards on either side nodded to the woman and they opened them for her without question, which made me curious as to her identity. She and I dismounted the sea horse and walked into a great hall of sorts. There were three thrones at the far end. She asked one of the guards something and moments later, two people walked into the hall.

The woman was tall and slender with long black hair and brown eyes. She was covered in turquoise scales. The man had long white hair tied in a braid and blue eyes. He was covered in umber scales. They wore rings and had pierced ears as well. The two took a seat and gave me a look somewhere between interest and disgust. After all, I was still in just my soaked undergarments that left nothing to the imagination.

"My King and Queen," the woman said, bowing. I did the same. "We have a visitor from the surface. She seeks an audience with you regarding your son, Thomas."

"What have you to say about my son?" the woman asked coldly.

I licked my chapped lips, my teeth chattering. "Y-Your Majesties..."

I paused as one of the guards came forward with a silver cloak. It had lining on the inside, some kind of animal pelt, and I wrapped it around me, thanking him. It helped me stop shivering so much. "Prince Thomas has been our traveling companion for some time now. We were ambushed by pirates and they took our ship, kidnapped him, and sailed away. We seek your help in rescuing him."

"Pirates," the king sneered. "Heartless, cut-throat cowards, the lot of them. He should have known better than to cavort around with your kind—"

"Elian," the queen said quietly. "Do not be uncouth. He made a mistake, as we all do. Do not punish him for not walking your path."

She turned to me. "I am Queen Meredith, Thomas' mother. Who are you to him?"

"He is mine and another's lover and friend. I care for him deeply. I wish to return him to Atlantis after he has been rescued, for I know now that I can't protect him the way I thought I could."

"You ask for our help after endangering him?" King Elian snapped. "You have some nerve, human."

"She risked her life coming down here," the woman beside me said. "You know no surface dweller has ever reached Atlantis alive and yet you condemn her?"

"Evey, that is enough. Your cousin's foolishness has finally caught up with him. It's high time he learn the consequences of his actions."

Evey gritted her teeth. "It is not a crime to wonder about the world above. If you will do nothing, I will go myself. Thomas has always been there for me in a way that you never have. We are blood. I will not let him suffer at the hands of a bloodthirsty pirate."

Queen Meredith raised her hand before King Elian could get another word out. She looked at me. "Do you understand what you are asking, young one? If you return him here, he will never again be allowed to leave Atlantis."

I swallowed hard. "Yes, Your Majesty. I...love him. And I just want him to be safe."

She studied me. "How many pirates abducted our son?"

"At least ten, Your Majesty."

She gestured to the nearest guard. "Gather your men. Return to the surface and find our son."

The guard bowed his head. "As you wish, Your Majesty."

"I will go with them," Evey said. "And I will bring him home."

"If he does not agree to return," King Elian said, his eyes narrowing at me. "Then he will be exiled from Atlantis. Do you understand?"

"Yes, Your Highness. Might I make a suggestion?"

"If you must."

"There may be ten or more men waiting. I wish no harm to come to your guards. You know what we need."

Elian smirked. "Very well."

He gestured to the guard captain. "Send in the Kraken."

* * *

Thomas was a smart merman. If Brolin went for the nearest treasure hunt, then I knew where Thomas would lead them if there was any chance for a rescue. There was a ship that had sunk with rumors of French currency less than a day's journey from the cliffs where they'd caught us. The reason we'd never bothered with it was the current was too strong for me to swim and Thomas couldn't haul it out alone. The pirates wouldn't know that.

And it would give Thomas the time to stall.

A merman could swim against a strong current, but it took time and effort. More than likely, they'd put him in chains so he couldn't escape and posted a man as a lookout while he was underwater. He would have just under an hour to try to trick them into staying put long enough for us to find him.

There was only one way to take back the ship. It couldn't be a man at a time—we'd have to hit them all at once and overpower them.

And that's where the merfolk came in handy.

Aside from the man holding onto Thomas' chains, there were four posted on the deck to check for any approaching ships. It was nighttime now. The current below them made the ship rock back and forth even though it was anchored.

The perfect time to strike.

The first guard didn't even get out a scream when a tentacle the size of a tree trunk lifted out of the water, crushed his windpipe, and dragged him into the briny deep. The second one went the exact same way. The third and fourth guards were talking to each other on the other side of the deck, but then one noticed the two men were missing and asked the man on watch if he'd seen them. He said no. They walked over to the edge of the ship, calling for them.

Which gave Kida the cover to climb up the side of the ship and slit the watchman's throat.

I caught the corpse so it wouldn't make a splash as it tipped over the side of the ship. I tried not to groan as the weight of his heavy body nearly made me drop to the sea as well, but I stayed the course until I heard the splash of the Kraken snatching the other two men off the deck. I let the body hit the water and climbed up onto the deck beside Kida, offering my hand to Evey to help her up as well. She helped the captain of the guard, Reed, and his other four men aboard and we headed for the lower deck.

Unfortunately, one of the drunken pirates stumbled out of the lower deck and spotted us.

"We're under attack—" He died instantly as one of the guard's harpoons impaled him.

Chaos erupted.

The rest of the pirates spilled out from the lower deck and charged us. Kida and I took the lead with swords in hand, slaying them left and right until the deck was splattered with blood. The merfolk joined in. An unearthly vibration shook the night air as the Kraken below the ship began thrashing around snatching pirates off to drag them down into its hungry mouth under the surface. The sea boiled and the ship rocked on the waves in the midst of the chaos.

"Where is he?" I snarled into the man at the end of my blade. "Where is Brolin?"

He gasped like a landed fish and pointed to the living quarters. I snatched the blade out of his stomach and marched forward, Kida at my side.

I kicked the door open.

Brolin stood in the center of the room, cutlass in hand, a nasty smirk on his lips. "So. Apparently, you're both hardheaded women."

"Oh, you have no idea," Kida snarled as she kicked the door shut behind us.

"We can always be diplomatic about this," Brolin said. "Call a truce and part ways since you didn't have the decency to die on that beach."

I laughed. "We are way past a truce. Best prepare to meet your maker. You'll be seeing him shortly."

I charged. Brolin parried, but Kida was right on my heels, slashing at his left side. He dodged and spun to my right, aiming for my neck. I blocked and shoved him away from me, regaining my balance. Kida led, her cutlass glinting in the candlelight, her small body swift and deadly in her sword strokes. I circled Brolin and closed in from behind, forcing him to draw a second smaller blade to counter me. He did well, for a pirate.

But not well enough.

Kida landed the first cut across his upper arm. I scored another across the top of his left thigh. He kept going, fighting harder, but as his blood painted the floor of our bedroom, we attacked in unison to drive him back against the wall. He fell to one knee at first. Kida kicked at his kneecap and dislodged it. He screamed and tried to balance on it, but failed. He collapsed on his backside and I slapped the swords from his grip one at a time. He slumped to the wall, bleeding profusely, clutching the injured leg, while my lover and I stood above him, our swords at his throat.

Brolin let out a wet cough and grinned. "I guess true love really does conquer all."

"Goddamn right it does," I whispered.

Our swords swung together and beheaded him.

\* \* \*

The relief on my love's face was a moving thing when we pulled Thomas onto the ship. He wrapped his long arms around me and Kida and we embraced him back, huddling together in a shaking wet pile.

"My loves," he whispered. "Why? Why did you come for me? You risked everything for me. You could have died."

I drew back and brushed the soaked dark hair from his face, smiling through my tears. "You silly merman. Haven't you figured it out yet?"

Thomas frowned. "Figured what out?"

Kida kissed his forehead. "For want of treasure. It's not about the gold, Thomas. You are our treasure. Always."

He bowed his head, humbled by our words, and held us tighter. No one said anything for a minute, just letting us hold him.

We helped him up. He bowed formally to his cousin Evey and the guards. "I thank you for risking your lives to help my beloved ladies."

"It was nothing," Evey said, smiling at us. "They are valiant women."

Thomas sighed. "I suppose the King and Queen have demanded I return home or face exile."

"Indeed they have."

"We'll miss you," I said, squeezing his fingers. "But it's for the best."

"You will not miss me, for I am not going anywhere."

"Thomas, please," Kida said. "You must listen to reason. Atlantis is your home. Your family can keep you safe and you will never again be in danger."

"And," he said. "I will never have a life of my own. I will be a fish in a bowl, forever swimming in circles, safe...and trapped and unhappy."

He faced me and my lover, holding our hands. "I disobeyed the royal family and came to the surface seeking adventure." Thomas smiled softly. "And found love instead. Atlantis holds many wonders, but that is what it lacks. I would trade safety for true love any day. You are worth it, both of you. Always."

Kida and I shared an intimate look before I asked. "Are you sure?"

He kissed our hands where they were joined with his. "Absolutely certain, my treasures."

He glanced at Evey. "Do give the royal family my best, cousin."

Evey smiled and shook her head. "You always were a rebel, Thomas."

She lifted onto her tiptoes and kissed his cheek. "I'll miss you, but..." She smiled warmly at me and Kida. "...I know you are in good hands."

With that, she and the merfolk left *La Espada* and disappeared into the moonlit waters below.

We rid our ship of the pirates that had tainted her, then climbed into bed together. The sea led us into sleep with its lullaby, leaving us in peace at last.

Kyoko M. is the author of *The Black Parade* urban fantasy series, and the *Of Cinder and Bone* science-fiction series. She has appeared as a guest and panelist at such conventions as Geek Girl Con, DragonCon, Blacktasticon, JordanCon, ConCarolinas, MultiverseCon, and Momocon. She is also a contributor to Marvel Comics' *Black Panther: Tales of Wakanda* (2021) anthology.

# Haunting Georgie

Sara Codair

Sapphic Representation: Lesbian, Bi/Pan
Heat Level: Low
Content Warnings: Coarse Language, Death

It was a perfect day, so of course *The Classy Princess* had to break down. Georgie supposed she shouldn't be surprised. The boat had been cheap, even for used and old. There had to be more wrong with it than a crappy name and a loose wire in the starter. A wire she'd fixed before putting the boat in the water.

It had been running great all afternoon, so good that she'd decided to venture out of the harbor and into the ocean. It quit while passing a beach populated with kayakers and anchored boats. She tried restarting it again, but no matter how many times she turned the key, the engine wouldn't turn over.

This was why she had a kicker motor—a small outboard mounted to the back of the swim platform. It had just enough power to slowly push the boat. *That* started on the first try, coming to life full throttle and pushing the boat forward a little too enthusiastically. It turned hard, the handle flying free from Georgie's grip. The boat lurched toward the beach and Georgie wobbled. She reached for the rail, but her hand passed through cold air. She swayed, then fell, arms flailing into the cold water as the boat puttered forward.

"Shit!" Georgie shouted as she swam after the boat, which thankfully couldn't go too fast with the little eight-horsepower. Still, there were rocks between the boat and the beach it was now heading toward, and if it hit one...

The boat turned, effortlessly avoiding rocks that would have ripped a hole in the freshly painted hull. It was like something invisible was steering—angling the boat for a spot between a single kayaker and a child-infested Boston Whaler. And there was only one invisible thing Georgie thought might be steering a boat.

A ghost.

A freaking ghost.

She'd checked for ghosts before she bought the damned boat, but she lacked a medium's ability to sense just any ghost and equipment only detected malevolent spirits.

If her instruments didn't pick it up, that meant it was probably a friendly one, but regardless of its temperament, it was a dead thing that didn't belong here, and it was steering her boat. Apparently, she couldn't catch a break from the damned supernatural. Not even on the water.

George used to be a monster hunter. Raging, pissed off, murderous ghosts were a thing she used to deal with on a regular basis. But she retired when, well, things had gotten a bit out of hand. She'd lost her mentor and apprentice. Done things she regretted. She wanted no part of the supernatural now.

Muscles burned as she channeled all her rage into kicking her legs. Her hands cut into the water and hit a rock. Then, realizing it was shallow, she stood in waist-deep water and ran and flopped her way to the boat. Close to shore, the outboard sputtered and quit, and Georgie grabbed onto the swim ladder, folded it down, and climbed onto the narrow platform. Momentum carried the vessel forward while she scrambled into the boat and got the anchors out. She dropped one off the back, climbed between the windows to the bow, dropped the other down, lowered herself into ankle deep water, and carried the front anchor to shore, all the while hoping the ghost didn't mess with the rear anchor.

Friendly ghosts did exist, but it was mediums who usually dealt with them, not hunters. She'd probably need to hire a medium.

"Hello!"

Georgie jumped at the sound of a cheery voice. Maybe it was the kayaker the boat had pulled up next to.

"Hi!" She turned around and found herself being smiled at by a woman, standing a few feet away. Giant sunglasses covered her eyes, but that didn't dim the brightness of her smile. Wavy hair—light brown and streaked with gray—hung to her shoulders. She wore floral board shorts and an athletic bikini top that showed off a well-muscled abdomen.

A pit formed in Georgie's stomach as her cheeks heated up. She had a long history of being reckless around beautiful women and was committed to staying single while she figured out her new life. Leaving would be the logical thing to do, except her engine wasn't working, and God, that smile...

"Engine trouble?" asked the woman. "I noticed you came with your spare engine."

"Looks like it." It was entirely possible that the engine might start again in a few minutes and she'd make it home no problem, especially if the ghost—and not a mechanical problem—stalled the engine. Maybe the ghost had good intentions and didn't want Georgie to go out any further in the ocean because it knew something was wrong with the engine or sensed a storm the weather forecasters missed. Or maybe it was more selfish and wanted to stop at the beach, especially if it had been there before and had strong memories of it. Maybe the ghost was just as drawn to that smile...

And if the ghost gave her trouble the whole way back?

She suppressed a shudder. She'd gotten rid of ghosts before, by banishing them or burning their bones, which were the most painful ways to send them on. It was a task very few people were willing to do because it caused agony for the ghost, but Georgie had done it over and over again. She'd never forget the sounds of screaming as they were torn apart at a molecular level and ripped from this reality. The humane way to do it was to hire a medium to work their ghost therapist magic and talk it into moving on all on its own. And there had been far too many times Georgie hadn't done things the humane way.

"My nieces want me to have a boat like this." Grinning, the woman gestured to *The Classy Princess*. It was twenty-four feet long with a cabin big enough to sleep in, a tiny galley and bathroom, and enough seating for four to six people on the deck if Georgie wanted people on board, which she didn't. "But neither of my two brain cells is mechanically talented. I'll stick with my kayak."

A smile warmed Georgie's face and the present chased away old memories. "I think the fact that you chose something without an engine implies you have many more than two brain cells."

"Tell that to the cat who got dog food for breakfast this morning." The woman held a hand out to Georgie. "I'm Cali. She/her pronouns."

"Georgie. She/her." She shook the woman's hand, holding it a moment longer than she should have. It was calloused, presumably from lots of paddling, and her nails were trimmed short. "But did the dog get cat food? If so, I bet you had one happy doggo."

"Unfortunately, no." Cali's eyes smirked as they met Georgie's. "But he did steal half my scrambled eggs while I was getting the cat new food."

Laughter bubbled out of Georgie's mouth. "Your day sounds more chaotic than mine."

Cali put a hand to her chest. "I am the living embodiment of chaotic days." She swept her arms out toward *The Classy Princess*. "What do you think is wrong with your boat?"

"It could be anything." It wasn't exactly a lie. It could be anything even if it probably was a ghost. "She's more than twenty years old and I just bought her. The engine was running beautifully, then it stalled and wouldn't start up."

Cali's eyes wandered to the swim platform. She squinted and tilted her head. Georgie followed her gaze. Was that...smoke? She blinked. The air was clear. She inhaled salty air but didn't smell any smoke. Huh. She hoped the ghost wasn't trying to manifest. Only really, really strong, emotional ghosts could do that. Last time Georgie saw a ghost manifest, it had wrapped its cold, dead hands around her throat and tried to choke her. And while not all strong ghosts were violent or dangerous, the ones people hired her to go after were. And she'd had enough with violence.

But if this ghost was violent, Georgie's alarms would be blaring.

The alarms were silent.

Some ghosts were, allegedly, harmless. But that didn't mean they belonged in this world. At least, that's what everyone had always told Georgie. The dead didn't belong here, and it was the job of mediums and hunters to make sure they didn't stay here.

"Maybe it will start if you try again, after it's had a little break." Cali tilted her head, staring at the letters spelling out the boat's name.

"Maybe." Georgie squeezed her hands together behind her back and kept staring where she'd thought she saw the ghost. Nothing. Maybe her vision had just blurred.

"My late wife had a boat like this, only it was more colorful. *The Salty Unicorn.* Sometimes, the engine just got tired and demanded a break."

"I'll try starting it one more time." Georgie smiled at the word "wife," while a little panic fluttered in her chest. This woman was beautiful and queer and flirty. If she stayed here, her plans of staying single were doomed. She climbed up into the boat and turned the key. And the engine started right up, purring to life like nothing had ever been wrong with it. Maybe the ghost was now content to let Georgie leave.

She walked to the port side and looked down at Cali. "You know, I think I'm going to head home while it's running."

Georgie hoped the ghost would let her get home without problems. Then she could figure out what to do about it.

"Well, I'm here every Friday afternoon if you ever want to chat more." Cali waved. "Do you think you'll be back?"

"I guess that depends on what I find when I take this engine apart," said Georgie, uncertain whether a pretty, talkative woman meant she should definitely come back, or she should avoid this beach on Fridays. Flirting was fun, but it seemed like all her attempts at dating ended up disasters. Granted, some relationships, like the fling with the vampire, had been doomed from the start.

Georgie had spent twenty years hunting monsters for a living. It was hard to build relationships with people when she couldn't talk about something that had been her entire life for so long. And within the supernatural world? Well, Georgie had a bit of a reputation that colored the way people saw her. She was the one they called when a ghost couldn't be talked on, and they needed someone willing to banish it or torch its bones. She was the one who fought things like six-headed slime monsters and people-eating demons. When the job was messy, dangerous and morally ambiguous, you called Georgie Faust.

If she was going to start a relationship, which she wasn't, she didn't want that ruining her chance at love. She wasn't that person anymore.

It all seemed so impossible if she even wanted it, and she didn't, right? Right?

\* \* \*

Georgie closed the engine compartment and plopped down on the deck, though there was a seat a few feet away. She was too tired to move even that far. After retiring from monster hunting, she'd have been done with harsh physical labor if it weren't for this damned boat that she'd just had to have. But she'd wanted something big enough to sleep on if she wanted to travel...or if her anxiety over a vengeful ghoul sneaking past the wards on her house and murdering her in her sleep got too high. There was another reason not to date. What if some old enemy came back for revenge, like the poltergeist that shot acidic purple slime? That banishing had been sloppy. The cursed thing might piece itself back together one day to further torment Georgie.

She wiped sweat from her forehead. At least this ghost hadn't damaged anything when it made her boat stall out, and the lack of things wrong with the engine helped confirm that it had, indeed, been a ghost.

She heard a disembodied sound caught between a laugh and sob. Again.

She'd been hearing that noise all day, and assumed it was someone out on a boat or maybe on a dock across the river. But this time, the sound was close, like someone was with her on the dock.

"What's so funny?" she asked the disembodied voice.

"There is absolutely nothing wrong with this damned boat. Nothing. I took such good care of it." The words sounded far away, like there was water and air rushing between. These were words of the dead.

Georgie sat up straighter, hands reaching for a weapon she no longer carried before remembering that this ghost hadn't tripped her wards or sensors. It didn't mean any harm. "Then why did it stall out on me yesterday?"

Silence.

"You...you can...you can hear me?" asked the voice. "So far no one has heard me!"

"I can hear you." Not everyone could hear ghosts talk, but Georgie had always been able to hear the strong ones. "Why did you mess with the engine?"

"How do you know I messed with the engine?"

"You just said nothing was wrong with the boat," said Georgie. "Yet it stalled."

"Maybe I wanted you to meet that pretty lady you talked to." Pause. "You seemed lonely, and she was all alone."

"Do you have any idea what I did for a living?" Georgie smacked her forehead with her hands. Of course. Of course, she had to end up with a boat haunted by someone who wanted to play matchmaker from beyond the grave.

"Why does your old career matter?"

Georgie got to her feet and paced around the boat, wishing she knew exactly where the ghost was. "I hunted monsters. Raging ghosts. I probably still have dirt under my nails from all the graves I had to dig up. Who wants to date someone with grave dirt permanently embedded in their skin?"

"I bet you have a lot of fun stories to tell." She could hear the smirk in the ghost's voice even if she couldn't see it.

"Violent stories." Georgie shuddered, remembering being chased by kitchen knives and flying books. She remembered translucent monsters with half-a-dozen eyes and so many teeth that just sort of caved in and dissolved when she impaled them with an iron poker. The shriek of a ghost torn apart as she burned its bones. "Violence isn't fun."

"Are you sure about that? An awful lot of entertainment is full of it."

Georgie took a deep breath and stared down at the river, at the water rushing and swirling by on its race to the sea. She bit her lip. The problem was, Georgie wasn't sure. And that had been part of why she quit. Yes, she was tired of waking up sore from having to literally run for her life, get battered by flying objects, and dig up graves. She was tired of having to lie when people asked her what she did for a living, and feeling so disconnected from the mainstream world.

But she hated the fact that she wasn't tired of hearing ghosts scream when their bones burned or of decapitating ghouls or getting sprayed by guts when she stabbed some unnamed monstrosity. She didn't *want* to be the kind of person who *liked* doing all those things. And she certainly hadn't wanted to die how her mentor and apprentice both died.

So, she'd quit.

She had money saved but took a day job at a boating supply store to make sure she didn't go through her savings too quickly. Sometimes she liked it. Sometimes it was boring. Sometimes the customers were scarier than poltergeists.

"You liked it, didn't you?" There was something smug about the ghost's voice. "Hunting monsters. Fighting. Or whatever it was you did."

"That is none of your business. And neither is my love-life." Georgie's hands balled into fists and her lip snarled. "If you ever interfere with my engine and navigation again, I will exorcize you from this boat and send your ass packing to the great beyond. Are we clear?"

"Crystal," said the ghost with a tone that made Georgie think things were not clear at all.

* * *

Each night Georgie took the boat out after work. The ghost and the engine behaved, meaning the engine ran and the ghost didn't interfere or talk. Had Georgie not had a conversation with it, she would've doubted its existence.

Friday was her day off. She took the quickest route to the ocean—straight out on the river. Once past its mouth, she was greeted with a blast of fresh, cool ocean air. Her muscles tensed and her heart rate sped up. Her hand reached for the iron blade she used to carry.

Then she shook her head. Took a deep breath.

The temperature always dropped once you got out of the river and into the open ocean. It might have felt like walking into a cold pocket caused by a ghost, but the temperature change was because the ocean was just so damned cold. Georgie exhaled, slowly letting go of the tension in her body.

Ghosts, like most other supernatural creatures, couldn't cross running water unless they were somehow bound to an object. Like the way the ghost was bound to the *Princess*. And that wasn't the kind of angry ghost that would cause a cold pocket. Georgie was safe out here.

Sure, the sea held its own monsters, but they lurked far offshore in the deep dark places. Since Georgie had never hunted sea monsters, they wouldn't be seeking revenge against her for banishing their second cousin like a ghoul might.

Georgie shuddered at the memory of the last ghoul she'd banished. The poor thing hadn't really been hurting anybody, but ghouls don't belong in this dimension, and someone had paid Georgie a lot of money to get rid of it. It had fought so hard to stay Georgie wasn't sure it had survived the trip back to its home dimension.

* * *

After an hour or two on the ocean, her stomach was growling. She knew she'd stocked the galley before she left, but her sandwich was not in the fridge and the cupboards were empty. Maybe the ghost hadn't been so well behaved. Ghosts didn't eat, but if they were motivated, they could certainly feed Georgie's sandwich to the seagulls when she wasn't looking.

She turned around and started heading back home. It was probably better to not burn too much gas anyway, but she decided to go home through the back channel, where the water was calm and shallow, winding between islands, sandbars, and a bank populated with a mix of new McMansions and historic properties.

"Are you really going home?" The ghost's voice echoed all around Georgie.

"Yes. I'm hungry." And maybe a little nervous too. So, the ghost had finally woken up.

"I bet Cali has extra food. She'd share it with you."

Georgie shook her head. She wasn't going to ask some random person she'd only met once for food. "She goes to the beach in a kayak. And even if she had crammed extra food into that kayak, why would she share it with me?"

"Because that's the kind of person she is. I bet you don't even need to ask!"

"Do you know Cali?"

The ghost didn't respond, but the wheel turned hard, abruptly, sending the boat off course. Georgie tightened her grip as a bolt of fear stabbed her chest. The wheel slipped through her hands, friction burning them.

Fear and frustration brought a sharp edge to her words. "I warned you that if you messed—"

She stopped mid-sentence, cut off by the horrible grinding sound of her prop hitting a rock buried in muck.

"Shit." She shut the engine off and looked over the side. The stern was only in inches of water and the bow was completely beached in the sandbar that went all the way back to shore. She wasn't sure if she'd be able to push the boat off and the tide didn't turn for two more hours.

"Hey, Georgie, are you okay?"

The voice was familiar. Cali. Wearing a bright yellow, wide-brimmed hat, huge round sunglasses, and a rainbow tie-dye t-shirt.

The damned ghost had literally got her stuck in Cali's way. Fantastic. Why did it want them to meet so bad?

"Making me look like I don't know how to drive a boat is not going to make me look good to her," Georgie hiss-whispered to the ghost.

"So, does that mean you like her? You do want to see her?"

"If you ever do anything like this again, I am going to torch your bones." Georgie scowled, but her chest felt as hollow as the threat. She'd torched dozens of ghost bones, but she swore she'd never do it again.

She plastered on a fake cheery voice, turned toward the water, and greeted Cali. "Last week I had engine trouble. This week it's the steering."

"You are really making me appreciate my kayak." Cali paddled up to the sandbar, beaching the bow of her kayak.

"You know, something about this boat looks familiar," said Cali.

"We met last week," said Georgie.

"I mean it looked familiar then too," said Cali. "You need a hand pushing her back into the water?"

"I think I need a dozen hands." Georgie had to stop herself from making a joke about needing a hydra that could grow hands instead of heads. Or a maybe a tamed kraken.

"Well, it doesn't hurt to try, right?" Cali stepped out of her kayak and pulled it further up. Mud squirted her shin and onto her blue and white floral board shorts. "Worst case scenario, you have to wait for the tide, right?"

"Right." Georgie wondered if she should get out of the boat, join Cali in the muddy sand, and actually try to push, or invite her up into the boat.

"It's almost like the beach, but well, you sink a little." Cali looked down at her dirty legs and frowned.

"And people looking at me like the fool I am."

She shook her head. "What, you're a fool for not predicting your steering was going to have an issue at this exact moment?"

"Yes? I did take the whole thing apart this weekend and missed something important, apparently."

Cali rolled her eyes. "You're no fool."

Georgie disagreed. She was both a fool and apparently a liar now, because she knew darn well that her steering was fine, and the ghost was the problem. But why was the ghost so fixated on Cali?

"I'd offer you a tow, if I were in a big boat," said Cali. "And I am guessing you need one, because even if you get off the mudflat, and your steering is busted, you can't just drive back. And who knows what damage you did to your prop."

"I'm afraid to look." The brand-new prop was probably all warped. Hopefully nothing on the outdrive's shaft was damaged.

*If you weren't dead, I'd murder your ass,* Georgie thought loudly at the ghost in case it was one of the telepathic kinds, but it didn't respond. So maybe it wasn't, which was a good thing, she supposed. Less likely to turn into a brain mulching poltergeist that way. She'd fought a telepathic poltergeist once while it shouted profanity and insults into her brain. She'd had such a headache after blowing up and banishing that one.

"I'll keep you company until the tow boat arrives," said Cali. "You do have towing insurance, right?"

"I do," she admitted. She had signed up for it right away, because she rightfully didn't trust cheap old boats with bad names. "But I'll be fine waiting alone."

"Yes, but you might also be bored. Or you might decide to just try and fix the boat out here instead of calling for a tow and then the tide would come in while you're working on it and you might forget to put an anchor down and float away, or not be able to fix it before dark and then it will be late and harder to get a tow."

"Um." Georgie took a minute to let her brain try to make sense of what Cali said and then form coherent words. Cali clearly wasn't going to just leave, so Georgie decided to go with the current instead of fighting it. There was something alluring about her smile, her easygoing way of talking, and her cheeriness. "You want to come aboard?"

"I'd love to." Cali paused, looking at the name of the boat with her brows furrowed before stepping into the shallow water and climbing onboard.

"So did the cat get cat food or dog food this morning?" Georgie asked while looking around for her phone.

"Cat food. Today was too calm, actually. Insufficient chaos until now." Cali smiled, but there was something sad about her eyes and the way she looked around. Almost like she'd been here before. And if she had, maybe the ghost knew her.

Georgie called the tow boat and found out she was going to have to wait an hour.

"Well, I've got plenty of snacks in the kayak if you get hungry." Cali looked past Georgie toward the cabin door. "When my wife and I had a boat this size—the galley was always stocked with snacks."

"It's empty." A hollow pit formed in Georgie's stomach. Cali used to have a boat like this and a wife. Now she had neither and the boat had a ghost. A ghost who knew Cali would have snacks. "I bet you and your wife had some good times on the boat."

"So many." Cali wiped a tear out of her eye. "We got the boat when they were diagnosed with cancer. Even used in rough shape, it was expensive, but we knew we'd only have a few years on it. Still, we customized the upholstery and the paint—really personalized everything. And it was worth every penny. We were out on it more than we were home. Sometimes I regret selling it, but the upkeep was so much work, so much money...and it was really their thing."

Georgie studied the upholstery for a moment. The seats were plain white and blue on the deck and gray in the cabin. They didn't look anything how Georgie imagined Cali or her wife decorating. But that didn't mean it wasn't the same boat. It just meant the last owner had changed more than the name.

Georgie wanted a moment to process everything, but Cali had tears in her eyes. Thoughts about the ghost and its motive could wait.

With her heart racing, she reached out and gently squeezed Cali's hand. "If you want to talk more about it, I'm happy to listen. But if you want a distraction, let me know and I'll change the subject."

Cali smiled at Georgie, and this time, the brightness reached her eyes. "How about you tell me a little about yourself. What do you do for work? And fun?"

"I work at East Marine Supply. And lately seem to spend most of my free time trying to keep this boat running smoothly." Georgie loved being able to answer that question honestly. "What about you?"

"I'm a therapist," said Cali. "But I only work three days a week now and make sure I spend my free time paddling around the harbor or walking my dog."

"Where do you walk?" Georgie asked to keep the conversation going.

She told herself that just this once she'd let herself relax and enjoy the woman's company, but that was it. There was something freeing and intoxicating about being with Cali. About the way Cali looked at her like she was a normal, innocent person who had never burned ghost bones because it was the easiest way to get rid of it, like she'd never enjoyed tearing monsters apart with iron blades, and forcing other creatures from this dimension. But the thing was, Georgie had done those things, and it made her feel like every interaction with Cali was a lie.

* * *

"You're Cali's wife, aren't you?" Georgie said as soon as her boat was safely back at the dock. She was ninety-nine percent certain, but needed confirmation from the ghost.

"So what if I am?" the voice echoed all around the boat.

Georgie opened her mouth to answer, but realized she didn't have the words.

"She's not meant to be alone," said the ghost.

"There are millions of other people out in the world. Why me?" Georgie looked around, wishing she could see the ghost.

"Aside from you being the only one who hears me so far?"

"Yes, because that would be a pretty bad reason." Georgie hoped the ghost had a better one.

"I've had nothing better to do than watch you work on this boat, and I've noticed that when you dedicate yourself to something, like the boat, you really go all in. You don't give up when things go wrong. And you care about other people. Last week, you weren't sure the engine was ready, but when someone broke down in the middle of the river, you still went out and towed them back to your dock. You gave them water and food while they waited for the towboat. Oh, and you have this kind of brooding energy too, like you have secrets and A History. Cali is into that too."

Georgie gaped at the compliments. They felt undeserved, but still somehow true. "You don't really know me."

"I don't, yet. But Cali could get to know you, and then make her own decision. You could get to know her and make your own decision. Give it a chance, Georgie."

But she was afraid to.

\* \* \*

"I knew you were bluffing about banishing me," said the ghost as Georgie worked on replacing the prop a day after the incident at the mudflat. She still didn't have an appointment with a medium, though this time it wasn't for lack of trying. So many of the good ones had been booked months and months out that she'd gotten overwhelmed, taken a break from looking, and had yet to go back to it. "I'm still here and now you have Cali's number."

"Why do you want me to see her so badly? She's your wife!" Georgie put down her wrench on the swim platform and looked around. She could see the river rushing past her house across the yard and no neighbors were around to think she was talking to herself. She took her phone out and put it on the platform, just in case.

"Why are you so resistant? You clearly like her." The ghost's voice seemed to come from right in front of Georgie, like the boat itself was talking. "And I think she likes you."

"She is nice, but I'm not in the right place for a relationship," said Georgie. "My life was so entrenched in the supernatural for so long and now I'm *trying* to disentangle myself from it. I need to be on my own for a bit. Build a life in the regular world. Figure out who I am."

"Ah, so this is a midlife crisis? Change careers, insist on staying single, buy a boat...it would be better without the staying single part. Let's change it to 'find the love of your life and make my former wife happy!' Or at least be friends, if you don't want romance."

"Let's not interfere with my life if you want to continue to avoid the afterlife," said Georgie. "And I wasn't bluffing. I'm giving you one more chance. Three strikes and you're out."

"I'm only at one strike. My first interference was before you warned me, so it doesn't count!"

Georgie snorted. "Fine, you have two strikes left before I banish you."

She didn't mention that as soon as she was in the house, she was logging back onto the p'net and finding a medium. The ghost needed to be gone, but in a humane way.

\*\*\*

Thanks to a cancellation, Georgie was able to get a consultation with Liddia Grayson, one of the few mediums Georgie had never actually met. Mediums tended not to like hunters and avoided them until the hunter ended up having to save a medium from a ghost it lost control of, but Liddia had never needed rescuing by Georgie or any other hunter.

But even that appointment was three weeks away, which meant that Georgie was going to have to live with this ghost in the meantime.

She could have—probably should have—tried ignoring the ghost.

But some nights, she got lonely.

The good and bad thing about living on the water was the evenings were seldom quiet.

A few houses down, people were having a party. The glow of their fire reflected off the water and their voices carried down to where Georgie sat alone in her boat, nursing a bottle of red wine. The raucous voices annoyed her, but she couldn't tell if it was because she was lonely and just wished she was part of the group, or if it was because that group included members whose voices grated on her brain. Whatever the case, the party left her unsettled and lonely, like she didn't want to stay and listen but didn't want to leave either.

So, she started talking to the ghost.

"I wonder how they find so many things to talk about." The one time Georgie had gone to a fire with some people in the neighborhood, she'd sat around and hardly said a word while she struggled to follow the conversation. But these people didn't seem to have even the smallest lull, though the distance made it hard for Georgie to really hear the details of the conversation. "I can't tell if I'm just bad at conversation or if I wasted so much of my life hunting monsters that I can't interact with normal people anymore."

Georgie's wine bottle twitched and fell over.

"Normal is a crappy word," said the ghost. "People who know about the supernatural and people who don't can be equally normal or not normal, if normal even exists, which I don't think it does."

"No, but when people talked about work, I always had to lie." Georgie folded her arms and looked up at the sky. There were strict rules in the supernatural community about who could know what when, mostly to protect supernatural beings and regular people from each other. And that always made things complicated for people like hunters or mediums who were human but with a connection to the supernatural. "And when people asked about bruises, about injuries, I always had to lie. Do you know how many ridiculous stories I made up about how I broke my arm or got stitches? I still have to lie if people ask about my scars."

And Georgie had scars. Some were hidden by clothing. Some weren't visible at all. Some were in plain sight, across her knuckles and stretching from her eyebrow to her hairline.

Silver white light coalesced into the shape of a person: short with a pixie haircut, cargo shorts and a V-neck t-shirt. Their clothes were colorless, but every part of them glowed as if it were made from moonlight.

Georgie stared at them, mouth hanging open. There was something calm and serene about how they stood, moved, and stared at Georgie, unlike any ghost she'd ever seen.

"Your history doesn't have to define your present," said the ghost after a while.

"But how can it not?" Georgie said, unable to take her eyes off the ghost. "That part made me who I am now."

"But are we still living in the past?" The ghost put their hands on their hips and stared into Georgie's eyes.

"No." She couldn't think of anything else to say. She was too busy marveling over seeing a ghost manifest that wasn't trying to kill her.

"Then accept what it did and let it go. Let *now* define you and your choices."

Georgie took a long drink of wine, gathering her thoughts while she adjusted to the ghost's new form. "But even if I do that, even if I choose not to let the past define my present, it doesn't change the fact that I spent so much of my life working a secret job that I can't tell people about. How do you think Cali would react if I just started telling her all about my life? She'd probably think I was making things up."

The air temperature dropped as the ghost stood rigid and glared. "Be careful what you assume about people."

Georgie tensed. "What's that supposed to mean?"

The ghost crossed their arms. "You can't just assume everyone who is nice to you isn't part of that community and that everyone who knows your past is going to judge you for it."

Georgie put her wine glass down and crossed her arms. "Who says I am doing that?"

The ghost got quiet.

They vanished.

Georgie was jealous. Maybe she'd participate in more conversations if she could just disappear when the discussion got tough.

* * *

"Now you're not going to mess with my navigation today, right?" asked Georgie as she untied from the dock. She'd been talking to the ghost almost every night for a week, and hoped they'd reached an understanding.

Of course, the ghost didn't answer.

"Ghost? Did you hear me?" Georgie had not asked the ghost's name because she didn't want to get attached, but maybe she needed it if she was going to get the ghost to listen. If she was stuck with them for weeks before a medium could even get started.

"What's your name?" Georgie shifted into reverse, backing away from the dock into the current rushing downriver toward the ocean.

"Bianca," said the ghost. "I'm surprised it took you so long to ask."

Georgie didn't have an answer that wasn't potentially hurtful. "What pronouns should I use for you?"

"I use they and she pronouns, with a slight preference for they/them," said Bianca.

"Thank you for telling me that." A flash of yellow caught Georgie's eye and she looked down just as a yellowjacket landed on her hand. She took it off the wheel in a moment of panic, and the thing stung her. Georgie cursed. The current caught the boat. But the wheel turned before she got her hand back on it, steering away from the rocks just downstream of the dock and directing the boat out into the main channel.

"I can steer for a few minutes if you need to take care of the sting." Bianca manifested in her monochrome moonlight form.

"Thanks." She looked down at her hand. She wasn't usually allergic to stings, but it still hurt like hell. She grabbed some ice out of the fridge and put it on the rapidly forming welt while Bianca had the wheel.

She had to admit that it was nice having someone else around. Without Bianca, she probably would've hit the rocks and wrecked her hull. Something about her felt a little lighter as she sped downstream, opening the engine up full throttle. The wind whipped her hair and when she went over bigger waves—mostly wake from other boats—the salt sprayed her face.

"Thank you, again, Bianca." She slowed down as she went under the second bridge. She had to decide soon whether she was heading straight out to the ocean or going to take the meandering backway through the harbor and by the beach where she knew Cali would be, since it was a Friday.

She knew which way the ghost wanted to go. She was curious to see if, now that they'd been talking, Bianca would still try to force her to see Cali. She wanted to see if she could drive right by the beach without the ghost interfering.

It was a beautiful day, and she was looking forward to finally getting the boat out of the harbor and into the open ocean. No wind. Hardly a cloud in the sky. The marine forecast said the ocean was calm. Bianca was quiet for most of the drive, but when Georgie passed by the beach, the steering wheel jerked.

"This is strike two," said Georgie through gritted teeth as she turned the wheel in the opposite direction the ghost was trying to turn it.

But Bianca was strong.

And despite Georgie's efforts to correct course, despite her empty threats about banishment and burnt bones, they zigzagged their way toward the spot where Cali's kayak was beached.

"Still having trouble with your steering?" Cali shouted from shore.

"It's a long story." Georgie gave up fighting Bianca and dropped anchor just offshore since the tide was going out. She secured her anchors, then climbed down the swim platform into waist deep water. It was cool, but not as cold as it would be if the tide was coming in. At least it was a good day for swimming.

"I'm planning on staying out here all afternoon," said Cali. "And I enjoy long stories."

Georgie froze, because the truth was the kind of thing that could turn Cali's world upside down. But she liked Cali, and didn't want to lie to her, either. Her heart raced. Seaweed brushed against her legs. She took a deep breath and walked the rest of the way to shore.

She wasn't supposed to tell humans about the supernatural in general, but ghosts were a bit of a gray area. Some people believed in ghosts, and something Bianca had said about assumptions made Georgie wonder if Cali already knew.

Cali's hand landed on her shoulder as her feet hit the beach. "Hey, what's wrong?"

"What..." Georgie took a deep breath. "What would you say if I told you the boat was haunted?"

"I guess that'd depend on how serious you were." Her eyes narrowed as she studied the boat. "And on if you really believed it was haunted."

"Say I did believe." Standing knee-deep in water, Georgie made eye contact, maybe for the first time, noticing Cali's eyes were a vibrant blue.

"I think I'd dig out my business card," Cali said in a much more serious tone. "If you've got a ghost, it's a strong one."

"So, you believe in ghosts?"

"Believing in ghosts is part of my job." Cali dug around in her backpack, grabbing a card and her phone. She handed the card to Georgie and started scrolling through her phone. "I'm more than just a therapist for living. I'm also a professional medium."

Georgie exhaled—half laughing, half wanting to cry. There was a strange feeling creeping into her chest. It was a lightness of relief but also twisting embarrassment. And fear. Because Georgie had just lost her number one excuse for avoiding Cali.

Now Georgie was faced with another decision: whether to tell Cali who the ghost was or wait for the ghost to reveal themself.

Georgie looked down at the card.

Liddia Grayson.

"I use a different name for my medium work. It helps keep things as simple as they can be when you have two jobs."

Cali was the medium Georgie had an appointment with.

Cali, whom Georgie had been telling herself she couldn't date because she didn't know about the supernatural, was a medium. Someone who would probably know of Georgie's reputation when she connected Georgie to the G. A. Faust on her appointment roster.

But would Cali care that at some point in the past, Georgie had been cruel? Reckless? Or would she only care about who Georgie was now?

How was Cali going to react when she learned who the ghost was?

Georgie didn't know whether it was better to just blurt it now or wait. Cali hadn't seemed to notice the boat was haunted before, which meant that Bianca had been hiding from her.

Cali squeezed Georgie's hand. "Have you talked to the ghost at all?"

"I have." Georgie's throat was tight. Her palms were sweating from more than just the summer heat.

Cali leaned in closer. "Do you have any idea what it wants?"

"They wanted me to meet you." Georgie's cheeks heated up. "And date you."

"That's unusual." Cali's cheeks flushed bright red. "I don't think I've met a match-making ghost before, and I've met a lot of ghosts. Is this your first time seeing one?"

Georgie shook her head. "No. But they are certainly the friendliest. I, um, used to be a hunter, but I don't do that anymore. My full name is Georgina A. Faust, and I actually have an appointment with you already, but I didn't realize who you were."

Cali tensed. Her eyes narrowed. "Booking an appointment with me was the right thing to do. Hunter methods of getting rid of ghosts are..."

"Inhumane? Cruel?" Georgie took a step back and shook her head. "I would never just banish a ghost that wasn't hurting anyone."

"Good." Cali's shoulders relaxed. "You know, I don't usually work on Fridays, but if you're around tonight, at sunset, I could come have a chat with the ghost."

"I'm free." The piece of truth Georgie had yet to reveal conjured tension in her shoulders and lurched in her gut. But something...fear? A sense of respect for the ghost? Something held her back.

"Good. Where should I meet you?"

"My place is fine. The boat will be docked there." Georgie gave out her address and watched Cali type it into her phone.

"You know, I only live a few streets away from you." Cali's cheeks flushed.

"Nice." Georgie looked around. "Um, should I cancel my other appointment with you?"

"We'll see how it goes tonight."

There was a part of her that hoped one session was enough, so she could just move on with her summer. But another part tugged against that one—one that hoped it would take many, many sessions to talk Bianca onto the afterlife. Because she wanted to spend more time with both Bianca and Cali.

* * *

Cali showed up ten minutes before sunset, wearing an ankle-length, patchwork skirt and bright yellow shirt. She had a tray of brownies in one hand and a bottle of wine in the other. "The wine and dessert are for after I talk to the ghost."

"I wouldn't judge you if you drank first." Georgie took the bottle and brownies to the counter, wondering just how long Cali planned to stick around. This was supposed to be business, not a date. But—if Cali could somehow get past Georgie's monster hunter reputation and the fact they were brought together by her late wife's ghost—Cali was funny and pretty, and Georgie wouldn't have to lie to her if she asked about her scars. Maybe she wanted it to be a date after all.

"I bet you worked with a lot of mediums in your old job, right?"

"Some." Georgie tensed. "But usually, I was the last resort."

"You were smart to retire early." Cali leaned against the counter. "A lot of people in your former line of work don't make it to retirement."

"That's true." Georgie's mentor had been impaled with a rake on what was supposed to be his last gig. The apprentice they'd started training had died when a ghost realized its telekinesis worked on lungs.

"You're shaking, Georgie." Cali's voice was gentle, her hand warm and soothing on Georgie's shoulder.

"Some people in my old field think it's their duty to protect humans from monsters," Georgie whispered. "But it can also make us monsters. I never want to be the monster."

"I don't think you're a monster." Cali smiled at Georgie.

"Thank you." Georgie exhaled, but her body remained wracked with tension. She might not be a monster, but she still hadn't told Cali who the ghost was. "But I think it's time for you to talk to Bianca."

Cali's hand tightened on Georgie's shoulder. "Bianca? That's...that's the ghost's name?"

"It is." Georgie met Cali's eyes. "I couldn't find the right words to tell you, but you know them."

Cali backed up. "Where did you get that boat?"

"Some guy down near Boston. He let it go cheap because he couldn't get it to start."

"From a marina across from the airport?" Cali asked, face pale, looking out the river facing window, where she could see the boat tied up at the dock. "Was it you or him that took all the color out of the boat and changed her name?"

"Him. Changing the name is bad luck." Georgie moved toward Cali and put a hand on her arm. "Do you want to go down to the boat now?"

"Yes, please." Cali took a deep breath. "I think it's time I have a chat with my wife."

When she arrived at the boat, Bianca was there, sitting cross legged on the back seat, a smug smile lighting up her face. "I knew you two would hit it off if you just gave each other the time of day."

Cali smiled and shook her head. Tears glimmered in her eyes. "And how did you know that, Bianca?"

"Because I know you, Cali." The ghost floated off the chair, over to Georgie, who was torn between watching things play out and running away so they could argue in private.

Cali wiped a tear from her eye and crossed her arms. "How long have you known Georgie?"

"I only met her when she bought the boat," admitted Bianca. "But I could tell after watching her for ten minutes that she was our type."

"Our type?" Cali took a deep breath.

"Stubborn? Crafty? Tenacious? A bit brooding with A History." Bianca floated up, so they were hovering mere inches from Cali.

Now Georgie wanted to slink away, maybe into the water, and just never see this ghost or medium again.

"Why are you here, Bianca? You promised, *promised* you'd move on."

"I did. And I meant to. But I just wanted to make sure you were okay, and that you were also moving on, but then I saw how sad you were, and the door closed and then I was lost."

Tears dripped down Cali's face as she reached out. Her hand passed through Bianca's face. "Oh, Bee. I wish you'd found me sooner."

"I tried to move on, but I couldn't leave the boat, and then when I finally did see you, it was daytime and you couldn't see me, and I just couldn't bring myself to say something. Plus, I was afraid if you saw me, you'd never even give Georgie a chance and she...she is amazing, Cali. An amazing woman."

Georgie was surprised to hear that anyone who spent half their time silently spying on her could possibly think she was amazing...but that was what was happening. And despite feeling like an intruder in this personal moment, Georgie was pretty sure she thought both of the other two people were also amazing. Maybe Bianca didn't need to leave quite yet.

"You know, if we start dating now, it is going to seem like we are doing it to get rid of you, now that you've said why you pushed us together," said Georgie.

"Yes...maybe." Bianca turned their attention to Georgie. "Do you actually want to get rid of me, though?"

Georgie wasn't sure how to answer that. "It's been nice having you around, but the dead don't belong in the world of the living."

The words felt hollow. Parroted. She'd believed them because she'd only ever seen the worst of the dead, but what if they were wrong? What if the dead could stick around?

"But it isn't so easy for the dead to let go, and it takes more than one heart-to-heart, sometimes, for them to move on." Cali looked at Georgie.

Georgie smiled. "So how long were you two together?"

"We'd have been married seven years if I hadn't gotten that cancer," said Bianca. "Seven years. And we dated three years before that."

Somehow condolences didn't seem like the appropriate response, so Georgie stayed silent. But so did the others and it was an awkward silence, loaded with grief and realizations.

Georgie didn't really want the ghost—Bianca—to leave.

Georgie really did want to get to know Cali more.

And in an ideal world, one where cancer hadn't stolen Bianca's life prematurely, she thought she would've enjoyed getting to know them both together in a lot of different ways.

"Maybe tonight doesn't have to be about heart-to-hearts and moving on," said Georgie. "Maybe that will need to happen one day, but maybe tonight, the three of us can just sit out on the boat and enjoy the evening."

"I'd like that," said Bianca, as close to solid as a ghost could get.

And so, the three of them sat out under the stars. Maybe Bianca would need to move on, sooner than later, but it didn't have to be tonight or even this week or this month.

Sara Codair is the author of *The Evanstar Chronicles, Earth Reclaimed,* and an assortment of odd short stories. Check out *Power Surge, Life Minus Me,* and *Power Inversion,* available from most major book retailers. Learn more at **www.saracodair.com**. Follow Sara on Twitter and Instagram **@shatteredsmooth** for updates, cats, and dogs.

# Caught

Margaret Adelle

Sapphic Representation: Lesbian
Heat Level: Hot!
Content Warnings: Coarse Language

In another life, she was Countess Victoria Artham de LaCont, daughter of nobility. Word had it she was the treasure of whatever royal courts she waltzed through. Until she married some old geezer for his riches, they said. And then the old man tried to do her in for an even younger wife with a bigger dowry. He left her for dead in some godsforsaken wilderness. So, she commandeered her own ship. She stole from every merchant her dear old husband invested in. By the time he died, her husband was a shadow of a man and his new widow, penniless.

"A cruel conniving witch," they said.

"A horrible chit of a captain," they said.

*The strongest woman in the world*, I thought.

I watched her stride across the deck, giving every crewmember a sharp look as she passed. She'd never glare at them; Captain LaCont didn't need to glare at her crew. Just a look would tell you what you did wrong. Her fiery red hair streamed behind her as she walked, as if she dared the wind to tangle it.

If I looked closely enough, I could see the woman that would have taken tea in the parlor, or whatever it was a noble did. Her chin was always up, her shoulders always just a bit back—as if she could never quite forget her breeding. But the iron in her gray eyes...that was pure pirate.

A first mate wasn't supposed to stare at the captain from across the deck. A first mate wasn't supposed to think about the captain at night or look too long at the captain's lips. Not only was it bad luck, it was impossible.

The captain was a gilded lily turned jewel of the sea. I was the cast off of some unknown sailor, born in a port town brothel. I was raised to follow my mother's line of work. But while I loved my mother dearly, no amount of coin would ever be enough to let a man lie on top of me.

"Gail," the captain called as she approached. I stood up a bit straighter, cursing my heart for beating so fast. She barely paused as she passed, headed for the door of her office.

"Follow me," she said.

*To the ends of the earth,* I thought.

\* \* \*

"You need to keep on an eye on the new cabin boy when we go through the straits," the captain announced as we entered her office. She walked around the giant wooden desk to her chair, sliding into it with a heavy sigh. I didn't know what a pirate captain needed with a desk, but she always kept it clean.

"What's wrong with him?"

"He's gotten it into his head that he's going to listen to the sirens," she said dryly. "Apparently he thinks he's safe."

I grimaced. We went through the straits often enough that I could almost forget how dangerous they were. But without your ears stopped up against the damnable song, you were begging for death.

The captain nodded as if I'd spoken.

"My thoughts exactly," she continued. She leaned back in her chair. "Apparently someone told him a legend about how to listen to the song safely." She cleared her throat and recited in a dramatic voice. "'The sirens' song cannot ensnare a heart that is already caught.'" She scoffed. "And apparently he has a girl back on the mainland that'll keep him safe."

"You don't believe he really loves her?" I couldn't help but think of all the men that would stumble out of my mother's room with a dopey grin on their face...then walk into another woman's arms on their next visit.

"Being in love and being caught are two different things," the captain said with a sad smile. "The first one is much easier."

I didn't understand what she meant. But seeing as I was the one to suggest she hire the cabin boy, he was my responsibility.

"I'll be on the lookout, Captain," I gave a sharp salute, the kind that always made her grin. Gods above, her smile.

"I can always rely on you, Gail." She spoke in a warm voice that did weird things to my insides. But I kept my face flat as I nodded and headed out.

I stumbled into the salty sea air, taking deep breaths. I tried to push the captain's face out of my head, but it was fixed there. I gritted my teeth and headed across the deck in search of the cabin boy. We would see whose heart was "caught."

* * *

Ike the cabin boy's thin and scrappy frame was the result of a hard life, but he smiled as he ran around the mess with a bucket in his hands. The cook stood nearby, glaring occasionally as the boy passed, but didn't say anything.

"Ike," I called. The boy skidded to a stop and turned to stare at me with wide eyes. I beckoned him with a hand. He gave one last look to the cook before muttering a "yes ma'am" and making his way over. I squared my shoulders.

"What's this I hear about you thinking about listening to the siren song?" I asked with a raised brow. Ike ducked his head, his mop of brown hair falling over his face. The cook looked over sharply, but I waved him off.

"Beryl said that I would be safe," Ike muttered.

"Beryl's your girl?" I asked. He nodded.

"She says we caught each other's hearts, so I would be fine," he mumbled.

"And how would she know that?"

"Her grandmother knows things." He looked up at me with wide, open eyes. "She was always good at reading people and learning things no one else knows. She swears it's true."

I held in a curse. The boy was so damned hopeful.

"You need to keep your ears stopped up," I insisted. "The captain doesn't want to lose anyone to the straits. That includes you."

"But I'm safe!" Ike insisted. "My heart's caught, I swear!"

I sighed and sat heavily at one of the mess tables. Ike followed me over with those same wide eyes.

"She makes my heart beat like...like a galloping horse," he began. "And when I'm with her, it's like nothing else matters." He put a hand over his chest with a grin. I kept my face firm, lips pressed just like the captain did when giving the crew a dressing down.

"Sounds like you're sweet on her," I replied. "But that don't mean you're caught."

"I can't imagine being without her," he insisted.

"You're without her now."

"Well, yes, but..." He looked around as if an answer would pop up. "Have you ever felt like just being able to see someone makes your whole day better? Like...just the look of their face and it's all okay?"

I sat still, trying to keep all thoughts of her flaming red hair out of my mind.

"That doesn't mean—"

"And just the thought of 'em makes you want to smile," Ike continued. "I know we're separated now, but Beryl and me, we're gonna make it work. I'll make my fortune and go back to her, I swear."

"I don't doubt you love your girl," I said with a sigh. "But ya still gotta keep your ears stopped up. No need to risk anything."

"I promised her I would listen," Ike said in a quiet voice. "She said she wanted to know what they sounded like."

"Just tell her...you can't describe them," I stammered. "They're...otherworldly, not for human ears."

Ike rubbed the back of his head.

"Lie to her, ya mean?" he muttered. "Mama always said a good man was honest."

I stared at him blankly.

"You're training to be a pirate, boy," I said flatly. "Lying's part of the job." He flinched.

"Aye," he mumbled.

"It's alright." I gave him a slow pat on the shoulder. "Sometimes keeping a secret is the best thing for it. Trust me."

* * *

The Siren Strait was a thin passageway between two sheer cliffs of dark gray stone. The waters churned and frothed between the giant rock faces. It was just big enough for one ship to pass through at a time.

The strait's namesakes kept to the crevasses of the rocks, crooning out their songs to those that passed. Those unlucky enough to hear would find themselves jumping overboard to drown in the waves or bash their heads open on the rocks.

Merchant ships didn't dare attempt the crossing, instead going the long way around and adding days or weeks to their passage. But pirates were a tougher breed. And Captain LaCont was the toughest of them all.

"Steady, Hank," she called to the helmsman. "Keep to the center, if you please."

The large man behind the helm glared out at the horizon. He knew the center had the worst of the rapids. He also knew he'd get a lashing if he tried to argue with the captain.

"Alright, everyone," the captain called in a calm voice. "To your stations." She reached into the pocket of her deep blue coat and pulled out two pieces of cotton. "Prepare yourselves." She pressed the cotton into her ears, and everyone followed.

I hated the feeling of cotton in my ears. Made the whole world feel off-kilter in a way I could never explain. Or maybe that was the rapids. Either way, I stuffed the things in and walked among the crew as they furiously tried to keep the ship under control among the rapids. Hank sweated at the wheel, Nadia and Sybil were tying everything down as the ship listed to the side.

A feeling in my gut told me I should find Ike. I didn't trust how quickly he'd agreed to abandon his plan. Lovestruck cabin boys were never much good at following orders.

I found him at the aft. He jumped slightly as she saw me, a bucket in his hands. He freed a hand to point to his ears. I could make out the cotton just peeking out. I nodded and headed back to the main deck.

The sight of the captain stopped me in my tracks.

Her red hair whipped around her in the wind, like tentacles that might snatch a man off his feet at any moment. But no matter how hard the wind blew, no matter how hard the ship rocked, she kept her feet. She glared at the strait as we came closer. And then she turned that gaze to me.

Her eyes were like two churning, gray storm clouds. I held my breath, like I expected something to happen. My own, much shorter brown locks were doing their best to whip me in the face. Trying to tell me to get my head out of my arse, I expected.

The captain raised a brow and nodded toward Ike. I pointed to my ears and nodded. She gave me a small smile. She never smiled very wide. But it warmed my insides just the same. Then the ship lurched, and it was all I could do to stay on my feet.

Passing through the straits was like being swallowed by some giant, gaping mouth. The sky between the cliff faces felt miles away. The rocks, on the other hand, felt close enough to touch. If I stared too long, I could start imagining all the blood splatters from poor souls that tried to make the crossing before us.

I shook my head. None of those thoughts. We'd done this passing a dozen times and the captain had never led us wrong before. I wasn't gonna start doubting her now.

Everyone besides Hank and the captain stared at the stone around us. No one had ever seen the sirens, but there were always stories. I found a dark crack high up. When I squinted, I could have sworn I saw something move.

And then I realized we were over halfway across, and I hadn't checked on Ike. I cursed my distraction and went back to the aft...just in time to find him trying to climb over the railing.

"Ike!" I yelled, my own voice muffled to my ears. Stupid to yell, when everyone's got their ears stopped up, I thought. But then I noticed the two pieces of cotton lying on the deck. I swore and raced forward, yanking him back from the edge.

The cabin boy might have been thin, but he was feisty. He fought as I pulled him back from the railing. We fell to the deck hard, but he jumped up again in an instant and rushed to the railing with wild eyes.

"Caught my arse," I muttered. I followed after and grabbed him again. This time he turned all the ferocity on me, scratching at my face and pulling at my hair. I held him off, even as I wanted to deck him. His hand caught my right ear and suddenly the world became a whole lot louder.

I could hear the rushing of the waves beneath us. The creaking of the ship as Hank struggled to keep her in place.

And I heard the songs.

It sounded like it was coming from everywhere, slipping from the stones itself. There were dozens of voices at once, but I couldn't make out any single one. There wasn't even a language to it, not one I recognized at least. But it was smooth and silky, like it was made to just slide in your ears.

I froze in horror. Ike took the opportunity to elbow me in the gut in another dash to go over the side. So, I did the only sensible thing: I decked him.

Ike was a lightweight and went down pretty easy. He slumped to the deck, dazed but not out. I swore and shook my hand.

The captain took that moment to come walking to the aft. She froze when she saw us. I thought she might be readying to rake the cabin boy over the coals for daring to take the cotton out. But it wasn't Ike she was staring at. She was looking at me.

No, not looking. *Glaring.*

I'd never seen her look so upset before. My stomach lurched like the ship. I opened my mouth to say something, but what was there to say? I couldn't even think of what I'd done wrong. She turned and stormed off, leaving me with the passed-out cabin boy and an aching heart.

\* \* \*

"Who is it, then?" Hank had found me in the cargo hold of the ship not an hour later, as I was pretending to check on the goods we were ferrying through the straits.

"Whatcha mean?" I asked lightly. He snorted.

"Whoever's caught your heart," he sat on one of the crates. The whole thing creaked its protest, but he was grinning. "Ike's been whining to the whole crew about it. His own heart isn't with his beloved, but yours is."

"Or maybe the whole thing's a myth," I snapped. "Maybe old grandmothers don't know nothing about sirens."

The helmsman just grinned wider.

"So, there is someone," he said. "You should probably tell the captain soon. She's on one."

I winced before I could catch it. He chuckled.

"Why does she care?" I muttered, half to myself.

"Probably doesn't want complications on the ship," he shrugged his massive shoulders. "You know her. Likes everything neat and tidy. Two of her crew being in love makes for a mess if something goes awry."

I glared at him, but he made sense.

"It won't be messy," I growled. "Because there's nothing about it. Just a myth."

"Fine, keep your secrets," he shrugged again and climbed off the crate. "The captain'll get it out of you eventually." He turned and sauntered out of the cargo hold.

"That's what I'm worried about," I muttered.

* * *

There was only a day's worth of sailing from the straits to the nearest port city and I'd already decided to make myself scarce for all of it. It was hard to avoid the captain entirely, being the first mate. But I made sure we spoke just about the business of the cargo and the ship. She barely looked at me, staring more at the horizon or the sails. I could see the countess she once was. And she was ordering me around like the scum I would always be.

I made a point of checking in on Ike. He was beside himself, crying about how much he'd betrayed his girl. The cook stared at him in disgust.

"I'm sure she'll understand," I muttered, but my heart wasn't in it.

"No, she won't," he wailed. "I've never lied to her, not the month we've known each other."

"Month?" I echoed. "One month?" He nodded, tears still streaming down his cheeks. I swore.

"You've known this girl for a month and you're crying about not being caught?" I rolled my eyes. "You can hardly blame yourself. You haven't even given your heart time to be caught."

"How long did it take you?"

I held in a grimace. Word traveled quickly on a ship. At this point, half the crew was smirking at me.

"I ain't caught," I snapped. He ducked his head, sniffling pathetically. I sighed.

"*If* you'd been caught...it wouldn't have been a single month." I scoffed. "It would have come on slowly—little things that you suddenly start noticing." Like how the captain never let her shoulders relax until she was in her office. Or the wry smile on her face when she told me that a royal ship was on our tail and another game of chase was on.

"And then what?" Ike asked. He looked up at me with those shining eyes. I cleared my throat and turned my gaze to the far wall.

"And then...you start realizing how much you like those things," I muttered. "And how each one of them makes your day a little brighter. Then you realize even the bad things about them aren't so bad." Like when she ordered the crew around in that way that was just a bit too haughty—learned from a youth I'd never understand. It should have annoyed me. But she'd always shake her head and give the order again in a way befitting a pirate captain.

"You think I'll get there with Beryl?" he asked.

"I'm sure," I said. "And if it makes you feel better, at least you can tell your girl what they sound like."

His head suddenly whipped around, and he stared up at me with those wide, childlike eyes.

"It was a wonderful song, wasn't it?" he murmured. "Like all the best sounds of the world rolled into one."

"What?" I scoffed. "It was a bit of pretty music. Not much more. Honestly, can't see why people make such a big fuss over it." There'd been stories of men tying themselves down to the ship so they could listen to the sirens as they passed. Sometimes they would go mad. It seemed like so much of a risk for such a little reward.

Ike stared at me in horror.

"You can't be serious," he choked the words out. "It was the most magical song there's ever been!"

"Hardly," I shrugged. "I've heard better from drunks at a tavern. At least then there's lyrics you know." Ike made another choked noise, while the cook chuckled. I glared at him.

"I think the boy's right," Cook said. "Your heart's caught like no other."

I scowled at the two of them. Before I could come up with a good insult, Eliza rushed into the mess.

"Captain's asking for you," she said in a breathless voice. I stiffened, then forced myself to relax my shoulders.

"Of course," I muttered. "We should be making it to port soon."

I stuck my hands in the pockets of my trousers and walked out of the mess at a slow pace. There was a rule I'd learned early on as a first mate. You never let the crew know when you're scared out of your wits.

* * *

I'd walked to the captain's quarters hundreds of times. This time it felt like walking to the gallows. My heart hammered in my chest. My hands kept twitching at my sides. It was like the first time I met her, when I was all hands and feet and stammering.

The captain was her normal self. She sat behind her desk with straight shoulders and an ocean-sized glare. And when she narrowed that glare at me, it felt like I was standing in front of my mother after punching Bobby Figgins in the face.

"You asked for me, Captain?" I began quietly. I clenched my hands into fists to stop their shaking. Her gaze flickered downward.

"We're about to come to port," she said stiffly. "I'd like you to stay aboard when the crew goes off doing...whatever it is they do." She was stiffer than usual, almost sneering.

"Aye, Captain," I muttered.

"Ike needs watching," she continued. "And since you did so well the *last time*, you can continue it."

"Aye, Captain."

I waited for the dismissal, but it never came. She just kept staring at me. Like she could see through me.

*Oh, gods above,* I thought. *She knows.*

She had to know. And it must have made her angry. Who was I to her? A useful hand on a ship. And yet I was walking around like I had any right to be by her side. A countess doesn't fall into bed with an urchin.

"Do you remember what I said to you when we first met?" she asked suddenly.

"I...uh..." I stammered. The memory had been fixed in my head clear as day, but suddenly I couldn't recall.

"I said that a first mate was someone a captain needed to trust implicitly."

I winced. The memory came back then. The crew was greener than grass at the time—mostly former merchants. Few weathered pirates wanted to work for a countess. By nature of being the one with experience sailing under a dark flag, I was named to the position.

"I remember," I muttered.

"And for years now, I have trusted you," she said quietly. "You have stayed with me through every step, teaching me how to be the best captain."

My jaw dropped. Me? Teach her?

"You...you were *made* to be captain," I sputtered. "I just told you some things the lifelong pirates know. That's all."

She waved her hand.

"Hardly," she sniffed. "I was a dreadful captain at first and you know it. Could barely convince anyone to follow an order. It was you they followed. I was just the pretty face at the head."

She stood up suddenly and walked around the desk. I resisted the urge to step back. My fingers itched to reach out and touch her.

"But now I find that you've been keeping secrets from me," she murmured in a low voice that made me weak in the knees, even as my heart was pounding. "I don't appreciate you keeping secrets."

"I—"

"Do you think I don't know my own ship?" she continued. "I hear every creaking board, every whisper, every bawdy tavern song that damnable cook sings under his breath. And you thought you could keep this from me?"

"I...I didn't think you'd want to hear it, Captain," I stammered. She stood up to her full height, then looked down her nose at me.

"I suppose not," she said in a curt voice. My heart sank. She walked back to her chair and the space between us felt like an abyss.

"Make sure Ike stays on the boat for the duration of the stay. I don't need him running around talking about the siren song." Under her breath, she added, "Enough fools trying to listen already."

"Aye, Captain," I stood as straight as I could and walked out on wooden legs.

* * *

I could take my lumps with the best of them, but that stay on the ship was hard. Most of the crew was off, save those that stayed to keep everything secure. Even the captain, who was known to almost always keep to her quarters, went off to the local pub.

I tried not to imagine her sitting in some dark tavern corner, drinking rum and making eyes at a man. Whatever poor excuse of a sailor she picked would happily fall into bed with her to boot. She could charm anyone.

Ike was miserable. When he wasn't moping, he was asking about relationships and being "caught at heart." No amount of snapping at him would call him off it, either. I hoped Beryl was ready for the sad puppy dog she was getting back. Might anger her more than the sirens.

I wasn't much better than the cabin boy. I kept turning over the captain's words in my head and stabbing myself in the heart every time.

She knew I loved her, and she didn't want to know it. Gods, it stung. Where could I go from here? We'd sailed together through worse storms than the straits, but I couldn't imagine she'd want me around after this. Maybe that's why she wanted me to stay on the ship. Didn't want me to know she was looking for a new first mate. She'd be stupid to pick one from a random port, but then that's how she'd found most of the crew.

Somewhere between my own pints of ale, I decided I wasn't going to let her toss me out. The second she walked back on the ship I'd march up to her and tell her I was leaving. Then I'd walk off into the port and find a new crew. Captain LaCont might have her naysayers, but hers was still a fierce enough reputation. A first mate that sailed under "La Cunt" could still find good work. I would find a new crew and sail off with them.

I hoped it wouldn't shatter the rest of me.

\* \* \*

I never got the chance to storm up to the captain as she boarded. Instead, I found myself waking up with a beast of a headache in the cargo hold. I groaned and I sat up slowly. Ike snored nearby. It had taken only two pints to knock him down. Cabin boys couldn't hold their ale.

I climbed to my feet. It took me several seconds to realize the room wasn't spinning, but rocking as the ship sailed. I climbed up the stairs as quickly as I could, holding my head. I got to the top deck in time to watch the port disappearing over the horizon.

"Shite," I grumbled.

"Sleep well?" asked a laughing voice. I winced and turned to face the helmsman.

"Shut it," I snapped. He just kept smiling.

"You and Ike drowning your sorrows, then? Where'd you leave him?"

I gestured vaguely back down to the decks below.

"I'd get him up and going soon," he crossed his arms over his chest. "Captain's been in a sour mood."

I stilled.

"Did she say why?" I asked in a low voice. He raised a brow.

"Wouldn't say," he replied. "Just nursed a pint in the corner of a pub for hours, lazing around." He shrugged. "That's what you get when the captain comes from nobility."

"Shut yer mouth," I snapped, louder this time. "That's your captain."

And there it was, that wide grin again.

"Ah, I knew it," he said with a chuckle. I scoffed and rolled my eyes, storming away. His laughter chased after me.

\* \* \*

With the captain still in her office, I took to overseeing the crew. They were experienced deck hands by now and understood how the captain liked things. Still, the walk in the fresh air helped clear my head.

How did Hank know my secret? Did the captain tell him? Was she already telling others, preparing to drop me off at the next port without warning?

The idea made my head spin. I gripped the railing, praying none of the crew saw. The first mate had to have her dignity.

Eventually, my fear bled out into anger. How dare she tell other people my secret? She didn't even want to know it. And if she was so unhappy about it, why hadn't she tossed me out at the last port? Find herself some new first mate that wouldn't make big, wide eyes at her. Instead, she was keeping me around, leaving me on the ship just to remind me of my place.

Before I knew it, I was walking with purpose toward her office. To hell with it. I'd head back to port in a rowboat if I had to. I couldn't keep this in any longer.

I opened the door, letting it slam against the wall with a satisfying *bang*. The captain jolted upward. It was the first time I'd caught her unawares in years.

"Was that really necessary?" she asked in a tired voice. I didn't let myself dwell on the circles under her eyes or the surprising number of tangles in her hair.

"Yes," I snapped. But after a moment, I turned and shut the door. Better to let us both have some dignity when this all came out.

"And what grievance is it that you've come to air, exactly?" she asked dryly. She leaned back in her seat, the same haughty air. It would have been more effective if her shirt wasn't wrinkled.

"I'm quitting," I forced the words out before I could second guess them. She stared at me with an expressionless face. I could have sworn I saw a twinge in her cheek, but the rest of her was stone.

"I suppose I shouldn't be surprised," she said in an even tone. "With everything that's happened. And I suppose your lover will want their leave as well."

The world stopped for a moment while I gaped at her.

"Well?" she asked with another raised brow. "I can't imagine you'll want to leave them behind, whoever they are." Her tone turned icier by the second. "Although I would like to know exactly what crew member I'll be losing, if you don't mind."

She didn't know?

*She didn't know.*

"You...I...what?" I stammered. She rolled her eyes.

"I wouldn't tear apart a pair of lovebirds," she continued. She stood up and walked around the desk. Her gait was careful, leaving plenty of space between us. "Even *I'm* not that heartless."

If there were words to say, I couldn't find them. I reeled at the stoic look on her face.

"So?" The captain leaned against the desk, crossing her arms over her chest. I was distracted for a moment by the sight of her breasts pressed upward. "Who is it?"

My legs did the replying for me. I was suddenly rushing across the room. But just as I neared her, I came to my senses. This was the *captain*. Kissing her was like trying to kiss Aphrodite. I skidded to a halt, breathing hard. That's when I noticed how wide her eyes were.

"What is this?" she hissed. I might have caught a hitch in her voice, but I was distracted by how furious she looked. "Are you trying to fight me on my own ship?"

"No!" I yelled, holding my hands up in defense.

"Do I need to leave you hog-tied in the cargo hold?"

"No, no, I swear!" I tried to ignore the sensations that appeared in the pit of my stomach at the idea of being tied up. Now was not the time. "I wasn't trying to fight you, I swear?"

"Then what in the abyssal hells were you trying to do?"

The words tumbled out before my scrambled mind could catch them. "I was trying to kiss you!"

Silence came down heavy and thick between the two of us. She just stared at me for a long moment.

"Kiss me?" she echoed in a quiet voice. Her shoulders had yet to relax, but her expression had gone slack.

"It's you, alright?" I continued. "It's you."

For a second, I could see the thoughts swirling behind her iron eyes. But then the mask came down again and I went cold. What if she was even angrier at this? What if—

Before I could finish the thought, she grabbed my arms and yanked me forward. I crashed into her with all the grace of a flopping fish, but I couldn't find the breath to right myself. And then she was kissing me.

It was every bit as fierce and dominant as I hoped. Her lips were soft, but firm, taking control of the kiss. When she slipped her tongue past my lips, I melted into her with a moan.

I don't know how long we stood like that. When I came up for air, it felt like the whole world was a different color. Brighter, somehow. When I looked up at her face, her eyes were sparking.

"I can't believe you never told me," she murmured, brushing a hand against my cheek.

"You never told me either," I replied. She chuckled.

"True." She nodded. After a moment, the look on her face changed. It reminded me of the expression she wore when we were heading into the strait. She grabbed my shoulders and pushed me back slightly.

"Remember one of the first things you told me?" she asked in a slightly louder voice. "When I tried asking the helmsman for help navigating that first day. You said..."

"The captain doesn't ask for suggestions," I finished. "She gives orders." She nodded, with a devious grin on her face.

"You are going to find a bit of rope. Then, you are going to go to my cabin and remove every last scrap of clothing from your person. Am I clear?"

My head was reeling with the command.

"But the crew is still—" She grabbed my chin and forced my head up to look in her eyes. The steely determination nearly undid me on the spot.

"You leave the crew to me. I want you squirming and screaming underneath me within the hour. Is that clear?"

Gods, everything in me burned up at the order.

"Aye, Captain."

\* \* \*

The captain's bunk was nearly the same as everyone else's, save for the size. But it felt like a foreign place as I walked in and closed the door behind me. There wasn't anything fancy about the place—the captain kept her nicest things for the office. But my skin was crawling, like my own body was trying to tell me I didn't belong here.

I placed the rope in a small coil at the foot of the bed. Just the sight of it was enough to put an ache in my lower belly.

I stripped slowly and climbed onto the bed. It felt like intruding.

*Captain's orders,* I reminded myself. But thinking of her words just made my heart pound. I fidgeted on the bed. I knew the covers were the same everywhere else on the ship, but these felt so much better. Everything about this room was better because it was *hers*.

* * *

The door slowly creaked open and I stiffened, but I didn't look. I couldn't see her looking at me like this. So, I stared at the ceiling, listening to the sounds of clothing hitting the floor. It wasn't until she stood next to the bed that I finally looked over.

My mouth ran dry. She was looking down, staring at me, but all I could see was her creamy skin. She was dotted with freckles in the strangest of places, including a smattering across her breasts. And those breasts...full and round, but so very far away. I opened and closed my mouth several times, but I couldn't get sound out. I finally forced my gaze up to her face to find her smirking at me.

"I don't think I've ever seen you so speechless before," she murmured. She reached down and brushed a lock of hair away from my face. Her own hair was its usual glorious auburn. I slowly reached up to run my fingers through it. It was every bit as soft as I'd hoped. Her smirk deepened into a smile.

"All this time," she whispered. "And you never said anything."

"The first mate isn't supposed to fall in love with the captain," I muttered back.

"I'm not the captain in here," she replied. "Just a woman who's going to make you squirm." Her hands slowly drifted down my jaw, to my collar bone. Her fingertips barcly grazed my nipple, but it was enough to make me gasp. She chuckled.

"How long has it been for you?" she asked.

"A while," I admitted. "Being with someone else...it didn't feel honest."

"Then let me make this worth it." I expected her fingers to continue their path, prayed for it even, but she suddenly pulled away. Instead, she walked to the end of the bed and picked up the rope.

"Ah, not quite long enough for the real fun," she said in a light tone. "But we'll have time for that later."

"Real fun?" I couldn't tell if my voice was shaking from need or nerves. Maybe both.

"We'll have time to discuss it later. For now, something simple." She walked up to the top of the bunk. "Hands together." She ordered. I obeyed the command without a second thought.

"Good girl," she purred. My skin flushed with the praise. She wrapped the rope around my wrists and tied it, with a long tail of rope left over.

"That hurt?" she asked. I shook my head. "Good." And she pulled the rope up to a small hook sitting just above the bunk, tying the rope around it with practiced movements.

"I...I thought that was for hanging your hat on," I stammered. She smirked.

"It is...and for other things."

I tugged on the rope. Loose enough that it didn't chafe the skin. But tight enough that I wasn't going anywhere.

She could do anything to me. I was at her mercy. My cunt clenched.

The captain seemed content to take her time, slowly walking around the bed and admiring her handiwork. I tried not to fidget. But her gaze felt like a physical thing, brushing against me.

Then finally, she touched me. I bit my lip to keep from squirming. Her fingers made their way slowly down my stomach, brushing over my navel, almost touching the hair between my thighs. I tensed, taking a breath. But her fingers instead slowly made their way back up. I forced an exhale.

"Captain?" I asked nervously.

"Hush," she replied. I pressed my lips together as her fingers continued to brush gently across my stomach, coming slightly lower each and every time. I was strung out like a sail, but I kept quiet. Until finally her fingers reached my clit. I arched my back, but she moved them up again.

"Patience, darling," she cooed. "You must have patience."

I stared at the ceiling, trying to slow my breathing. It felt like I was moments from snapping when her fingers suddenly slipped inside. I gasped, jerking under her grasp.

"So wet already?" she teased. "You've been waiting for me, haven't you?"

"Yes," I breathed. She moved her fingers slowly, tormenting me.

"Please," I begged. "More, please." But she kept at the same pace, rocking her fingers inside me like she had all the time in the world. I dared a look at her face, but she was still smirking and self-satisfied.

"Oh, you'll take what you're given, darling," she said in a low voice. "I've waited so long for this; I'm going to take my time."

I groaned, but the torture was exquisite. More than just her fingers, it was the knowledge that she'd been waiting for me as well. I could only risk little glances at her face. Anything more seemed too much.

"Oh, gods...Cap—" I blushed as she suddenly ducked forward and kissed my cheek.

"In here, it's just Vic," murmured. "Or Mistress, if you prefer." Her fingers suddenly picked up speed and I groaned again. Her palm rubbed against the outside of my cunt and my hips bucked in response. She chuckled again and leaned in close to my ear.

"Come for me," she demanded. "Now."

I never could say no to her. The winding, coiling tension had sunk into my bones. I felt my face flushed as the ache between my thighs grew. Then finally, it snapped. There was a sudden rush of pleasure that had me crying out. I pulled on the ropes without thinking, but I was well and truly bound. I screamed. The captain smirked.

Then the cap— I mean, Vic, withdrew her fingers. My body immediately felt the lack.

"Is that all the sound you could muster?" she asked quietly. "I'll have to try harder next time." The idea of a next time had everything inside me already clenching. But there were other fantasies. Fantasies that could finally come to be.

"Could...could I have a turn?" I asked quietly. She raised a brow. "Please, Mistress?" Her smile grew and did strange things to my heartbeat. She reached up and untied the knot.

"You remember how many times I had problems with knots?" she asked. "I never understood sailors and their obsessions with ropes." I grinned as my hands came free.

"Aye," I replied. "But most sailors don't use rope the way you do."

"Oh, that was just a test run, love." Her smirk turned darker. "You haven't seen what I can really do with rope yet." She reached over to my wrists and rubbed them gently. "Are you alright?"

I was already wound up again from her comments, but I nodded.

"And what is it you want from me?" she asked lightly.

"You," I muttered without thinking. She shook her head, tutting. And for a moment, she was a countess again.

"Come now, darling. We must communicate with each other, mustn't we?"

"Aye," I muttered and licked my lips nervously. "I...I want to taste you."

In seconds, the countess was gone, replaced by a dark pirate queen.

"Of course, Pet," she said in a low voice. Vic laid flat on her back, stretching out as if she hadn't a care in the world. I wanted to study her, the way she studied me. But the sight of all that skin, the plump breasts, her fiery hair spread across the pillow...my patience disappeared.

I eagerly climbed over her. I reached down to kiss her lips lightly before my mouth began to wander. I brushed over her breasts, and her navel, drinking in her moans. Despite the years of hard living, her skin was still soft everywhere.

I continued down to the apex between her thighs and finally tasted her. It was light at first, just testing the boundaries with my tongue. But then she gasped and grabbed a fistful of my hair, giving a delicious sting. I began to devour her, moving my tongue as fast as I could. Her taste, her sounds, the slight ache of her fingers digging into my scalp...it was heaven.

I should have drawn it out, the way she did mine. But I never had Vic's patience and the taste and sounds were too much to resist.

*Next time,* I promised myself. And the very idea that there could be a next time had me digging my fingers into the soft flesh of her thighs. Vic must have been in a similar state, because it was only moments later that she came on my tongue with a loud moan. I lapped up what I could and waited until her grip on my head eased before I finally pulled back.

With her face flushed and her auburn curls tossed carelessly across the pillow, she'd never looked more beautiful. She stared up at me through hooded eyes. I should have been too caught up in the bliss to think about anything else. I should have been enjoying the moment. But then a question suddenly popped into my mind.

*There* will *be a next time...right?*

Maybe if I brought it up coyly? Ask her how much rope she thought we'd need for the "real fun." But when I opened my mouth to speak, the words that came tumbling out were: "What are we?"

I cursed my brain for even coming up with that. It was desperate. A grasping, groping question just trying to latch on to her when things were just beginning. What if she got angry?

"I'm sorry, I didn't mean to—" I moved to the side, hoping I could grab my clothes and leave with whatever dignity I had left. But Vic suddenly sat up and grabbed my face between her hands. When she spoke, it was soft. But the words sliced through me like a cutlass.

"We are forever."

* * *

I don't know how or when the crew found out. One day everything was normal, the next everyone was smirking at me and making comments about how "dedicated" I was to my job. Hank was the worst of the lot. I even decked him after one comment too many, but the damn blighter just kept smiling.

They were always careful not to say anything to the captain directly, of course. But she laughed about it all in the privacy of her cabin. The cabin we now shared.

It was surreal. Things were as they always had been before. We traveled to various ports, relieving some merchant ships of their cargo as we went, and did the usual smuggling. But everything felt different. I spent my days on deck, yelling at the crew as they grinned at me. And my nights pressed up against Vic.

"We'll be at the strait again soon," she said softly one night. I shrugged as well as I could, with my arms wrapped around her. She idly ran her fingers through my hair.

"What, no big plans?" she teased. "I figured you'd want to hear the full song with both ears this time."

"I guess," I muttered. "But honestly, it's nothing. Just some pretty notes." She chuckled.

"I don't know, I think they're pretty special," she said in a low voice. "We might have been as we were forever if not for them."

She had a point. And as we passed through the strait once again, I grasped her hand as the song started up. There was a moment where I was afraid the captain might take for the railing. But she stayed right where she was, hand in mine.

The notes coming through my ears still did little for me. But the look on her face, the way she looked at me, and knowing what it meant that she didn't move an inch...

I decided the siren's song was pretty damn special anyway.

"Caught" is a short story by Margaret Adelle. You can check out her indie book reviews at
www.youtube.com/channel/UC5dF0Io4_1kbB4IZXgkBPzQ

Please take a moment to review this book at your favorite retailer's website, Goodreads, or simply tell your friends!

# ABOUT THE AUTHORS

**J.S. Fields** (@Galactoglucoman) is a scientist who has spent too much time around organic solvents. They enjoy roller derby, woodturning, making chainmail by hand, and cultivating fungi in the backs of minivans. J.S. lives with their wife and daughter in the Pacific Northwest, along with a Flemish giant rabbit named Sir Chip Edmonton III.

Fields' writing spans across science and science fiction / fantasy. Their *Ardulum* series was a Forewords INDIES finalist in science fiction, and a Gold Crown Literary Society finalist in science fiction. Their YA fantasy *Foxfire in the Snow* was also a Foreword INDIES finalist in YA. All of their writing, from published to drafting, is available on their Patreon: http://www.patreon.com/jsfields. You can keep up to date on their work at http://www.jsfieldsbooks.com/

**Sarah Day's** debut novella, *Greyhowler*, is forthcoming from Underland Press. You should pre-order it. Sarah is an author of horror, sci-fi, fantasy, and many other flavors of speculative fiction. Her work is heavily influenced by festival culture, body modification, mental illness, non-traditional relationships, and scary ghosts. She's always down to watch a monster movie. She's currently working on a novella about a city powered by the dead, and is drafting a novel with her frequent collaborator Tim Pratt. Sarah lives in the San Francisco Bay Area with her cat and many LED lights. Follow Sarah on Twitter @scribblingfox, or read more of her fiction at sarahday.org.

**Tim Pratt** is a Hugo Award-winning SF and fantasy author, and has been a finalist for World Fantasy, Philip K. Dick, Sturgeon, Stoker, Mythopoeic, and Nebula Awards, among others. He is the author of more than 30 books, most recently multiverse adventures *Doors of Sleep* and *Prison of Sleep*. His stories have appeared at Tor.com, Lightspeed, Clarkesworld, Asimov's, and other nice places. He's a senior editor and occasional book reviewer at Locus, the magazine of the science fiction and fantasy field. Since 2013 he's published a new story every month at www.patreon.com/timpratt, and he tweets incessantly at twitter.com/timpratt. He lives in Berkeley, CA.

**William C. Tracy** writes tales of the Dissolutionverse: a science fantasy series about planets connected by music-based magic instead of spaceflight. He also has an epic fantasy available about a land where magic comes from seasonal fruit, and two sisters plot to take down a corrupt government. He is currently writing a space colony trilogy set on a planet entirely covered by a sentient fungus.

William is a North Carolina native with a master's in mechanical engineering, and has both designed and operated heavy construction machinery. He has also trained in Wado-Ryu karate since 2003, and runs his own dojo in Raleigh, NC. In his spare time, he cosplays with his wife, and they enjoy putting their pets in cute little costumes and making them pose for the annual Christmas card. Follow him on Twitter (@tracywc) for writing updates, cat pictures, and thoughts on martial arts. You can also visit him online at www.williamctracy.com or www.patreon.com/wctracy.

**N.L. Bates** is a Canadian author of science fiction, fantasy, and slipstream stories, and is the moderator of the long-running critique group Reading Excuses. When not writing stories, she enjoys biking, dancing, and tabletop RPGs. She also writes and performs music as her alter ego, Natalie Lynn and filks occasionally, usually by accident. Connect with her on Twitter (@nlbateswrites) or find her at her website, www.nlbates.com.

**Kim Pritekel** was born and raised in Colorado, where she still lives. She's been a published author for twenty years with more than twenty-five titles under belt. She's also a songwriter and filmmaker. Come say hello on Facebook or her website at: http://www.kimpritekel.com.

**Robin C.M. Duncan** is a Scot born and living in Glasgow. A Civil Engineer by profession, he has been writing for decades, but seriously only for the last ten years. Robin has completed various novels, numerous short stories, novellas, novelettes, and poems, with copious other projects in different stages of incompletion.

Robin's first novel *The Mandroid Murders* was published in August 2022. His first published works, "Dew Diligence" and "The Bibliothek Betrayal", appear in the *Distant Gardens* anthology of 2021, available from Space Wizard Science Fantasy. Robin's short story "The NEU Oblivion" was long-listed for the 2019 James White Award.

Robin belongs to the Glasgow Science Fiction Writers' Circle, the Reading Excuses critique group, the British Fantasy Society, and the British Science Fiction Association. Robin likes LEGO, gardening, heavy metal, football (soccer), and long walks on the beach. Robin does not own a cat, but is slightly acquainted with one. News and blogging at robincmduncan.com. Active twit @ROBINSKL.

**Vanessa Ricci-Thode's** life seldom strays from the world of books, especially during winter hibernation. Even her volunteer work revolves around the literary world, with involvement in National Novel Writing Month as long-time municipal liaison to her region, and as co-founder of KW Writers Alliance. She is also a member of SFWA and TWUC.

When she's not being bookish, she's into astronomy, hiking, gardening, and has a personal goal to visit all the national parks. Don't ask her about her love of trees unless you've got some time. She loves

Halloween and hates to be cold. Vanessa lives in Waterloo (no, the other one) with her husband, daughter, and dogs. To learn more, visit www.thodestool.ca or follow her on Twitter & Instagram @VRicciThode.

**Kyoko M.** is a USA Today bestselling author and a fangirl. She is the author of *The Black Parade* urban fantasy series and the *Of Cinder and Bone* science-fiction series. *The Black Parade* has been reviewed by Publishers Weekly and New York Times bestselling author Ilona Andrews. *Of Cinder and Bone* placed in the Top 30 Books in Hugh Howey's 2021 Self Published Science Fiction Contest. Kyoko M. has appeared as a guest and panelist at such conventions as Geek Girl Con, DragonCon, Blacktasticon, Momocon, JordanCon, ConCarolinas, and MultiverseCon. She is also a contributor to Marvel Comics' *Black Panther: Tales of Wakanda* (2021) anthology. She has a Bachelor of Arts in English Lit degree from the University of Georgia.

**Sara Codair** is a community college English professor and author of speculative short stories and novels, including *The Evanstar Chronicles* and *Earth Reclaimed*. They partially owe their success to their faithful feline writing partner, Goose the Meowditor-In-Chief, who likes to "edit" their work by deleting entire pages. You can follow Sara and Goose's writing journey on Twitter and Instagram (@shatteredsmooth). You can also learn more about Sara on their website, www.saracodair.com.

**Margaret Adelle** worked with indie authors for three years before she finally decided to become one herself. While this is her first published work, she's been writing for over a decade and plans to continue publishing in the future. Mostly stories about women in love with each other.

Margaret currently resides with her husband in Davenport, Iowa. She has a Bachelor's degree in History and a Master's in Museum Studies, though uses neither of them at her job as a Special Education Paraeducator. When not corralling young children, she's playing Dungeons and Dragons, running the merch table at a local pro wrestling promotion, LARPing on the internet, and crocheting about a million scarves. You can follow her on Twitter (@margaret_adelle) and TikTok (@callmemirabel).

Made in the USA
Columbia, SC
11 November 2022

70642861R00202